NEGIMA! 4

Ken Akamatsu

TRANSLATED BY
Douglas Varenas

ADAPTED BY
Peter David and Kathleen O'Shea David

LETTERED BY
Steve Palmer

DEL
REY

BALLANTINE BOOKS · NEW YORK

Translator—Douglas Varenas
Adaptors—Peter David and Kathleen O'Shea David
Lettering—Steve Palmer
Cover Design—David Stevenson

This is a work of fiction. Any resemblance to actual persons, living or dead, is unintentional and purely coincidental.

A Del Rey® Book
Published by The Random House Publishing Group

Copyright © 2005 Ken Akamatsu. All rights reserved.
This publication—rights arranged through Kodansha Ltd.

All rights reserved.

Published in the United States by Del Rey Books,
an imprint of The Random House Publishing Group, a division
of Random House, Inc., New York, and simultaneously in
Canada by Random House of Canada Limited, Toronto.
First published in serial form by Shonen Magazine Comics and subsequently
published in book form by Kodansha, Ltd., Tokyo in 2004.
Copyright © 2004 by Ken Akamatsu.

Del Rey is a registered trademark and the Del Rey colophon is a
trademark of Random House, Inc.

www.delreymanga.com

Library of Congress Control Number: 2004091099

ISBN 0-345-47784-7

Manufactured in the United States of America

First Edition: January 2005

7 8 9

A Word from the Author

Finally, here's Volume 4 of *Negima!* Between trying to guide his tumultuous group of students through a wild field trip in Kyoto and Nara and dealing with a new menace, Negi-sensei has his hands full! (The field trip will continue into the next book.)

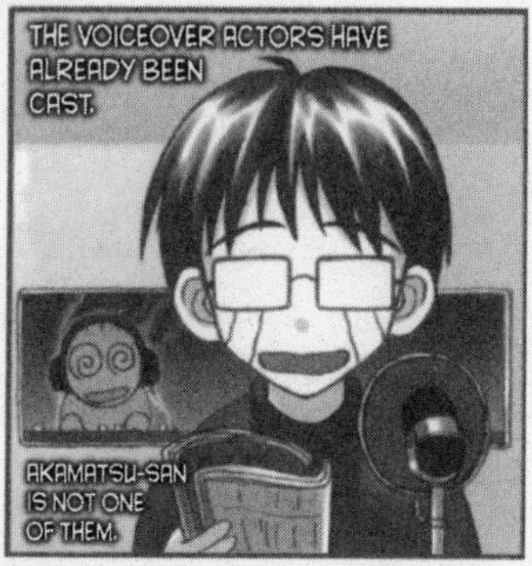
THE VOICEOVER ACTORS HAVE ALREADY BEEN CAST.
AKAMATSU-SAN IS NOT ONE OF THEM.

By the way, the "Character CD" of the digitized classmates of *Negima!* is now on sale. We've got thirty-one talented voice actors helping create a maxi CD single packed with imaging, mini-dramas, and more of each character. As a bonus, we included a Pactio Card (Probationary Contract). Don't miss it! For more information, check out my website.

Ken Akamatsu
http://www.ailove.net

Honorifics

Throughout the Del Rey Manga books, you will find Japanese honorifics left intact in the translations. For those not familiar with how the Japanese use honorifics, and more important, how they differ from American honorifics, we present this brief overview.

Politeness has always been a critical facet of Japanese culture. Ever since the feudal era, when Japan was a highly stratified society, use of honorifics — which can be defined as polite speech that indicates relationship or status — has played an essential role in the Japanese language. When addressing someone in Japanese, an honorific usually takes the form of a suffix attached to one's name (example: "Asuna-san"), or as a title at the end of one's name or in place of the name itself (example: "Negi-sensei," or simply "Sensei!").

Honorifics can be expressions of respect or endearment. In the context of manga and anime, honorifics give insight into the nature of the relationship between characters. Many translations into English leave out these important honorifics, and therefore distort the "feel" of the original Japanese. Because Japanese honorifics contain nuances that English honorifics lack, it is our policy at Del Rey not to translate them. Here, instead, is a guide to some of the honorifics you may encounter in Del Rey Manga.

-*san*: This is the most common honorific, and is equivalent to Mr., Miss, Ms., Mrs., etc. It is the all-purpose honorific and can be used in any situation where politeness is required.

-*sama*: This is one level higher than -*san*. It is used to confer great respect.

-*dono*: This comes from the word *tono*, which means *lord*. It is an even higher level than -*sama*, and confers utmost respect.

-kun: This suffix is used at the end of boys' names to express familiarity or endearment. It is also sometimes used by men among friends, or when addressing someone younger or of a lower station.

-chan: This is used to express endearment, mostly toward girls. It is also used for little boys, pets, and even among lovers. It gives a sense of childish cuteness.

Bozu: This is an informal way to refer to a boy, similar to the English term "kid" or "squirt."

Sempai: This title suggests that the addressee is one's "senior" in a group or organization. It is most often used in a school setting, where underclassmen refer to their upperclassmen as *sempai*. It can also be used in the workplace, such as when a newer employee addresses an employee who has seniority in the company.

Kohai: This is the opposite of *sempai*, and is used toward underclassmen in school or newcomers in the workplace. It connotes that the addressee is of lower station.

Sensei: Literally meaning "one who has come before," this title is used for teachers, doctors, or masters of any profession or art.

-[blank]: Usually forgotten in these lists, but perhaps the most significant difference between Japanese and English. The lack of honorific means that the speaker has permission to address the person in a very intimate way. Usually, only family, spouses, or very close friends have this kind of permission. Known as *yobisute*, it can be gratifying when someone who has earned the intimacy starts to call one by one's name without an honorific. But when that intimacy hasn't been earned, it can also be very insulting.

魔法先生

ネギま!

4

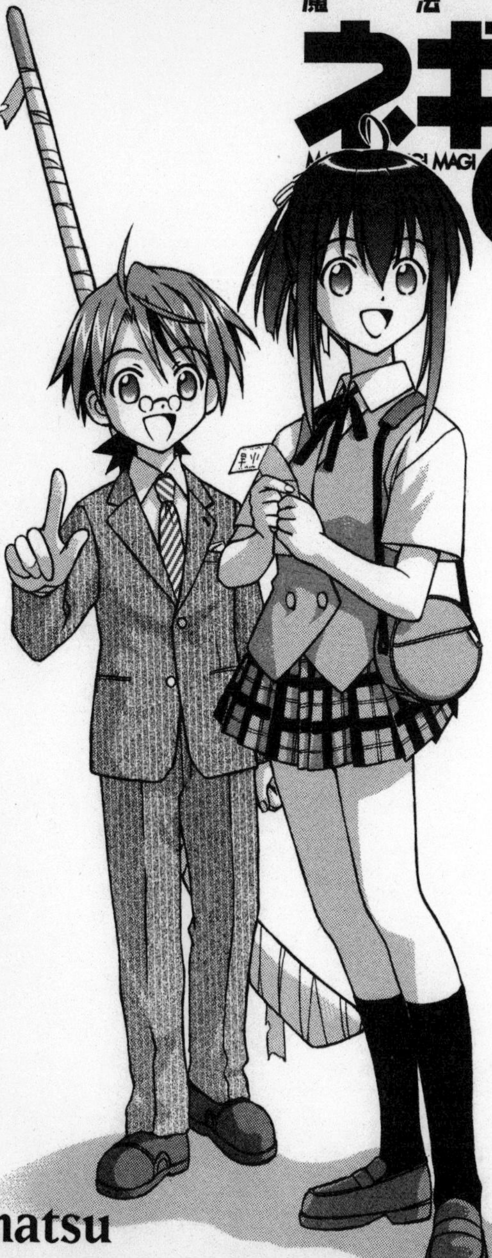

赤松健

Ken Akamatsu

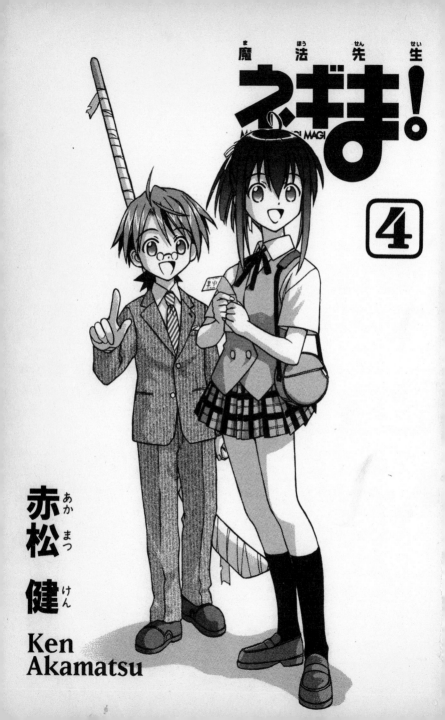

CONTENTS

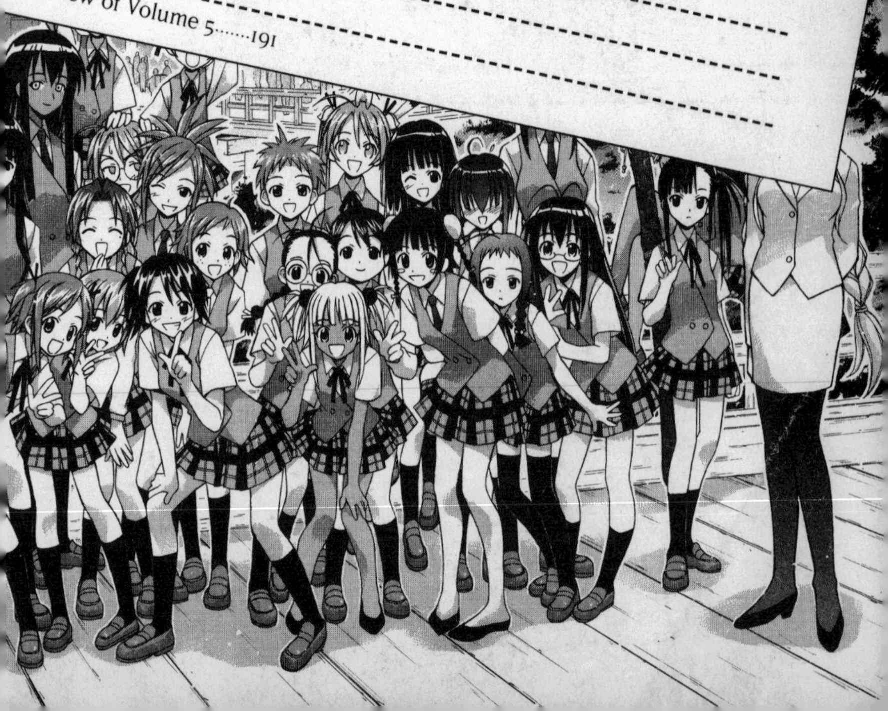

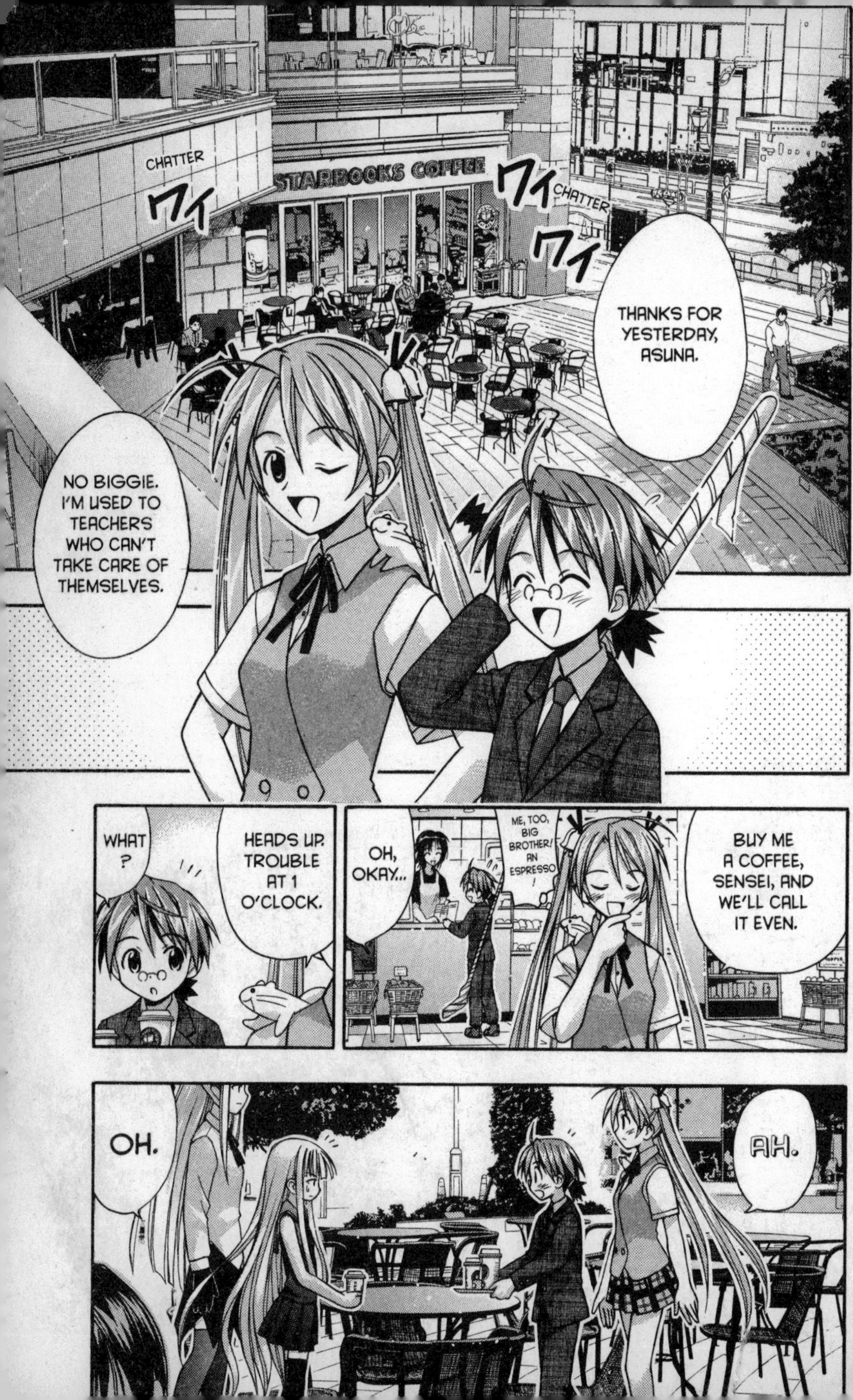
STARBOOKS COFFEE
ワイ
CHATTER
ワイ
CHATTER
ワイ
THANKS FOR YESTERDAY, ASUNA.
NO BIGGIE. I'M USED TO TEACHERS WHO CAN'T TAKE CARE OF THEMSELVES.
BUY ME A COFFEE, SENSEI, AND WE'LL CALL IT EVEN.
ME, TOO, BIG BROTHER! AN ESPRESSO!
OH, OKAY...
HEADS UP. TROUBLE AT 1 O'CLOCK.
WHAT?
AH.
OH.

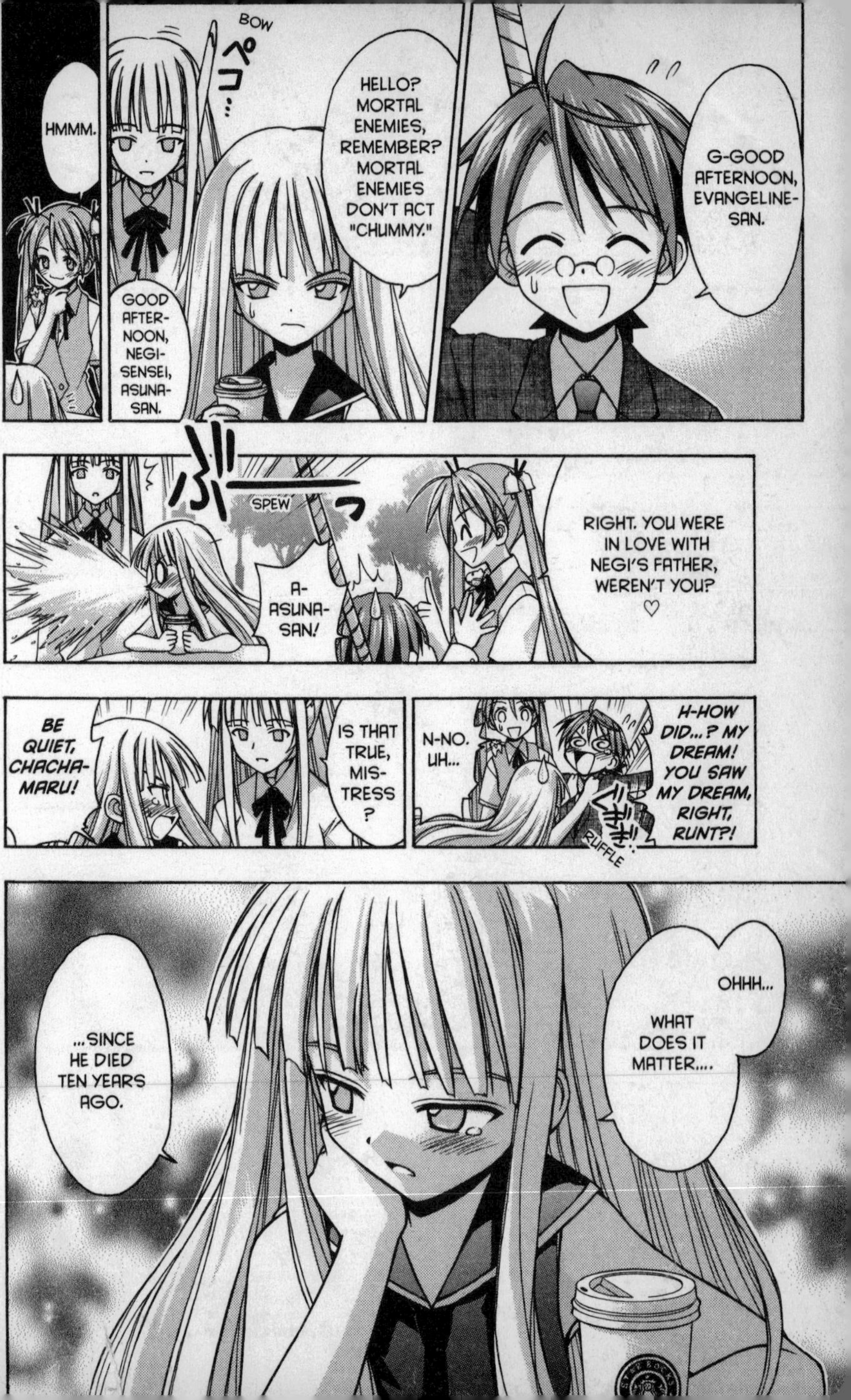
G-GOOD AFTERNOON, EVANGELINE-SAN.
HELLO? MORTAL ENEMIES, REMEMBER? MORTAL ENEMIES DON'T ACT "CHUMMY."
BOW
GOOD AFTERNOON, NEGI-SENSEI, ASUNA-SAN.
HMMM.
RIGHT. YOU WERE IN LOVE WITH NEGI'S FATHER, WEREN'T YOU? ♡
A-ASUNA-SAN!
SPEW
H-HOW DID...? MY DREAM! YOU SAW MY DREAM, RIGHT, RUNT?!
RUFFLE
N-NO. UH...
IS THAT TRUE, MISTRESS?
BE QUIET, CHACHAMARU!
OHHH...
WHAT DOES IT MATTER....
...SINCE HE DIED TEN YEARS AGO.

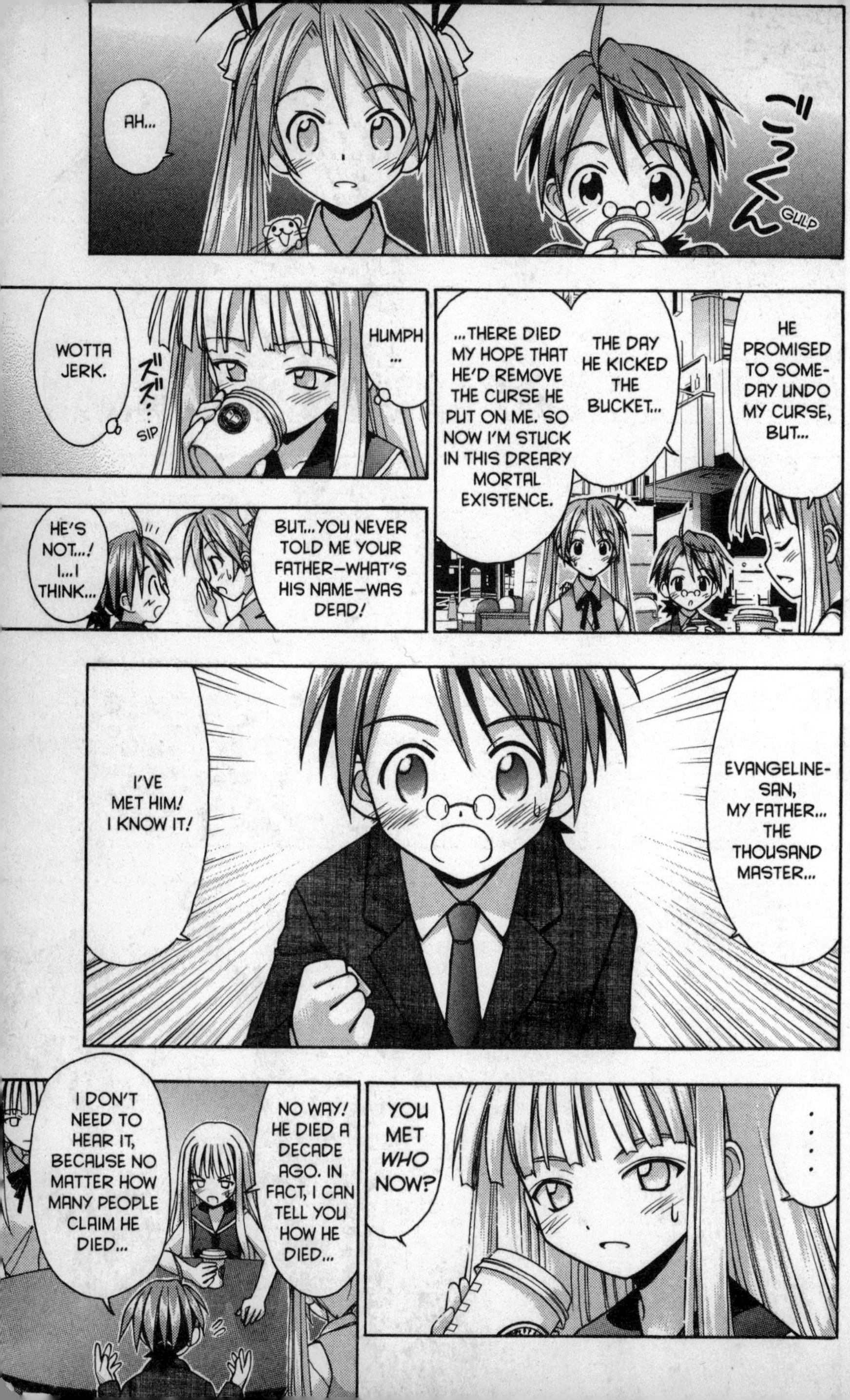
ごっくん
GULP
AH...
HE PROMISED TO SOMEDAY UNDO MY CURSE, BUT...
THE DAY HE KICKED THE BUCKET...
...THERE DIED MY HOPE THAT HE'D REMOVE THE CURSE HE PUT ON ME. SO NOW I'M STUCK IN THIS DREARY MORTAL EXISTENCE.
HUMPH...
ズズ...
SIP
WOTTA JERK.
BUT...YOU NEVER TOLD ME YOUR FATHER—WHAT'S HIS NAME—WAS DEAD!
HE'S NOT...! I...I THINK...
EVANGELINE-SAN, MY FATHER... THE THOUSAND MASTER...
I'VE MET HIM! I KNOW IT!
. . . .
YOU MET *WHO* NOW?
NO WAY! HE DIED A DECADE AGO. IN FACT, I CAN TELL YOU HOW HE DIED...
I DON'T NEED TO HEAR IT, BECAUSE NO MATTER HOW MANY PEOPLE CLAIM HE DIED...

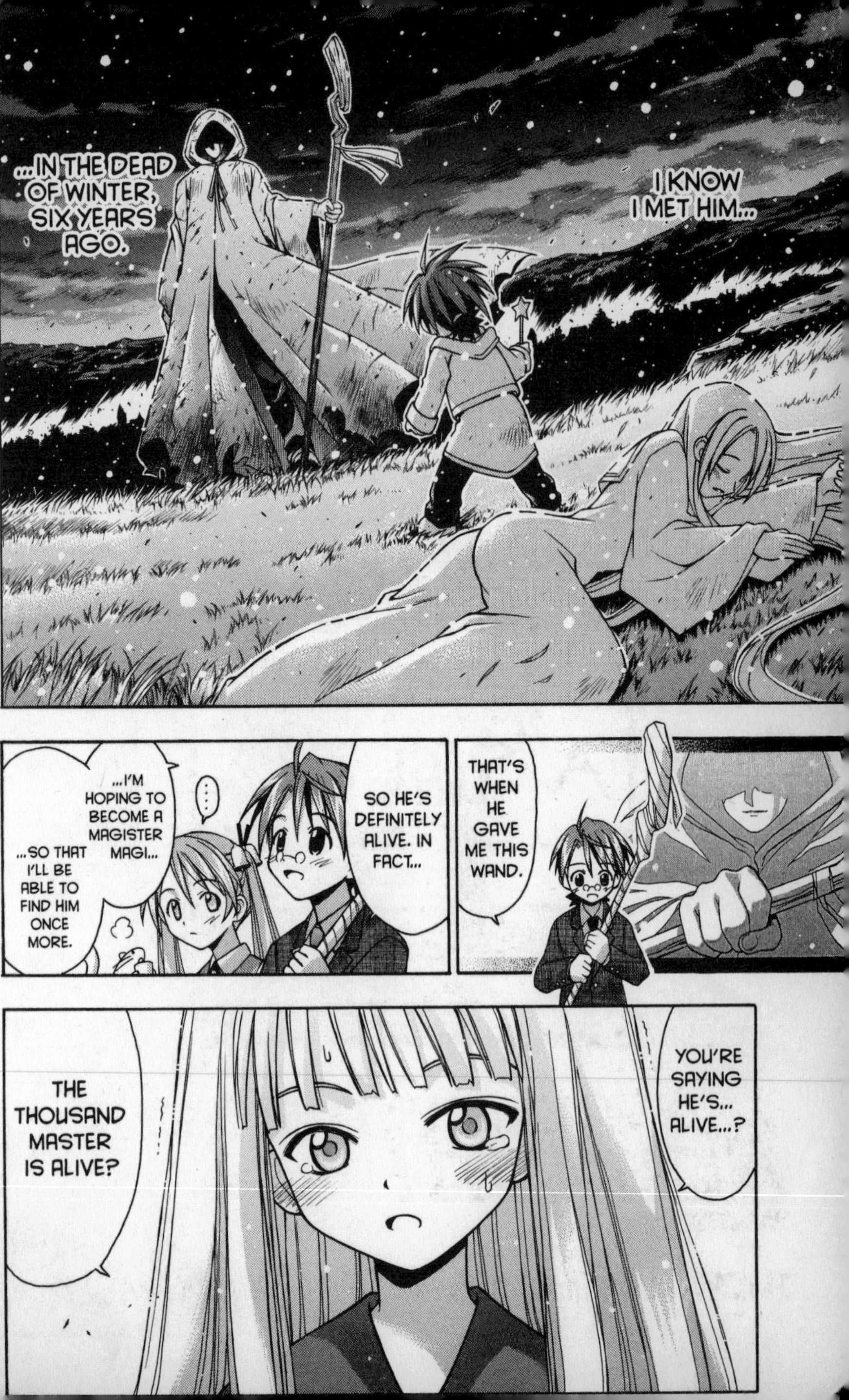
I KNOW I MET HIM...
...IN THE DEAD OF WINTER, SIX YEARS AGO.
THAT'S WHEN HE GAVE ME THIS WAND.
SO HE'S DEFINITELY ALIVE. IN FACT...
...
...I'M HOPING TO BECOME A MAGISTER MAGI...
...SO THAT I'LL BE ABLE TO FIND HIM ONCE MORE.
YOU'RE SAYING HE'S... ALIVE...?
THE THOUSAND MASTER IS ALIVE?

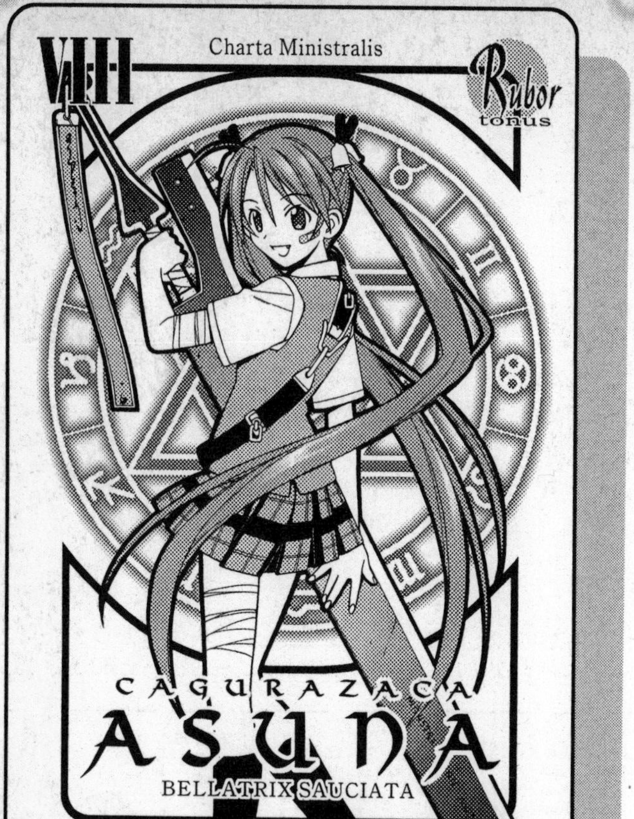
Charta Ministralis
Rubor
tonus
CAGURAZACA
ASUNA
BELLATRIX SAUCIATA
virtus
audacia
astralitas
directio
oriens
Mars

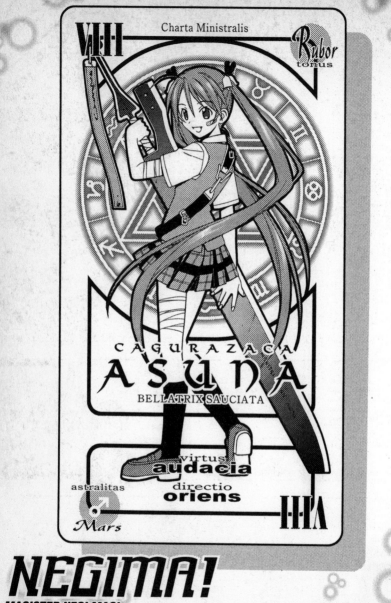

NEGIMA!

MAGISTER NEGI MAGI

TWENTY-SIXTH PERIOD: PROOF OF A CONTRACT!?

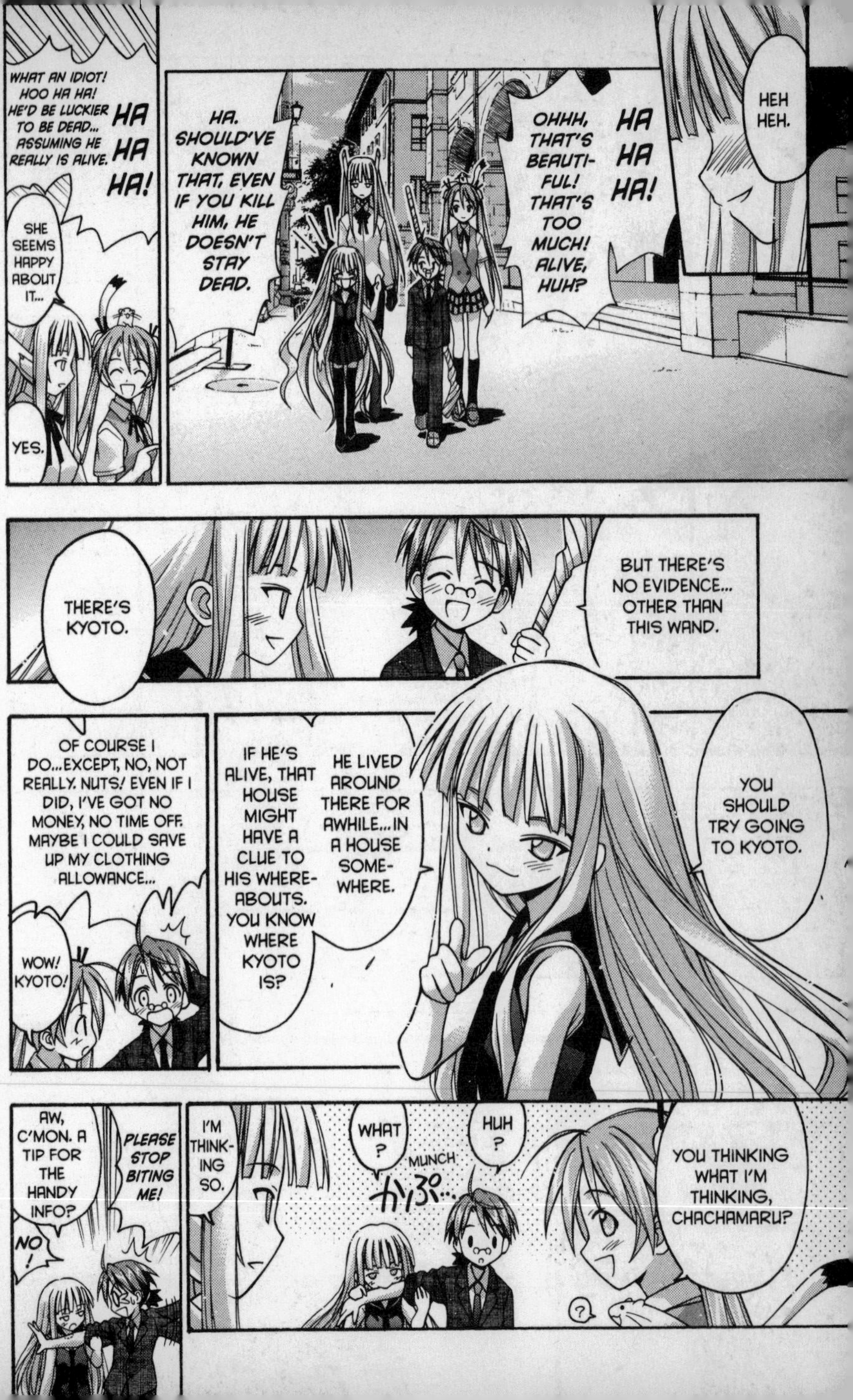
HEH HEH.
OHHH, THAT'S BEAUTI-FUL! THAT'S TOO MUCH! ALIVE, HUH?
HA HA HA!
HA. SHOULD'VE KNOWN THAT, EVEN IF YOU KILL HIM, HE DOESN'T STAY DEAD.
WHAT AN IDIOT! HOO HA HA! HE'D BE LUCKIER TO BE DEAD... ASSUMING HE REALLY IS ALIVE.
HA HA HA!
SHE SEEMS HAPPY ABOUT IT...
YES.
BUT THERE'S NO EVIDENCE... OTHER THAN THIS WAND.
THERE'S KYOTO.
YOU SHOULD TRY GOING TO KYOTO.
HE LIVED AROUND THERE FOR AWHILE...IN A HOUSE SOME-WHERE.
IF HE'S ALIVE, THAT HOUSE MIGHT HAVE A CLUE TO HIS WHERE-ABOUTS. YOU KNOW WHERE KYOTO IS?
OF COURSE I DO...EXCEPT, NO, NOT REALLY. NUTS! EVEN IF I DID, I'VE GOT NO MONEY, NO TIME OFF. MAYBE I COULD SAVE UP MY CLOTHING ALLOWANCE...
WOW! KYOTO!
YOU THINKING WHAT I'M THINKING, CHACHAMARU?
HUH?
WHAT?
MUNCH
かぷ...
?
I'M THINK-ING SO.
PLEASE STOP BITING ME!
AW, C'MON. A TIP FOR THE HANDY INFO?
NO!

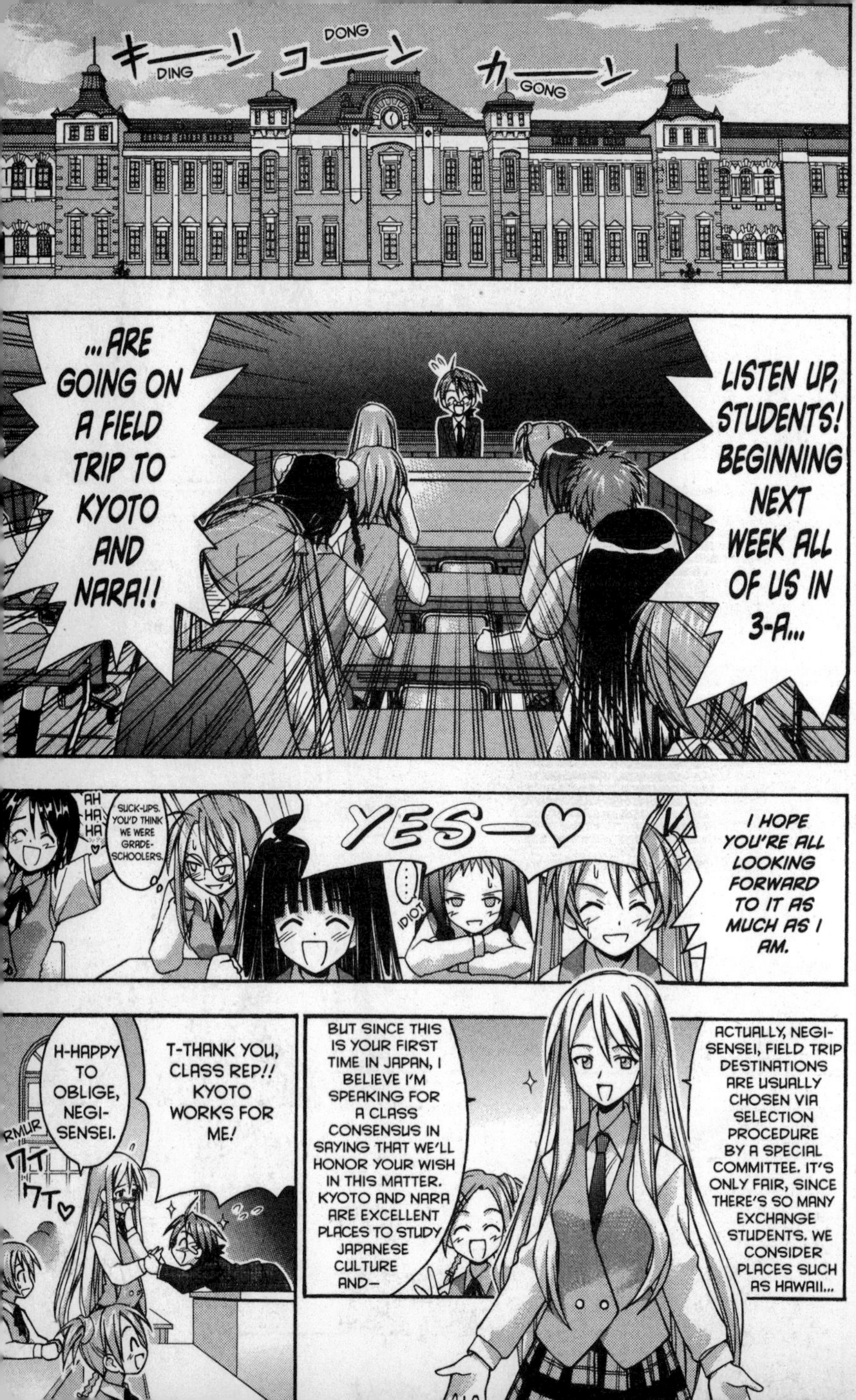
キーーン DING
コーーン DONG
カーーン GONG
LISTEN UP, STUDENTS! BEGINNING NEXT WEEK ALL OF US IN 3-A...
...ARE GOING ON A FIELD TRIP TO KYOTO AND NARA!!
I HOPE YOU'RE ALL LOOKING FORWARD TO IT AS MUCH AS I AM.
YES—♡
IDIOT
...
SUCK-UPS. YOU'D THINK WE WERE GRADE-SCHOOLERS.
AH HA HA ♡
ACTUALLY, NEGI-SENSEI, FIELD TRIP DESTINATIONS ARE USUALLY CHOSEN VIA SELECTION PROCEDURE BY A SPECIAL COMMITTEE. IT'S ONLY FAIR, SINCE THERE'S SO MANY EXCHANGE STUDENTS. WE CONSIDER PLACES SUCH AS HAWAII...
BUT SINCE THIS IS YOUR FIRST TIME IN JAPAN, I BELIEVE I'M SPEAKING FOR A CLASS CONSENSUS IN SAYING THAT WE'LL HONOR YOUR WISH IN THIS MATTER. KYOTO AND NARA ARE EXCELLENT PLACES TO STUDY JAPANESE CULTURE AND—
T-THANK YOU, CLASS REP!! KYOTO WORKS FOR ME!
H-HAPPY TO OBLIGE, NEGI-SENSEI.
RMUR
ワT ワT ♡

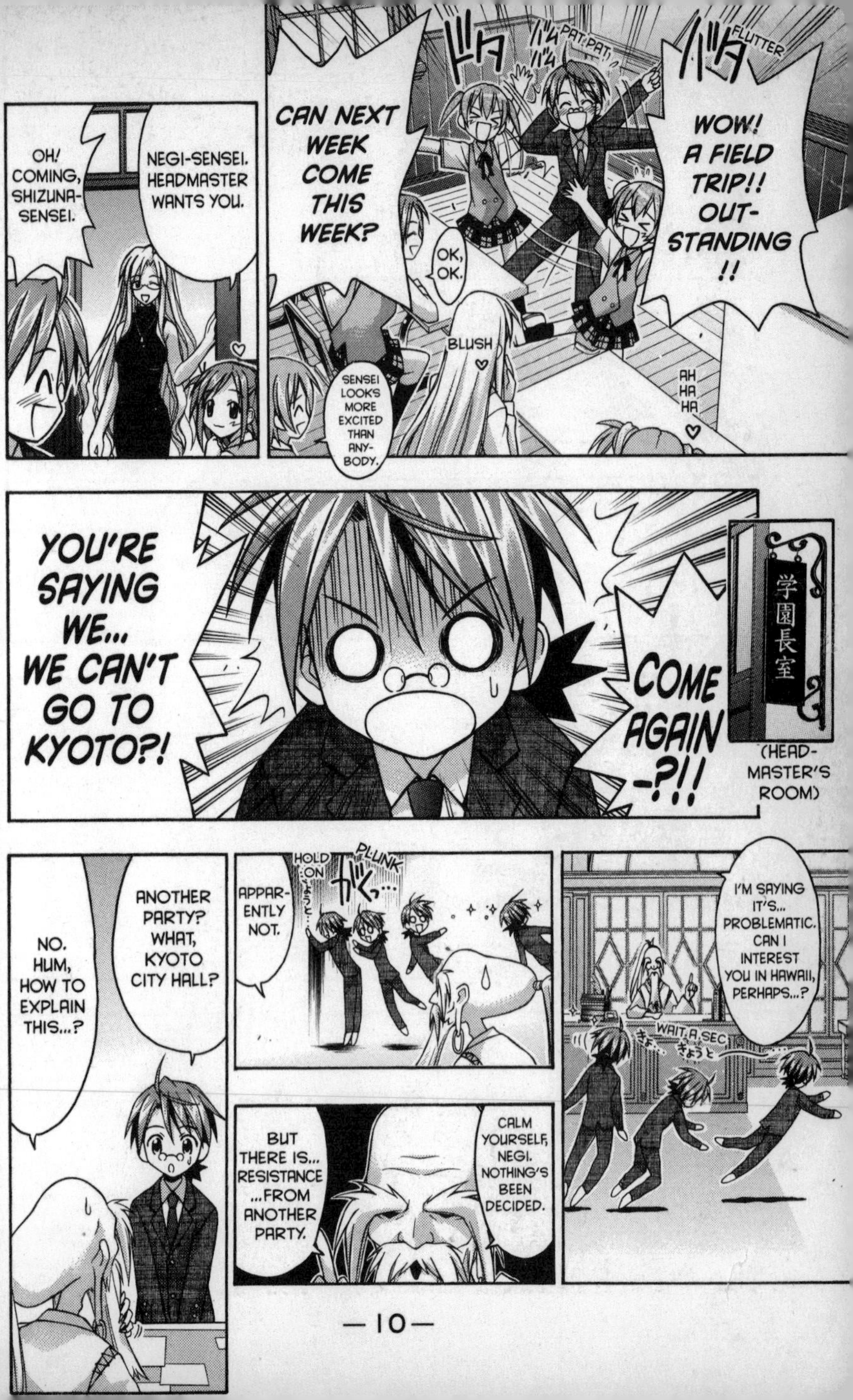

バタ
FLUTTER
WOW! A FIELD TRIP!! OUT-STANDING!!
バムバム
PAT PAT
ドタ
CAN NEXT WEEK COME THIS WEEK?
OK, OK.
BLUSH
AH HA HA
SENSEI LOOKS MORE EXCITED THAN ANY-BODY.
NEGI-SENSEI. HEADMASTER WANTS YOU.
OH! COMING, SHIZUNA-SENSEI.
学園長室
(HEAD-MASTER'S ROOM)
COME AGAIN-?!!
YOU'RE SAYING WE... WE CAN'T GO TO KYOTO?!
I'M SAYING IT'S... PROBLEMATIC. CAN I INTEREST YOU IN HAWAII, PERHAPS...?
WAIT A SEC
きょうと
PLUNK
がくっ…
HOLD ON
APPAR-ENTLY NOT.
CALM YOURSELF, NEGI. NOTHING'S BEEN DECIDED.
BUT THERE IS... RESISTANCE ...FROM ANOTHER PARTY.
ANOTHER PARTY? WHAT, KYOTO CITY HALL?
NO. HUM, HOW TO EXPLAIN THIS...?

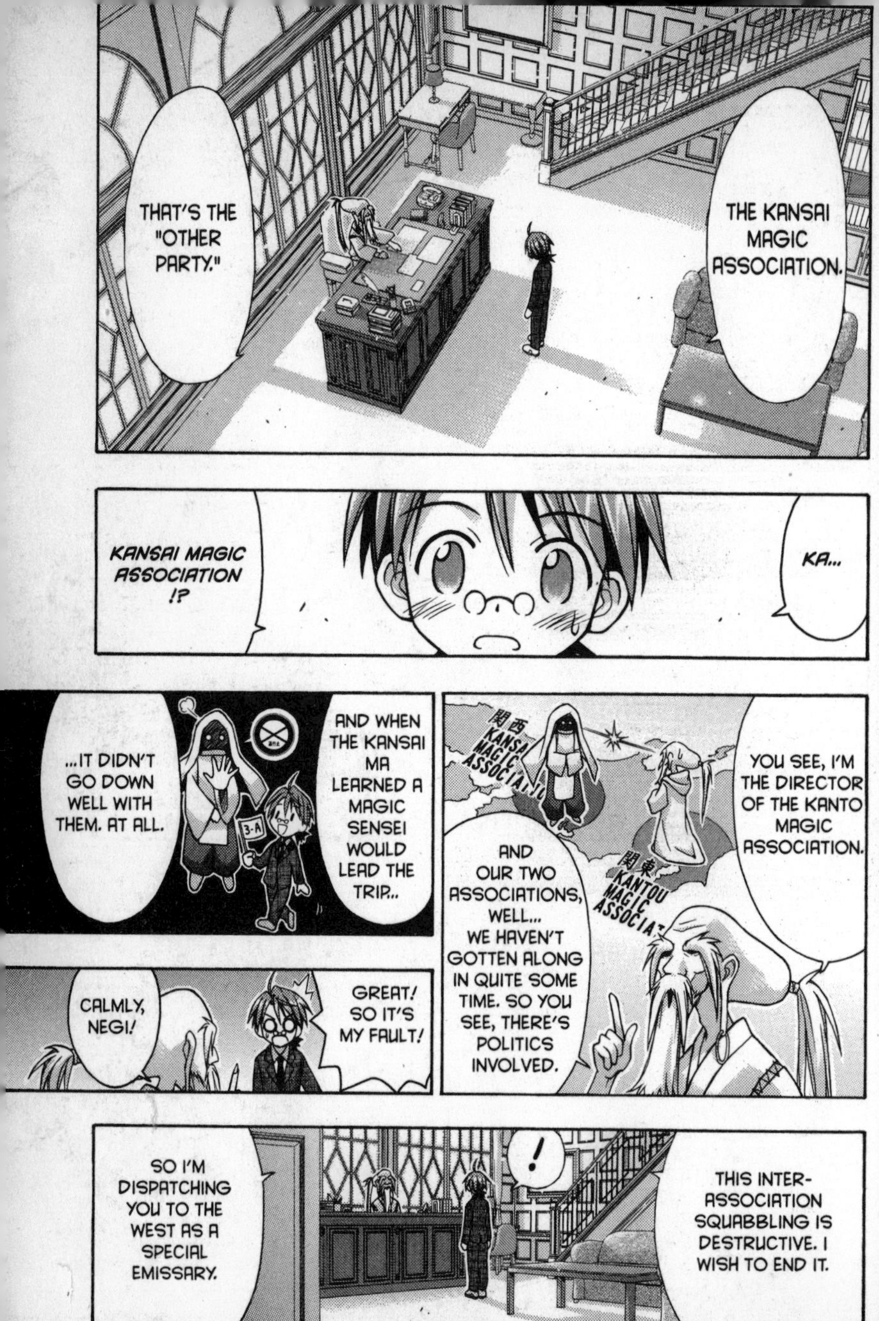
THE KANSAI MAGIC ASSOCIATION.
THAT'S THE "OTHER PARTY."
KA...
KANSAI MAGIC ASSOCIATION !?
YOU SEE, I'M THE DIRECTOR OF THE KANTO MAGIC ASSOCIATION.
関西
KANSAI MAGIC
関東
KANTOU MAGIC
AND OUR TWO ASSOCIATIONS, WELL... WE HAVEN'T GOTTEN ALONG IN QUITE SOME TIME. SO YOU SEE, THERE'S POLITICS INVOLVED.
AND WHEN THE KANSAI MA LEARNED A MAGIC SENSEI WOULD LEAD THE TRIP...
3-A
...IT DIDN'T GO DOWN WELL WITH THEM. AT ALL.
GREAT! SO IT'S MY FAULT!
CALMLY, NEGI!
THIS INTER-ASSOCIATION SQUABBLING IS DESTRUCTIVE. I WISH TO END IT.
!
SO I'M DISPATCHING YOU TO THE WEST AS A SPECIAL EMISSARY.

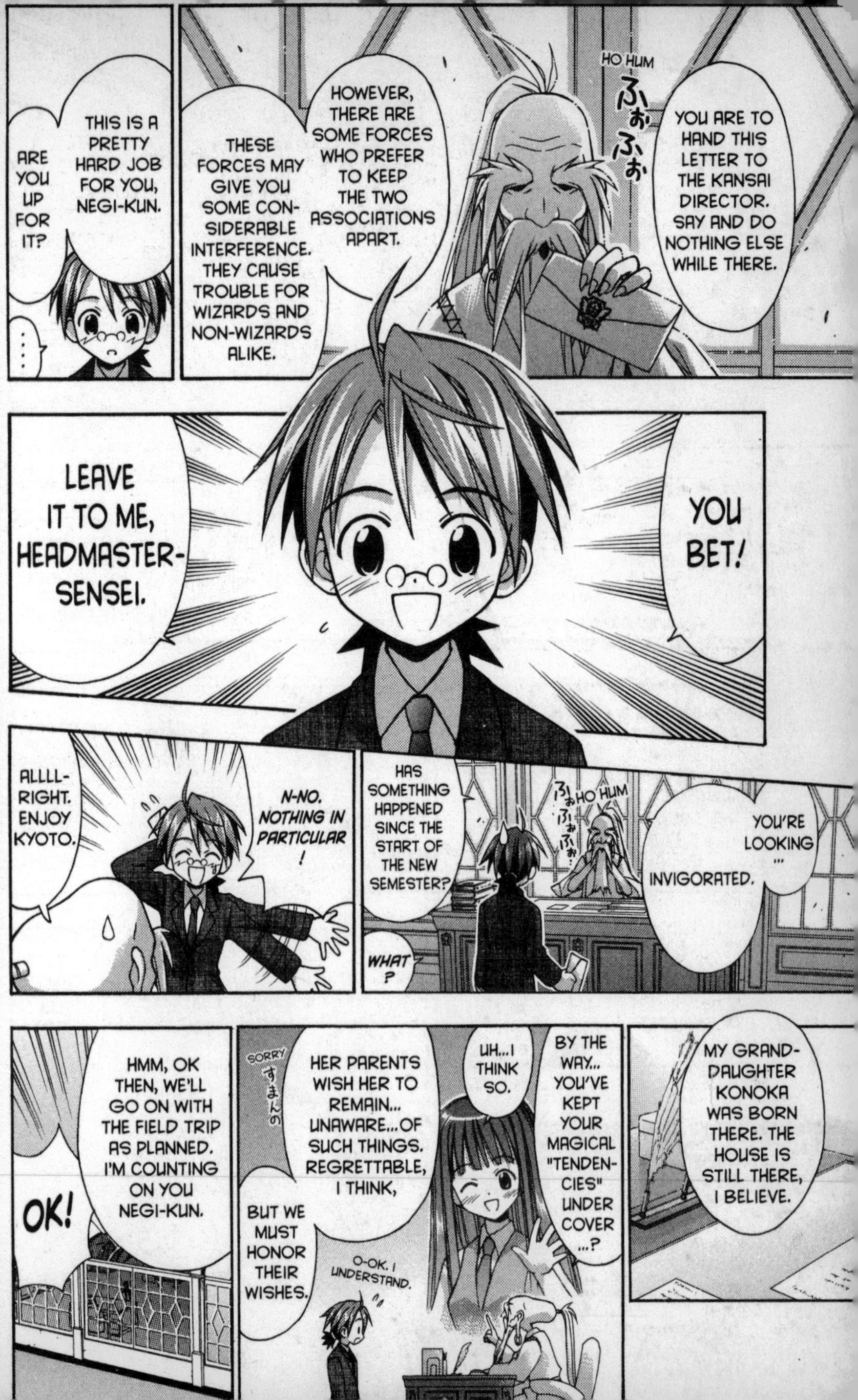
HO HUM
ふぉふぉ
YOU ARE TO HAND THIS LETTER TO THE KANSAI DIRECTOR. SAY AND DO NOTHING ELSE WHILE THERE.
HOWEVER, THERE ARE SOME FORCES WHO PREFER TO KEEP THE TWO ASSOCIATIONS APART.
THESE FORCES MAY GIVE YOU SOME CON-SIDERABLE INTERFERENCE. THEY CAUSE TROUBLE FOR WIZARDS AND NON-WIZARDS ALIKE.
THIS IS A PRETTY HARD JOB FOR YOU, NEGI-KUN.
ARE YOU UP FOR IT?
....
YOU BET!
LEAVE IT TO ME, HEADMASTER-SENSEI.
YOU'RE LOOKING ... INVIGORATED.
ふぉふぉふぉふぉ
HO HUM
WHAT?
HAS SOMETHING HAPPENED SINCE THE START OF THE NEW SEMESTER?
N-NO. NOTHING IN PARTICULAR!
ALLLL-RIGHT. ENJOY KYOTO.
MY GRAND-DAUGHTER KONOKA WAS BORN THERE. THE HOUSE IS STILL THERE, I BELIEVE.
BY THE WAY... YOU'VE KEPT YOUR MAGICAL "TENDEN-CIES" UNDER COVER ...?
UH...I THINK SO.
SORRY
すまんの
HER PARENTS WISH HER TO REMAIN... UNAWARE...OF SUCH THINGS. REGRETTABLE, I THINK,
BUT WE MUST HONOR THEIR WISHES.
O-OK. I UNDERSTAND.
HMM, OK THEN, WE'LL GO ON WITH THE FIELD TRIP AS PLANNED. I'M COUNTING ON YOU NEGI-KUN.
OK!

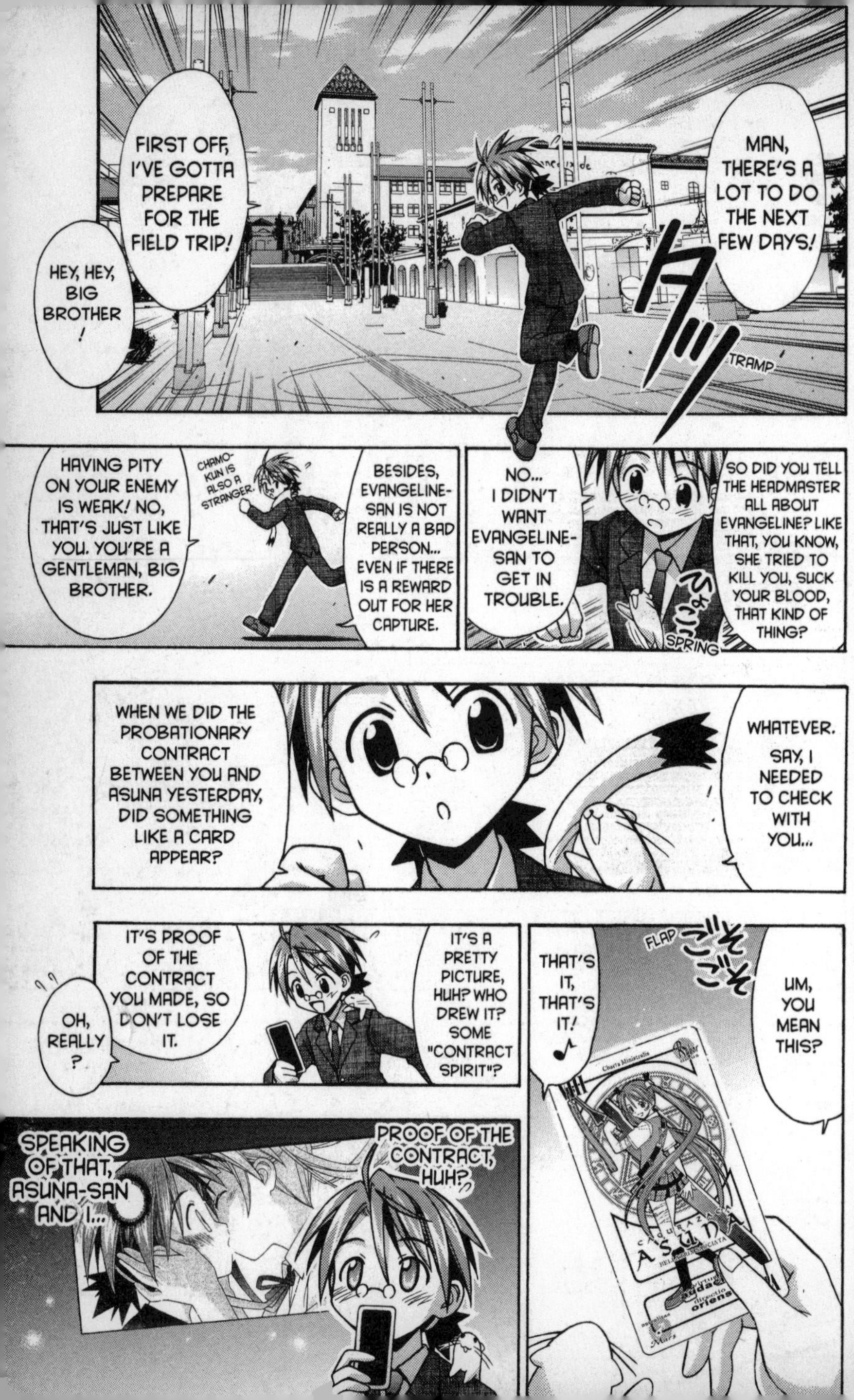
MAN, THERE'S A LOT TO DO THE NEXT FEW DAYS!
タッ
TRAMP
FIRST OFF, I'VE GOTTA PREPARE FOR THE FIELD TRIP!
HEY, HEY, BIG BROTHER!
SO DID YOU TELL THE HEADMASTER ALL ABOUT EVANGELINE? LIKE THAT, YOU KNOW, SHE TRIED TO KILL YOU, SUCK YOUR BLOOD, THAT KIND OF THING?
SPRING
NO... I DIDN'T WANT EVANGELINE-SAN TO GET IN TROUBLE.
BESIDES, EVANGELINE-SAN IS NOT REALLY A BAD PERSON... EVEN IF THERE IS A REWARD OUT FOR HER CAPTURE.
CHAMO-KUN IS ALSO A STRANGER.
HAVING PITY ON YOUR ENEMY IS WEAK! NO, THAT'S JUST LIKE YOU. YOU'RE A GENTLEMAN, BIG BROTHER.
WHATEVER.
SAY, I NEEDED TO CHECK WITH YOU...
WHEN WE DID THE PROBATIONARY CONTRACT BETWEEN YOU AND ASUNA YESTERDAY, DID SOMETHING LIKE A CARD APPEAR?
UM, YOU MEAN THIS?
FLAP
THAT'S IT, THAT'S IT! ♪
Charta Ministralis
audacia
directio
oriens
Mars
IT'S A PRETTY PICTURE, HUH? WHO DREW IT? SOME "CONTRACT SPIRIT"?
IT'S PROOF OF THE CONTRACT YOU MADE, SO DON'T LOSE IT.
OH, REALLY?
PROOF OF THE CONTRACT, HUH?
SPEAKING OF THAT, ASUNA-SAN AND I...

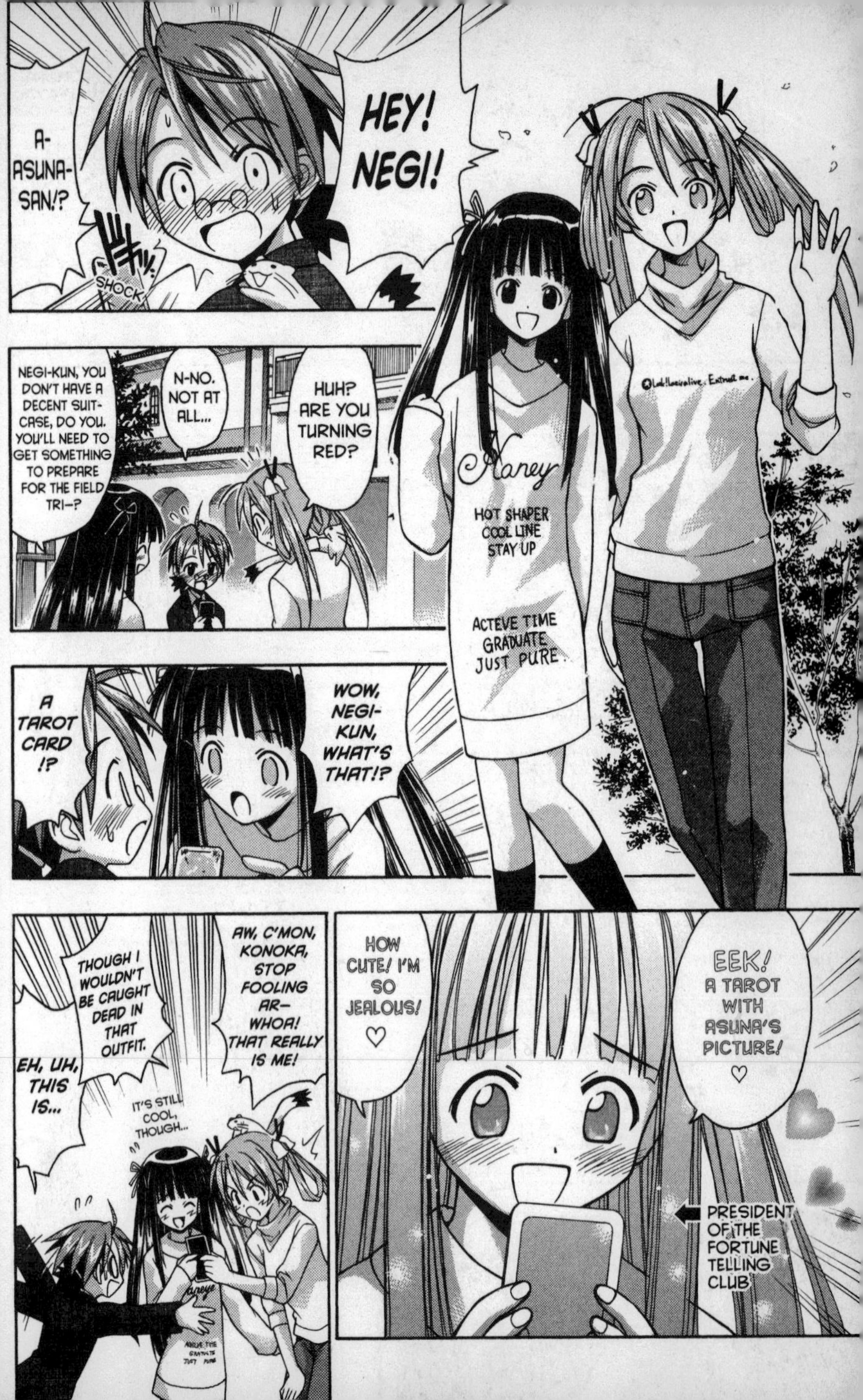
HEY! NEGI!
A-ASUNA-SAN!?
SHOCK
HOT SHAPER COOL LINE STAY UP
ACTEVE TIME GRADUATE JUST PURE
HUH? ARE YOU TURNING RED?
N-NO. NOT AT ALL...
NEGI-KUN, YOU DON'T HAVE A DECENT SUIT-CASE, DO YOU. YOU'LL NEED TO GET SOMETHING TO PREPARE FOR THE FIELD TRI—?
WOW, NEGI-KUN, WHAT'S THAT!?
A TAROT CARD !?
EEK! A TAROT WITH ASUNA'S PICTURE! ♡
HOW CUTE! I'M SO JEALOUS! ♡
PRESIDENT OF THE FORTUNE TELLING CLUB
AW, C'MON, KONOKA, STOP FOOLING AR— WHOA! THAT REALLY IS ME!
THOUGH I WOULDN'T BE CAUGHT DEAD IN THAT OUTFIT.
EH, UH, THIS IS...
IT'S STILL COOL, THOUGH...

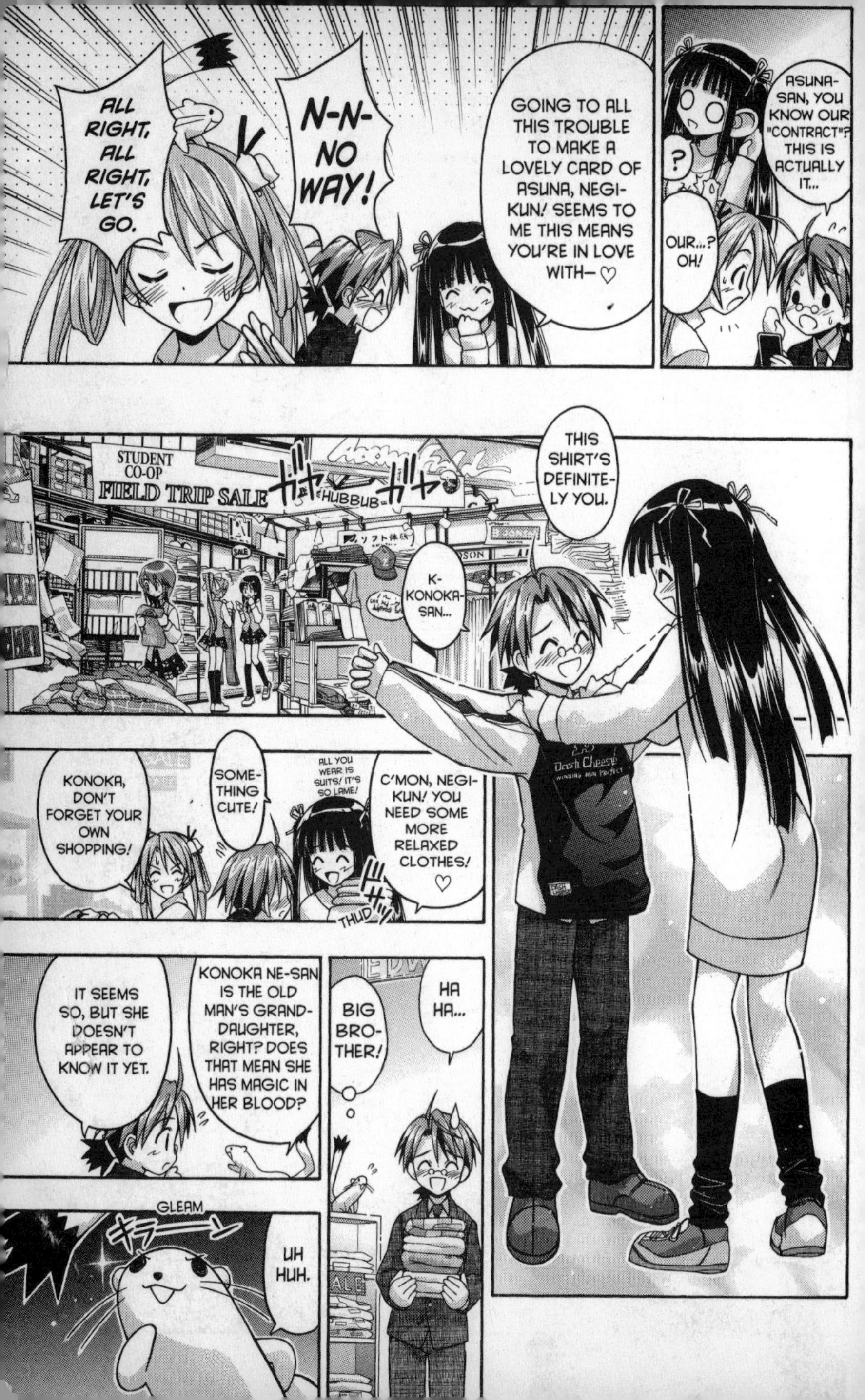
ASUNA-SAN, YOU KNOW OUR "CONTRACT"? THIS IS ACTUALLY IT...
?
OUR...? OH!
GOING TO ALL THIS TROUBLE TO MAKE A LOVELY CARD OF ASUNA, NEGI-KUN! SEEMS TO ME THIS MEANS YOU'RE IN LOVE WITH— ♡
N-N-NO WAY!
ALL RIGHT, ALL RIGHT, LET'S GO.
THIS SHIRT'S DEFINITE-LY YOU.
K-KONOKA-SAN...
STUDENT CO-OP FIELD TRIP SALE
HUBBUB
C'MON, NEGI-KUN! YOU NEED SOME MORE RELAXED CLOTHES! ♡
ALL YOU WEAR IS SUITS! IT'S SO LAME!
SOME-THING CUTE!
THUD
KONOKA, DON'T FORGET YOUR OWN SHOPPING!
HA HA...
BIG BRO-THER!
KONOKA NE-SAN IS THE OLD MAN'S GRAND-DAUGHTER, RIGHT? DOES THAT MEAN SHE HAS MAGIC IN HER BLOOD?
IT SEEMS SO, BUT SHE DOESN'T APPEAR TO KNOW IT YET.
GLEAM
UH HUH.

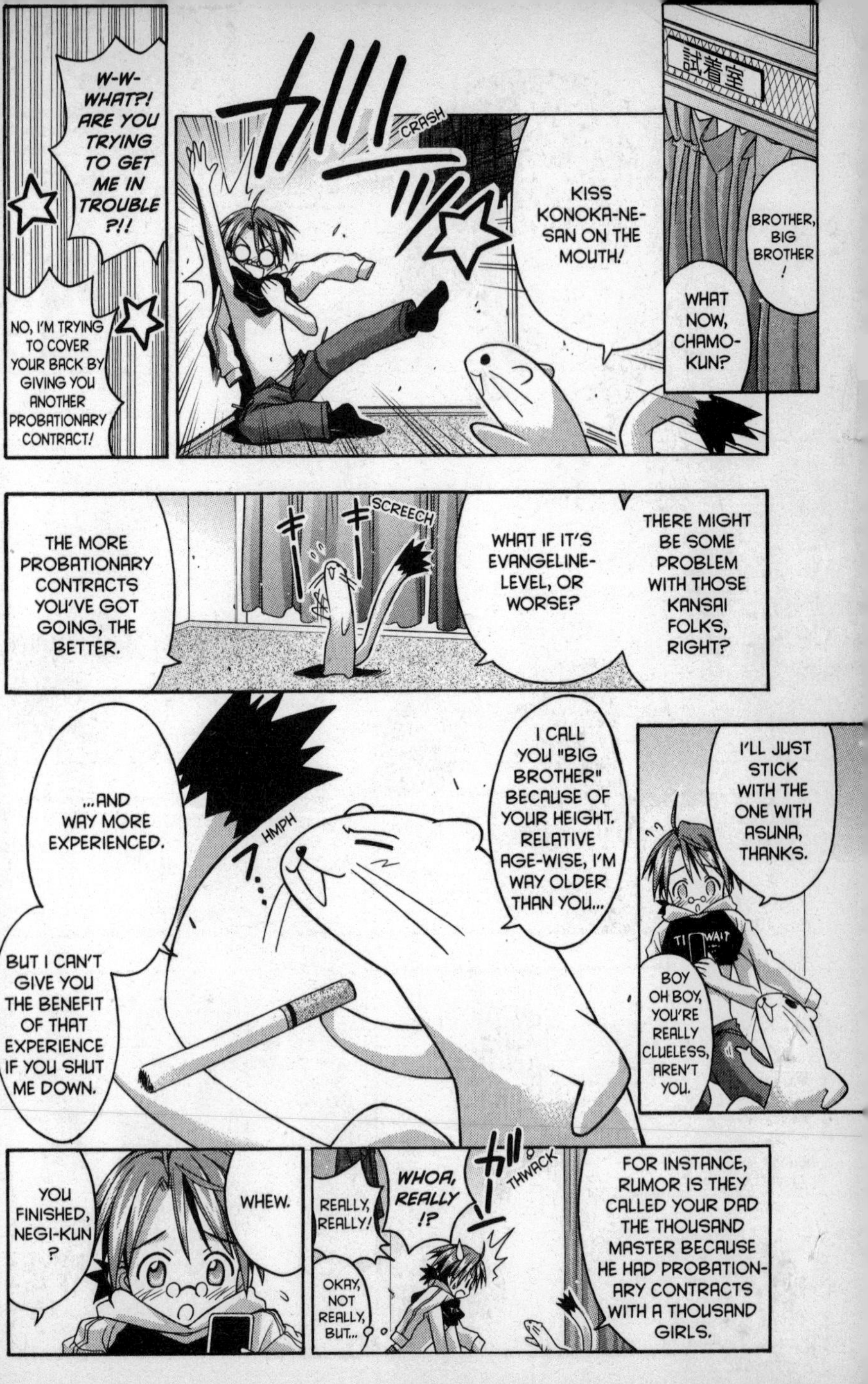
試着室
BROTHER, BIG BROTHER!
WHAT NOW, CHAMO-KUN?
KISS KONOKA-NE-SAN ON THE MOUTH!
CRASH
W-W-WHAT?! ARE YOU TRYING TO GET ME IN TROUBLE?!!
NO, I'M TRYING TO COVER YOUR BACK BY GIVING YOU ANOTHER PROBATIONARY CONTRACT!
THERE MIGHT BE SOME PROBLEM WITH THOSE KANSAI FOLKS, RIGHT?
WHAT IF IT'S EVANGELINE-LEVEL, OR WORSE?
SCREECH
THE MORE PROBATIONARY CONTRACTS YOU'VE GOT GOING, THE BETTER.
I'LL JUST STICK WITH THE ONE WITH ASUNA, THANKS.
BOY OH BOY, YOU'RE REALLY CLUELESS, AREN'T YOU.
I CALL YOU "BIG BROTHER" BECAUSE OF YOUR HEIGHT. RELATIVE AGE-WISE, I'M WAY OLDER THAN YOU...
HMPH
...AND WAY MORE EXPERIENCED.
BUT I CAN'T GIVE YOU THE BENEFIT OF THAT EXPERIENCE IF YOU SHUT ME DOWN.
FOR INSTANCE, RUMOR IS THEY CALLED YOUR DAD THE THOUSAND MASTER BECAUSE HE HAD PROBATIONARY CONTRACTS WITH A THOUSAND GIRLS.
THWACK
WHOA, REALLY!?
REALLY, REALLY!
OKAY, NOT REALLY, BUT...
WHEW.
YOU FINISHED, NEGI-KUN?

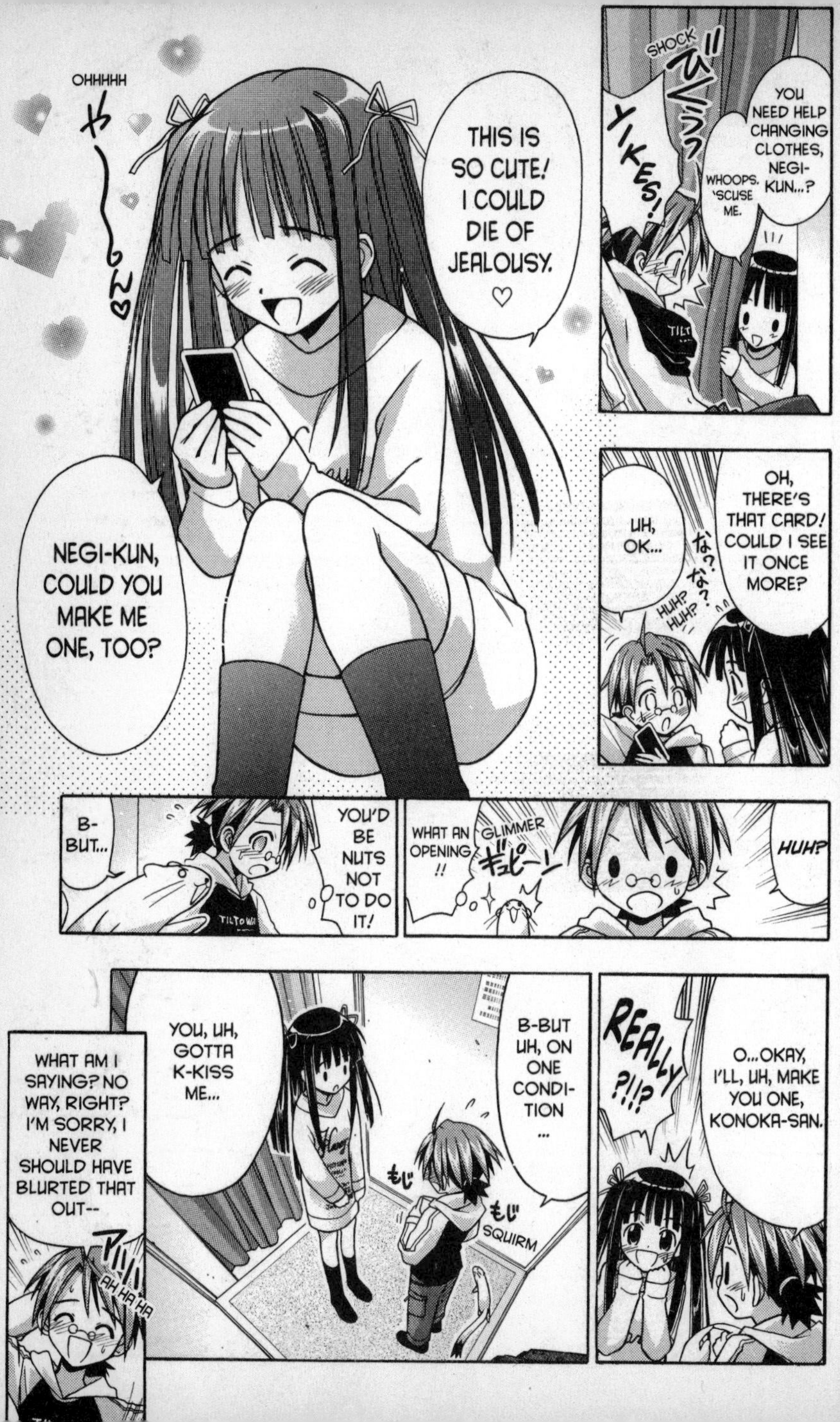
SHOCK
YOU NEED HELP CHANGING CLOTHES, NEGI-KUN...?
YIKES!
WHOOPS. 'SCUSE ME.
OH, THERE'S THAT CARD! COULD I SEE IT ONCE MORE?
なっ? なっ?
HUH? HUH?
UH, OK...
THIS IS SO CUTE! I COULD DIE OF JEALOUSY. ♡
OHHHHH
NEGI-KUN, COULD YOU MAKE ME ONE, TOO?
HUH?
GLIMMER
ギュピーン
WHAT AN OPENING !!
YOU'D BE NUTS NOT TO DO IT!
B-BUT...
O...OKAY, I'LL, UH, MAKE YOU ONE, KONOKA-SAN.
REALLY?!!?
B-BUT UH, ON ONE CONDITION...
YOU, UH, GOTTA K-KISS ME...
もじ
もじ
SQUIRM
WHAT AM I SAYING? NO WAY, RIGHT? I'M SORRY, I NEVER SHOULD HAVE BLURTED THAT OUT--
AH HA HA

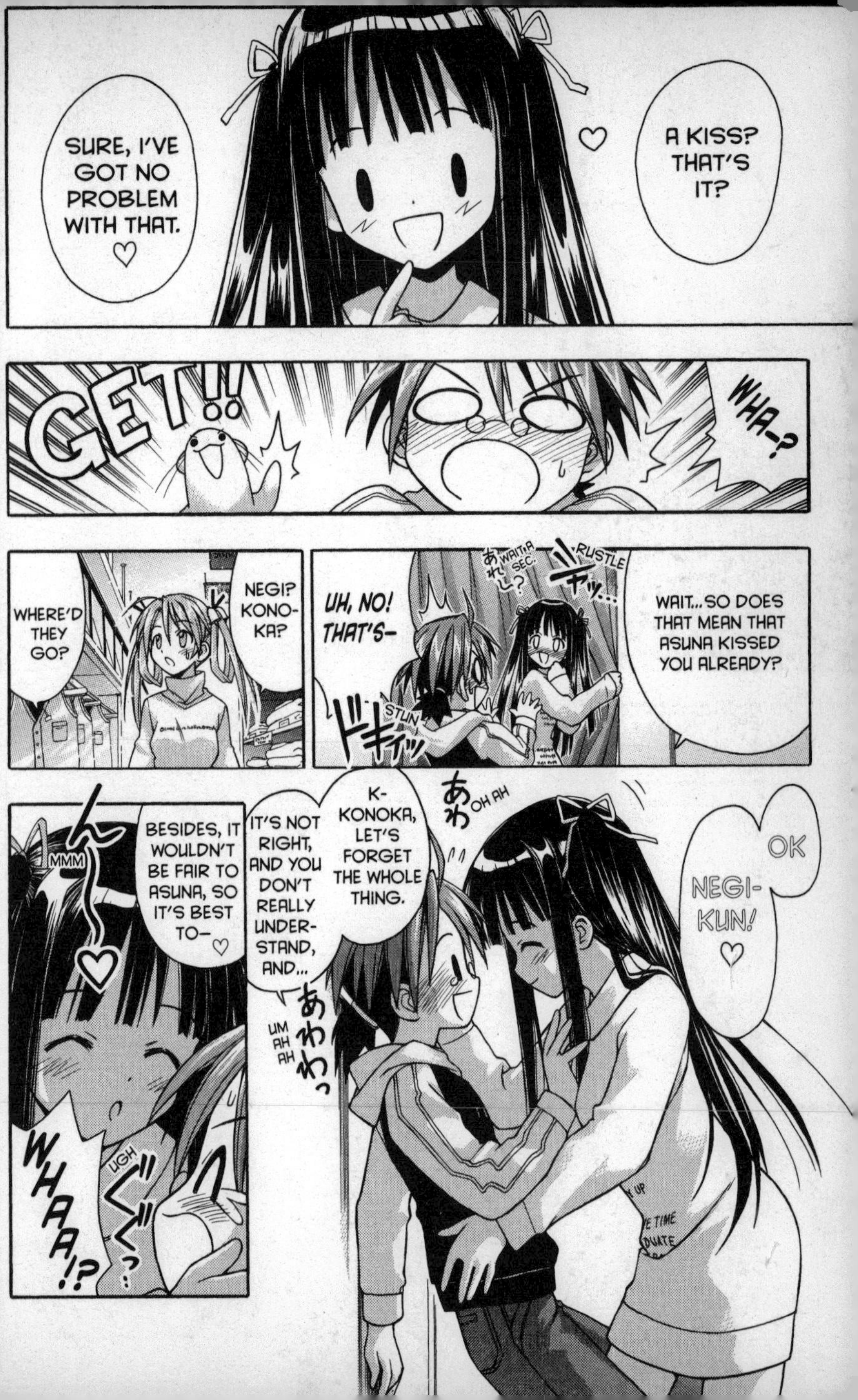
A KISS? THAT'S IT?
SURE, I'VE GOT NO PROBLEM WITH THAT. ♡
WHA-?
GET!!
WAIT...SO DOES THAT MEAN THAT ASUNA KISSED YOU ALREADY?
RUSTLE
WAIT, A SEC.
UH, NO! THAT'S-
STUN
NEGI? KONOKA?
WHERE'D THEY GO?
OK NEGI-KUN! ♡
OH AH
K-KONOKA, LET'S FORGET THE WHOLE THING.
IT'S NOT RIGHT, AND YOU DON'T REALLY UNDERSTAND, AND...
UM AH AH
BESIDES, IT WOULDN'T BE FAIR TO ASUNA, SO IT'S BEST TO— ♡
MMM
UGH
WHAA!?

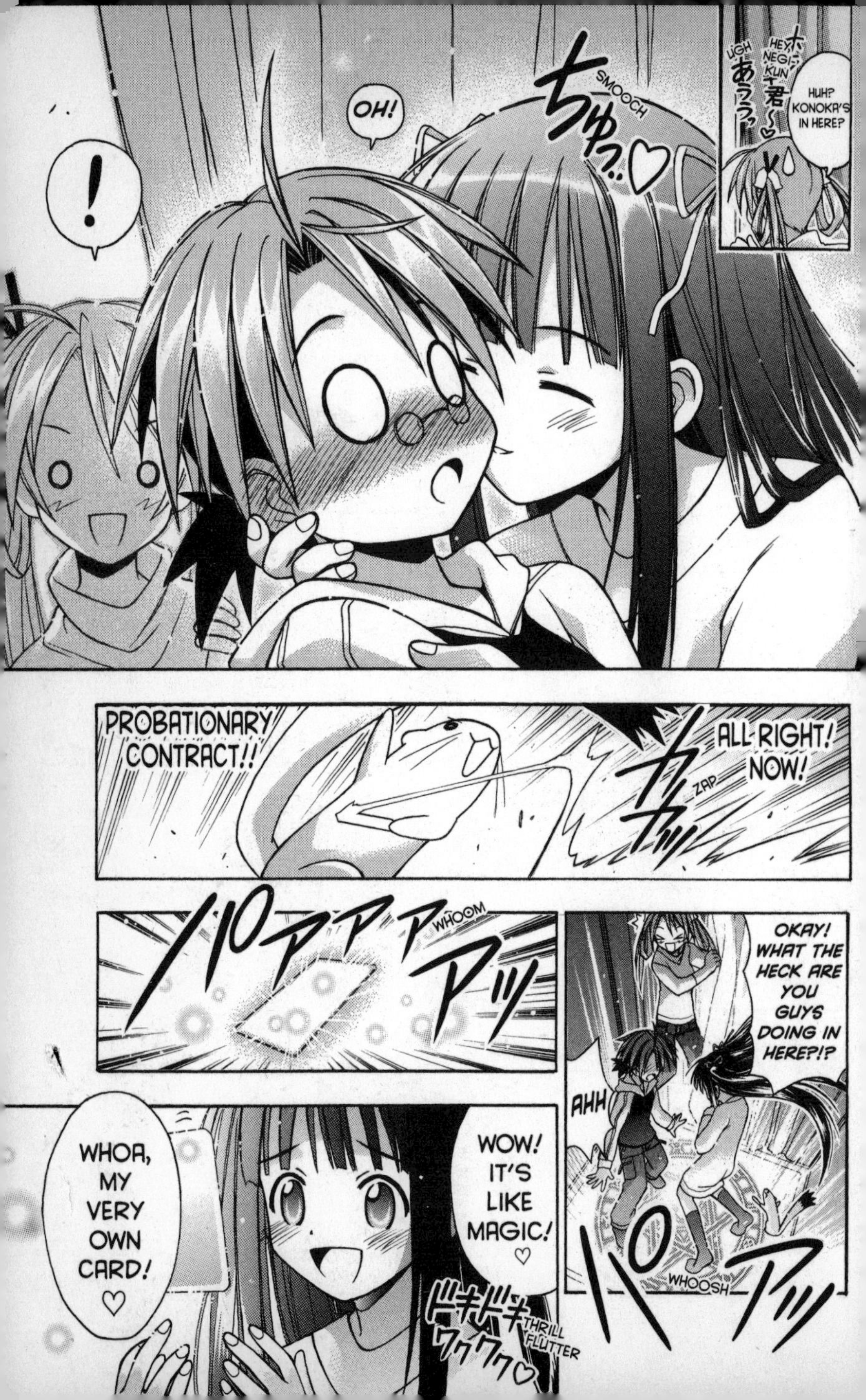
HEY NEGI-KUN ネギ君~♡
UGH あうう
HUH? KONOKA'S IN HERE?
SMOOCH
OH!
!
ALL RIGHT! NOW!
ZAP
PROBATIONARY CONTRACT!!
OKAY! WHAT THE HECK ARE YOU GUYS DOING IN HERE?!?
AHH
WHOOSH
WHOOM
WOW! IT'S LIKE MAGIC! ♡
WHOA, MY VERY OWN CARD! ♡
THRILL FLUTTER

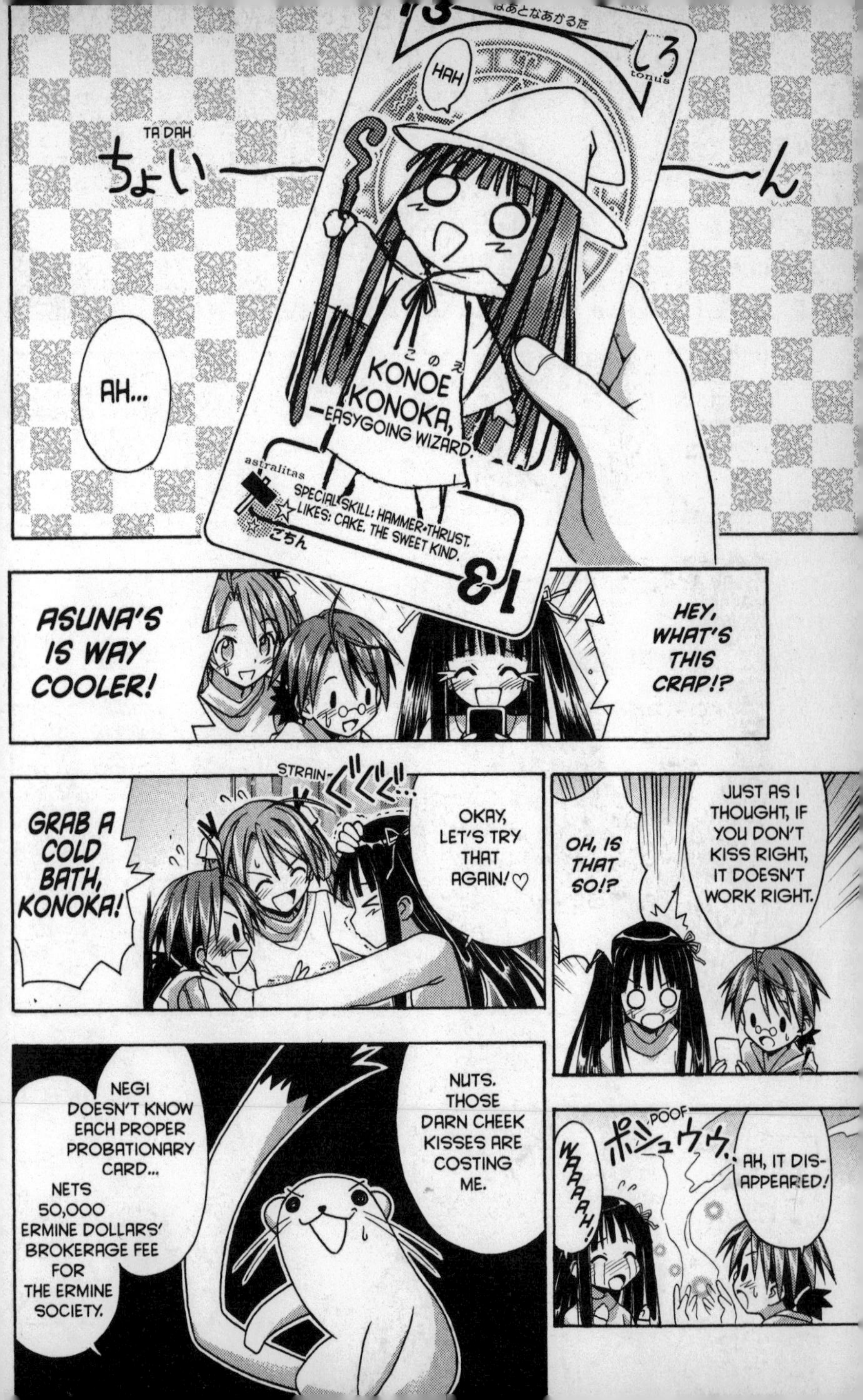
TA DAH
ちょい——ん
ぱあとなあかるた
しろ
tonus
HAH
こ の え
KONOE KONOKA, —EASYGOING WIZARD.
astralitas
SPECIAL SKILL: HAMMER-THRUST.
LIKES: CAKE. THE SWEET KIND.
こちん
13
AH...
HEY, WHAT'S THIS CRAP!?
ASUNA'S IS WAY COOLER!
JUST AS I THOUGHT, IF YOU DON'T KISS RIGHT, IT DOESN'T WORK RIGHT.
OH, IS THAT SO!?
STRAIN- ぐぐぐ...
OKAY, LET'S TRY THAT AGAIN! ♡
GRAB A COLD BATH, KONOKA!
POOF ポシュウウ...
AH, IT DIS-APPEARED!
WAAAAH!
NUTS. THOSE DARN CHEEK KISSES ARE COSTING ME.
NEGI DOESN'T KNOW EACH PROPER PROBATIONARY CARD... NETS 50,000 ERMINE DOLLARS' BROKERAGE FEE FOR THE ERMINE SOCIETY.

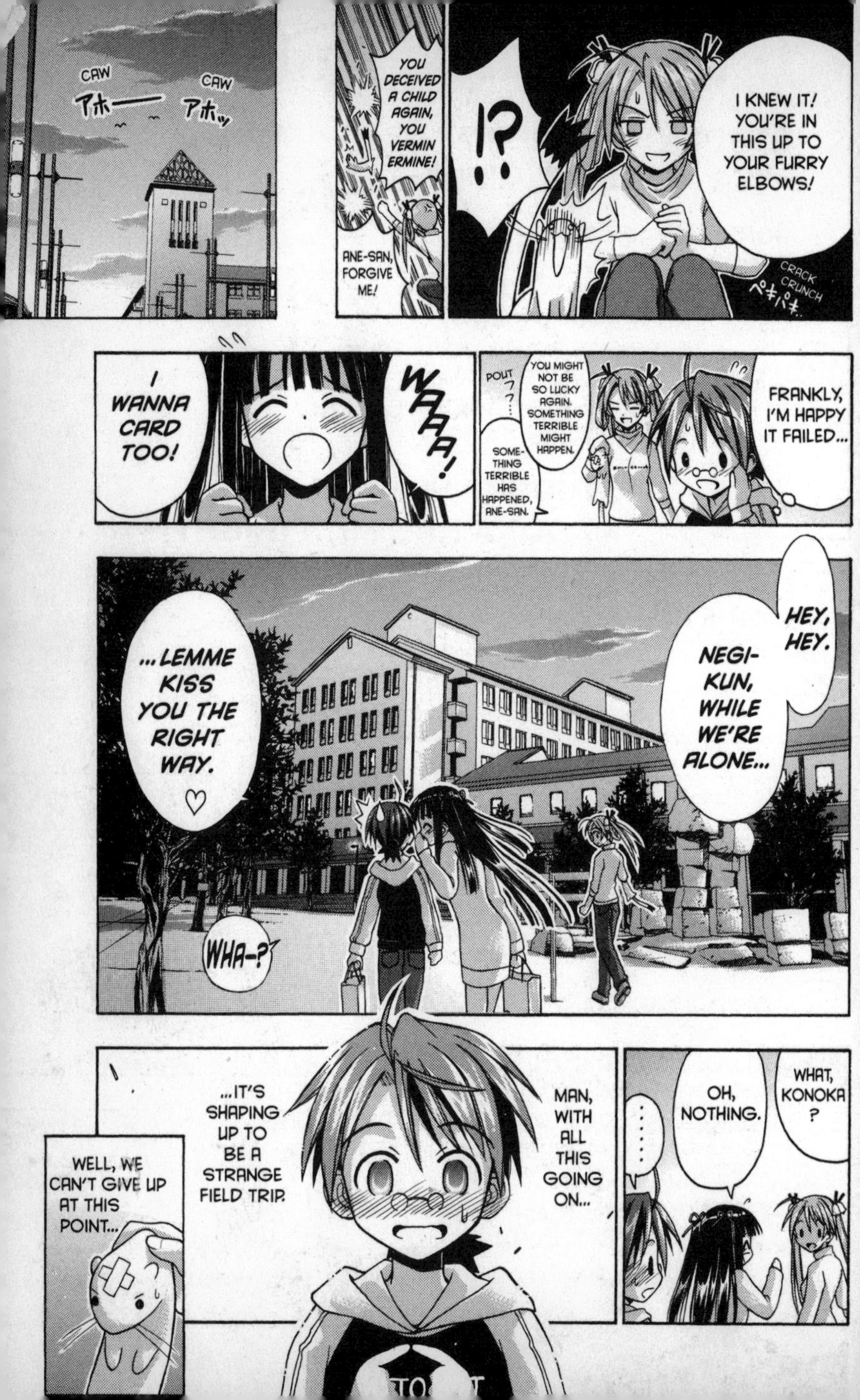
I KNEW IT! YOU'RE IN THIS UP TO YOUR FURRY ELBOWS!
!?
CRACK CRUNCH ペキパキ
YOU DECEIVED A CHILD AGAIN, YOU VERMIN ERMINE!
ANE-SAN, FORGIVE ME!
CAW アホッ
CAW アホー
FRANKLY, I'M HAPPY IT FAILED...
YOU MIGHT NOT BE SO LUCKY AGAIN. SOMETHING TERRIBLE MIGHT HAPPEN.
POUT
SOME-THING TERRIBLE HAS HAPPENED, ANE-SAN.
WAAA!
I WANNA CARD TOO!
HEY, HEY.
NEGI-KUN, WHILE WE'RE ALONE...
...LEMME KISS YOU THE RIGHT WAY. ♡
WHA-?
WHAT, KONOKA?
OH, NOTHING.
......
MAN, WITH ALL THIS GOING ON...
...IT'S SHAPING UP TO BE A STRANGE FIELD TRIP.
WELL, WE CAN'T GIVE UP AT THIS POINT...

3-A STUDENT PROFILE

STUDENT NUMBER 7
MISA KAKIZAKI (MIDDLE)

BORN: MAY 15, 1988
BLOOD TYPE: O
ASTROLOGICAL SIGN: TAURUS
LIKES: PRUNES, SHOPPING
      (EVERY WEEKEND DOWNTOWN)
DISLIKES: CARBONATED DRINKS
AFFILIATIONS: MAHORA CHEERLEADING,
      CHORUS CLUB

STUDENT NUMBER 11
MADOKA KUGIMIYA (RIGHT)

BORN: MARCH 3, 1989
BLOOD TYPE: AB
ASTROLOGICAL SIGN: PISCES
LIKES: MATSUYA BEEF BOWL, SILVER
      ACCESSORIES, WESTERN MUSIC
      (LATELY, IT'S AVRIL LAVIGNE)
DISLIKES: SHOWY GUYS THAT COME AND
      HIT ON HER, HAS A COMPLEX ABOUT
      HER OWN HUSKY VOICE
AFFILIATIONS: MAHORA CHEERLEADING

STUDENT NUMBER 17
SAKURAKO SHIINA (LEFT)

BORN: JUNE 9, 1988
BLOOD TYPE: B
ASTROLOGICAL SIGN: GEMINI
LIKES: KARAOKE, COOKIE AND BIKKE (HER CATS)
DISLIKES: BLACK FURRY THINGS STARTLING
      HER IN PLACES LIKE THE KITCHEN
      (SPECIFICALLY, HER CATS)
AFFILIATIONS: MAHORA CHEERLEADING,
      LACROSSE CLUB

NEGIMA!
MAGISTER NEGI MAGI

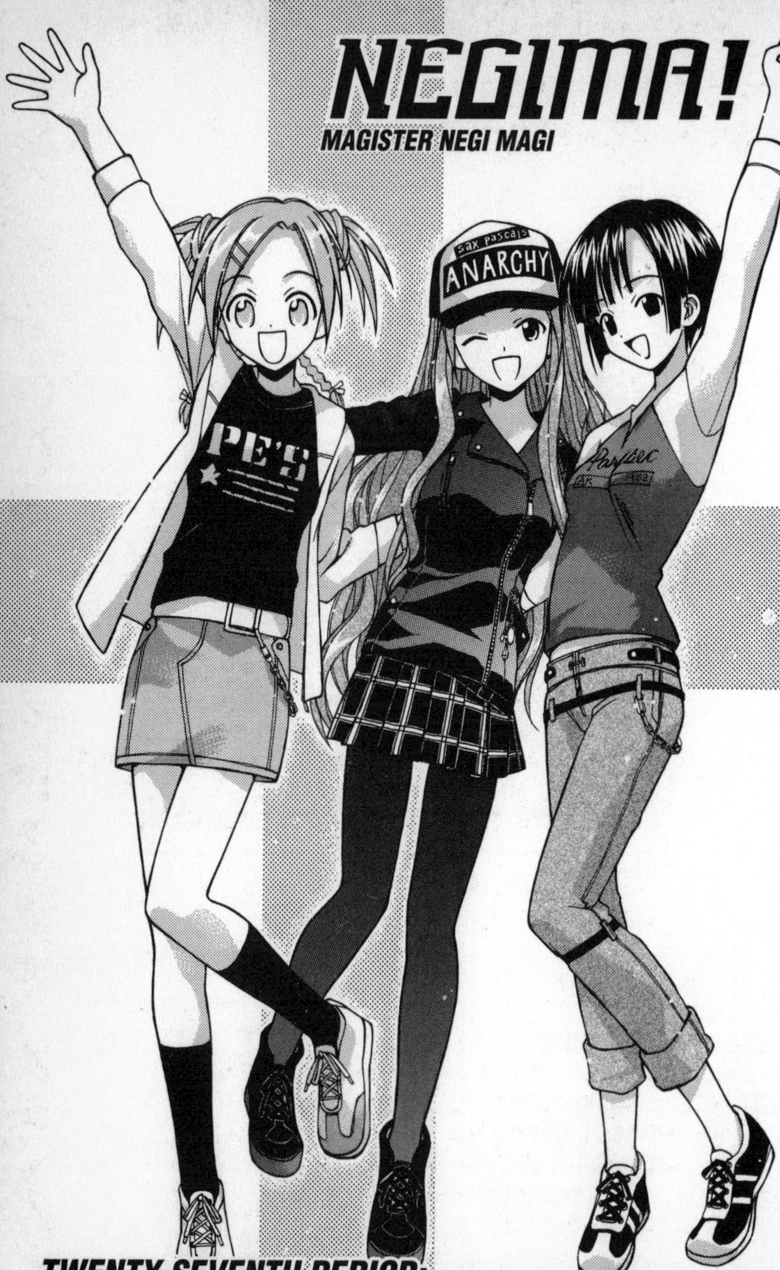
sax pascals
ANARCHY
PE'S

TWENTY-SEVENTH PERIOD:
A SECRET DATE!? CHEERLEADERS ATTACK!

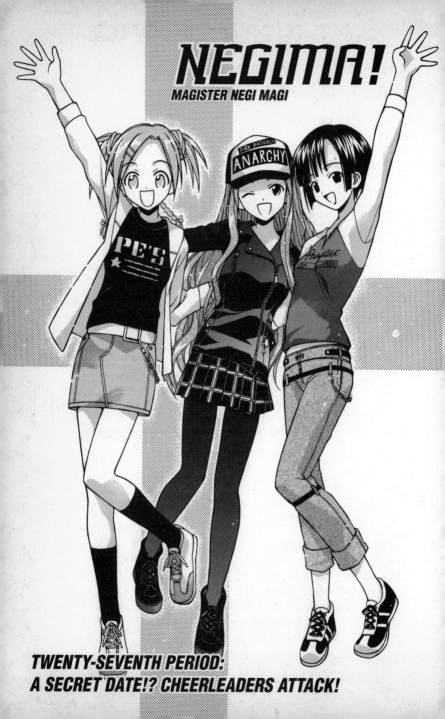

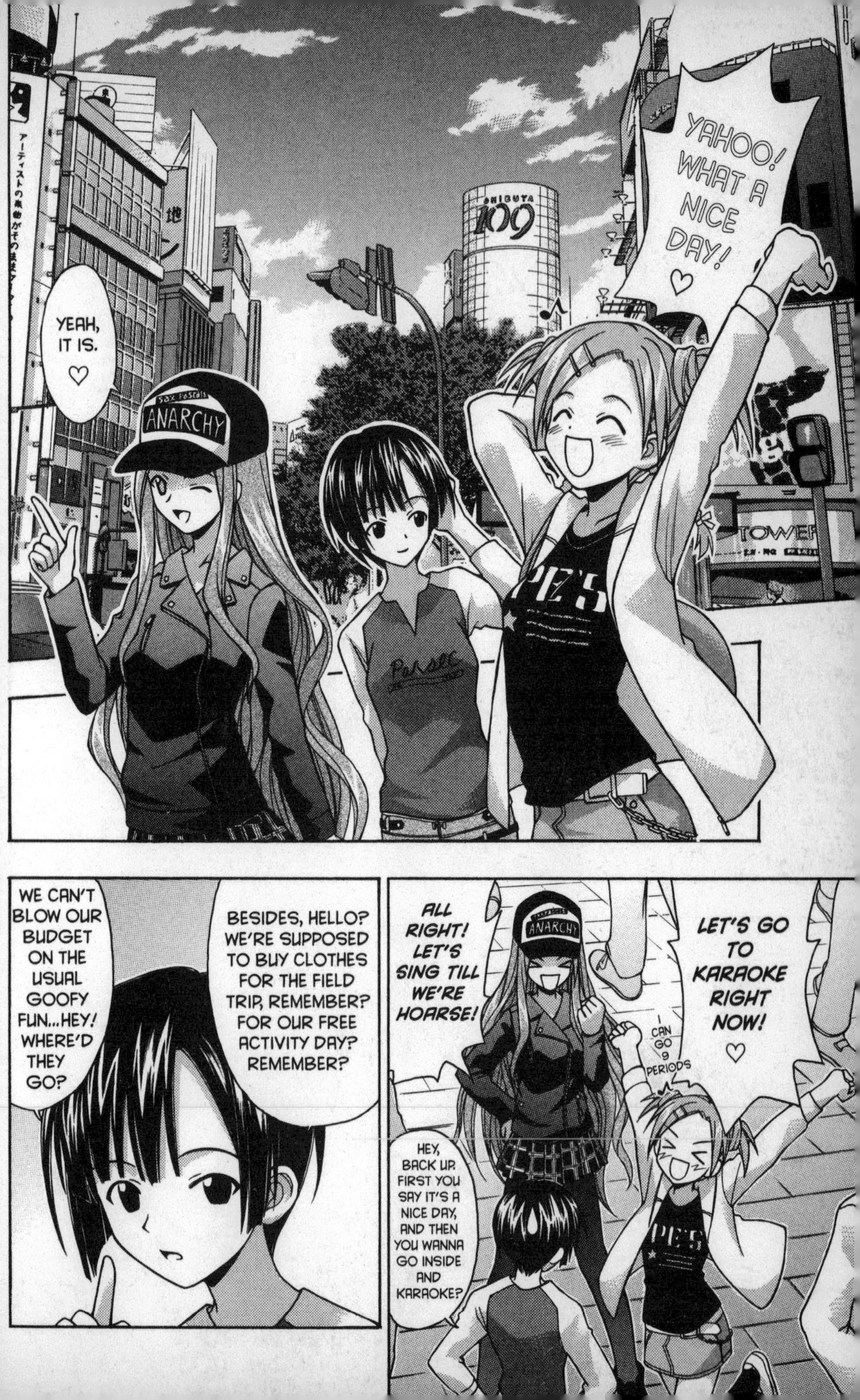
YAHOO! WHAT A NICE DAY! ♥
SHIBUYA 109
ANARCHY
TOWER
PE'S
YEAH, IT IS. ♥
LET'S GO TO KARAOKE RIGHT NOW! ♥
I CAN GO 9 PERIODS
ALL RIGHT! LET'S SING TILL WE'RE HOARSE!
HEY, BACK UP. FIRST YOU SAY IT'S A NICE DAY, AND THEN YOU WANNA GO INSIDE AND KARAOKE?
BESIDES, HELLO? WE'RE SUPPOSED TO BUY CLOTHES FOR THE FIELD TRIP, REMEMBER? FOR OUR FREE ACTIVITY DAY? REMEMBER?
WE CAN'T BLOW OUR BUDGET ON THE USUAL GOOFY FUN...HEY! WHERE'D THEY GO?

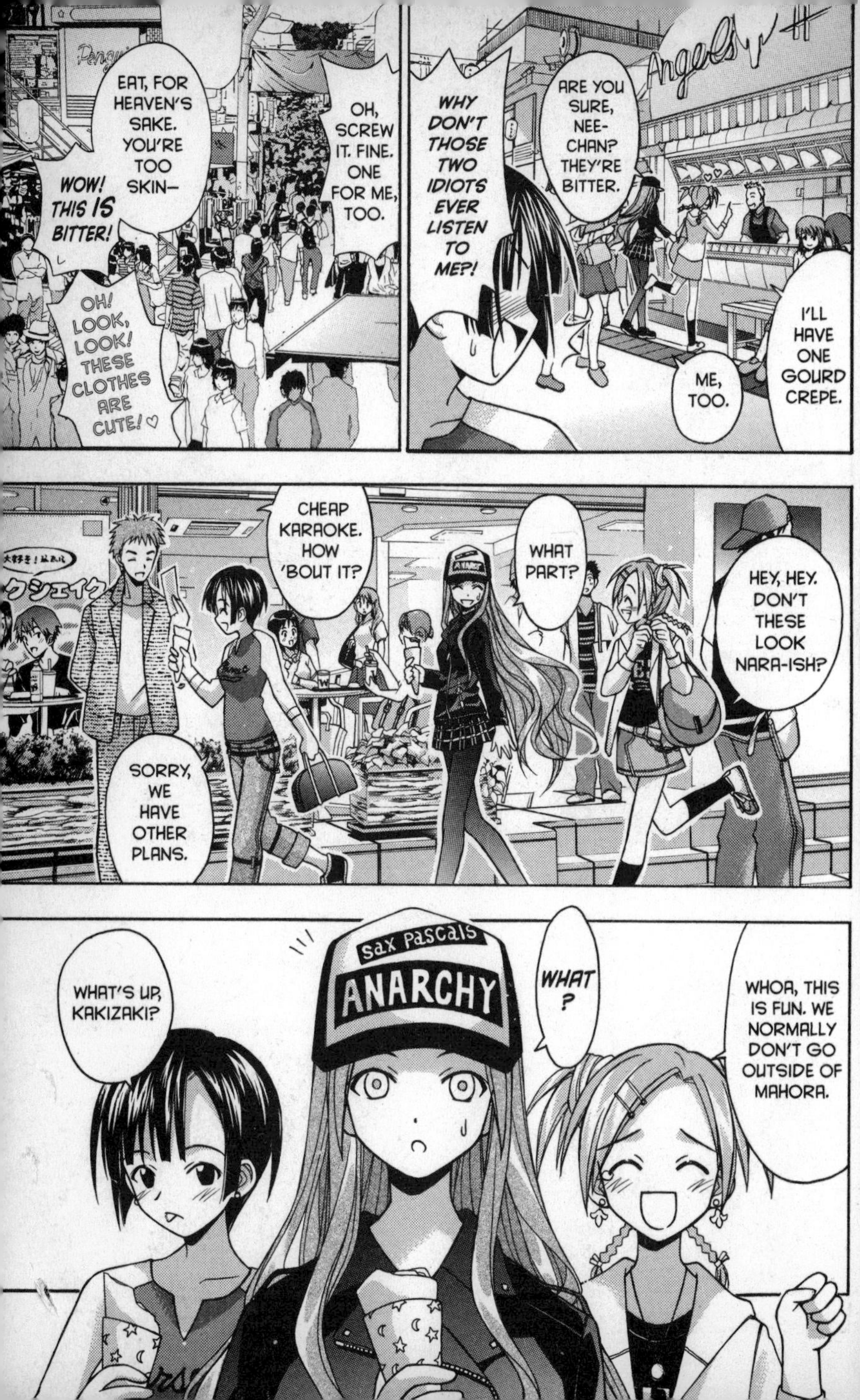
Angels
ARE YOU SURE, NEE-CHAN? THEY'RE BITTER.
WHY DON'T THOSE TWO IDIOTS EVER LISTEN TO ME?!
I'LL HAVE ONE GOURD CREPE.
ME, TOO.
OH, SCREW IT. FINE. ONE FOR ME, TOO.
EAT, FOR HEAVEN'S SAKE. YOU'RE TOO SKIN—
WOW! THIS IS BITTER!
OH! LOOK, LOOK! THESE CLOTHES ARE CUTE! ♡
HEY, HEY. DON'T THESE LOOK NARA-ISH?
WHAT PART?
CHEAP KARAOKE. HOW 'BOUT IT?
SORRY, WE HAVE OTHER PLANS.
WHOA, THIS IS FUN. WE NORMALLY DON'T GO OUTSIDE OF MAHORA.
WHAT?
sax pascals
ANARCHY
WHAT'S UP, KAKIZAKI?

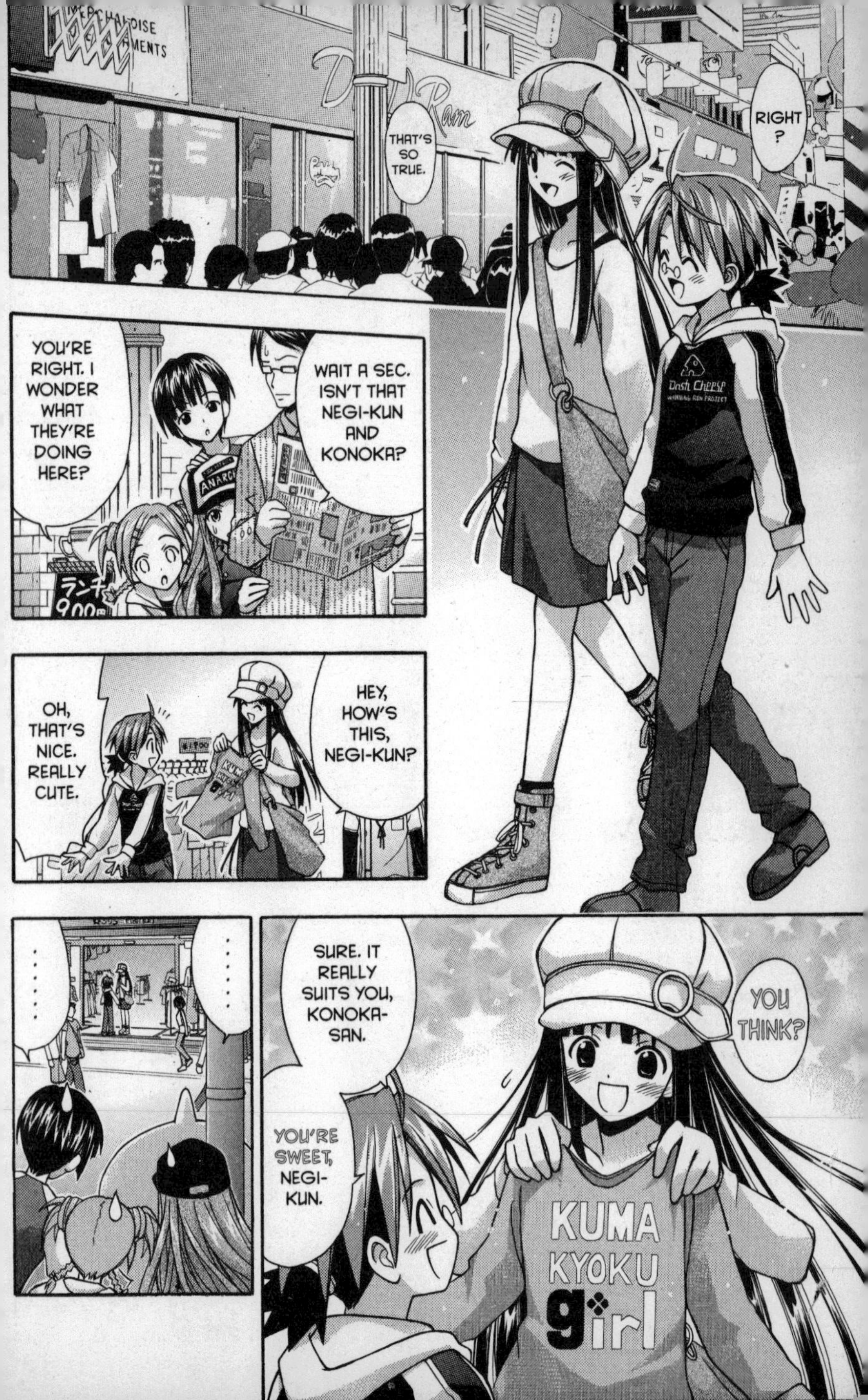
RIGHT ?
THAT'S SO TRUE.
WAIT A SEC. ISN'T THAT NEGI-KUN AND KONOKA?
YOU'RE RIGHT. I WONDER WHAT THEY'RE DOING HERE?
HEY, HOW'S THIS, NEGI-KUN?
OH, THAT'S NICE. REALLY CUTE.
YOU THINK?
SURE. IT REALLY SUITS YOU, KONOKA-SAN.
YOU'RE SWEET, NEGI-KUN.
KUMA KYOKU girl
......
......

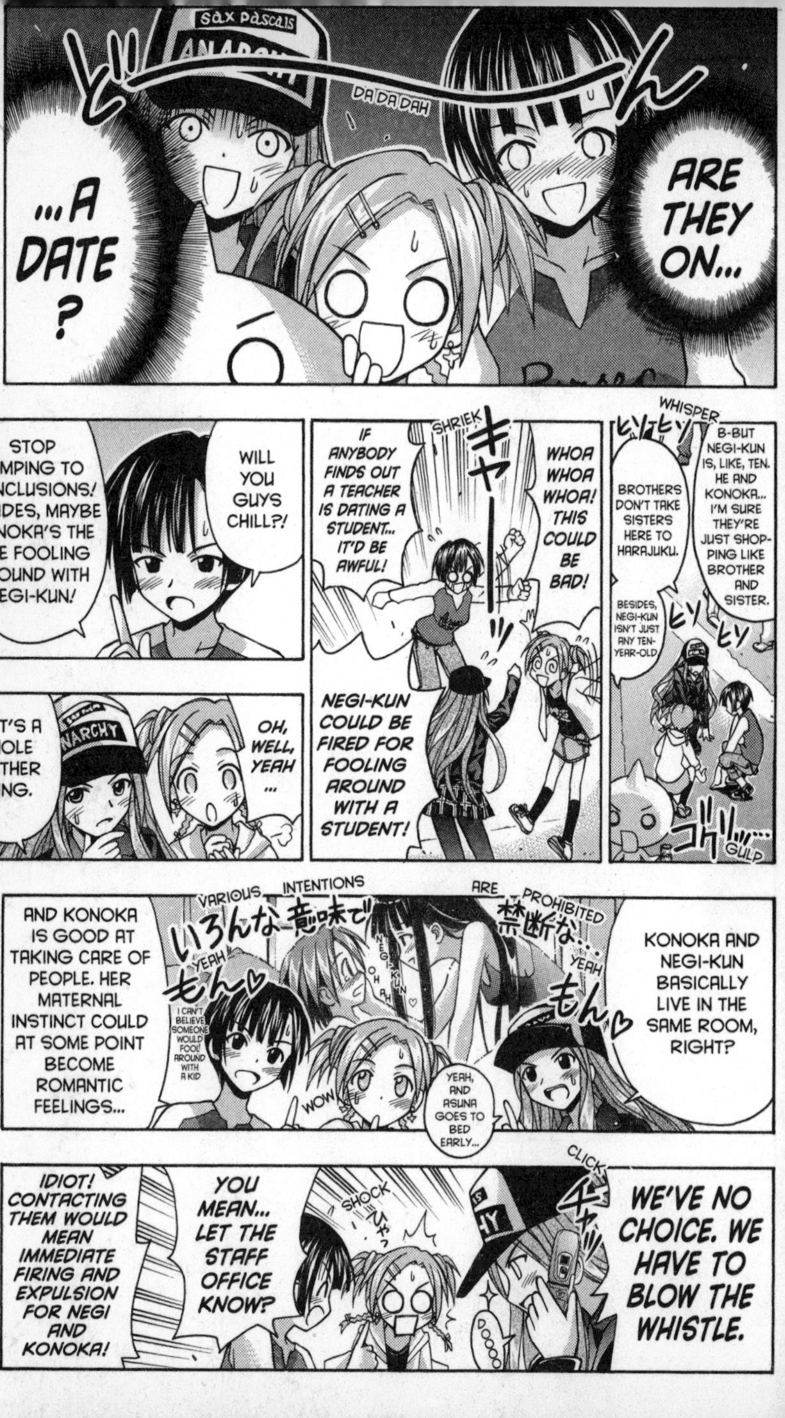

ARE THEY ON...
DA DA DAH
...A DATE?
WHISPER
B-BUT NEGI-KUN IS, LIKE, TEN. HE AND KONOKA... I'M SURE THEY'RE JUST SHOPPING LIKE BROTHER AND SISTER.
BROTHERS DON'T TAKE SISTERS HERE TO HARAJUKU.
BESIDES, NEGI-KUN ISN'T JUST ANY TEN-YEAR-OLD.
GULP
SHRIEK
WHOA WHOA WHOA! THIS COULD BE BAD!
IF ANYBODY FINDS OUT A TEACHER IS DATING A STUDENT... IT'D BE AWFUL!
NEGI-KUN COULD BE FIRED FOR FOOLING AROUND WITH A STUDENT!
WILL YOU GUYS CHILL?!
STOP JUMPING TO CONCLUSIONS! BESIDES, MAYBE KONOKA'S THE ONE FOOLING AROUND WITH NEGI-KUN!
OH, WELL, YEAH...
THAT'S A WHOLE 'NOTHER THING.
KONOKA AND NEGI-KUN BASICALLY LIVE IN THE SAME ROOM, RIGHT?
PROHIBITED
禁断な…
ARE
YEAH
もん♥
YEAH, AND ASUNA GOES TO BED EARLY...
NEGI-KUN OH AH
VARIOUS INTENTIONS
いろんな意味で
YEAH
もん♥
I CAN'T BELIEVE SOMEONE WOULD FOOL AROUND WITH A KID
WOW
AND KONOKA IS GOOD AT TAKING CARE OF PEOPLE. HER MATERNAL INSTINCT COULD AT SOME POINT BECOME ROMANTIC FEELINGS...
WE'VE NO CHOICE. WE HAVE TO BLOW THE WHISTLE.
CLICK
SHOCK
YOU MEAN... LET THE STAFF OFFICE KNOW?
IDIOT! CONTACTING THEM WOULD MEAN IMMEDIATE FIRING AND EXPULSION FOR NEGI AND KONOKA!

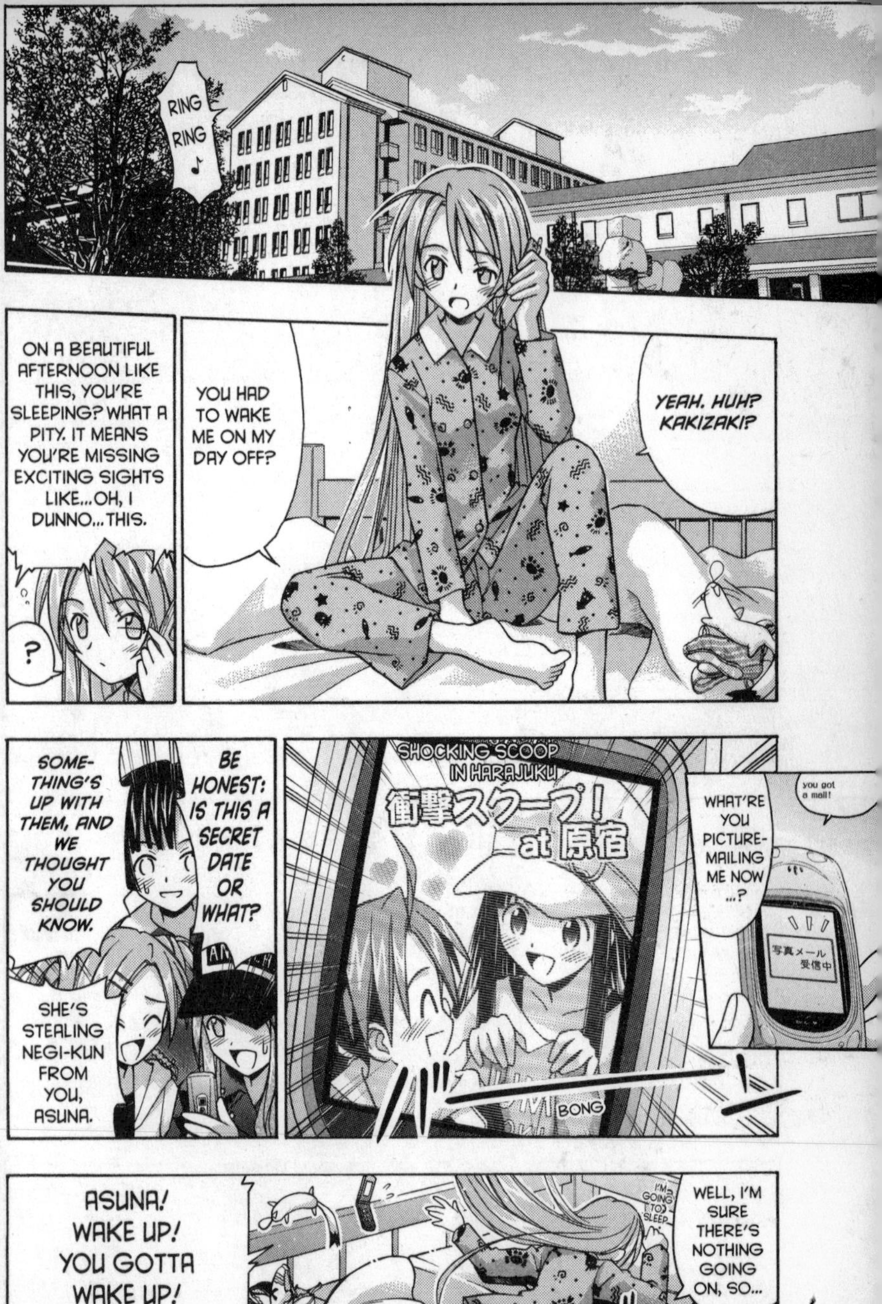
RING RING ♪
YEAH. HUH? KAKIZAKI?
YOU HAD TO WAKE ME ON MY DAY OFF?
ON A BEAUTIFUL AFTERNOON LIKE THIS, YOU'RE SLEEPING? WHAT A PITY. IT MEANS YOU'RE MISSING EXCITING SIGHTS LIKE...OH, I DUNNO...THIS.
?
you got a mail!
WHAT'RE YOU PICTURE-MAILING ME NOW ...?
写真メール 受信中
SHOCKING SCOOP IN HARAJUKU
衝撃スクープ! at 原宿
BONG
BE HONEST: IS THIS A SECRET DATE OR WHAT?
SOME-THING'S UP WITH THEM, AND WE THOUGHT YOU SHOULD KNOW.
SHE'S STEALING NEGI-KUN FROM YOU, ASUNA.
WELL, I'M SURE THERE'S NOTHING GOING ON, SO...
I'M GOING TO SLEEP.
ASUNA! WAKE UP! YOU GOTTA WAKE UP!
PLUNK
ボフッ

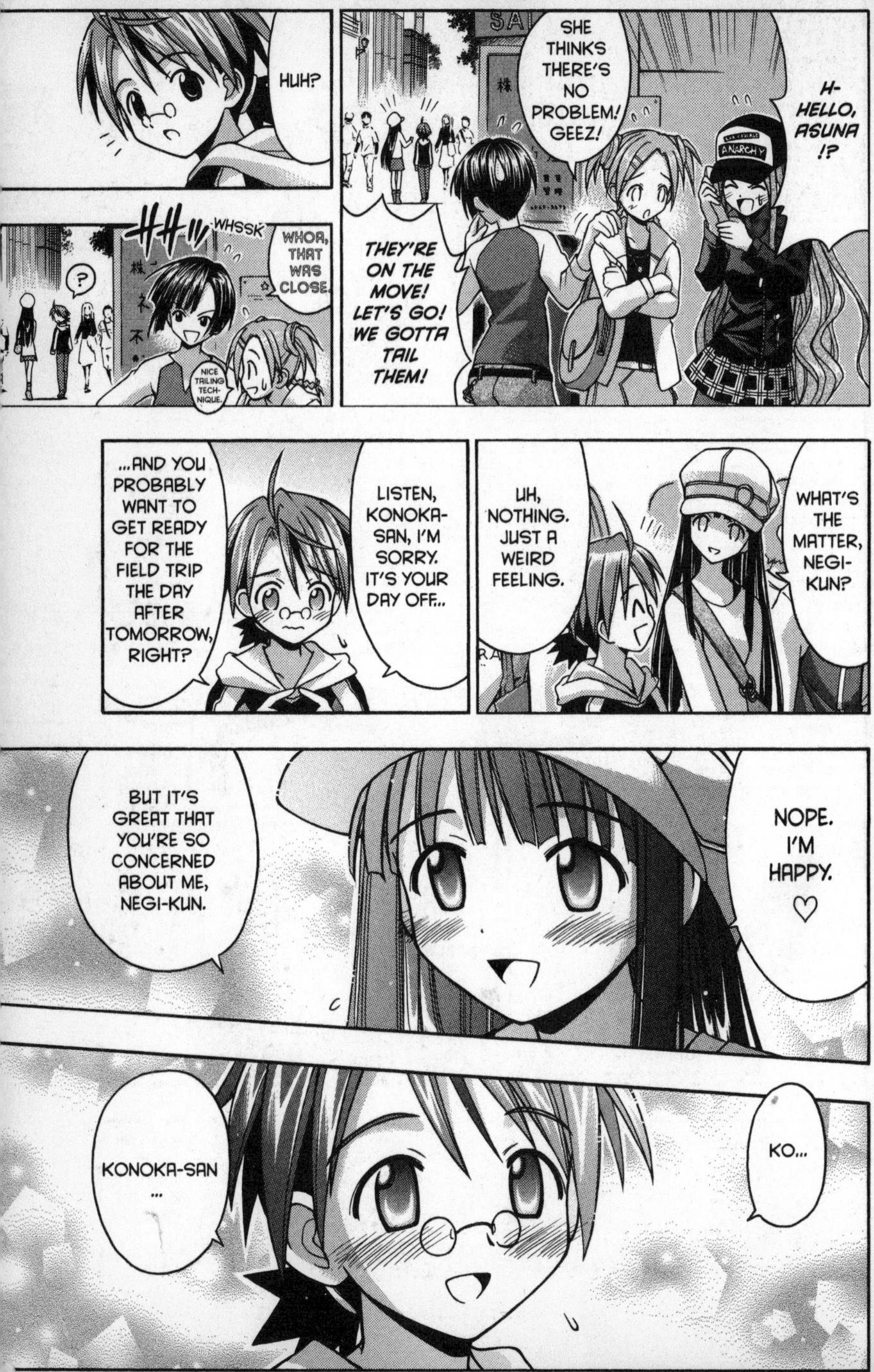
H-HELLO, ASUNA!?
SHE THINKS THERE'S NO PROBLEM! GEEZ!
THEY'RE ON THE MOVE! LET'S GO! WE GOTTA TAIL THEM!
HUH?
WHSSK
WHOA, THAT WAS CLOSE.
NICE TAILING TECHNIQUE.
WHAT'S THE MATTER, NEGI-KUN?
UH, NOTHING. JUST A WEIRD FEELING.
LISTEN, KONOKA-SAN, I'M SORRY. IT'S YOUR DAY OFF...
...AND YOU PROBABLY WANT TO GET READY FOR THE FIELD TRIP THE DAY AFTER TOMORROW, RIGHT?
NOPE. I'M HAPPY. ♡
BUT IT'S GREAT THAT YOU'RE SO CONCERNED ABOUT ME, NEGI-KUN.
KO...
KONOKA-SAN ...

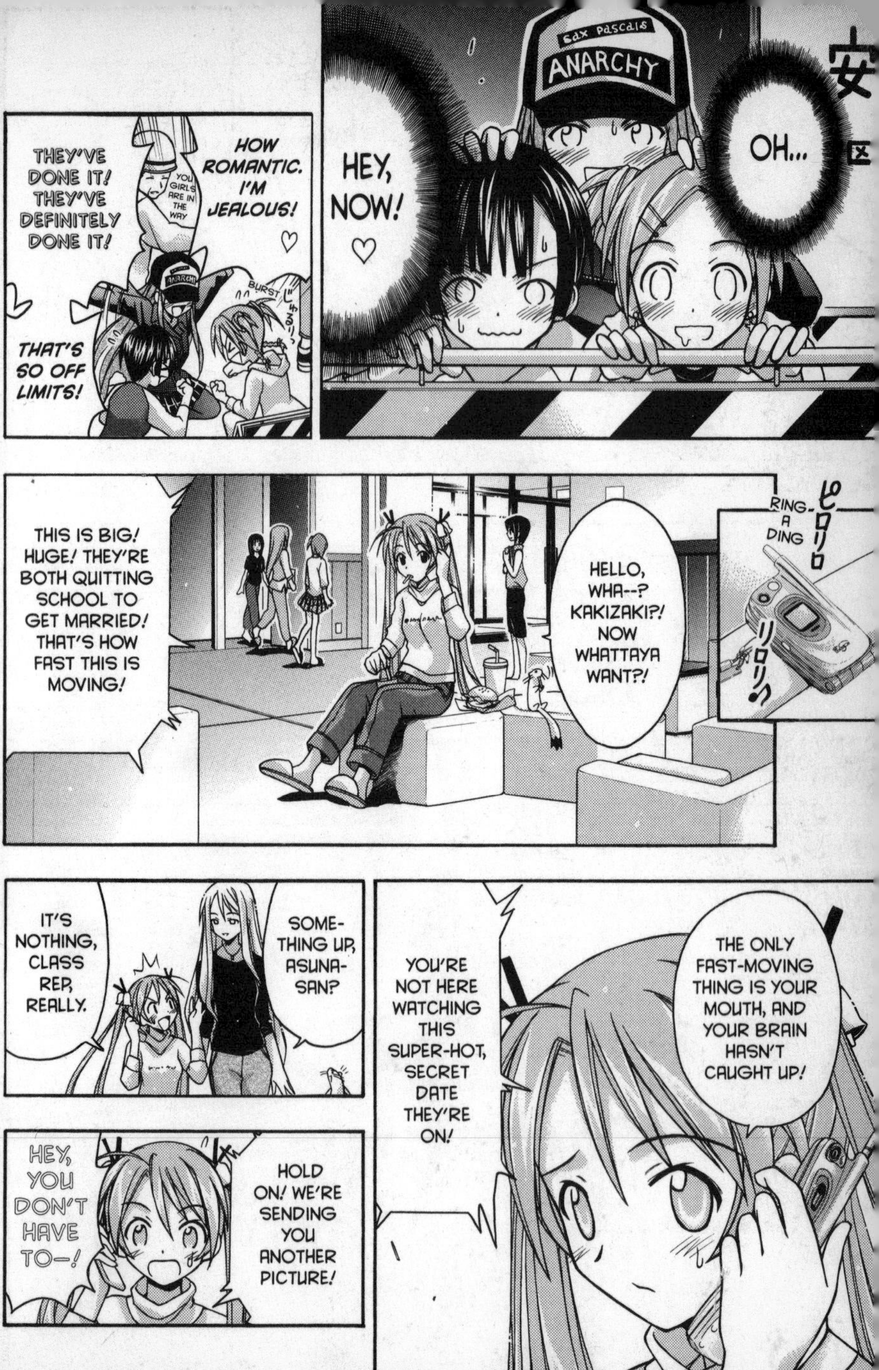
OH...
HEY, NOW! ♡
SAX PASCALS
ANARCHY
HOW ROMANTIC. I'M JEALOUS! ♡
THEY'VE DONE IT! THEY'VE DEFINITELY DONE IT!
YOU GIRLS ARE IN THE WAY
BURST
THAT'S SO OFF LIMITS!
RING-A DING
HELLO, WHA--? KAKIZAKI?! NOW WHATTAYA WANT?!
THIS IS BIG! HUGE! THEY'RE BOTH QUITTING SCHOOL TO GET MARRIED! THAT'S HOW FAST THIS IS MOVING!
THE ONLY FAST-MOVING THING IS YOUR MOUTH, AND YOUR BRAIN HASN'T CAUGHT UP!
YOU'RE NOT HERE WATCHING THIS SUPER-HOT, SECRET DATE THEY'RE ON!
SOME-THING UP, ASUNA-SAN?
IT'S NOTHING, CLASS REP, REALLY.
HOLD ON! WE'RE SENDING YOU ANOTHER PICTURE!
HEY, YOU DON'T HAVE TO—!

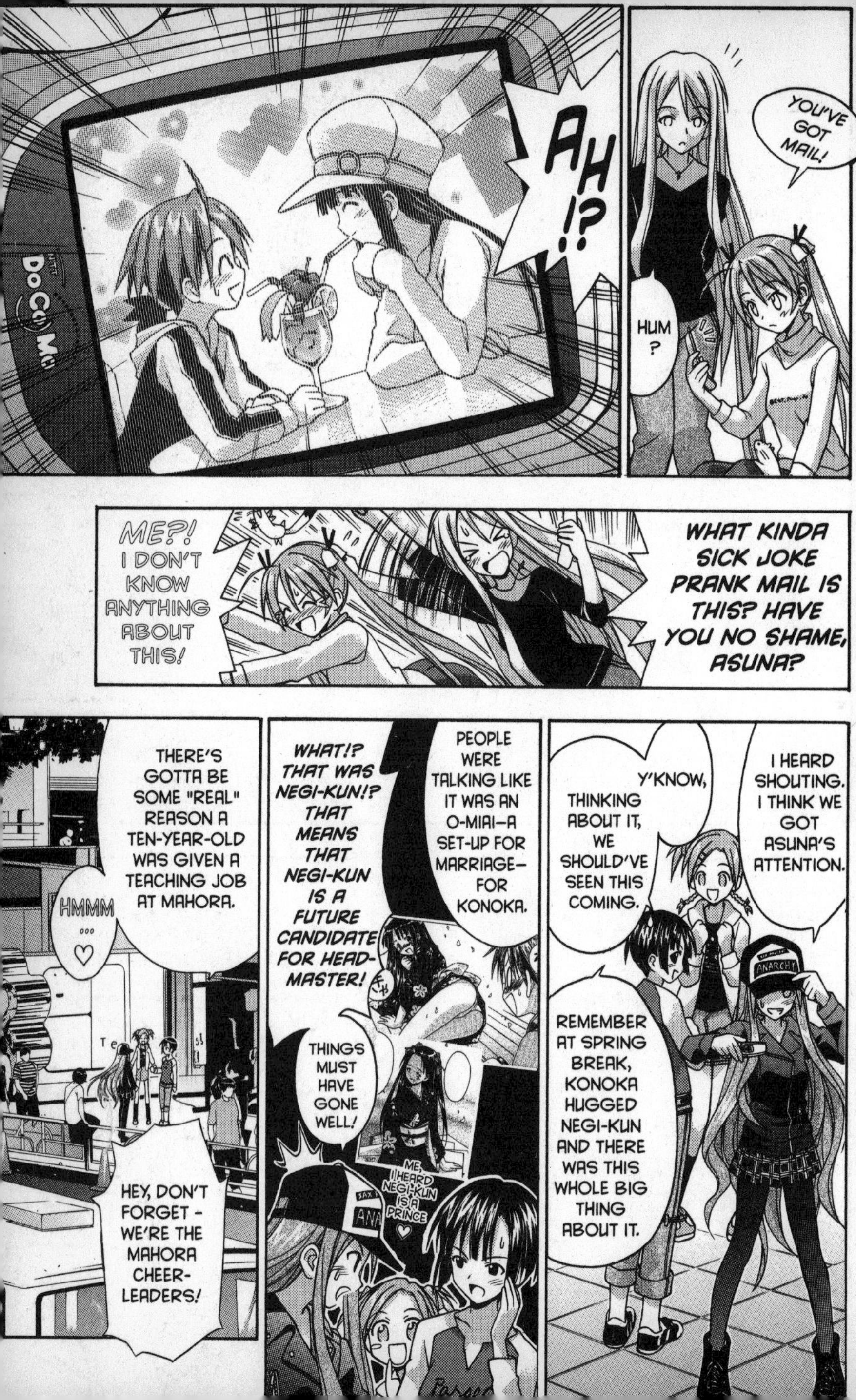
YOU'VE GOT MAIL!
HUM ?
AH !?
NTT DoCoMo
WHAT KINDA SICK JOKE PRANK MAIL IS THIS? HAVE YOU NO SHAME, ASUNA?
ME?! I DON'T KNOW ANYTHING ABOUT THIS!
I HEARD SHOUTING. I THINK WE GOT ASUNA'S ATTENTION.
Y'KNOW, THINKING ABOUT IT, WE SHOULD'VE SEEN THIS COMING.
ANARCHY
REMEMBER AT SPRING BREAK, KONOKA HUGGED NEGI-KUN AND THERE WAS THIS WHOLE BIG THING ABOUT IT.
PEOPLE WERE TALKING LIKE IT WAS AN O-MIAI—A SET-UP FOR MARRIAGE—FOR KONOKA.
WHAT!? THAT WAS NEGI-KUN!? THAT MEANS THAT NEGI-KUN IS A FUTURE CANDIDATE FOR HEAD-MASTER!
THINGS MUST HAVE GONE WELL!
ME, I HEARD NEGI-KUN IS A PRINCE ♡
THERE'S GOTTA BE SOME "REAL" REASON A TEN-YEAR-OLD WAS GIVEN A TEACHING JOB AT MAHORA.
HMMM... ♡
HEY, DON'T FORGET - WE'RE THE MAHORA CHEER-LEADERS!

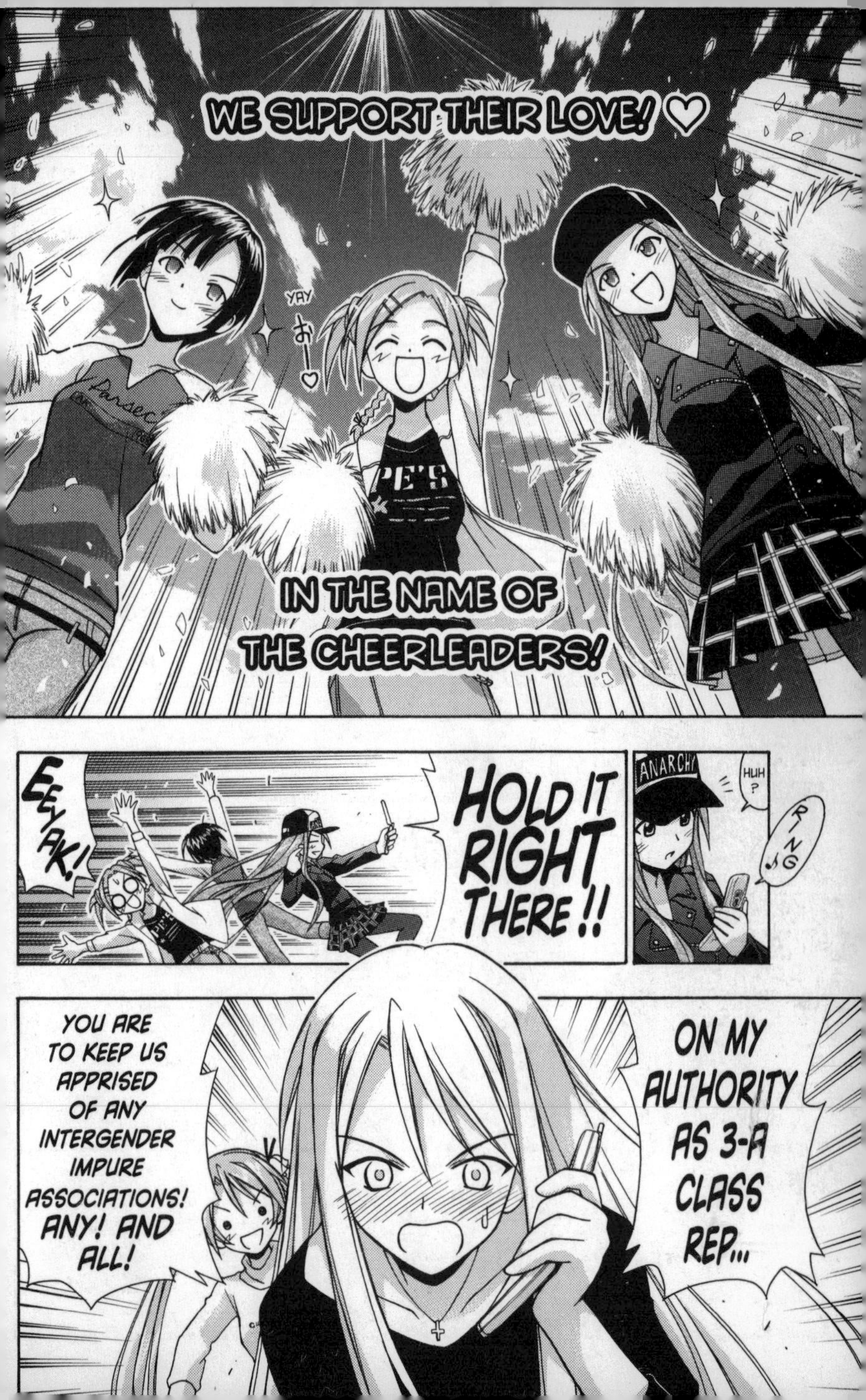
WE SUPPORT THEIR LOVE! ♥
YAY
お〜♥
IN THE NAME OF THE CHEERLEADERS!
ANARCHY
HUH?
RING
HOLD IT RIGHT THERE!!
EEYAAK!
ON MY AUTHORITY AS 3-A CLASS REP...
YOU ARE TO KEEP US APPRISED OF ANY INTERGENDER IMPURE ASSOCIATIONS! ANY! AND ALL!

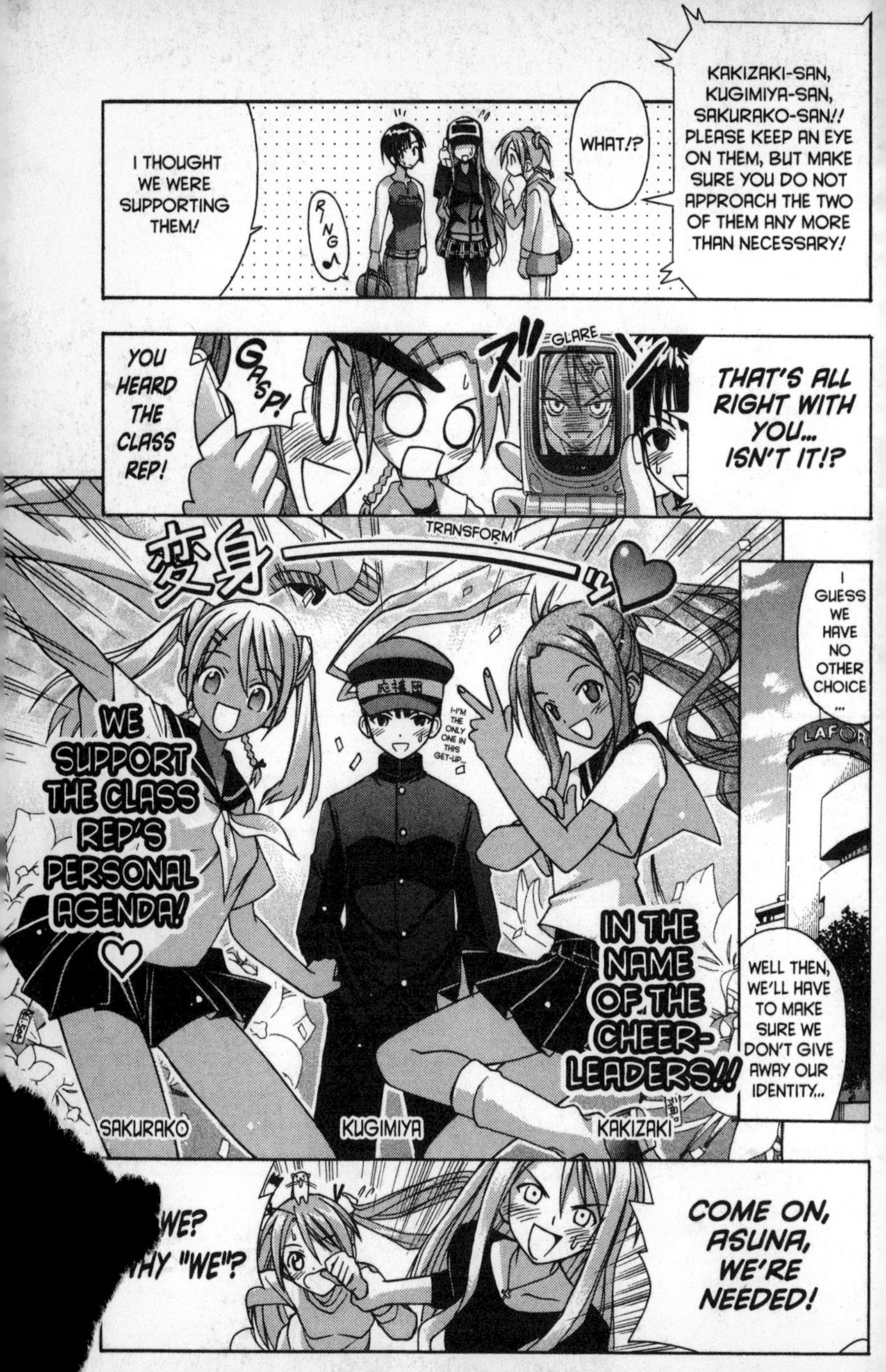

KAKIZAKI-SAN, KUGIMIYA-SAN, SAKURAKO-SAN!! PLEASE KEEP AN EYE ON THEM, BUT MAKE SURE YOU DO NOT APPROACH THE TWO OF THEM ANY MORE THAN NECESSARY!
WHAT!?
RING ♪
I THOUGHT WE WERE SUPPORTING THEM!
THAT'S ALL RIGHT WITH YOU... ISN'T IT!?
GLARE
GASP!
YOU HEARD THE CLASS REP!
I GUESS WE HAVE NO OTHER CHOICE...
WELL THEN, WE'LL HAVE TO MAKE SURE WE DON'T GIVE AWAY OUR IDENTITY...
変身
TRANSFORM
IN THE NAME OF THE CHEERLEADERS!!
I-I'M THE ONLY ONE IN THIS GET-UP...
WE SUPPORT THE CLASS REP'S PERSONAL AGENDA! ♡
KAKIZAKI
KUGIMIYA
SAKURAKO
COME ON, ASUNA, WE'RE NEEDED!
WE? WHY "WE"?

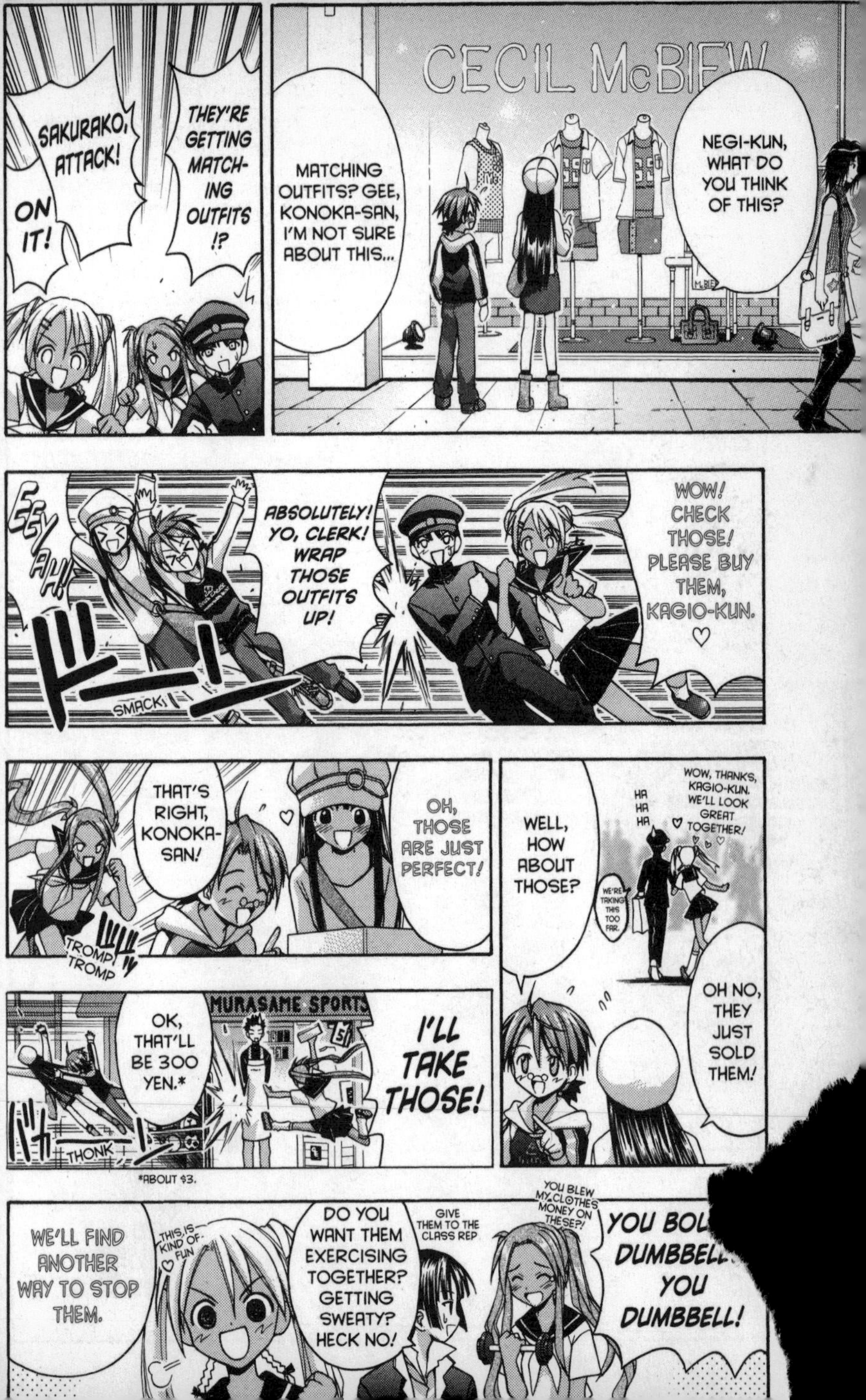
CECIL McBIEW
NEGI-KUN, WHAT DO YOU THINK OF THIS?
MATCHING OUTFITS? GEE, KONOKA-SAN, I'M NOT SURE ABOUT THIS...
THEY'RE GETTING MATCHING OUTFITS!?
SAKURAKO, ATTACK!
ON IT!
WOW! CHECK THOSE! PLEASE BUY THEM, KAGIO-KUN. ♡
ABSOLUTELY! YO, CLERK! WRAP THOSE OUTFITS UP!
SMACK
EEEYAAH!!
ドー
WOW, THANKS, KAGIO-KUN. WE'LL LOOK GREAT TOGETHER!
HA HA HA
WE'RE TAKING THIS TOO FAR.
WELL, HOW ABOUT THOSE?
OH NO, THEY JUST SOLD THEM!
OH, THOSE ARE JUST PERFECT!
THAT'S RIGHT, KONOKA-SAN!
TROMP TROMP
I'LL TAKE THOSE!
MURASAME SPORTS
OK, THAT'LL BE 300 YEN.*
THONK
YOU BOL
DUMBBEL
YOU DUMBBELL!
YOU BLEW MY CLOTHES MONEY ON THESE?!
GIVE THEM TO THE CLASS REP
DO YOU WANT THEM EXERCISING TOGETHER? GETTING SWEATY? HECK NO!
THIS IS KIND OF FUN
WE'LL FIND ANOTHER WAY TO STOP THEM.

*ABOUT $3.

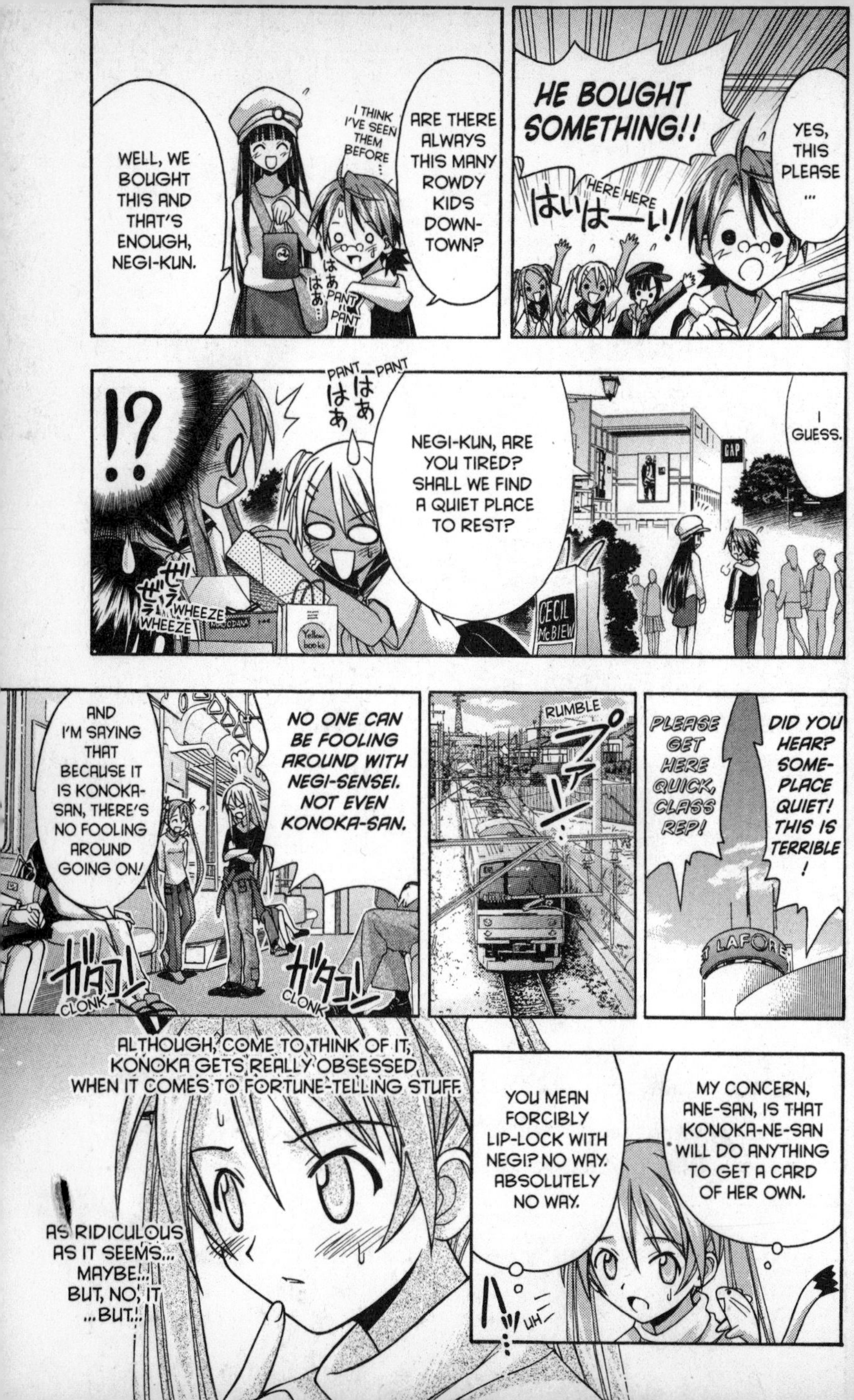
YES, THIS PLEASE ...
HE BOUGHT SOMETHING!!
はいはーい!
HERE HERE
ARE THERE ALWAYS THIS MANY ROWDY KIDS DOWNTOWN?
I THINK I'VE SEEN THEM BEFORE ...
はあ はあ
PANT PANT
WELL, WE BOUGHT THIS AND THAT'S ENOUGH, NEGI-KUN.
I GUESS.
GAP
NEGI-KUN, ARE YOU TIRED? SHALL WE FIND A QUIET PLACE TO REST?
はあ はあ
PANT PANT
CECIL McBIEW
Yellow books
!?
WHEEZE WHEEZE
DID YOU HEAR? SOME-PLACE QUIET! THIS IS TERRIBLE!
PLEASE GET HERE QUICK, CLASS REP!
LAFORE
RUMBLE
NO ONE CAN BE FOOLING AROUND WITH NEGI-SENSEI. NOT EVEN KONOKA-SAN.
AND I'M SAYING THAT BECAUSE IT IS KONOKA-SAN, THERE'S NO FOOLING AROUND GOING ON!
ガタコン
CLONK
ガタコン
CLONK
MY CONCERN, ANE-SAN, IS THAT KONOKA-NE-SAN WILL DO ANYTHING TO GET A CARD OF HER OWN.
YOU MEAN FORCIBLY LIP-LOCK WITH NEGI? NO WAY. ABSOLUTELY NO WAY.
UH
ALTHOUGH, COME TO THINK OF IT, KONOKA GETS REALLY OBSESSED WHEN IT COMES TO FORTUNE-TELLING STUFF.
AS RIDICULOUS AS IT SEEMS... MAYBE... BUT, NO, IT ...BUT...

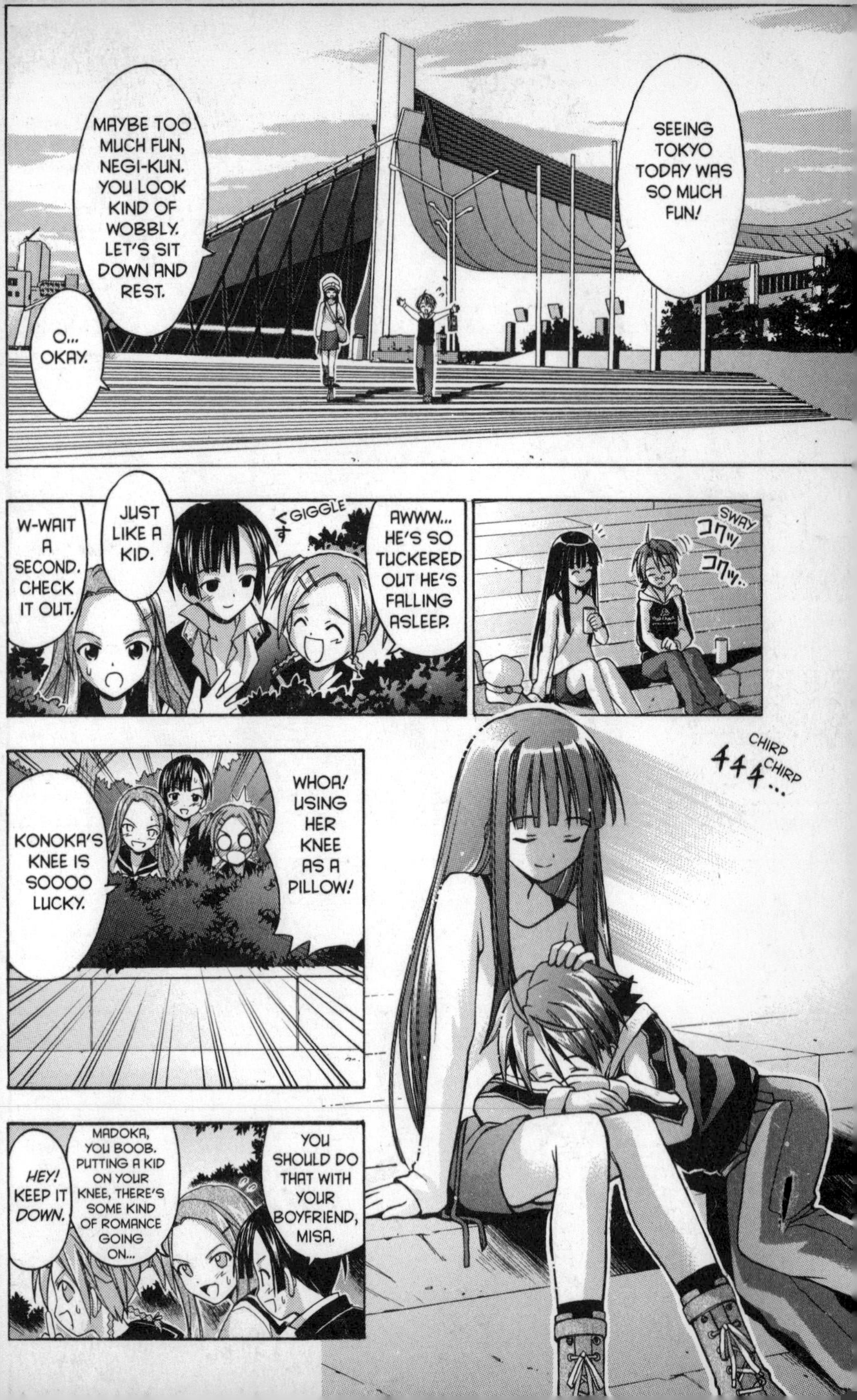
SEEING TOKYO TODAY WAS SO MUCH FUN!
MAYBE TOO MUCH FUN, NEGI-KUN. YOU LOOK KIND OF WOBBLY. LET'S SIT DOWN AND REST.
O... OKAY.
SWAY
コクッ
コクッ...
AWWW... HE'S SO TUCKERED OUT HE'S FALLING ASLEEP.
GIGGLE
JUST LIKE A KID.
W-WAIT A SECOND. CHECK IT OUT.
CHIRP CHIRP
WHOA! USING HER KNEE AS A PILLOW!
KONOKA'S KNEE IS SOOOO LUCKY.
YOU SHOULD DO THAT WITH YOUR BOYFRIEND, MISA.
MADOKA, YOU BOOB. PUTTING A KID ON YOUR KNEE, THERE'S SOME KIND OF ROMANCE GOING ON...
HEY! KEEP IT *DOWN.*

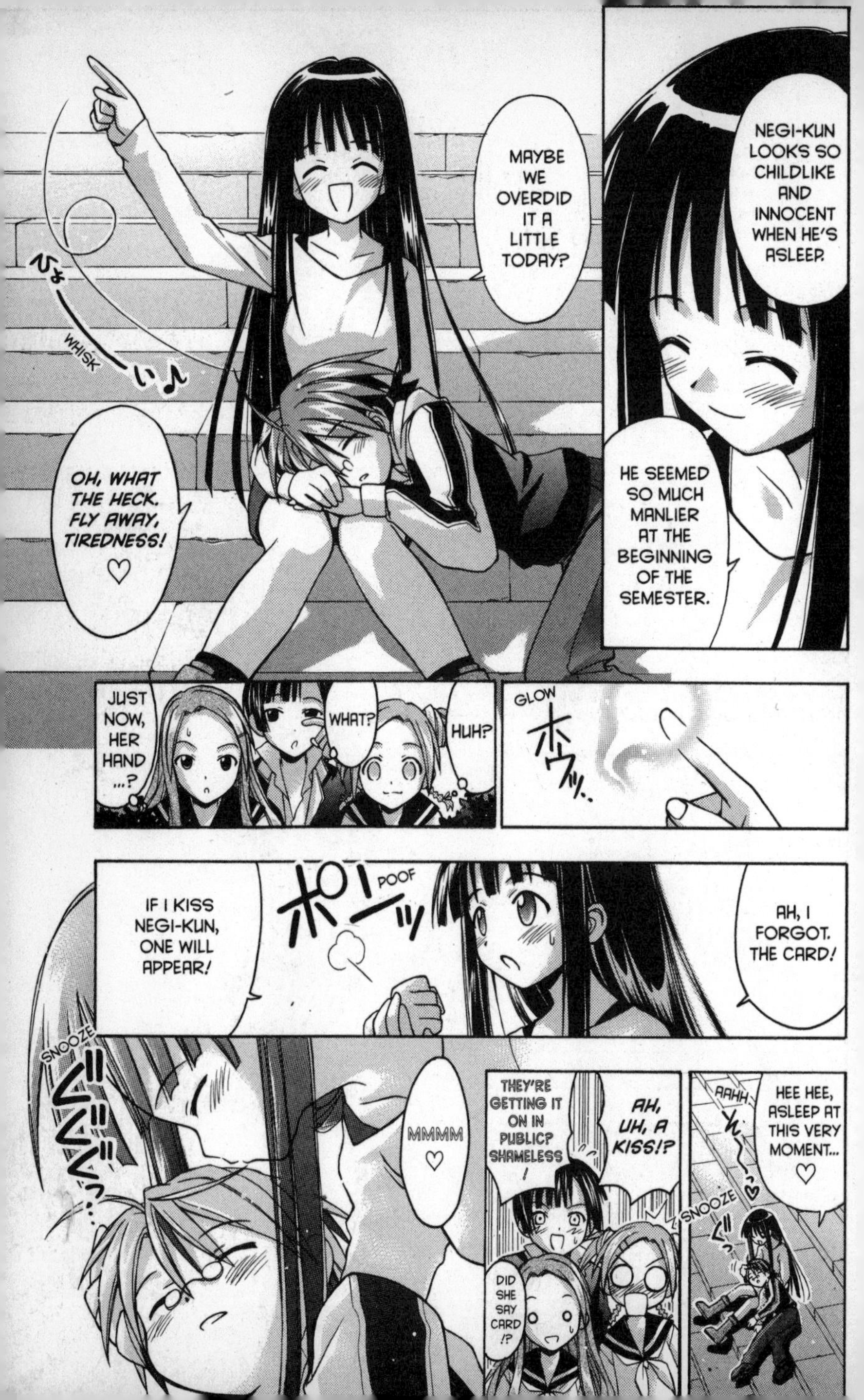
NEGI-KUN LOOKS SO CHILDLIKE AND INNOCENT WHEN HE'S ASLEEP.
HE SEEMED SO MUCH MANLIER AT THE BEGINNING OF THE SEMESTER.
MAYBE WE OVERDID IT A LITTLE TODAY?
ひょーーい♪
WHISK
OH, WHAT THE HECK. FLY AWAY, TIREDNESS! ♡
GLOW
ホウッ...
HUH?
WHAT?
JUST NOW, HER HAND ...?
AH, I FORGOT. THE CARD!
POOF
ポーッ
IF I KISS NEGI-KUN, ONE WILL APPEAR!
HEE HEE, ASLEEP AT THIS VERY MOMENT... ♡
AAHH
SNOOZE
AH, UH, A KISS!?
THEY'RE GETTING IT ON IN PUBLIC? SHAMELESS!
DID SHE SAY CARD!?
MMMM ♡
SNOOZE

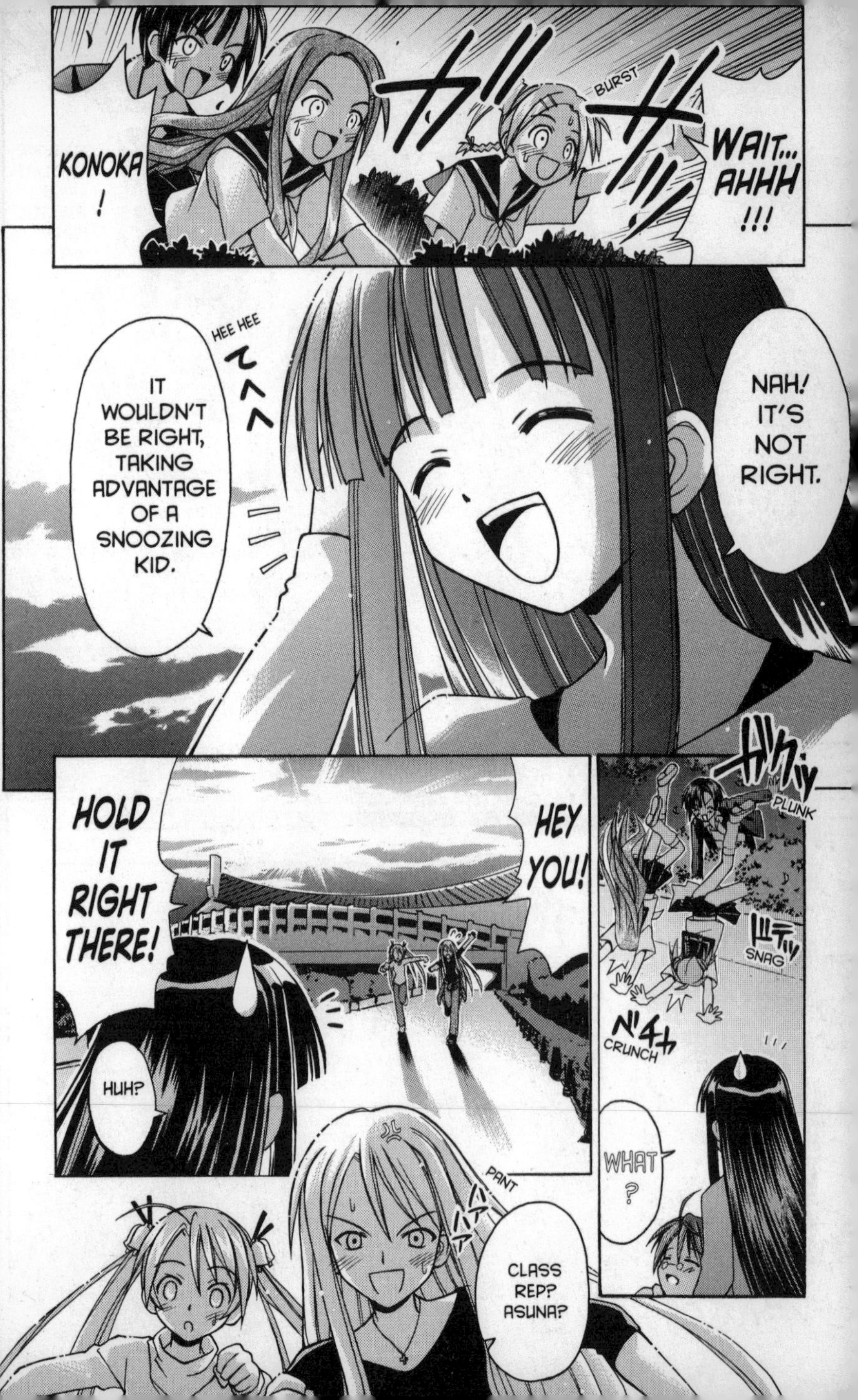
WAIT... AHHH!!!
BURST
KONOKA!
NAH! IT'S NOT RIGHT.
HEE HEE
てへへ
IT WOULDN'T BE RIGHT, TAKING ADVANTAGE OF A SNOOZING KID.
PLUNK
SNAG
CRUNCH
WHAT?
HEY YOU!
HOLD IT RIGHT THERE!
HUH?
PANT
CLASS REP? ASUNA?

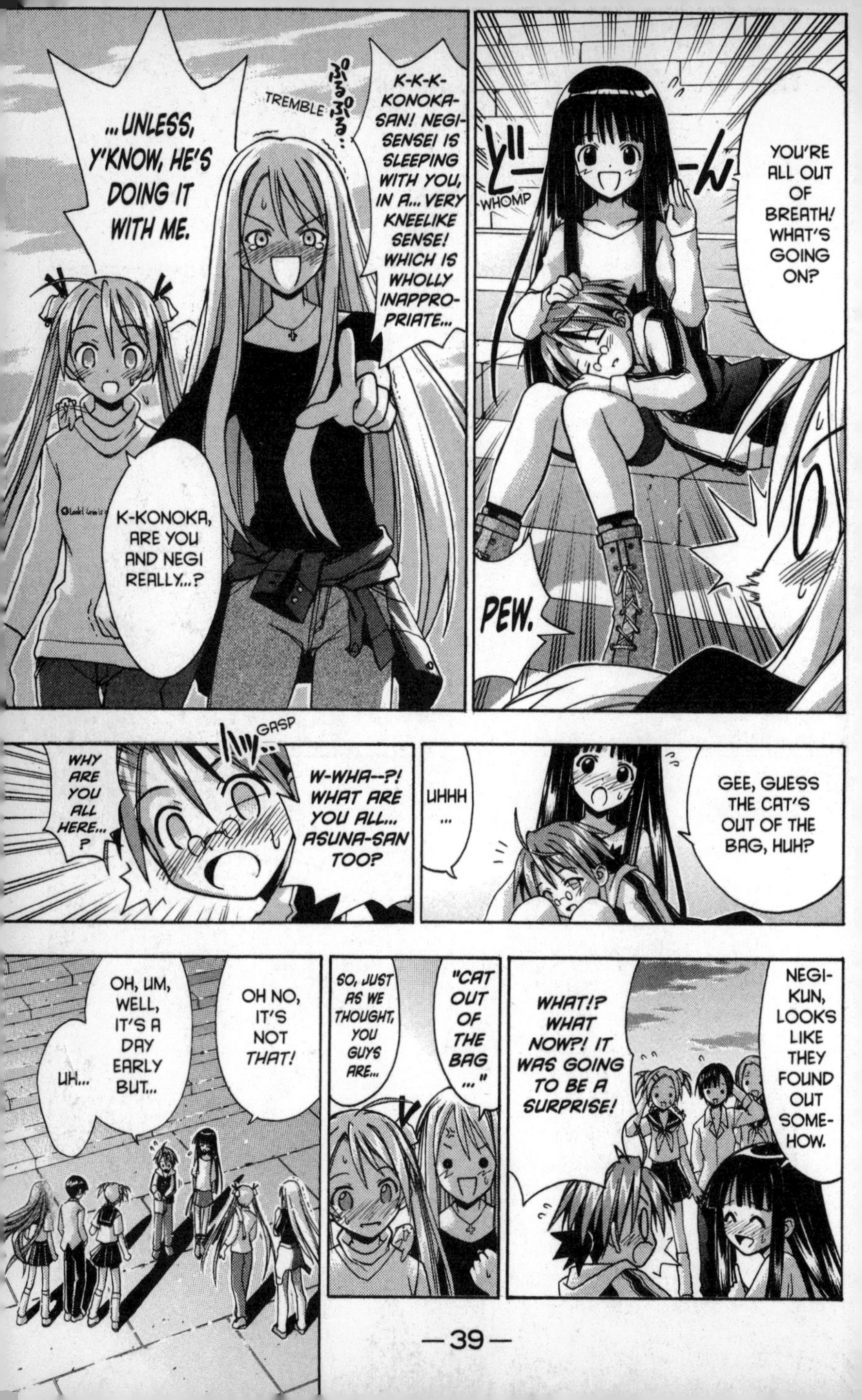
ドーン
WHOMP
YOU'RE ALL OUT OF BREATH! WHAT'S GOING ON?
PEW.
K-K-K-KONOKA-SAN! NEGI-SENSEI IS SLEEPING WITH YOU, IN A... VERY KNEELIKE SENSE! WHICH IS WHOLLY INAPPROPRIATE...
ぷるぷる…
TREMBLE
...UNLESS, Y'KNOW, HE'S DOING IT WITH ME.
K-KONOKA, ARE YOU AND NEGI REALLY...?
GEE, GUESS THE CAT'S OUT OF THE BAG, HUH?
UHHH ...
W-WHA--?! WHAT ARE YOU ALL... ASUNA-SAN TOO?
ハッ
GASP
WHY ARE YOU ALL HERE...?
NEGI-KUN, LOOKS LIKE THEY FOUND OUT SOMEHOW.
WHAT!? WHAT NOW?! IT WAS GOING TO BE A SURPRISE!
"CAT OUT OF THE BAG ..."
SO, JUST AS WE THOUGHT, YOU GUYS ARE...
OH NO, IT'S NOT THAT!
OH, UM, WELL, IT'S A DAY EARLY BUT...
UH...

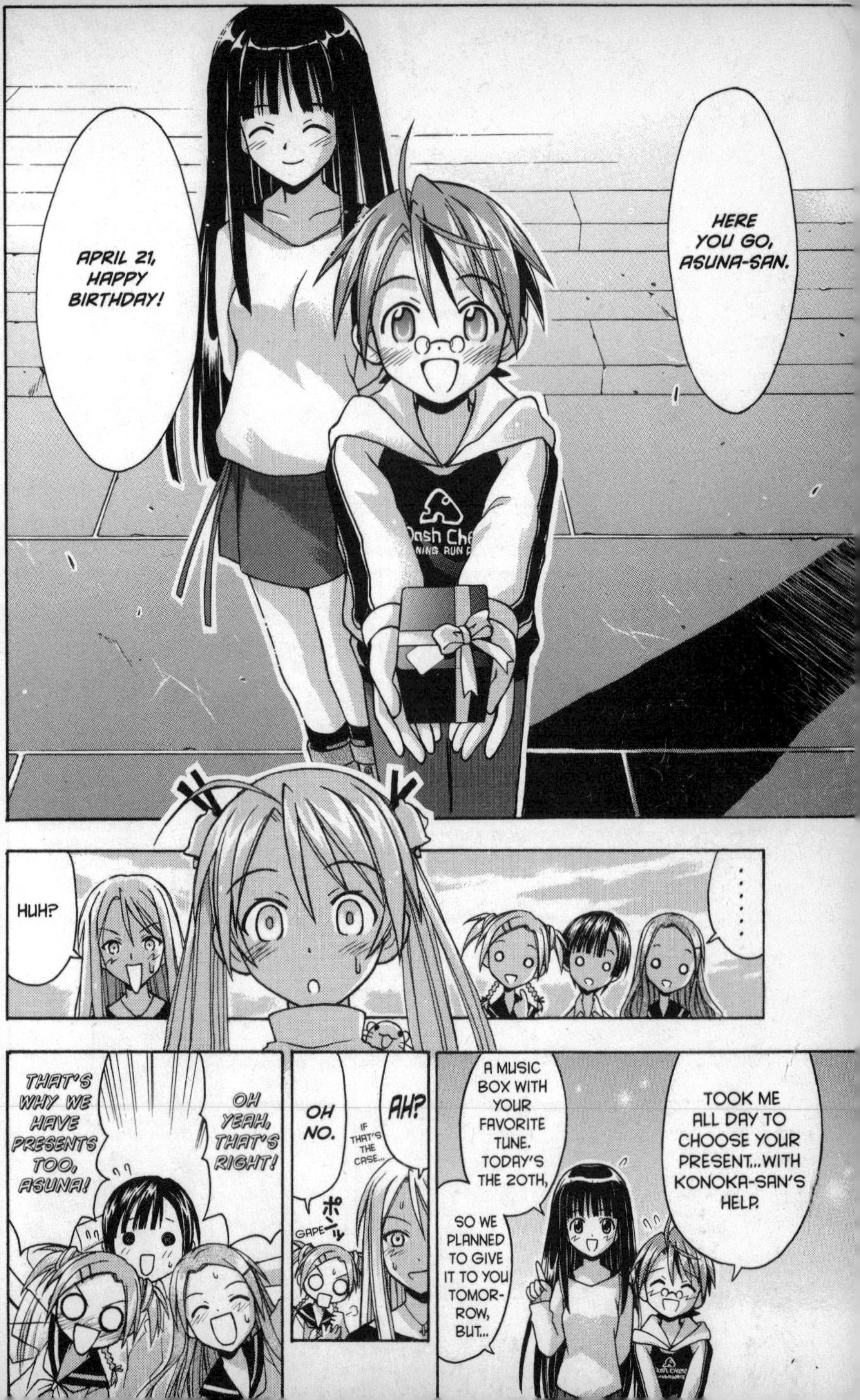
HERE YOU GO, ASUNA-SAN.
APRIL 21, HAPPY BIRTHDAY!
......
HUH?
TOOK ME ALL DAY TO CHOOSE YOUR PRESENT...WITH KONOKA-SAN'S HELP.
A MUSIC BOX WITH YOUR FAVORITE TUNE. TODAY'S THE 20TH,
SO WE PLANNED TO GIVE IT TO YOU TOMORROW, BUT...
AH?
IF THAT'S THE CASE...
OH NO.
GAPE
OH YEAH, THAT'S RIGHT!
THAT'S WHY WE HAVE PRESENTS TOO, ASUNA!

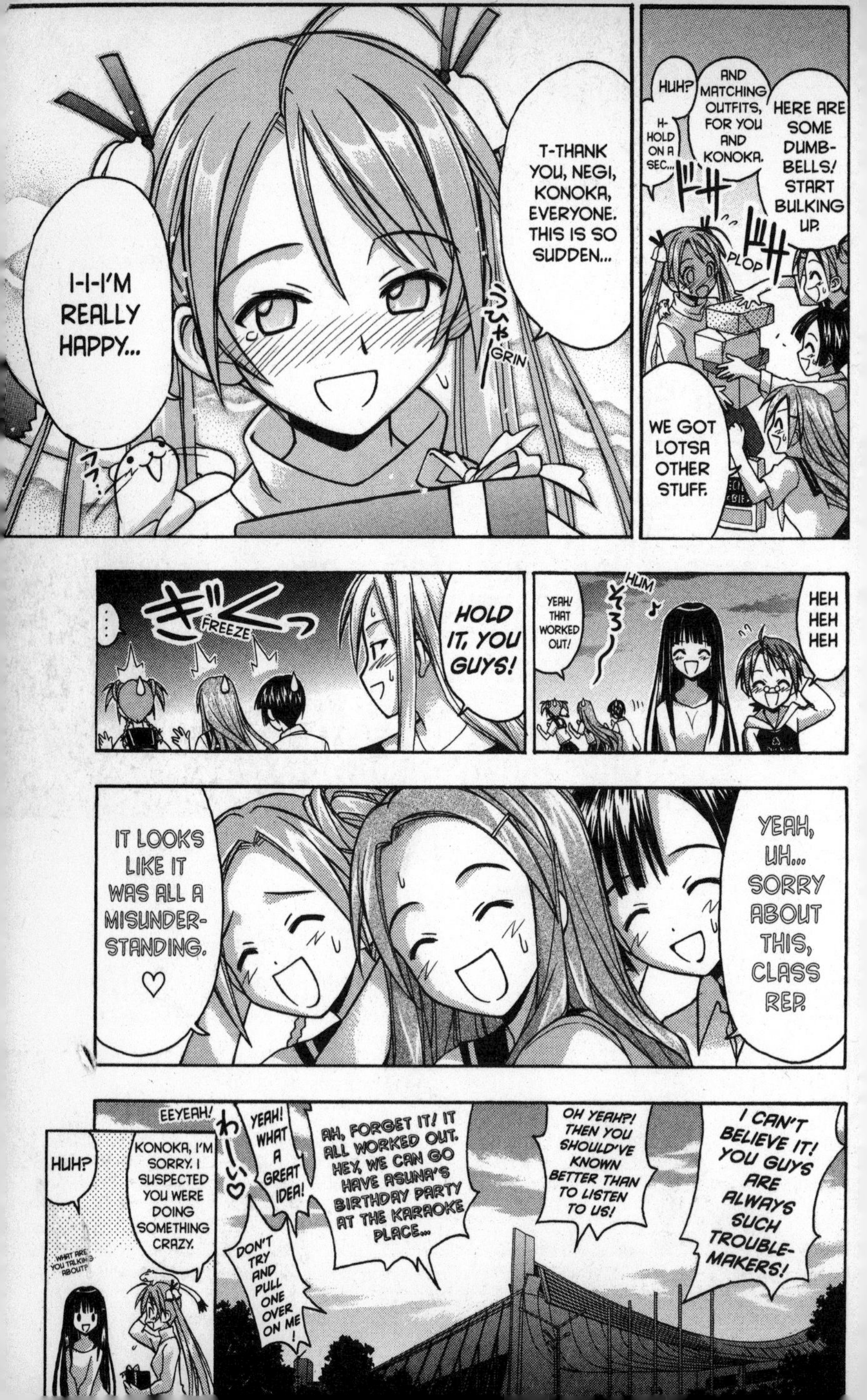
HERE ARE SOME DUMBBELLS! START BULKING UP.
AND MATCHING OUTFITS, FOR YOU AND KONOKA.
HUH?
H-HOLD ON A SEC...
PLOP
WE GOT LOTSA OTHER STUFF.
T-THANK YOU, NEGI, KONOKA, EVERYONE. THIS IS SO SUDDEN...
GRIN
I-I-I'M REALLY HAPPY...
HEH HEH HEH
HUM
YEAH! THAT WORKED OUT!
HOLD IT, YOU GUYS!
FREEZE
...
YEAH, UH... SORRY ABOUT THIS, CLASS REP.
IT LOOKS LIKE IT WAS ALL A MISUNDERSTANDING. ♡
I CAN'T BELIEVE IT! YOU GUYS ARE ALWAYS SUCH TROUBLE-MAKERS!
OH YEAH?! THEN YOU SHOULD'VE KNOWN BETTER THAN TO LISTEN TO US!
AH, FORGET IT! IT ALL WORKED OUT. HEY, WE CAN GO HAVE ASUNA'S BIRTHDAY PARTY AT THE KARAOKE PLACE...
DON'T TRY AND PULL ONE OVER ON ME!
YEAH! WHAT A GREAT IDEA!
EEYEAH!
KONOKA, I'M SORRY. I SUSPECTED YOU WERE DOING SOMETHING CRAZY.
HUH?
WHAT ARE YOU TALKING ABOUT?

STUDENT NUMBER 15
SETSUNA SAKURAZAKI

BORN: JANUARY 17, 1989
BLOOD TYPE: A
ASTROLOGICAL SIGN: CAPRICORN
LIKES: SWORD TRAINING, KONOKA
DISLIKES: INJUSTICE, CHATTING
AFFILIATIONS: KENDO CLUB
NOTES: BECAME A FOLLOWER OF SHINMEI RYU
      SCHOOL OF KYOTO AND IS A
      SWORDSMAN WISE IN THE WAY
      OF ONMYOU

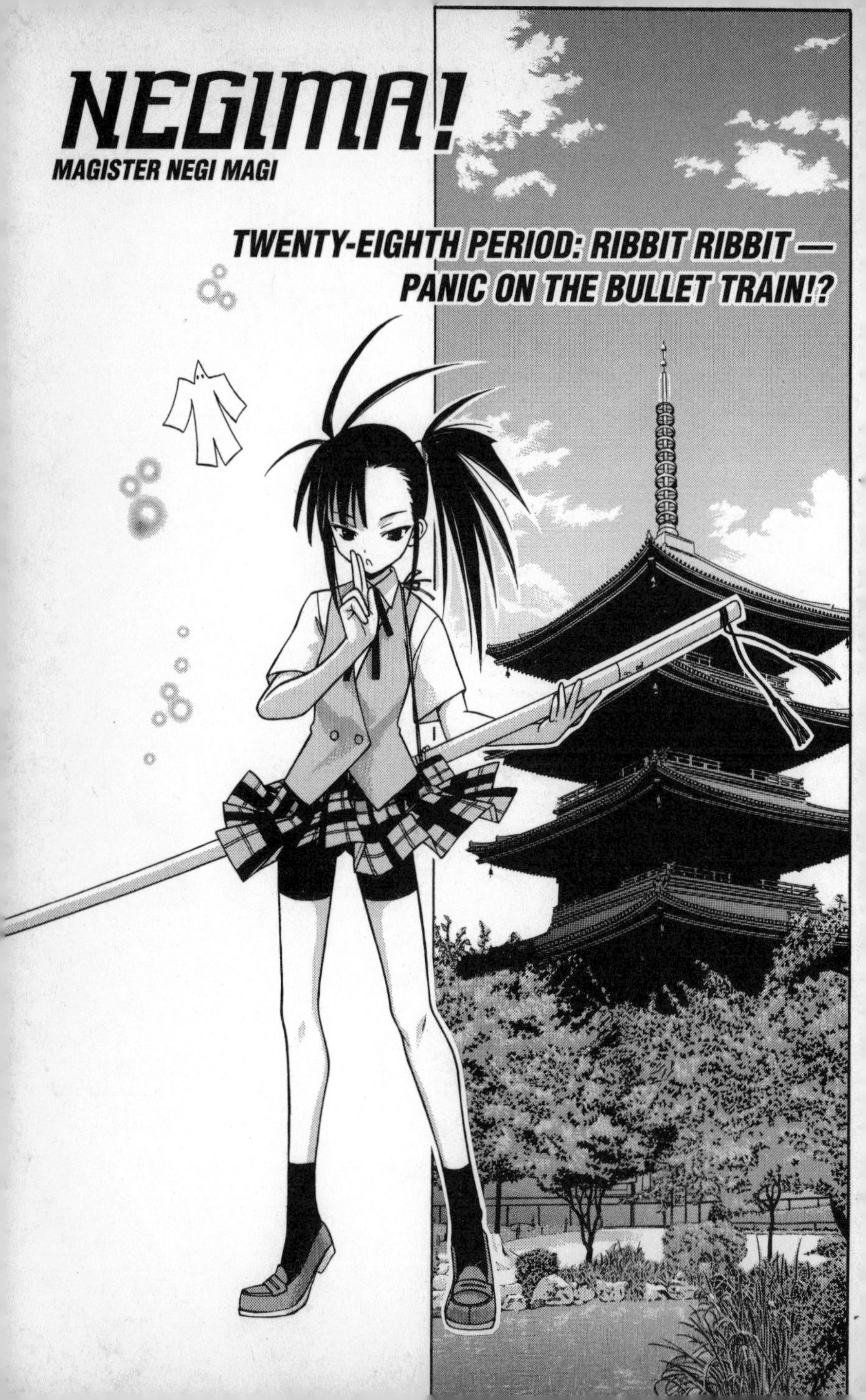
NEGIMA!
MAGISTER NEGI MAGI
TWENTY-EIGHTH PERIOD: RIBBIT RIBBIT —
PANIC ON THE BULLET TRAIN!?

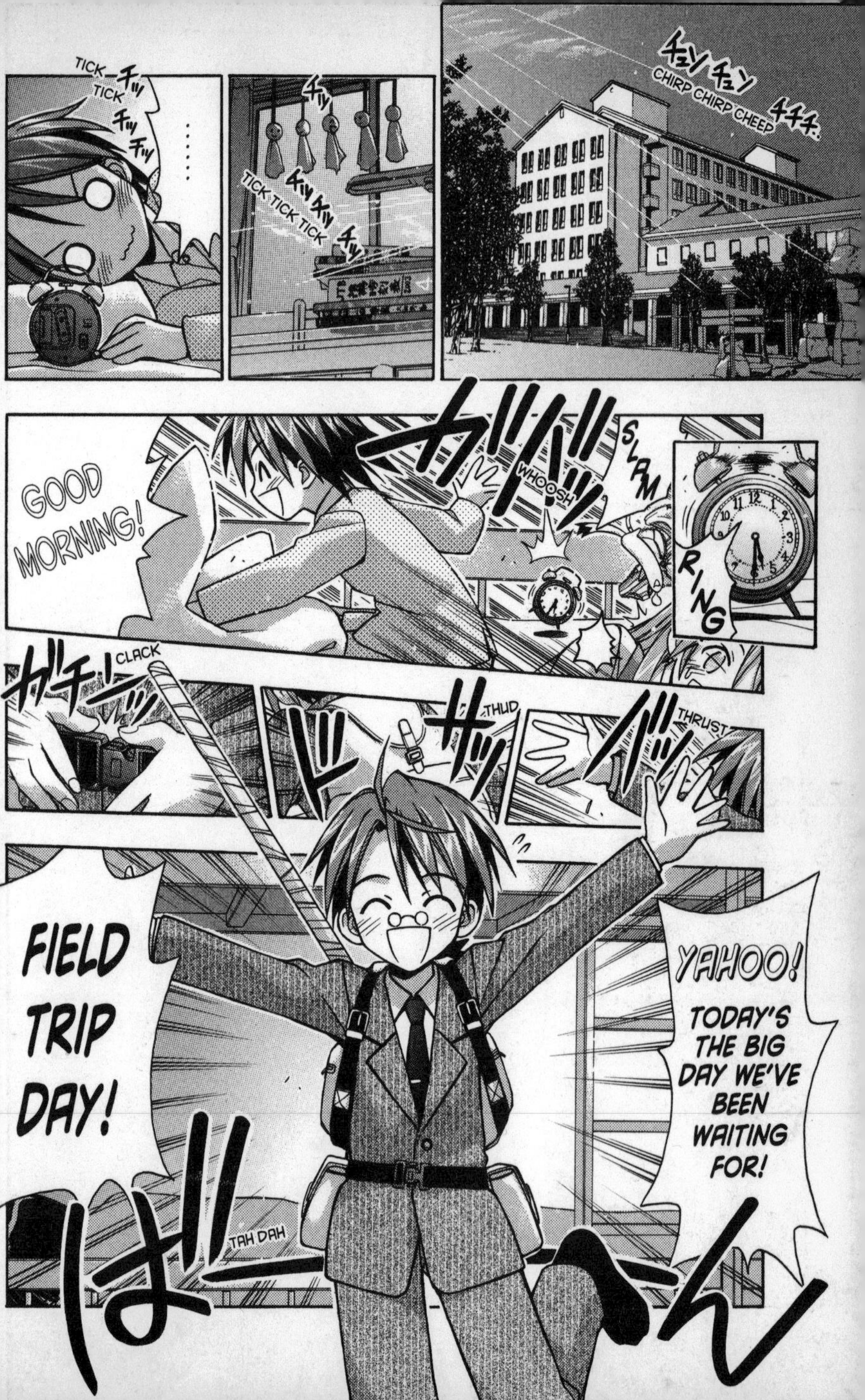
CHIRP CHIRP CHEEP
TICK TICK TICK
TICK TICK
....
RING
SLAM
WHOOSH
GOOD MORNING!
THRUST
THUD
CLACK
YAHOO!
TODAY'S THE BIG DAY WE'VE BEEN WAITING FOR!
FIELD TRIP DAY!
TAH DAH

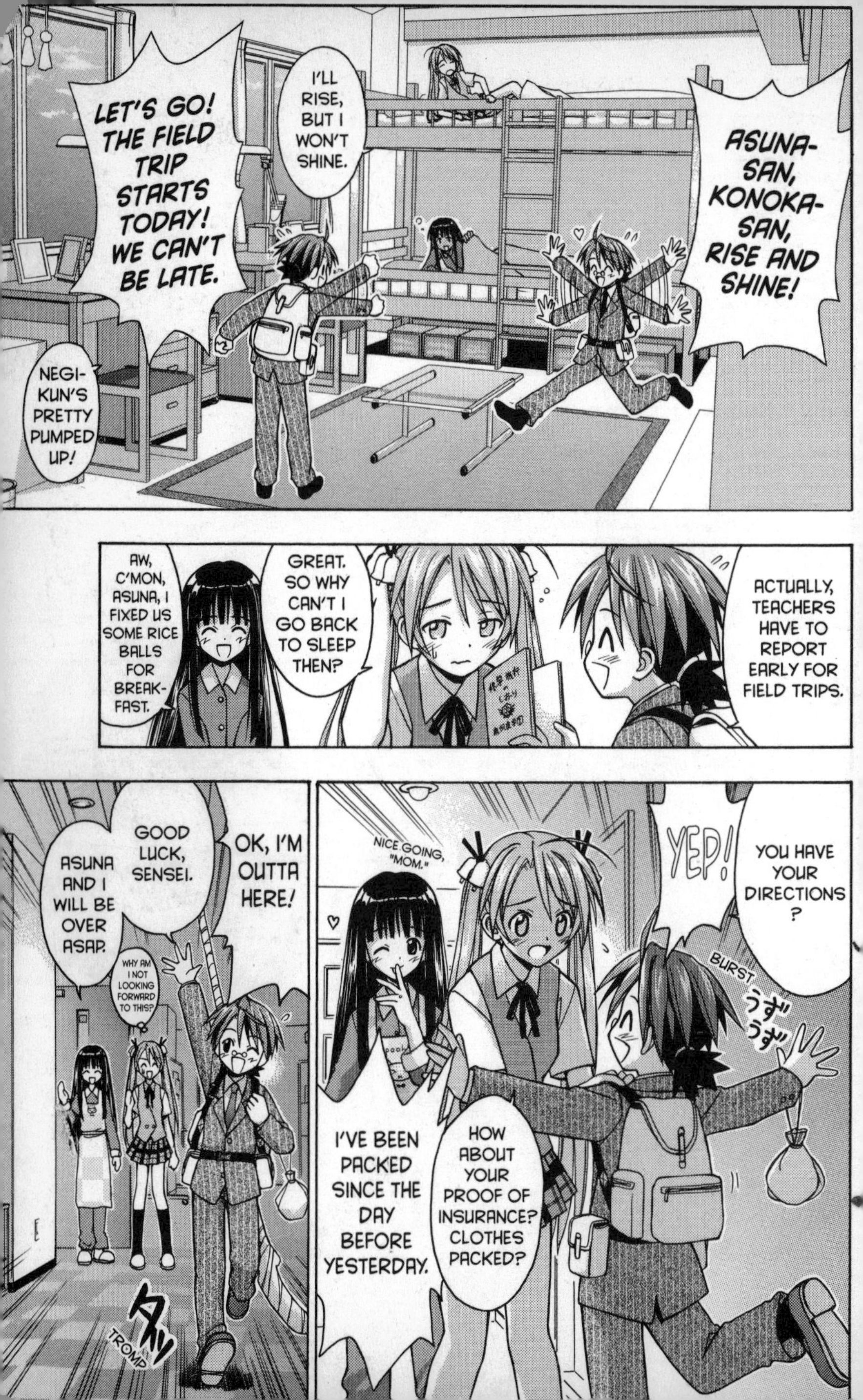
ASUNA-SAN, KONOKA-SAN, RISE AND SHINE!
I'LL RISE, BUT I WON'T SHINE.
LET'S GO! THE FIELD TRIP STARTS TODAY! WE CAN'T BE LATE.
NEGI-KUN'S PRETTY PUMPED UP!
ACTUALLY, TEACHERS HAVE TO REPORT EARLY FOR FIELD TRIPS.
GREAT. SO WHY CAN'T I GO BACK TO SLEEP THEN?
AW, C'MON, ASUNA, I FIXED US SOME RICE BALLS FOR BREAKFAST.
YOU HAVE YOUR DIRECTIONS?
YEP!
BURST うずうず
NICE GOING, "MOM."
HOW ABOUT YOUR PROOF OF INSURANCE? CLOTHES PACKED?
I'VE BEEN PACKED SINCE THE DAY BEFORE YESTERDAY.
OK, I'M OUTTA HERE!
GOOD LUCK, SENSEI.
ASUNA AND I WILL BE OVER ASAP.
WHY AM I NOT LOOKING FORWARD TO THIS?
タッ TROMP

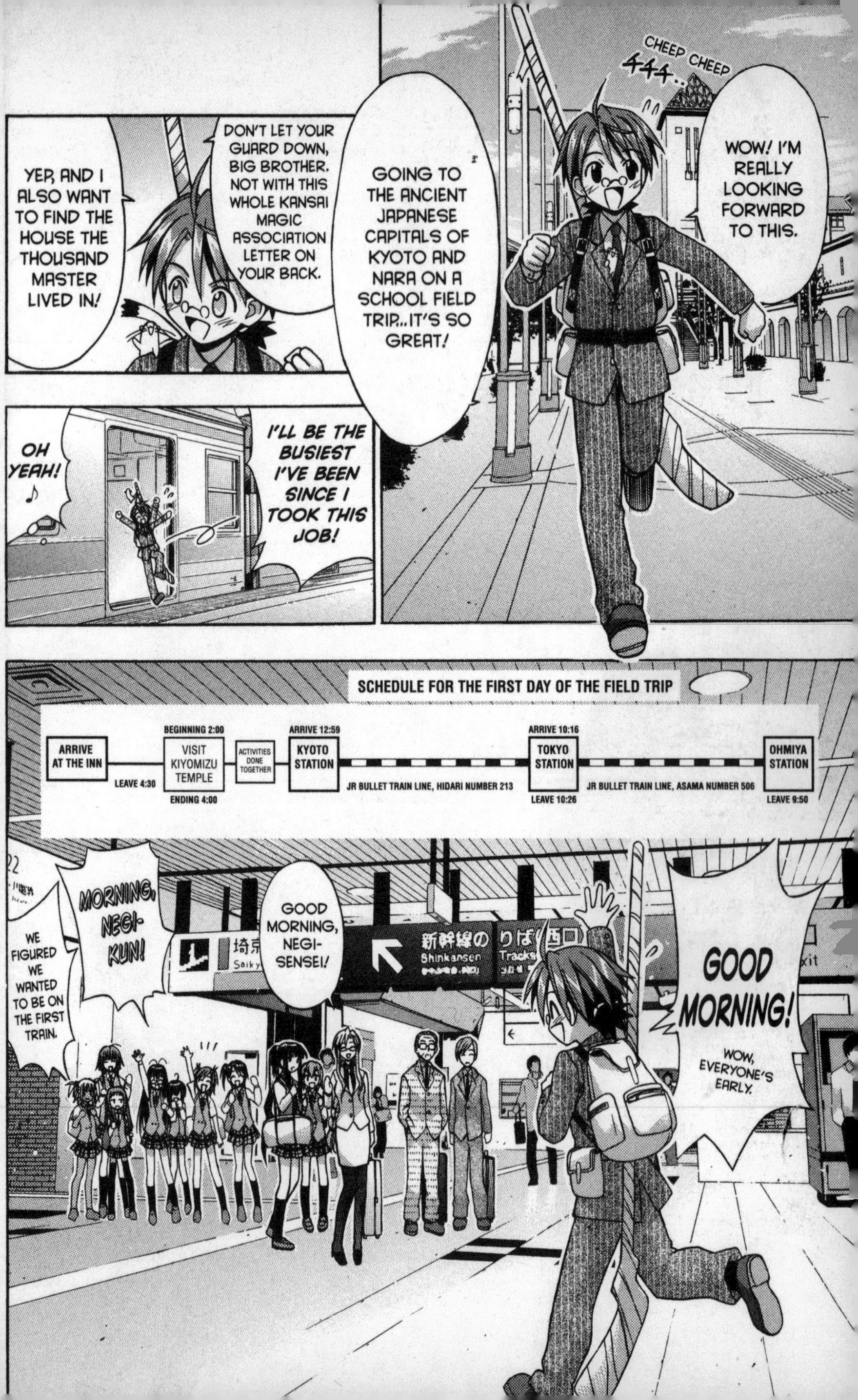
CHEEP CHEEP
WOW! I'M REALLY LOOKING FORWARD TO THIS.
GOING TO THE ANCIENT JAPANESE CAPITALS OF KYOTO AND NARA ON A SCHOOL FIELD TRIP...IT'S SO GREAT!
DON'T LET YOUR GUARD DOWN, BIG BROTHER. NOT WITH THIS WHOLE KANSAI MAGIC ASSOCIATION LETTER ON YOUR BACK.
YEP, AND I ALSO WANT TO FIND THE HOUSE THE THOUSAND MASTER LIVED IN!
I'LL BE THE BUSIEST I'VE BEEN SINCE I TOOK THIS JOB!
OH YEAH! ♪
SCHEDULE FOR THE FIRST DAY OF THE FIELD TRIP
ARRIVE AT THE INN
LEAVE 4:30
BEGINNING 2:00
VISIT KIYOMIZU TEMPLE
ENDING 4:00
ACTIVITIES DONE TOGETHER
ARRIVE 12:59
KYOTO STATION
JR BULLET TRAIN LINE, HIDARI NUMBER 213
ARRIVE 10:16
TOKYO STATION
LEAVE 10:26
JR BULLET TRAIN LINE, ASAMA NUMBER 506
OHMIYA STATION
LEAVE 9:50
新幹線の
Shinkansen
Tracks
GOOD MORNING!
WOW, EVERYONE'S EARLY.
GOOD MORNING, NEGI-SENSEI!
MORNING, NEGI-KUN!
WE FIGURED WE WANTED TO BE ON THE FIRST TRAIN.

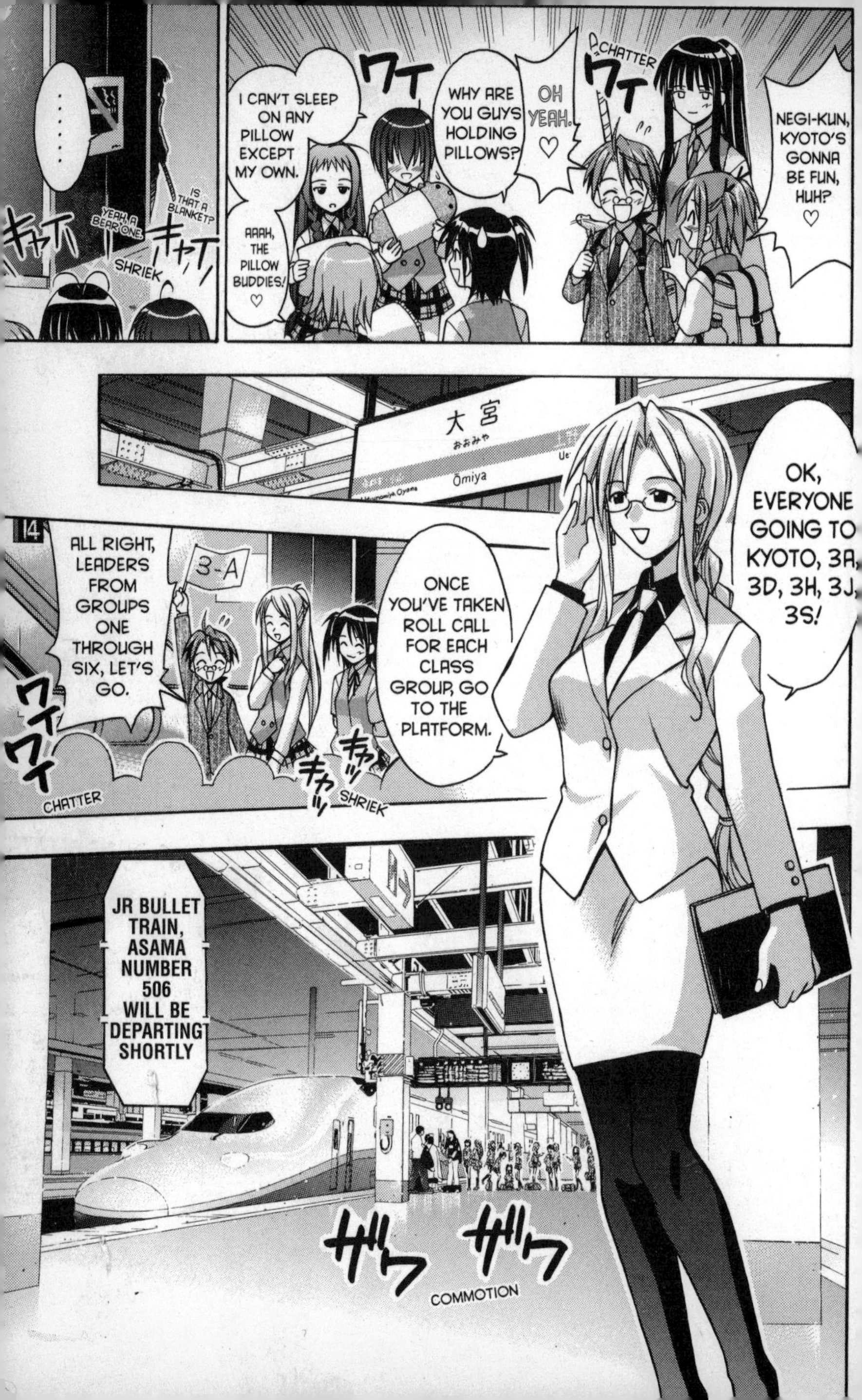
NEGI-KUN, KYOTO'S GONNA BE FUN, HUH? ♡
CHATTER
ワイ
OH YEAH. ♡
WHY ARE YOU GUYS HOLDING PILLOWS?
ワイ
I CAN'T SLEEP ON ANY PILLOW EXCEPT MY OWN.
AAAH, THE PILLOW BUDDIES! ♡
. . . . . .
IS THAT A BLANKET?
YEAH, A BEAR ONE.
SHRIEK
OK, EVERYONE GOING TO KYOTO, 3A, 3D, 3H, 3J, 3S!
ONCE YOU'VE TAKEN ROLL CALL FOR EACH CLASS GROUP, GO TO THE PLATFORM.
大宮
おおみや
Ōmiya
14
ALL RIGHT, LEADERS FROM GROUPS ONE THROUGH SIX, LET'S GO.
3-A
ワイ ワイ
CHATTER
SHRIEK
JR BULLET TRAIN, ASAMA NUMBER 506 WILL BE DEPARTING SHORTLY
ザワ ザワ
COMMOTION

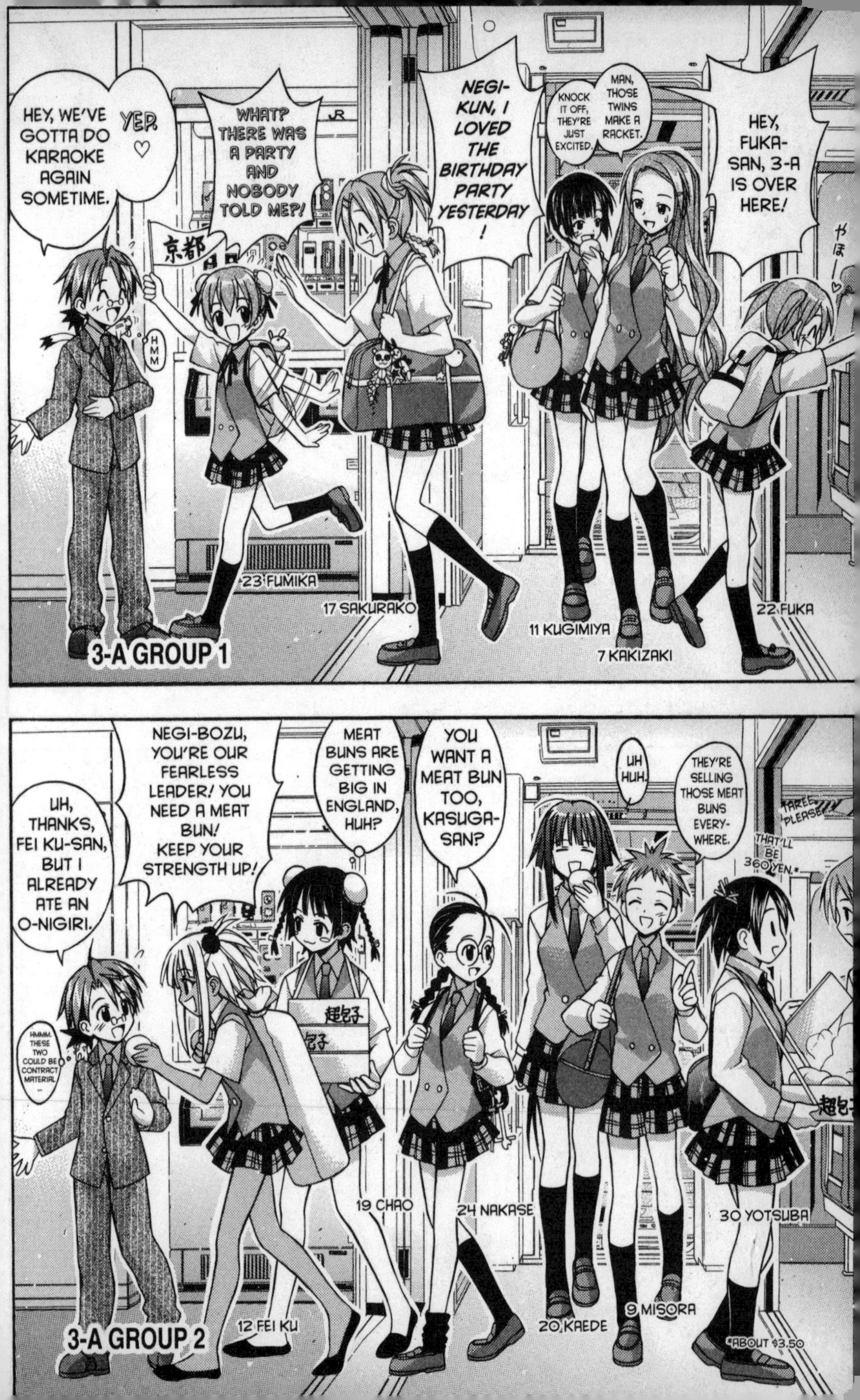

HEY, FUKA-SAN, 3-A IS OVER HERE!
やほー♡
MAN, THOSE TWINS MAKE A RACKET.
KNOCK IT OFF, THEY'RE JUST EXCITED.
NEGI-KUN, I LOVED THE BIRTHDAY PARTY YESTERDAY!
WHAT? THERE WAS A PARTY AND NOBODY TOLD ME?!
YEP. ♡
HEY, WE'VE GOTTA DO KARAOKE AGAIN SOMETIME.
HMM
京都
22 FUKA
7 KAKIZAKI
11 KUGIMIYA
17 SAKURAKO
23 FUMIKA
3-A GROUP 1
THREE PLEASE
THAT'LL BE 360 YEN.*
THEY'RE SELLING THOSE MEAT BUNS EVERYWHERE.
UH HUH.
YOU WANT A MEAT BUN TOO, KASUGA-SAN?
MEAT BUNS ARE GETTING BIG IN ENGLAND, HUH?
NEGI-BOZU, YOU'RE OUR FEARLESS LEADER! YOU NEED A MEAT BUN! KEEP YOUR STRENGTH UP!
UH, THANKS, FEI KU-SAN, BUT I ALREADY ATE AN O-NIGIRI.
HMMM. THESE TWO COULD BE CONTRACT MATERIAL...
超包子
30 YOTSUBA
9 MISORA
20 KAEDE
24 NAKASE
19 CHAO
12 FEI KU
3-A GROUP 2
*ABOUT $3.50

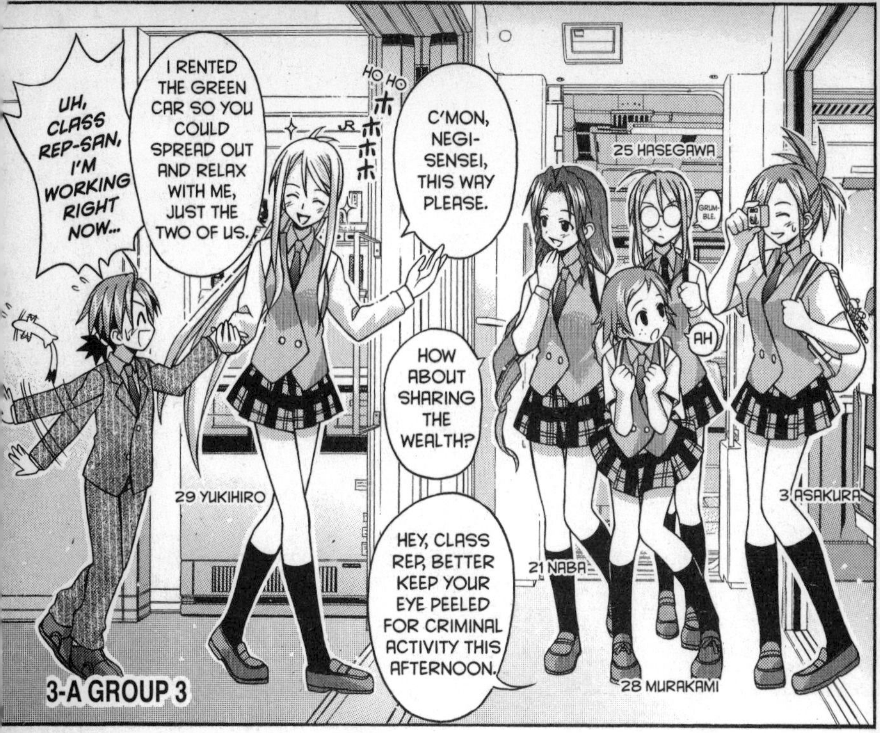
25 HASEGAWA
GRUMBLE.
3 ASAKURA
AH
C'MON, NEGI-SENSEI, THIS WAY PLEASE.
HO HO ホホホ
I RENTED THE GREEN CAR SO YOU COULD SPREAD OUT AND RELAX WITH ME, JUST THE TWO OF US.
UH, CLASS REP-SAN, I'M WORKING RIGHT NOW...
HOW ABOUT SHARING THE WEALTH?
HEY, CLASS REP, BETTER KEEP YOUR EYE PEELED FOR CRIMINAL ACTIVITY THIS AFTERNOON.
21 NABA
28 MURAKAMI
29 YUKIHIRO
3-A GROUP 3

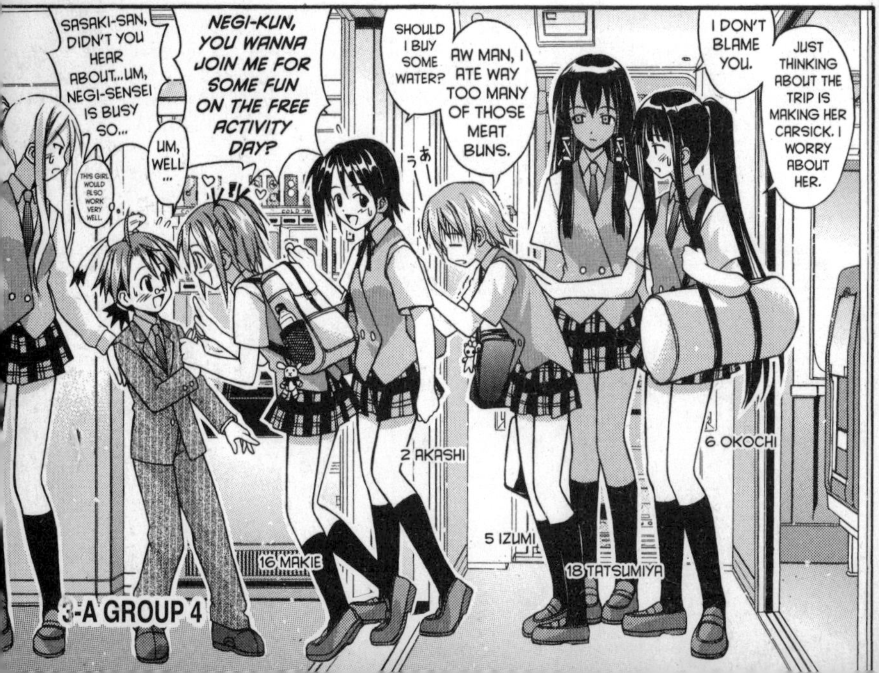
JUST THINKING ABOUT THE TRIP IS MAKING HER CARSICK. I WORRY ABOUT HER.
I DON'T BLAME YOU.
AW MAN, I ATE WAY TOO MANY OF THOSE MEAT BUNS.
SHOULD I BUY SOME WATER?
うあ
NEGI-KUN, YOU WANNA JOIN ME FOR SOME FUN ON THE FREE ACTIVITY DAY?
SASAKI-SAN, DIDN'T YOU HEAR ABOUT...UM, NEGI-SENSEI IS BUSY SO...
UM, WELL ...
THIS GIRL WOULD ALSO WORK VERY WELL.
6 OKOCHI
2 AKASHI
5 IZUMI
18 TATSUMIYA
16 MAKIE
3-A GROUP 4

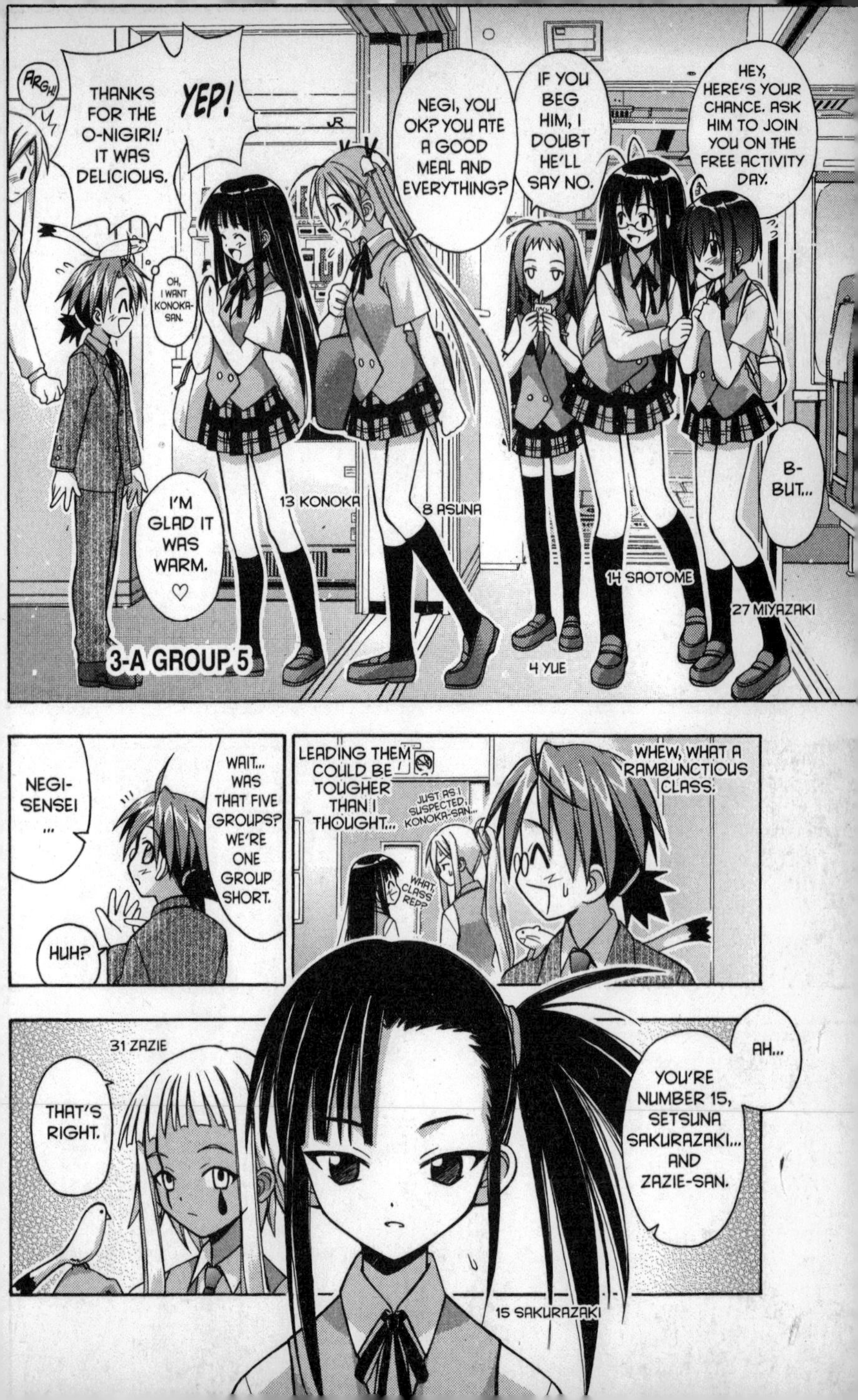
HEY, HERE'S YOUR CHANCE. ASK HIM TO JOIN YOU ON THE FREE ACTIVITY DAY.
IF YOU BEG HIM, I DOUBT HE'LL SAY NO.
NEGI, YOU OK? YOU ATE A GOOD MEAL AND EVERYTHING?
YEP!
THANKS FOR THE O-NIGIRI! IT WAS DELICIOUS.
ARGH!!
OH, I WANT KONOKA-SAN.
B-BUT...
I'M GLAD IT WAS WARM. ♡
27 MIYAZAKI
14 SAOTOME
4 YUE
8 ASUNA
13 KONOKA
3-A GROUP 5
WHEW, WHAT A RAMBUNCTIOUS CLASS.
JUST AS I SUSPECTED, KONOKA-SAN...
LEADING THEM COULD BE TOUGHER THAN I THOUGHT...
WHAT, CLASS REP?
WAIT... WAS THAT FIVE GROUPS? WE'RE ONE GROUP SHORT.
NEGI-SENSEI ...
HUH?
AH...
YOU'RE NUMBER 15, SETSUNA SAKURAZAKI... AND ZAZIE-SAN.
THAT'S RIGHT.
31 ZAZIE
15 SAKURAZAKI

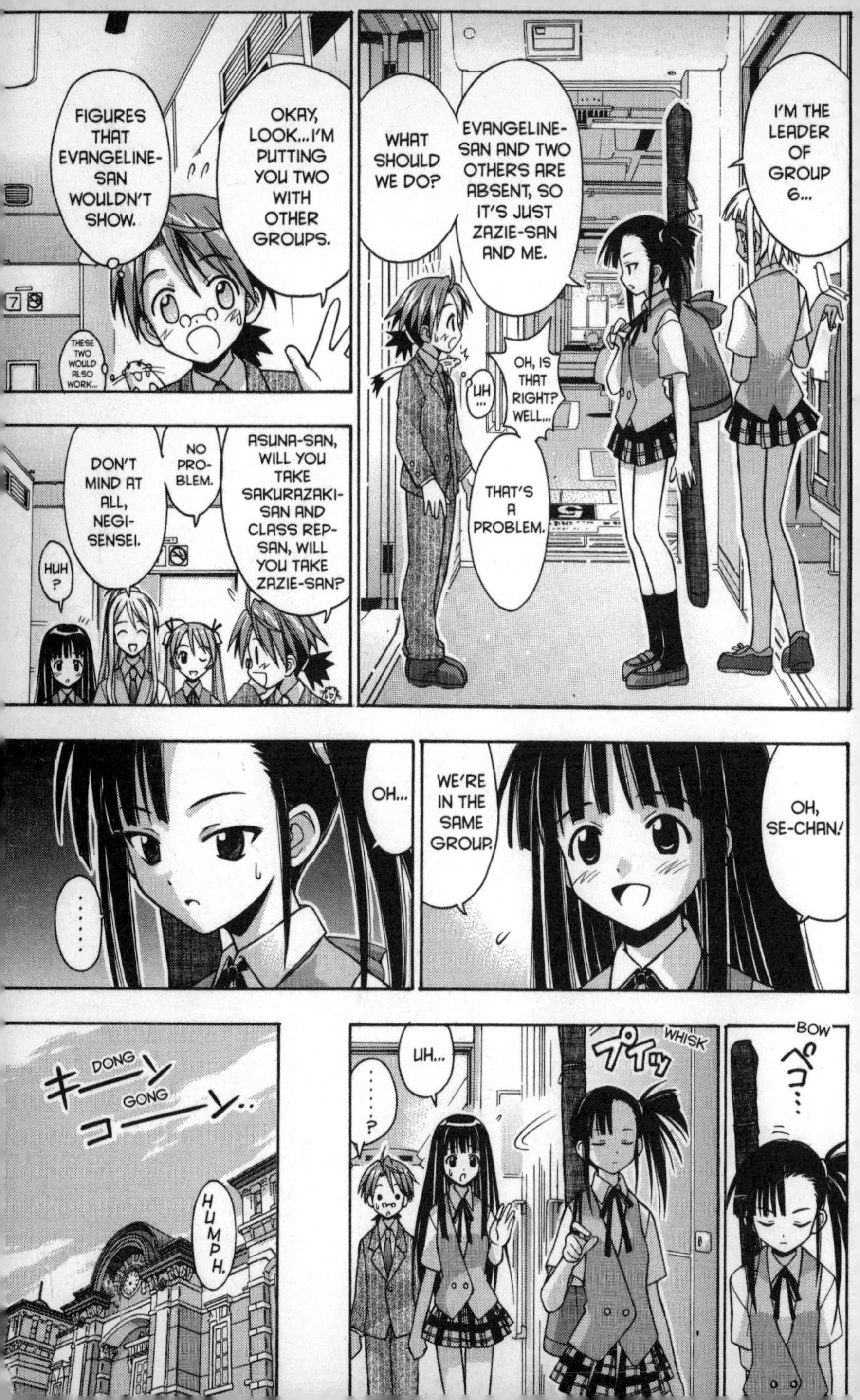
I'M THE LEADER OF GROUP 6...
EVANGELINE-SAN AND TWO OTHERS ARE ABSENT, SO IT'S JUST ZAZIE-SAN AND ME.
WHAT SHOULD WE DO?
OH, IS THAT RIGHT? WELL...
UH...
THAT'S A PROBLEM.
OKAY, LOOK...I'M PUTTING YOU TWO WITH OTHER GROUPS.
FIGURES THAT EVANGELINE-SAN WOULDN'T SHOW.
THESE TWO WOULD ALSO WORK...
ASUNA-SAN, WILL YOU TAKE SAKURAZAKI-SAN AND CLASS REP-SAN, WILL YOU TAKE ZAZIE-SAN?
NO PROBLEM.
DON'T MIND AT ALL, NEGI-SENSEI.
HUH?
OH, SE-CHAN!
WE'RE IN THE SAME GROUP.
OH...
......
BOW
WHISK
UH...
......?
DONG
GONG
HUMPH.

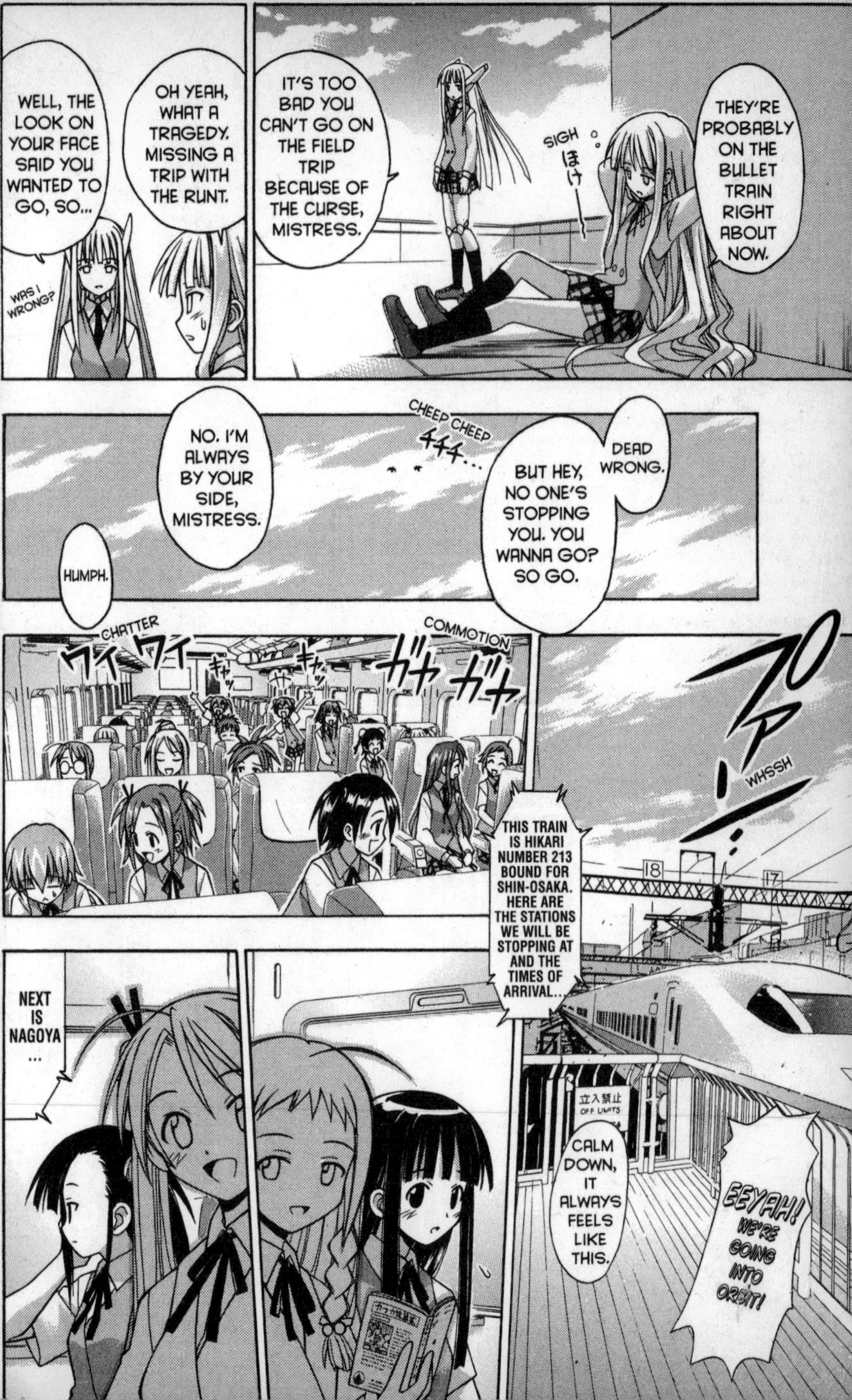
THEY'RE PROBABLY ON THE BULLET TRAIN RIGHT ABOUT NOW.
SIGH
ほけー
IT'S TOO BAD YOU CAN'T GO ON THE FIELD TRIP BECAUSE OF THE CURSE, MISTRESS.
OH YEAH, WHAT A TRAGEDY. MISSING A TRIP WITH THE RUNT.
WELL, THE LOOK ON YOUR FACE SAID YOU WANTED TO GO, SO...
WAS I WRONG?
DEAD WRONG.
BUT HEY, NO ONE'S STOPPING YOU. YOU WANNA GO? SO GO.
CHEEP CHEEP
チチチ...
NO. I'M ALWAYS BY YOUR SIDE, MISTRESS.
HUMPH.
WHSSH
18
17
THIS TRAIN IS HIKARI NUMBER 213 BOUND FOR SHIN-OSAKA. HERE ARE THE STATIONS WE WILL BE STOPPING AT AND THE TIMES OF ARRIVAL...
COMMOTION
ガヤガヤ
キャッ
キャッ
CHATTER
ワイワイ
EEYAH! WE'RE GOING INTO ORBIT!
立入禁止
OFF LIMITS
CALM DOWN, IT ALWAYS FEELS LIKE THIS.
NEXT IS NAGOYA ...

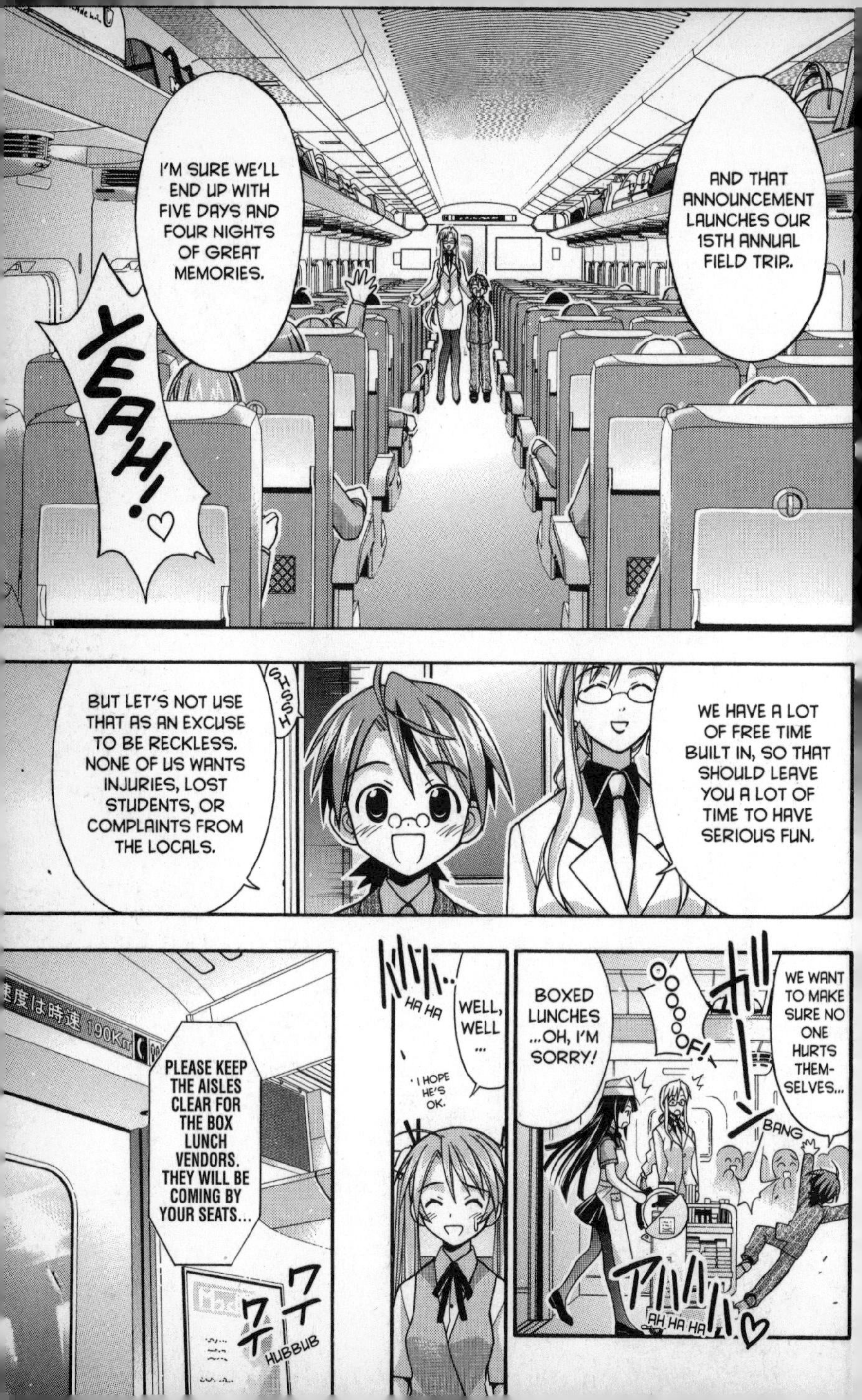
AND THAT ANNOUNCEMENT LAUNCHES OUR 15TH ANNUAL FIELD TRIP..
I'M SURE WE'LL END UP WITH FIVE DAYS AND FOUR NIGHTS OF GREAT MEMORIES.
YEAH!♡
WE HAVE A LOT OF FREE TIME BUILT IN, SO THAT SHOULD LEAVE YOU A LOT OF TIME TO HAVE SERIOUS FUN.
SHSSH
BUT LET'S NOT USE THAT AS AN EXCUSE TO BE RECKLESS. NONE OF US WANTS INJURIES, LOST STUDENTS, OR COMPLAINTS FROM THE LOCALS.
WE WANT TO MAKE SURE NO ONE HURTS THEMSELVES...
OOOOOF!
BANG
BOXED LUNCHES ...OH, I'M SORRY!
AH HA HA ♡
WELL, WELL ...
HA HA
I HOPE HE'S OK.
速度は時速 190Km
PLEASE KEEP THE AISLES CLEAR FOR THE BOX LUNCH VENDORS. THEY WILL BE COMING BY YOUR SEATS...
HUBBUB

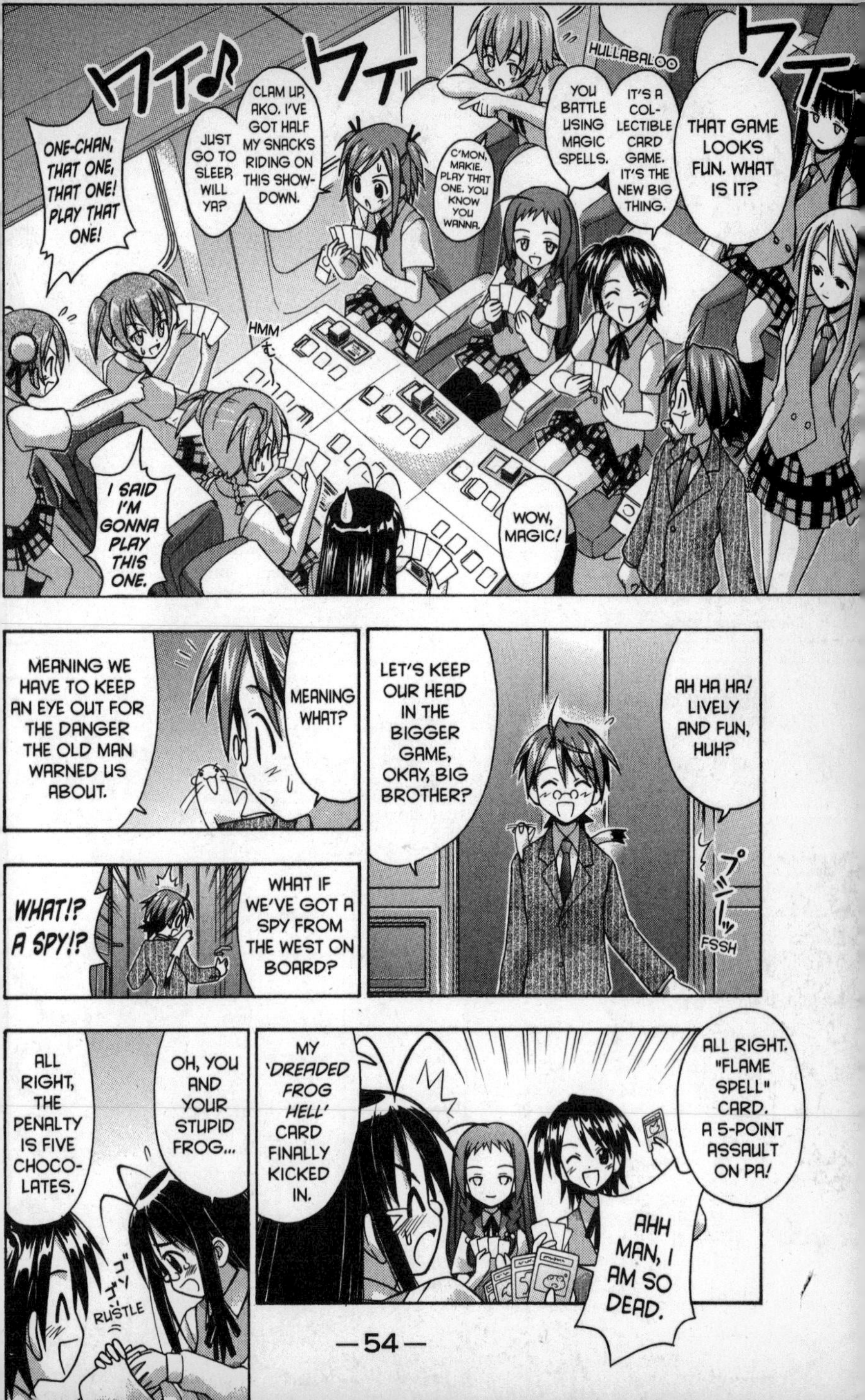
ワイ
HULLABALOO
THAT GAME LOOKS FUN. WHAT IS IT?
IT'S A COL-LECTIBLE CARD GAME. IT'S THE NEW BIG THING.
YOU BATTLE USING MAGIC SPELLS.
ワイ
C'MON, MAKIE. PLAY THAT ONE. YOU KNOW YOU WANNA.
CLAM UP, AKO. I'VE GOT HALF MY SNACKS RIDING ON THIS SHOW-DOWN.
JUST GO TO SLEEP, WILL YA?
ワイ♪
ONE-CHAN, THAT ONE, THAT ONE! PLAY THAT ONE!
HMM
WOW, MAGIC!
I SAID I'M GONNA PLAY THIS ONE.
AH HA HA! LIVELY AND FUN, HUH?
FSSH
LET'S KEEP OUR HEAD IN THE BIGGER GAME, OKAY, BIG BROTHER?
MEANING WHAT?
MEANING WE HAVE TO KEEP AN EYE OUT FOR THE DANGER THE OLD MAN WARNED US ABOUT.
WHAT IF WE'VE GOT A SPY FROM THE WEST ON BOARD?
WHAT!? A SPY!?
ALL RIGHT. "FLAME SPELL" CARD. A 5-POINT ASSAULT ON PA!
AHH MAN, I AM SO DEAD.
MY 'DREADED FROG HELL' CARD FINALLY KICKED IN.
OH, YOU AND YOUR STUPID FROG...
ALL RIGHT, THE PENALTY IS FIVE CHOCO-LATES.
RUSTLE

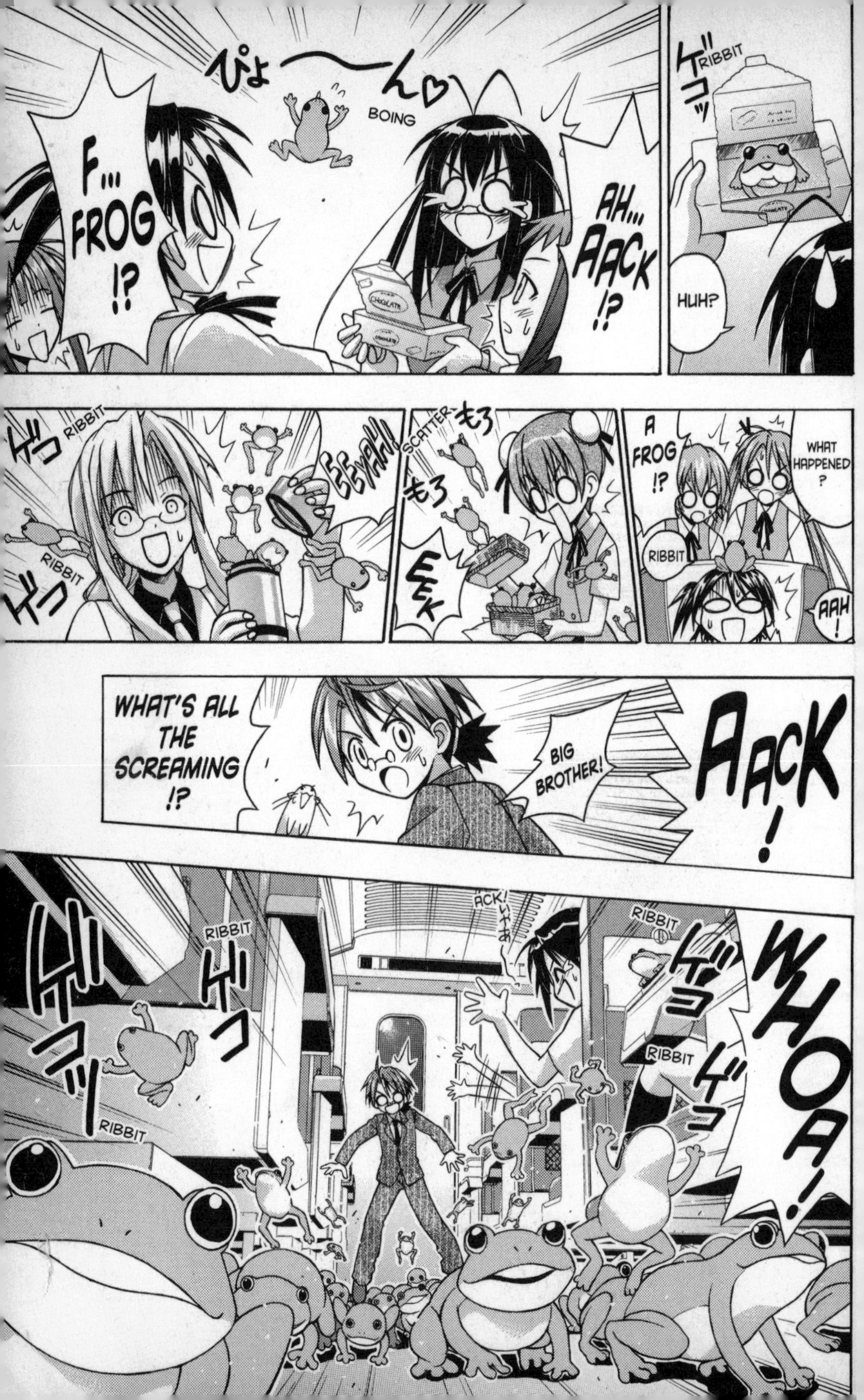
ゲコッ
RIBBIT
HUH?
AH... AACK !?
ぴょ〜〜ん♡
BOING
F... FROG !?
WHAT HAPPENED ?
A FROG !?
RIBBIT
AAH !
もろ
SCATTER
もろ
EEK
EEEYAH!!
ゲコ
RIBBIT
ゲコ
RIBBIT
AACK !
BIG BROTHER!
WHAT'S ALL THE SCREAMING !?
WHOA!!
ゲコ
RIBBIT
ゲコ
RIBBIT
ACK! いやあ
ゲコ
RIBBIT
ゲコッ
RIBBIT

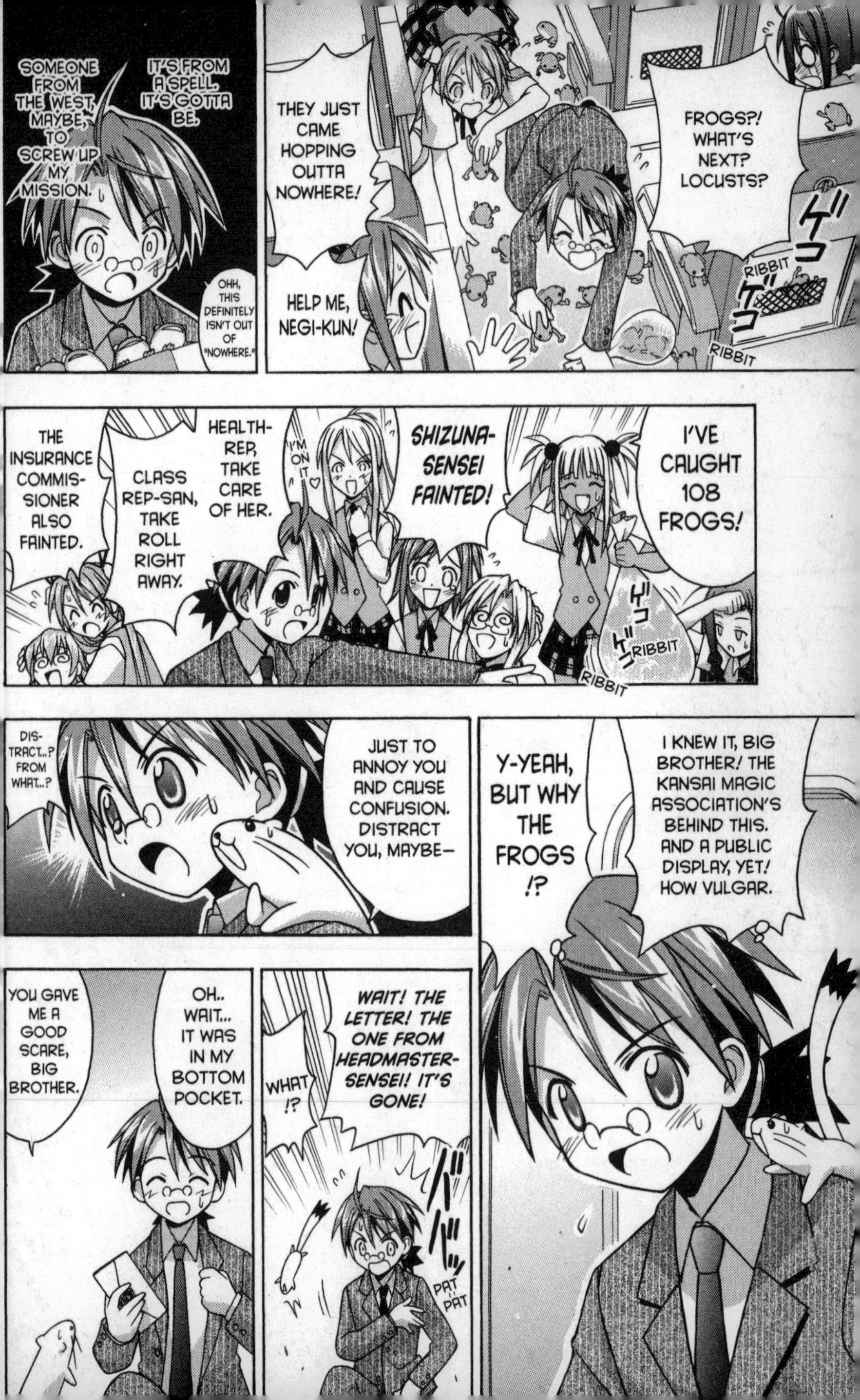
FROGS?! WHAT'S NEXT? LOCUSTS?
ゲコ
RIBBIT
ゲコ
RIBBIT
THEY JUST CAME HOPPING OUTTA NOWHERE!
HELP ME, NEGI-KUN!
IT'S FROM A SPELL. IT'S GOTTA BE.
SOMEONE FROM THE WEST, MAYBE, TO SCREW UP MY MISSION.
OHH, THIS DEFINITELY ISN'T OUT OF "NOWHERE."
I'VE CAUGHT 108 FROGS!
ゲコ
RIBBIT
ゲコ
RIBBIT
SHIZUNA-SENSEI FAINTED!
I'M ON IT ♡
HEALTH-REP, TAKE CARE OF HER.
CLASS REP-SAN, TAKE ROLL RIGHT AWAY.
THE INSURANCE COMMISSIONER ALSO FAINTED.
I KNEW IT, BIG BROTHER! THE KANSAI MAGIC ASSOCIATION'S BEHIND THIS. AND A PUBLIC DISPLAY, YET! HOW VULGAR.
Y-YEAH, BUT WHY THE FROGS!?
JUST TO ANNOY YOU AND CAUSE CONFUSION. DISTRACT YOU, MAYBE—
DISTRACT...? FROM WHAT...?
WAIT! THE LETTER! THE ONE FROM HEADMASTER-SENSEI! IT'S GONE!
WHAT!?
PAT PAT
OH.. WAIT... IT WAS IN MY BOTTOM POCKET.
YOU GAVE ME A GOOD SCARE, BIG BROTHER.

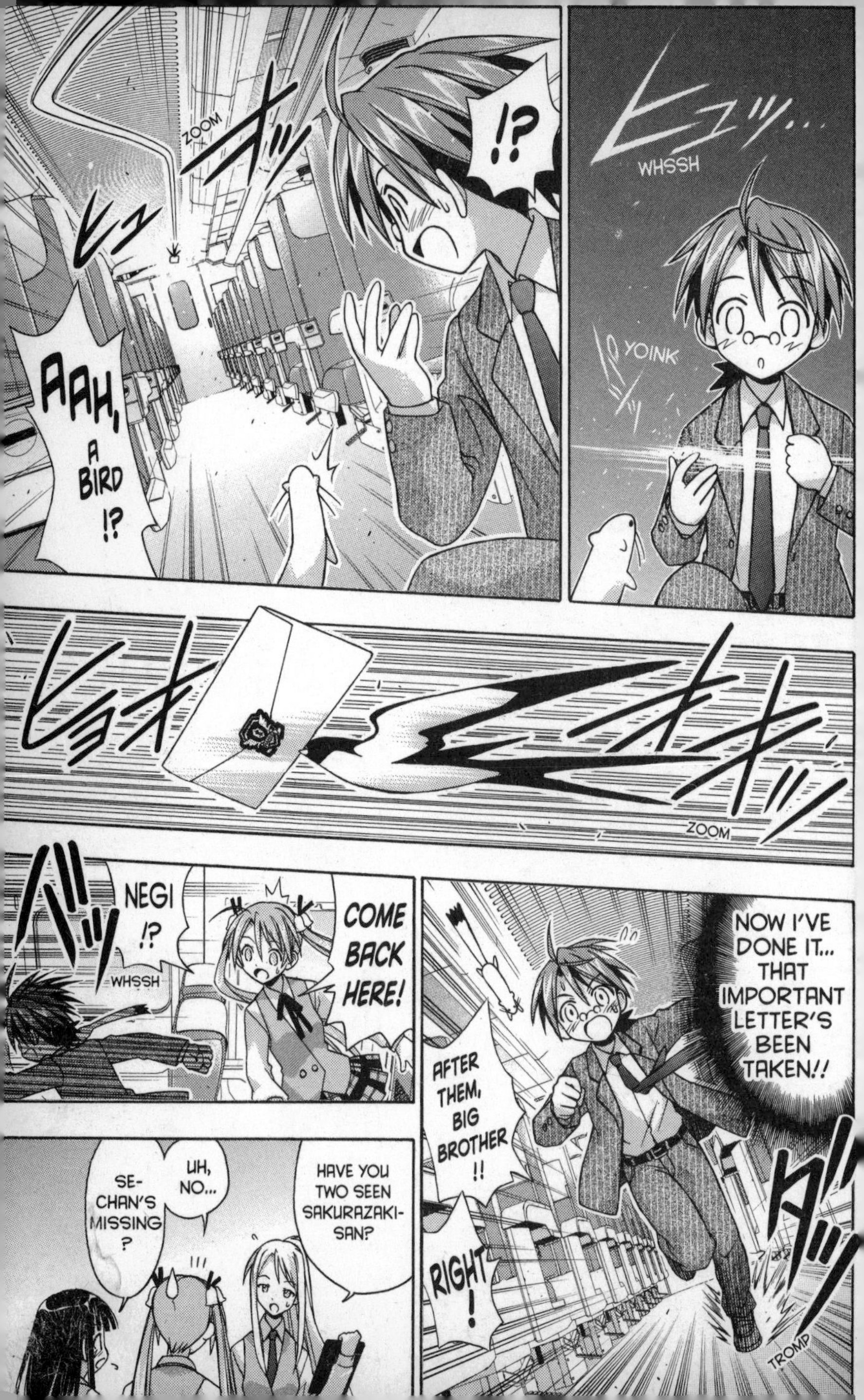

WHSSH
YOINK
!?
ZOOM
AAH, A BIRD !?
ZOOM
NOW I'VE DONE IT... THAT IMPORTANT LETTER'S BEEN TAKEN!!
AFTER THEM, BIG BROTHER !!
RIGHT !
TROMP
COME BACK HERE!
NEGI !?
WHSSH
HAVE YOU TWO SEEN SAKURAZAKI-SAN?
UH, NO...
SE-CHAN'S MISSING ?

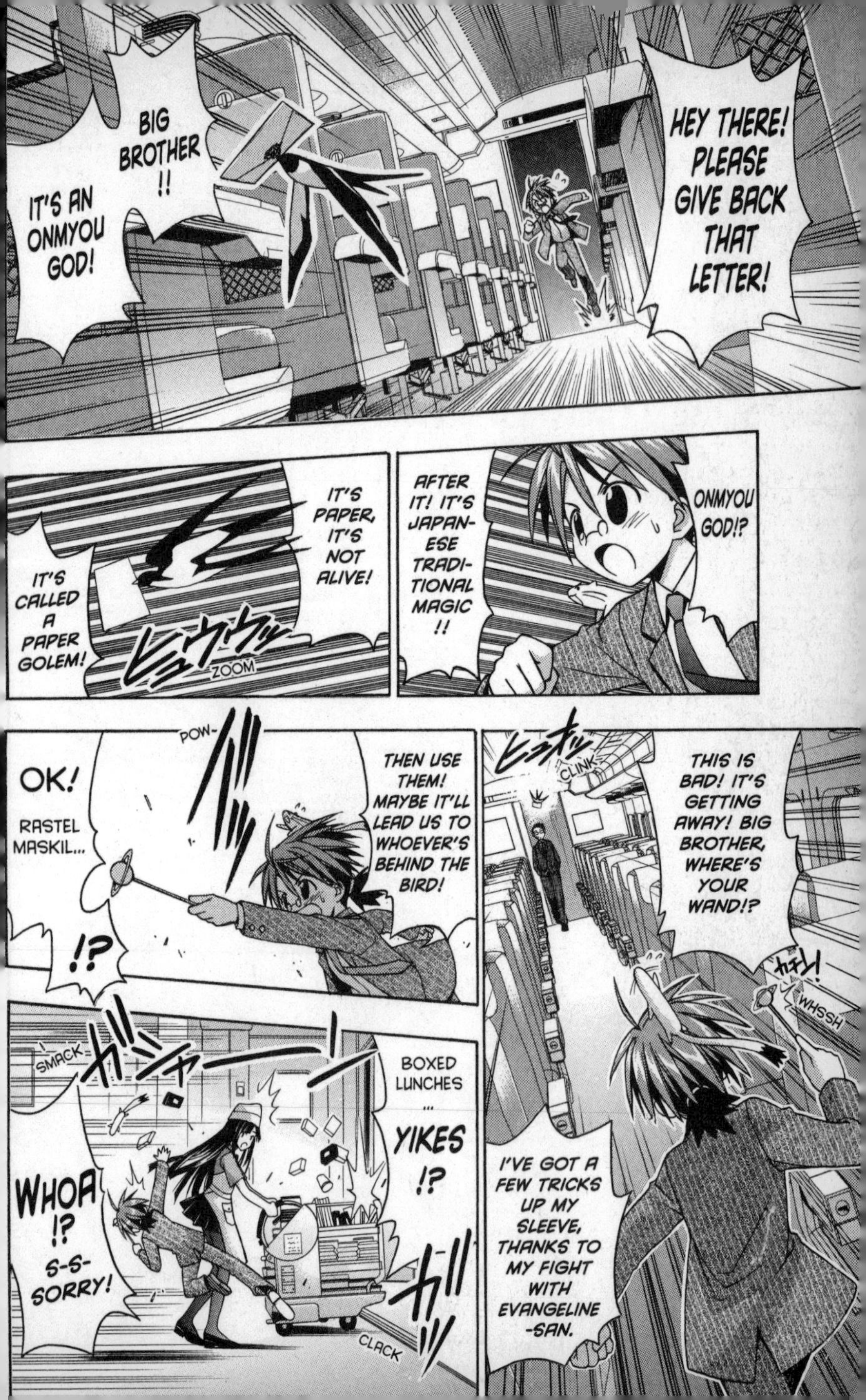
HEY THERE! PLEASE GIVE BACK THAT LETTER!
BIG BROTHER!!
IT'S AN ONMYOU GOD!
ONMYOU GOD!?
AFTER IT! IT'S JAPANESE TRADITIONAL MAGIC!!
IT'S PAPER, IT'S NOT ALIVE!
IT'S CALLED A PAPER GOLEM!
ZOOM
CLINK
THIS IS BAD! IT'S GETTING AWAY! BIG BROTHER, WHERE'S YOUR WAND!?
WHSSH
I'VE GOT A FEW TRICKS UP MY SLEEVE, THANKS TO MY FIGHT WITH EVANGELINE-SAN.
POW-
THEN USE THEM! MAYBE IT'LL LEAD US TO WHOEVER'S BEHIND THE BIRD!
OK!
RASTEL MASKIL...
!?
BOXED LUNCHES ...
YIKES!?
SMACK
WHOA!?
S-S-SORRY!
CLACK

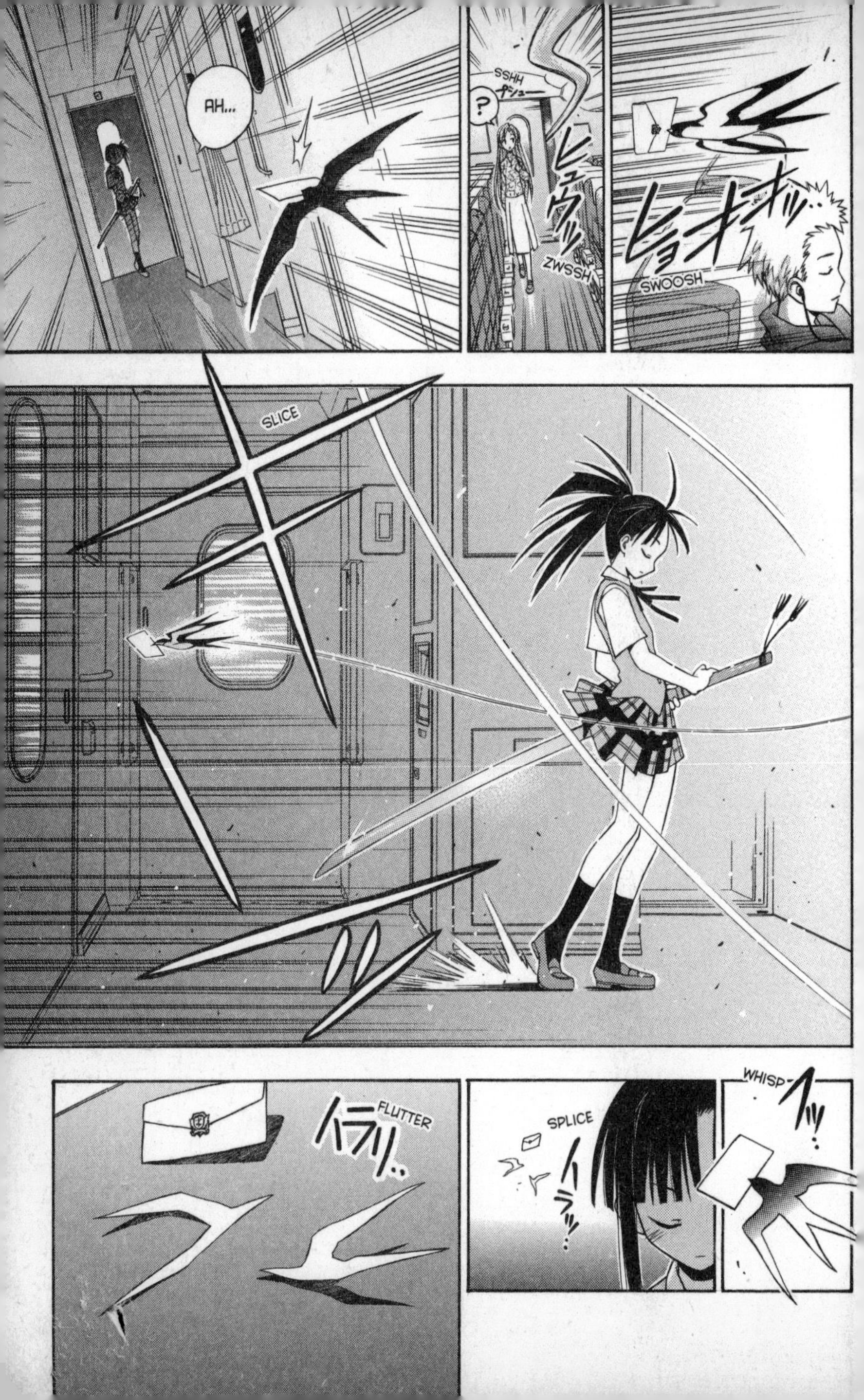
SWOOSH
SSHH
?
ZWSSH
AH...
SLICE
WHISP
SPLICE
FLUTTER

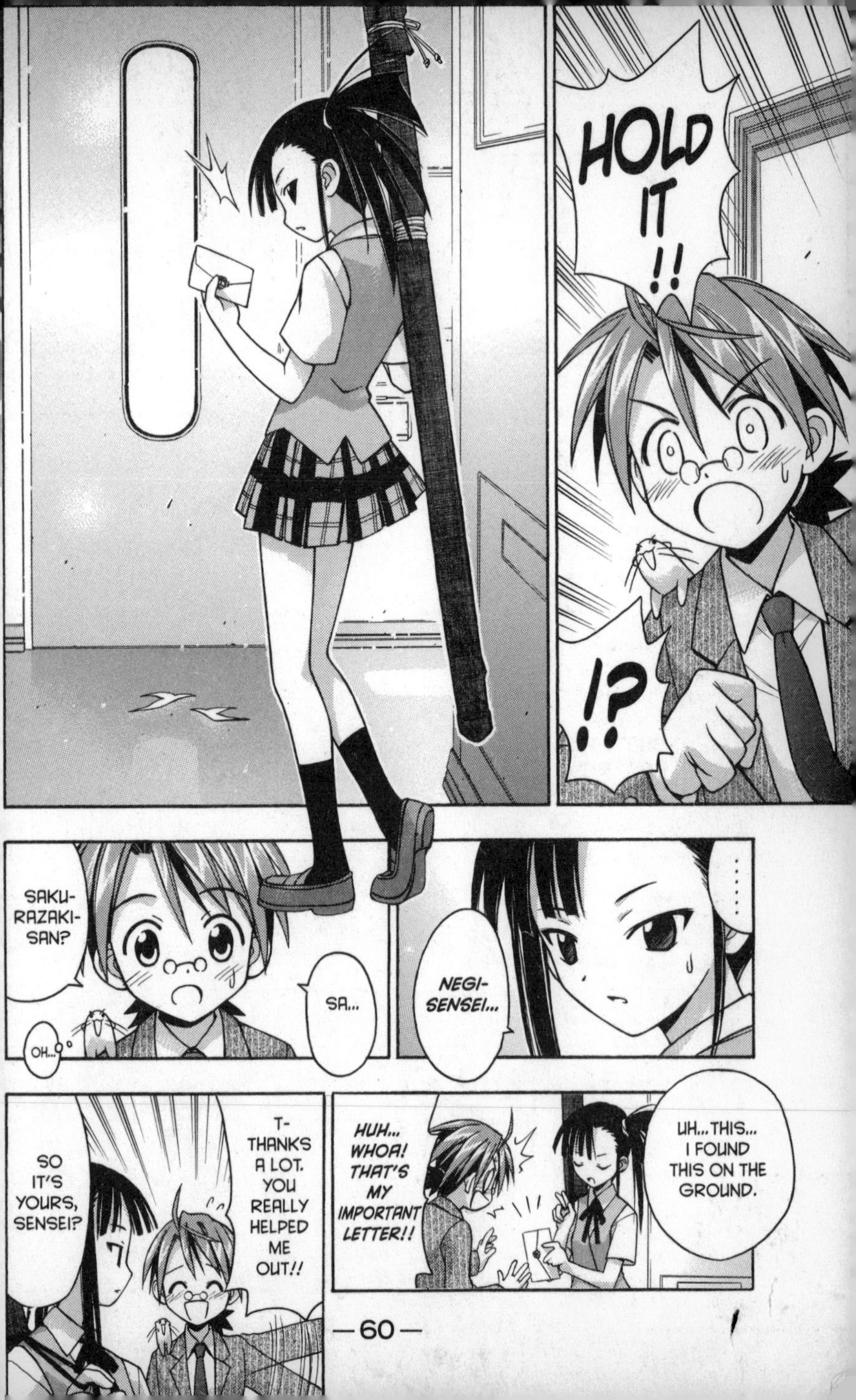
HOLD IT!!
!?
......
NEGI-SENSEI...
SA...
SAKU-RAZAKI-SAN?
OH...
UH...THIS... I FOUND THIS ON THE GROUND.
HUH... WHOA! THAT'S MY IMPORTANT LETTER!!
T-THANKS A LOT. YOU REALLY HELPED ME OUT!!
SO IT'S YOURS, SENSEI?

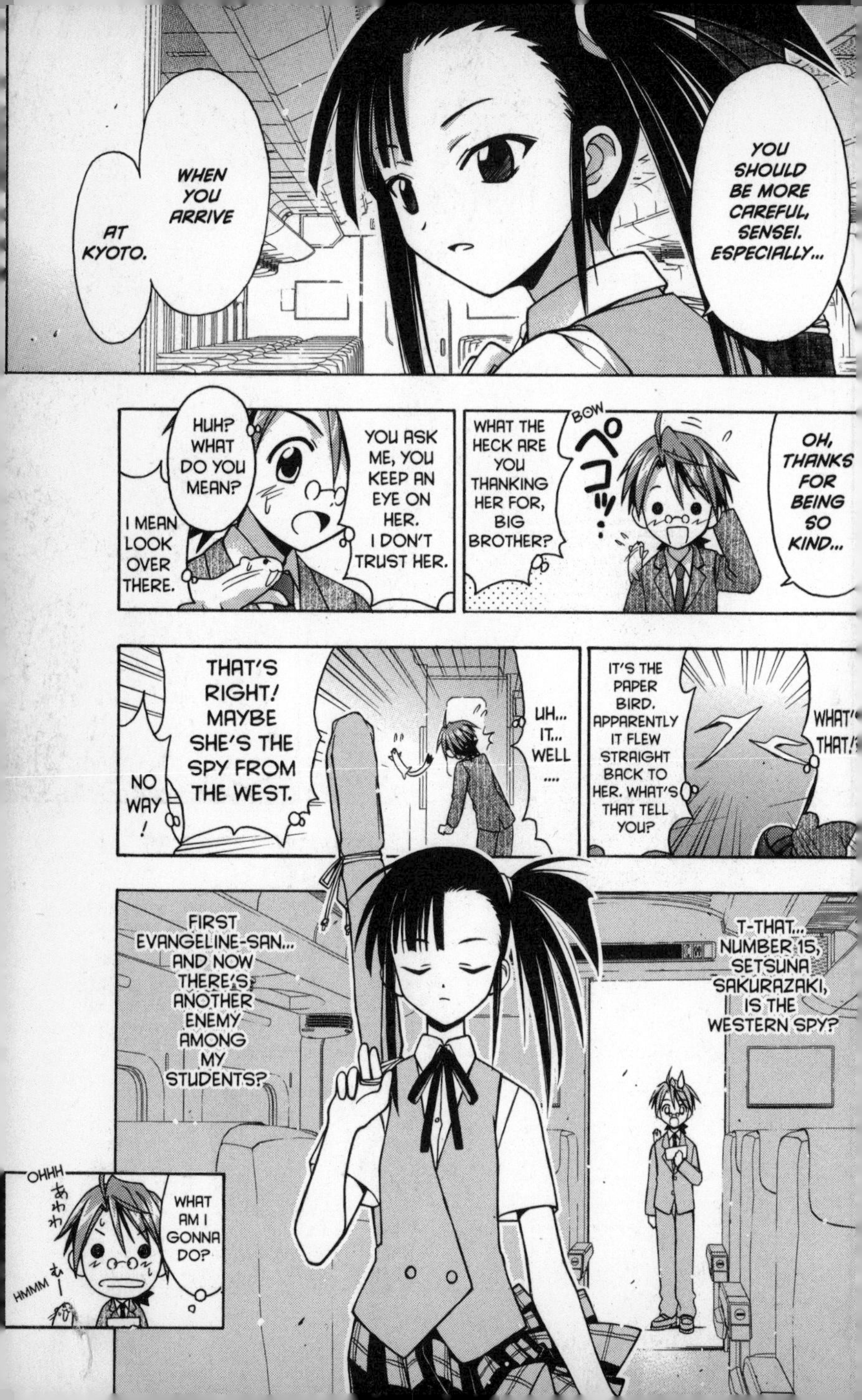
YOU SHOULD BE MORE CAREFUL, SENSEI. ESPECIALLY...
WHEN YOU ARRIVE AT KYOTO.
OH, THANKS FOR BEING SO KIND...
BOW ペコッ
WHAT THE HECK ARE YOU THANKING HER FOR, BIG BROTHER?
YOU ASK ME, YOU KEEP AN EYE ON HER. I DON'T TRUST HER.
HUH? WHAT DO YOU MEAN?
I MEAN LOOK OVER THERE.
WHAT'S THAT!?
IT'S THE PAPER BIRD. APPARENTLY IT FLEW STRAIGHT BACK TO HER. WHAT'S THAT TELL YOU?
UH... IT... WELL ....
THAT'S RIGHT! MAYBE SHE'S THE SPY FROM THE WEST.
NO WAY!
T-THAT... NUMBER 15, SETSUNA SAKURAZAKI, IS THE WESTERN SPY?
FIRST EVANGELINE-SAN... AND NOW THERE'S ANOTHER ENEMY AMONG MY STUDENTS?
OHHH あわわ
WHAT AM I GONNA DO?
HMMM むー

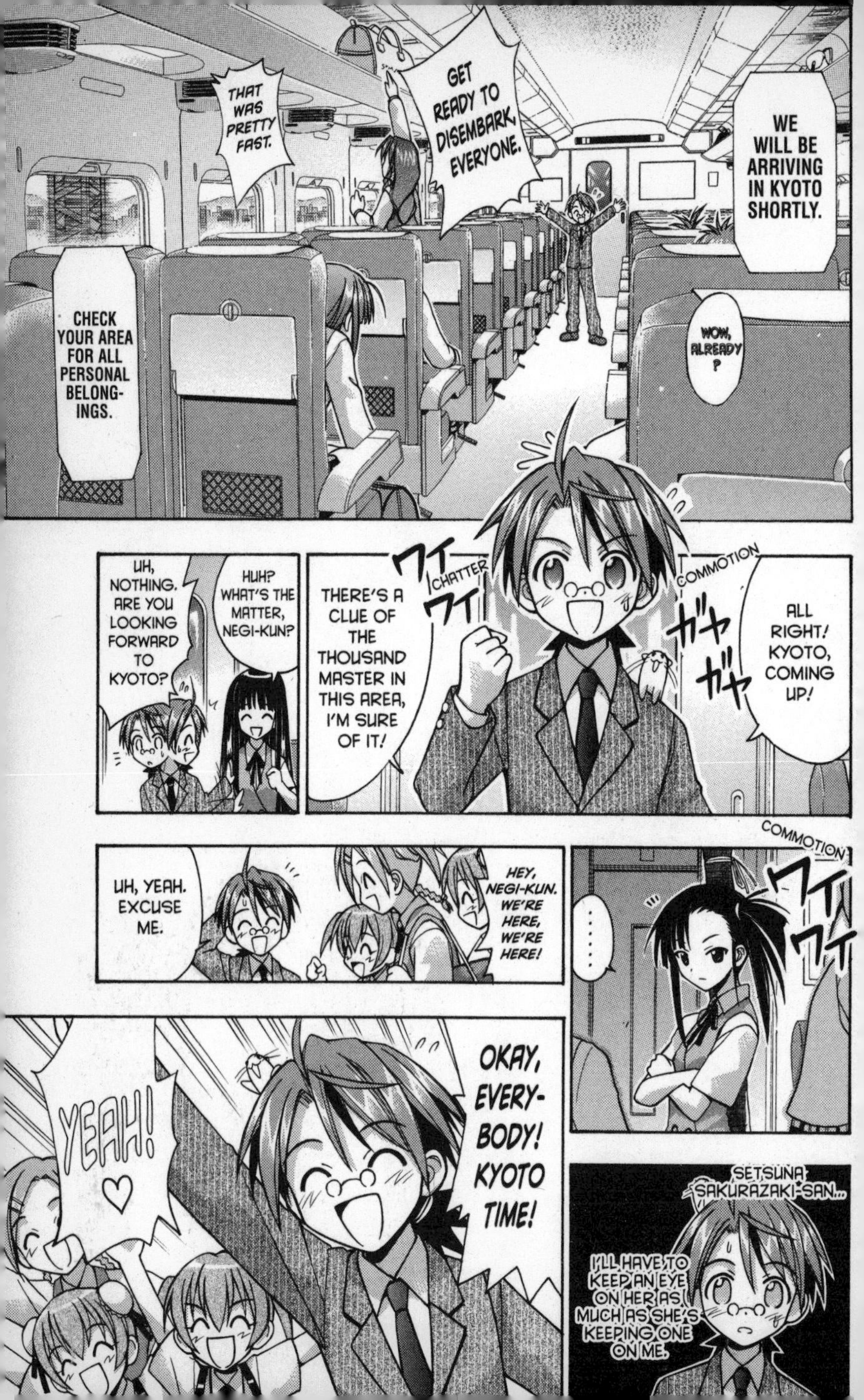
WE WILL BE ARRIVING IN KYOTO SHORTLY.
GET READY TO DISEMBARK, EVERYONE.
THAT WAS PRETTY FAST.
WOW, ALREADY?
CHECK YOUR AREA FOR ALL PERSONAL BELONGINGS.
COMMOTION
ガヤガヤ
ALL RIGHT! KYOTO, COMING UP!
ワイワイ
CHATTER
THERE'S A CLUE OF THE THOUSAND MASTER IN THIS AREA, I'M SURE OF IT!
HUH? WHAT'S THE MATTER, NEGI-KUN?
UH, NOTHING. ARE YOU LOOKING FORWARD TO KYOTO?
COMMOTION
ワイワイ
. . . . .
HEY, NEGI-KUN. WE'RE HERE, WE'RE HERE!
UH, YEAH. EXCUSE ME.
OKAY, EVERYBODY! KYOTO TIME!
YEAH! ♥
SETSUNA SAKURAZAKI-SAN...
I'LL HAVE TO KEEP AN EYE ON HER AS MUCH AS SHE'S KEEPING ONE ON ME.

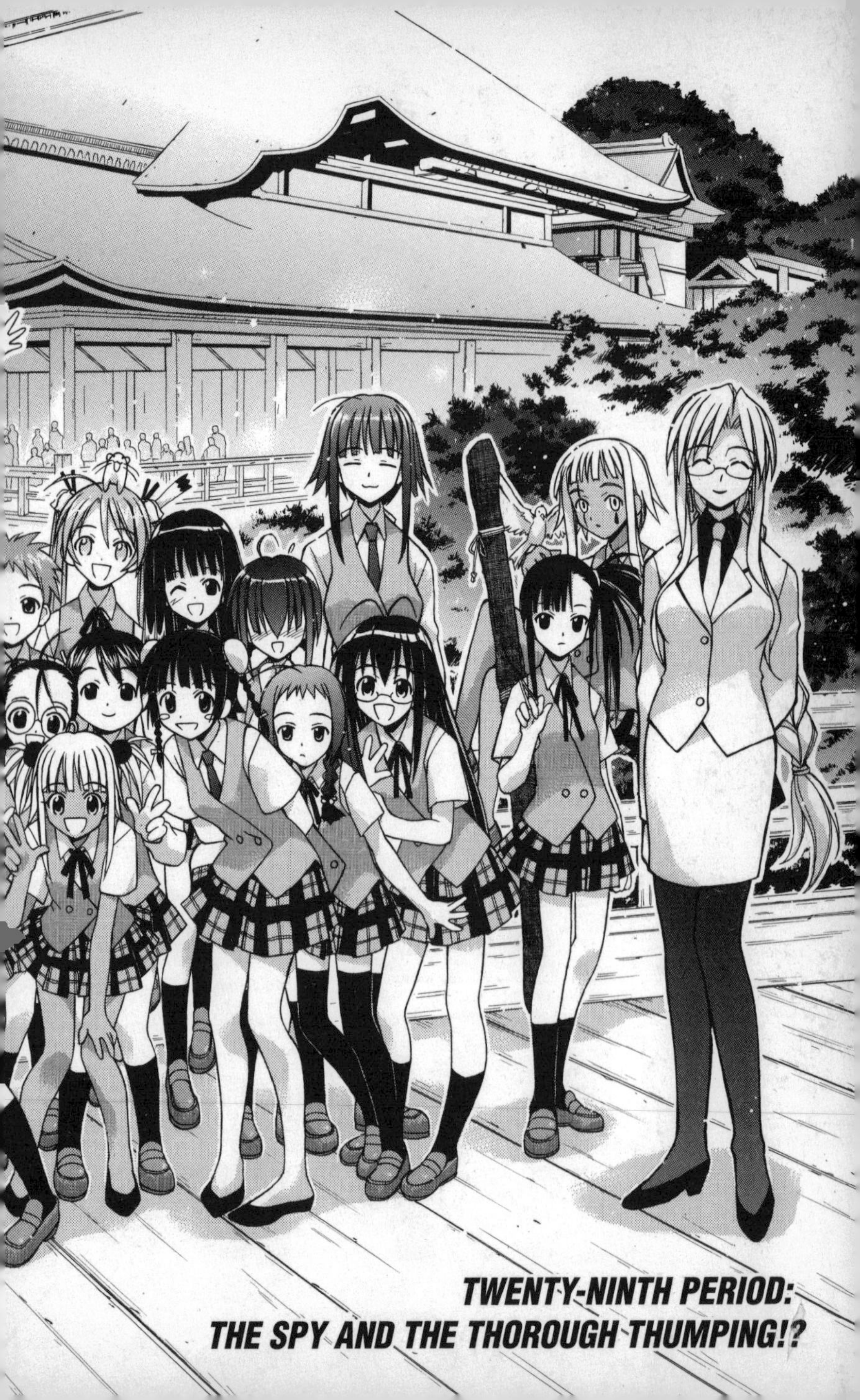

TWENTY-NINTH PERIOD: THE SPY AND THE THOROUGH THUMPING!?

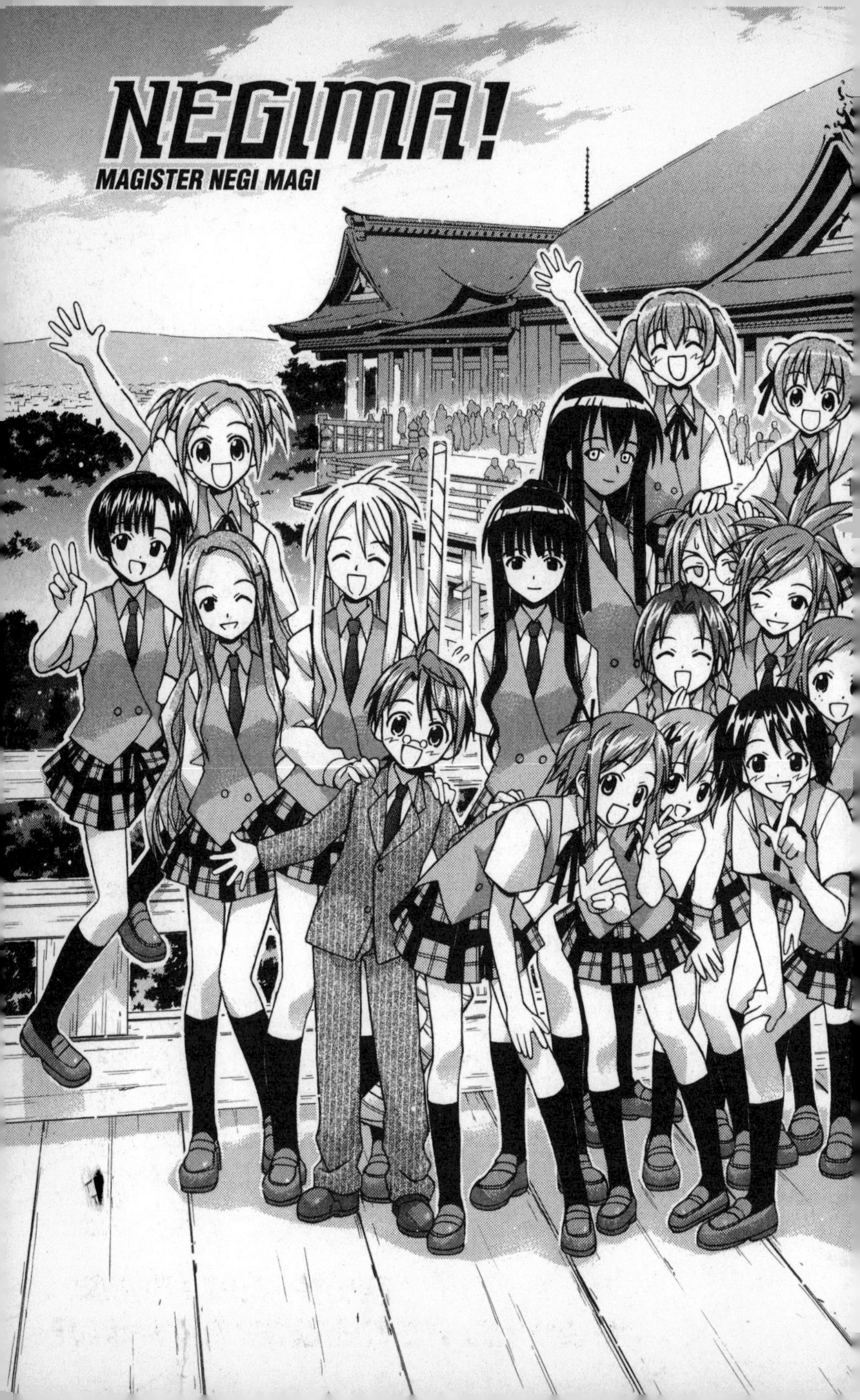
NEGIMA!
MAGISTER NEGI MAGI

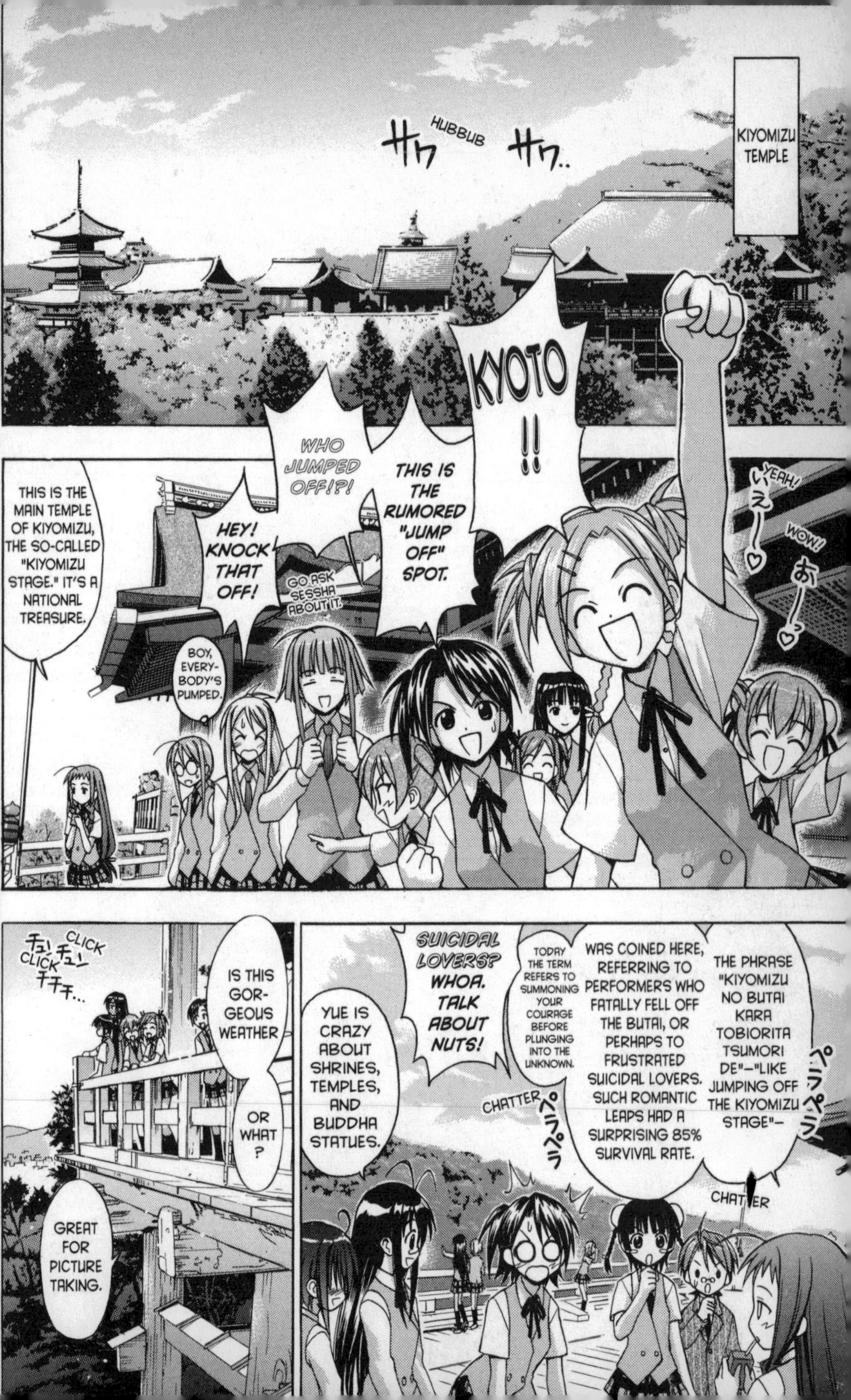
KIYOMIZU TEMPLE
HUBBUB
YEAH!
WOW!
KYOTO!!
THIS IS THE RUMORED "JUMP OFF" SPOT.
WHO JUMPED OFF!?!
GO ASK SESSHA ABOUT IT.
HEY! KNOCK THAT OFF!
BOY, EVERYBODY'S PUMPED.
THIS IS THE MAIN TEMPLE OF KIYOMIZU, THE SO-CALLED "KIYOMIZU STAGE." IT'S A NATIONAL TREASURE.
THE PHRASE "KIYOMIZU NO BUTAI KARA TOBIORITA TSUMORI DE"—"LIKE JUMPING OFF THE KIYOMIZU STAGE"—
WAS COINED HERE, REFERRING TO PERFORMERS WHO FATALLY FELL OFF THE BUTAI, OR PERHAPS TO FRUSTRATED SUICIDAL LOVERS. SUCH ROMANTIC LEAPS HAD A SURPRISING 85% SURVIVAL RATE.
TODAY THE TERM REFERS TO SUMMONING YOUR COURAGE BEFORE PLUNGING INTO THE UNKNOWN.
CHATTER
SUICIDAL LOVERS? WHOA. TALK ABOUT NUTS!
YUE IS CRAZY ABOUT SHRINES, TEMPLES, AND BUDDHA STATUES.
CHATTER
IS THIS GORGEOUS WEATHER
OR WHAT?
CLICK
CLICK
GREAT FOR PICTURE TAKING.

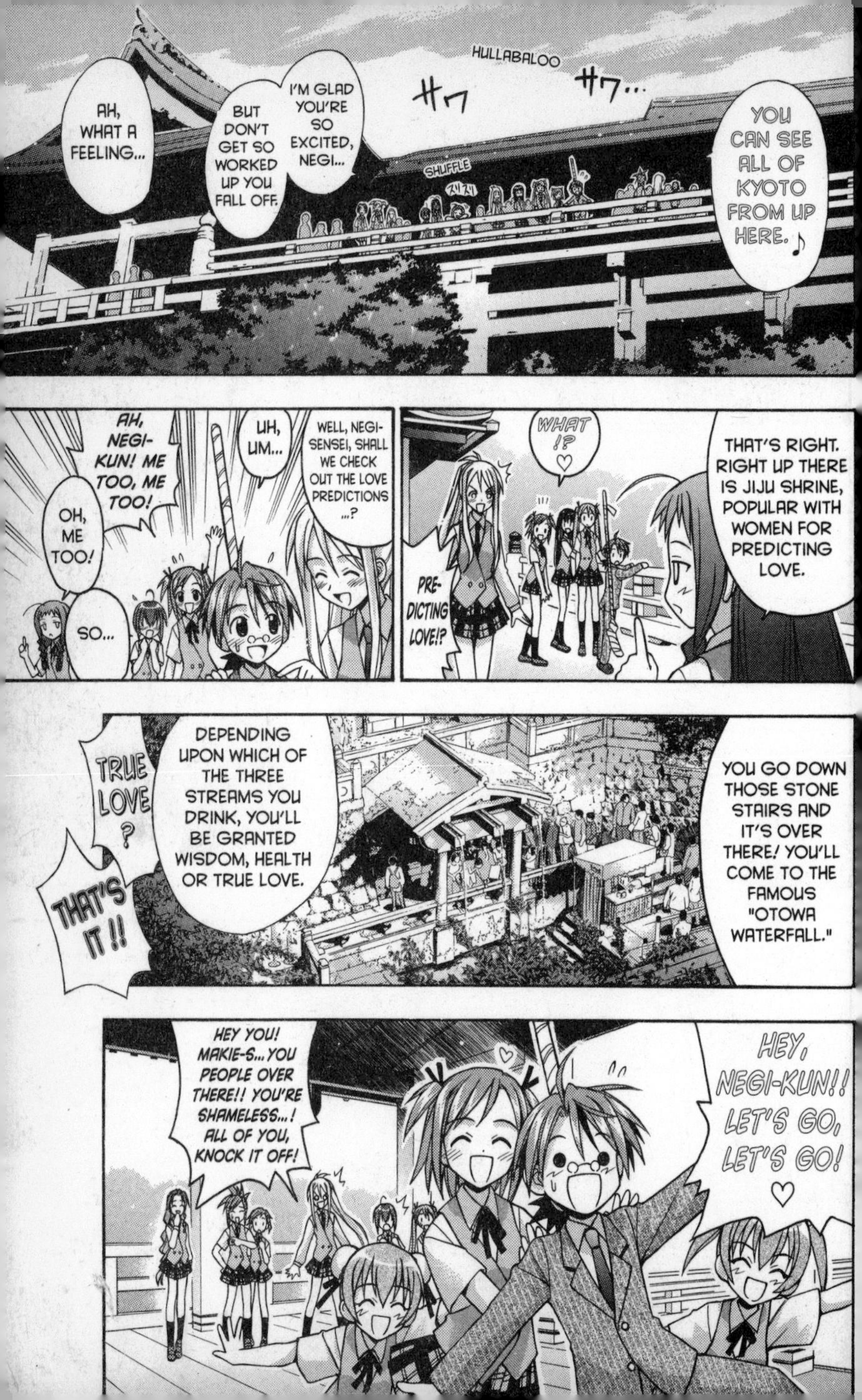
YOU CAN SEE ALL OF KYOTO FROM UP HERE. ♪
サワ…
HULLABALOO
サワ
I'M GLAD YOU'RE SO EXCITED, NEGI...
BUT DON'T GET SO WORKED UP YOU FALL OFF.
AH, WHAT A FEELING...
SHUFFLE
THAT'S RIGHT. RIGHT UP THERE IS JIJU SHRINE, POPULAR WITH WOMEN FOR PREDICTING LOVE.
WHAT !? ♡
PRE-DICTING LOVE!?
WELL, NEGI-SENSEI, SHALL WE CHECK OUT THE LOVE PREDICTIONS ...?
UH, UM...
AH, NEGI-KUN! ME TOO, ME TOO!
OH, ME TOO!
SO...
YOU GO DOWN THOSE STONE STAIRS AND IT'S OVER THERE! YOU'LL COME TO THE FAMOUS "OTOWA WATERFALL."
DEPENDING UPON WHICH OF THE THREE STREAMS YOU DRINK, YOU'LL BE GRANTED WISDOM, HEALTH OR TRUE LOVE.
TRUE LOVE ?
THAT'S IT !!
HEY, NEGI-KUN!! LET'S GO, LET'S GO! ♡
HEY YOU! MAKIE-S...YOU PEOPLE OVER THERE!! YOU'RE SHAMELESS...! ALL OF YOU, KNOCK IT OFF!

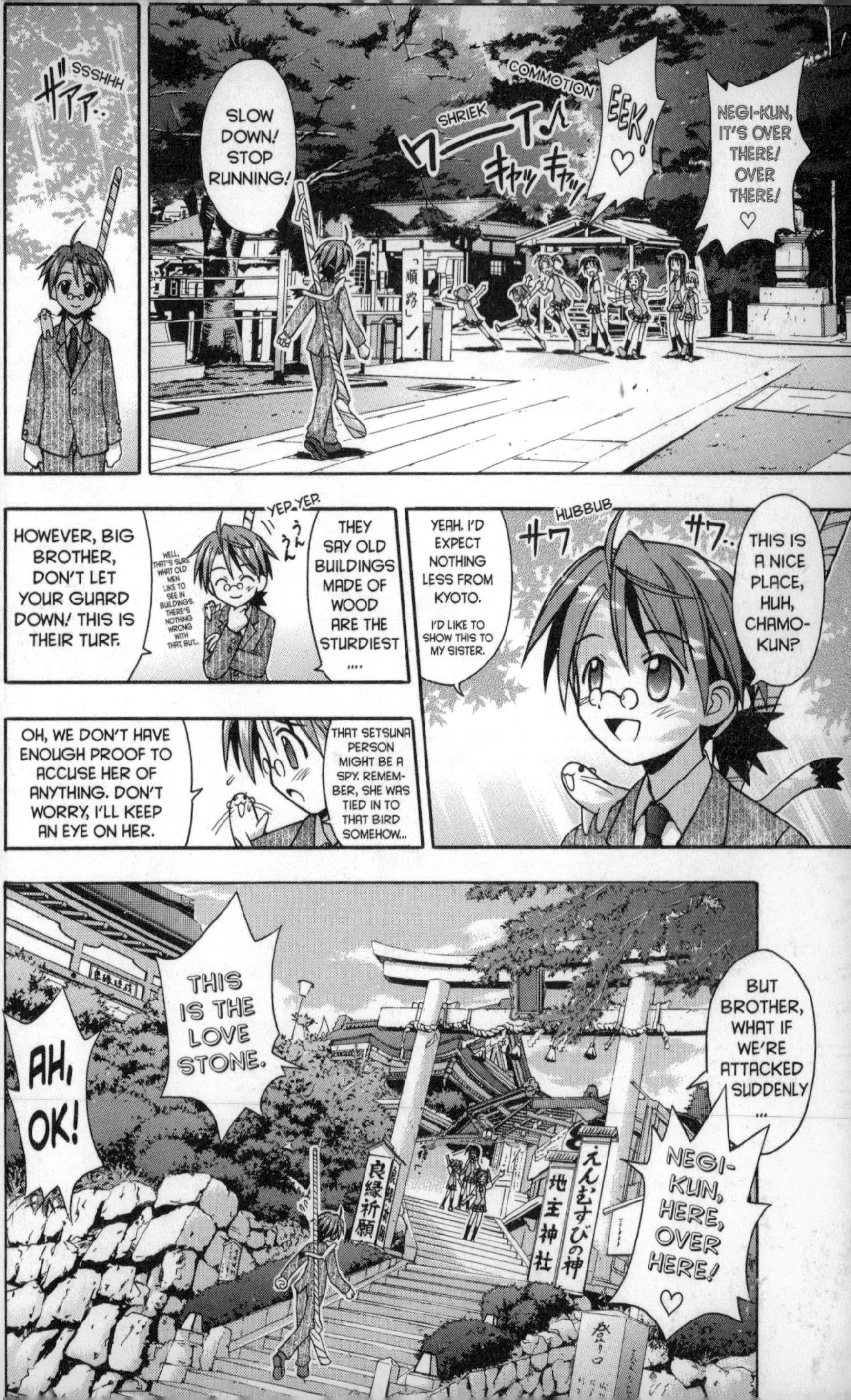
NEGI-KUN, IT'S OVER THERE! OVER THERE! ♡
EEK! ♡
COMMOTION
SHRIEK
SLOW DOWN! STOP RUNNING!
SSSHHH
THIS IS A NICE PLACE, HUH, CHAMO-KUN?
HUBBUB
YEAH. I'D EXPECT NOTHING LESS FROM KYOTO.
I'D LIKE TO SHOW THIS TO MY SISTER.
THEY SAY OLD BUILDINGS MADE OF WOOD ARE THE STURDIEST ....
YEP YEP.
WELL, THAT'S SURE WHAT OLD MEN LIKE TO SEE IN BUILDINGS. THERE'S NOTHING WRONG WITH THAT, BUT...
HOWEVER, BIG BROTHER, DON'T LET YOUR GUARD DOWN! THIS IS THEIR TURF.
THAT SETSUNA PERSON MIGHT BE A SPY. REMEMBER, SHE WAS TIED IN TO THAT BIRD SOMEHOW...
OH, WE DON'T HAVE ENOUGH PROOF TO ACCUSE HER OF ANYTHING. DON'T WORRY, I'LL KEEP AN EYE ON HER.
BUT BROTHER, WHAT IF WE'RE ATTACKED SUDDENLY ...
NEGI-KUN, HERE, OVER HERE! ♡
えんむすびの神
地主神社
良縁祈願
THIS IS THE LOVE STONE.
AH, OK!

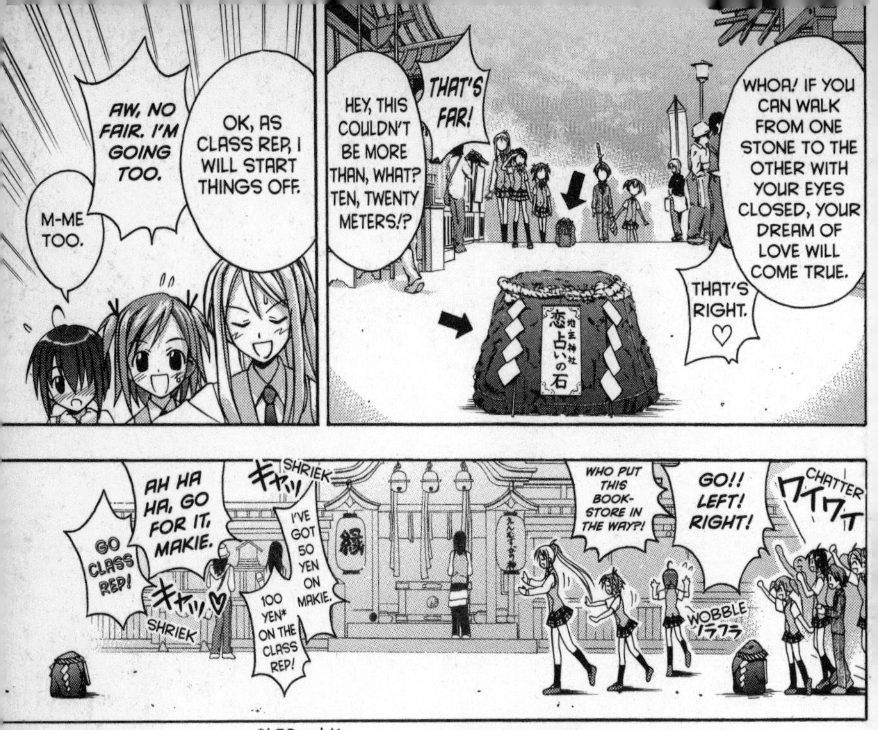
WHOA! IF YOU CAN WALK FROM ONE STONE TO THE OTHER WITH YOUR EYES CLOSED, YOUR DREAM OF LOVE WILL COME TRUE.
THAT'S RIGHT. ♡
地主神社 恋占いの石
THAT'S FAR!
HEY, THIS COULDN'T BE MORE THAN, WHAT? TEN, TWENTY METERS!?
OK, AS CLASS REP, I WILL START THINGS OFF.
AW, NO FAIR. I'M GOING TOO.
M-ME TOO.
ワイワイ CHATTER
GO!! LEFT! RIGHT!
WHO PUT THIS BOOK-STORE IN THE WAY?!
WOBBLE フラフラ
I'VE GOT 50 YEN ON MAKIE.
100 YEN* ON THE CLASS REP!
キャッ SHRIEK
AH HA HA, GO FOR IT, MAKIE.
GO CLASS REP!
キャッ♡ SHRIEK

*$.50 and $1.

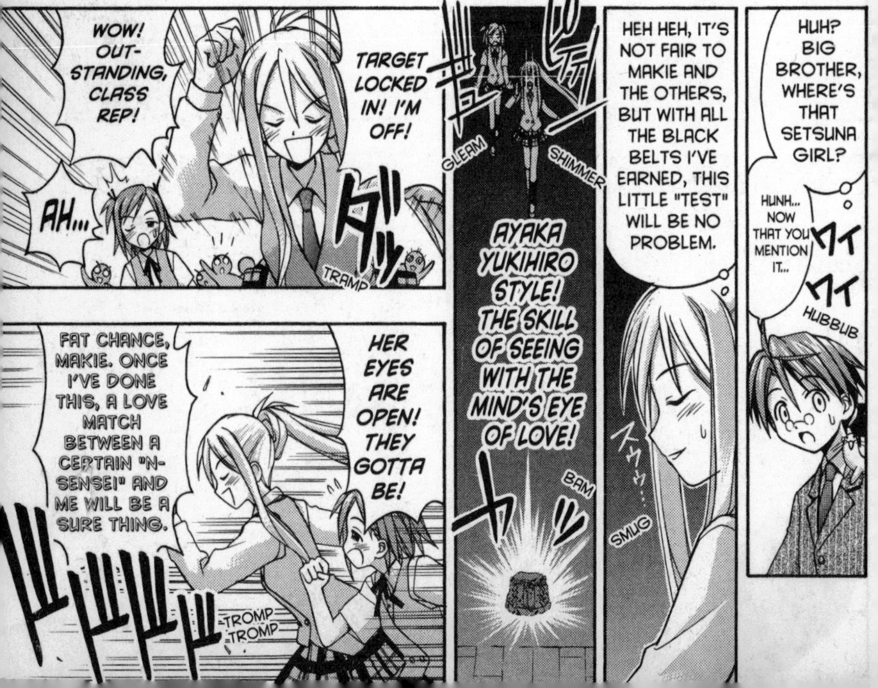
HUH? BIG BROTHER, WHERE'S THAT SETSUNA GIRL?
HUNH... NOW THAT YOU MENTION IT...
ワイワイ HUBBUB
HEH HEH, IT'S NOT FAIR TO MAKIE AND THE OTHERS, BUT WITH ALL THE BLACK BELTS I'VE EARNED, THIS LITTLE "TEST" WILL BE NO PROBLEM.
SMUG
GLEAM
SHIMMER
AYAKA YUKIHIRO STYLE! THE SKILL OF SEEING WITH THE MIND'S EYE OF LOVE!
BAM
TARGET LOCKED IN! I'M OFF!
WOW! OUT-STANDING, CLASS REP!
AH...
ダッ TRAMP
HER EYES ARE OPEN! THEY GOTTA BE!
FAT CHANCE, MAKIE. ONCE I'VE DONE THIS, A LOVE MATCH BETWEEN A CERTAIN "N-SENSEI" AND ME WILL BE A SURE THING.
TROMP TROMP

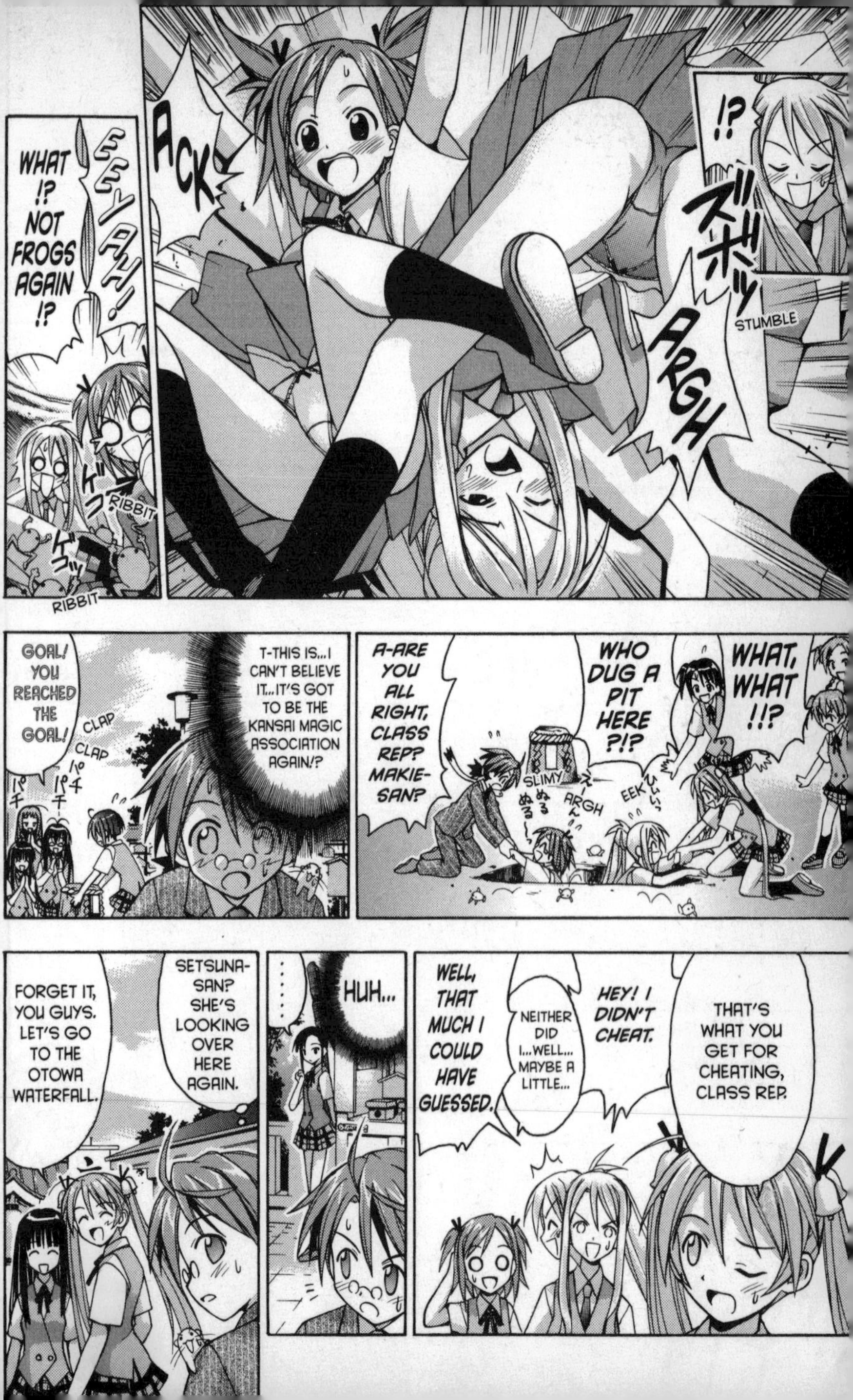
!?
STUMBLE
ARGH
ACK
EEYAAH!
WHAT!? NOT FROGS AGAIN!?
RIBBIT
RIBBIT
WHAT, WHAT!!?
WHO DUG A PIT HERE?!?
A-ARE YOU ALL RIGHT, CLASS REP? MAKIE-SAN?
EEK
ARGH
SLIMY
T-THIS IS...I CAN'T BELIEVE IT...IT'S GOT TO BE THE KANSAI MAGIC ASSOCIATION AGAIN!?
GOAL! YOU REACHED THE GOAL!
CLAP
CLAP
THAT'S WHAT YOU GET FOR CHEATING, CLASS REP.
HEY! I DIDN'T CHEAT.
NEITHER DID I...WELL... MAYBE A LITTLE...
WELL, THAT MUCH I COULD HAVE GUESSED.
HUH...
......
SETSUNA-SAN? SHE'S LOOKING OVER HERE AGAIN.
FORGET IT, YOU GUYS. LET'S GO TO THE OTOWA WATERFALL.

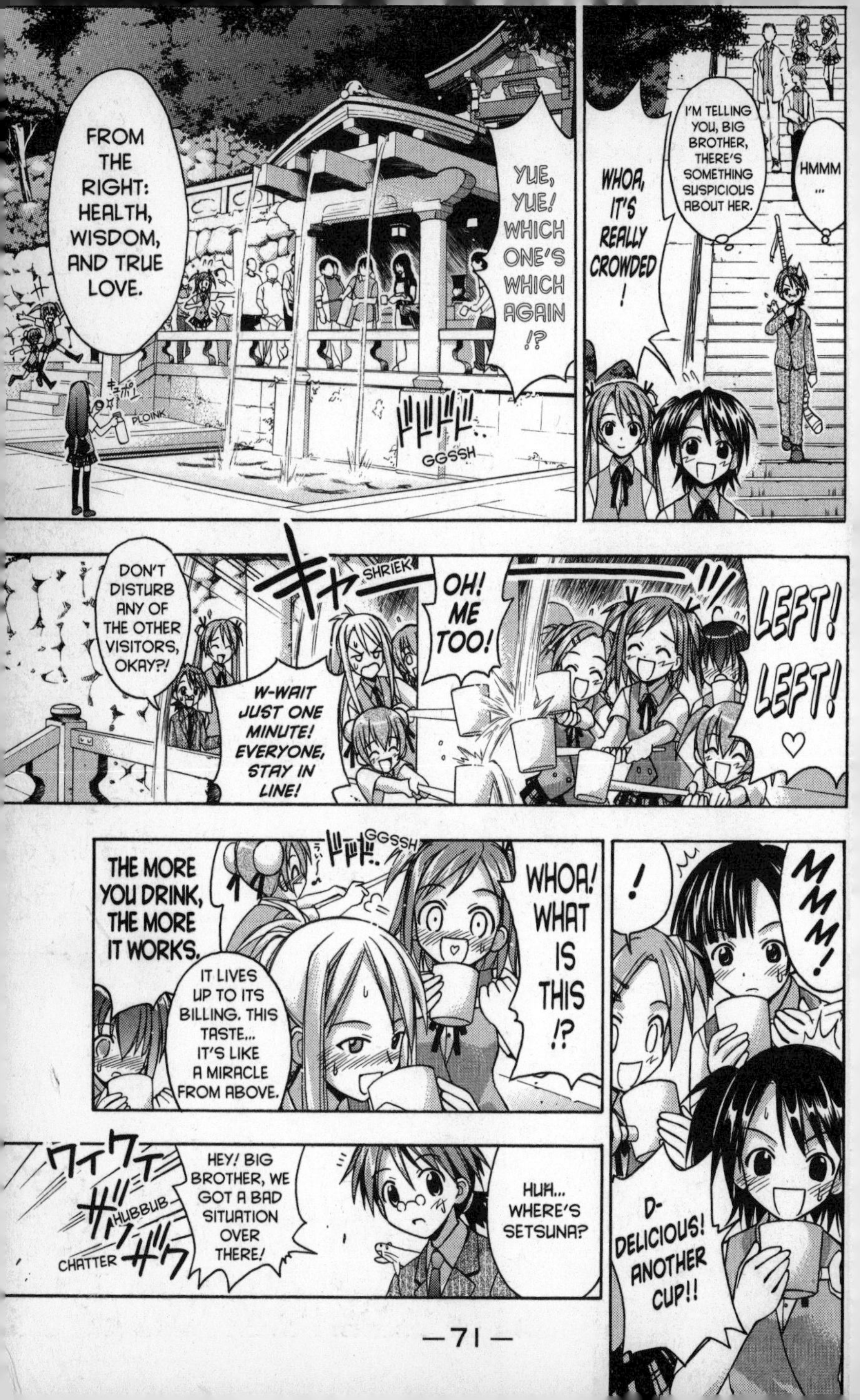
I'M TELLING YOU, BIG BROTHER, THERE'S SOMETHING SUSPICIOUS ABOUT HER.
HMMM...
WHOA, IT'S REALLY CROWDED!
YUE, YUE! WHICH ONE'S WHICH AGAIN!?
GGSSH
FROM THE RIGHT: HEALTH, WISDOM, AND TRUE LOVE.
PLOINK
LEFT! LEFT!
OH! ME TOO!
SHRIEK
W-WAIT JUST ONE MINUTE! EVERYONE, STAY IN LINE!
DON'T DISTURB ANY OF THE OTHER VISITORS, OKAY?!
MMMM!
!
D-DELICIOUS! ANOTHER CUP!!
WHOA! WHAT IS THIS!?
GGSSH
THE MORE YOU DRINK, THE MORE IT WORKS.
IT LIVES UP TO ITS BILLING. THIS TASTE... IT'S LIKE A MIRACLE FROM ABOVE.
HUH... WHERE'S SETSUNA?
HEY! BIG BROTHER, WE GOT A BAD SITUATION OVER THERE!
HUBBUB
CHATTER

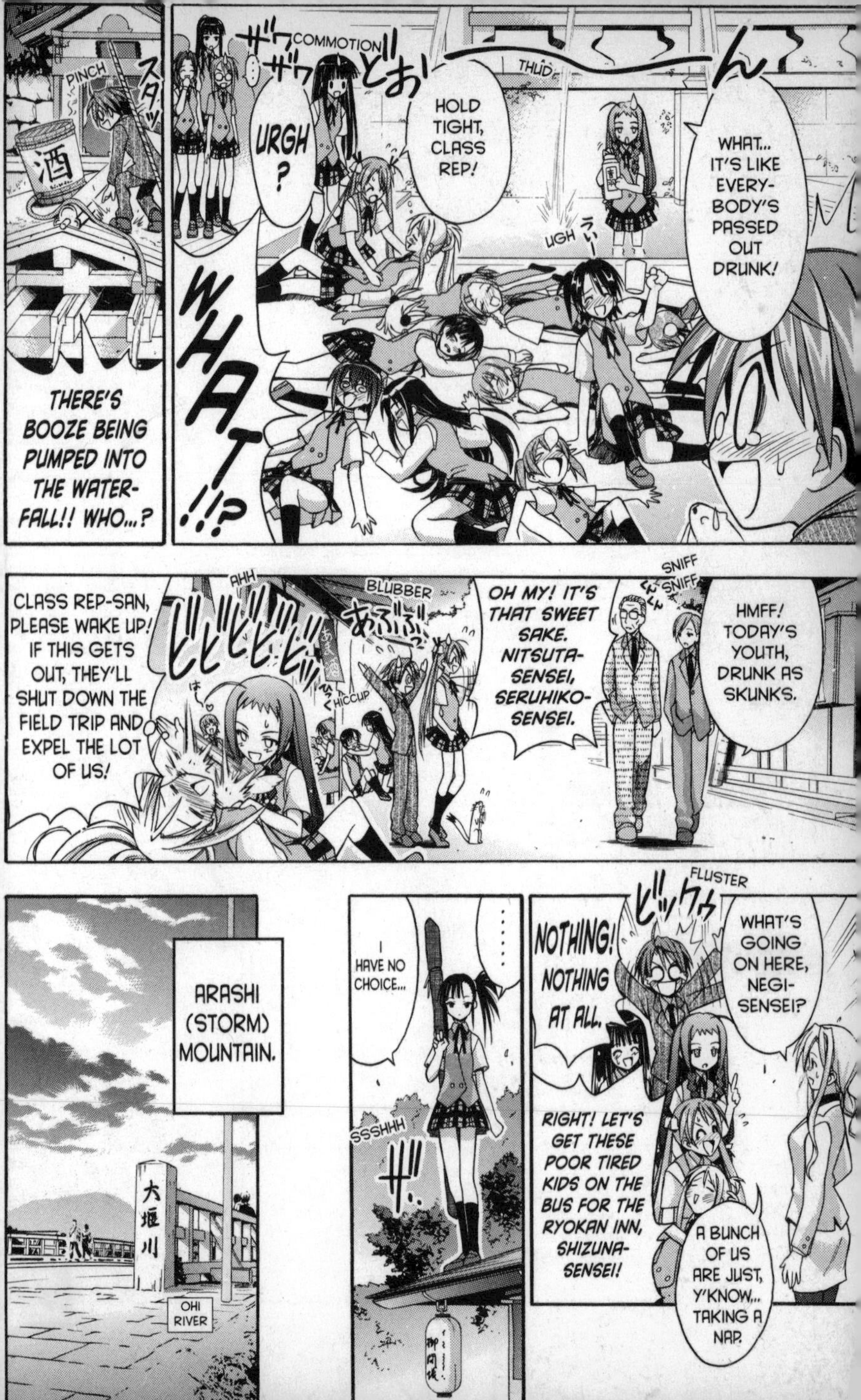

THUD
WHAT... IT'S LIKE EVERYBODY'S PASSED OUT DRUNK!
UGH
COMMOTION
HOLD TIGHT, CLASS REP!
URGH?
WHAT!!?
PINCH
酒
THERE'S BOOZE BEING PUMPED INTO THE WATERFALL!! WHO...?
HMFF! TODAY'S YOUTH, DRUNK AS SKUNKS.
SNIFF SNIFF
OH MY! IT'S THAT SWEET SAKE. NITSUTA-SENSEI, SERUHIKO-SENSEI.
BLUBBER
HICCUP
AHH
CLASS REP-SAN, PLEASE WAKE UP! IF THIS GETS OUT, THEY'LL SHUT DOWN THE FIELD TRIP AND EXPEL THE LOT OF US!
WHAT'S GOING ON HERE, NEGI-SENSEI?
FLUSTER
NOTHING! NOTHING AT ALL.
A BUNCH OF US ARE JUST, Y'KNOW... TAKING A NAP.
RIGHT! LET'S GET THESE POOR TIRED KIDS ON THE BUS FOR THE RYOKAN INN, SHIZUNA-SENSEI!
......
I HAVE NO CHOICE...
SSSHHH
ARASHI (STORM) MOUNTAIN.
大堰川
OHI RIVER

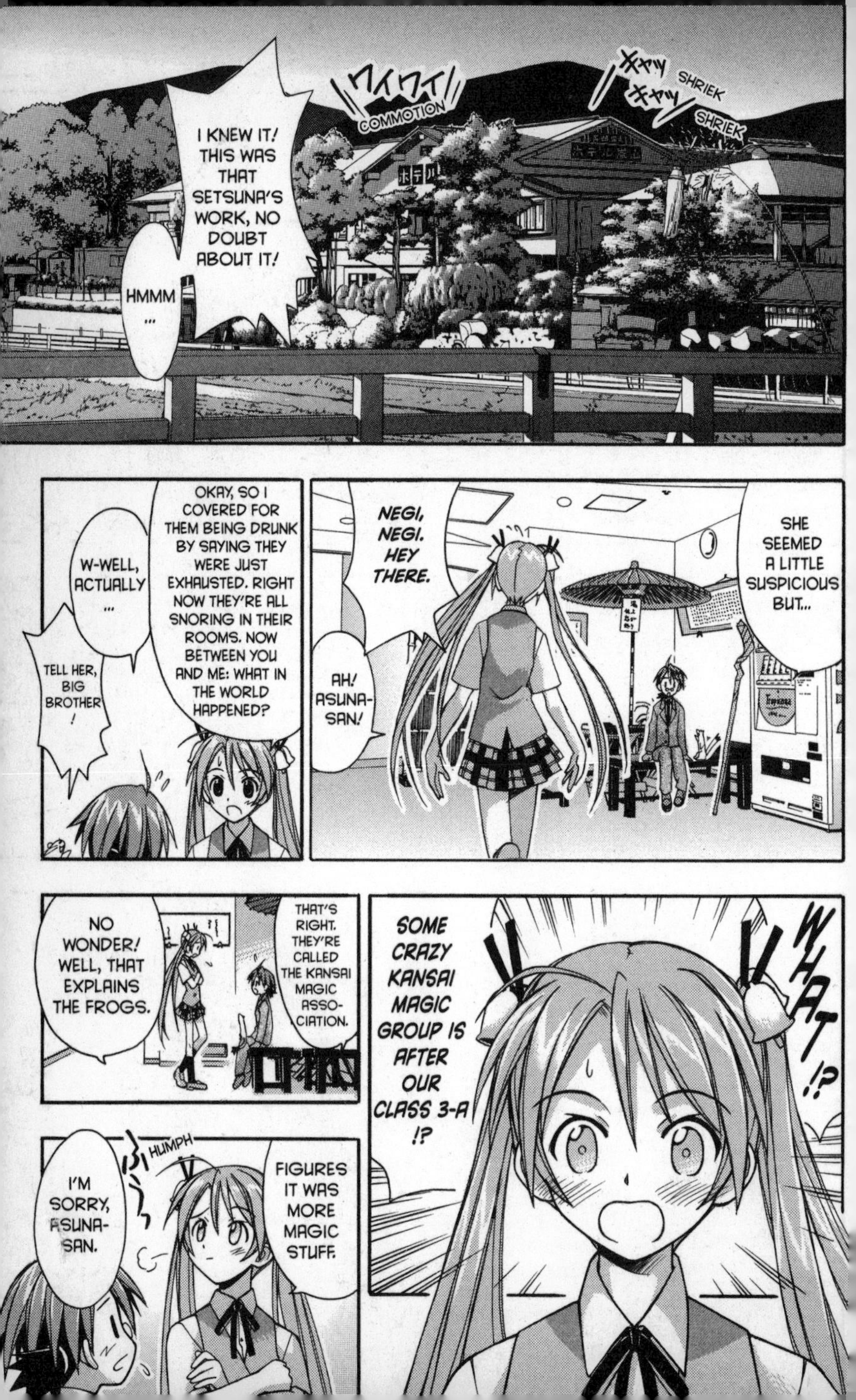
キャッ SHRIEK
キャッ SHRIEK
ワイワイ COMMOTION
I KNEW IT! THIS WAS THAT SETSUNA'S WORK, NO DOUBT ABOUT IT!
HMMM ...
SHE SEEMED A LITTLE SUSPICIOUS BUT...
NEGI, NEGI. HEY THERE.
AH! ASUNA-SAN!
OKAY, SO I COVERED FOR THEM BEING DRUNK BY SAYING THEY WERE JUST EXHAUSTED. RIGHT NOW THEY'RE ALL SNORING IN THEIR ROOMS. NOW BETWEEN YOU AND ME: WHAT IN THE WORLD HAPPENED?
W-WELL, ACTUALLY ...
TELL HER, BIG BROTHER!
WHAT!?
SOME CRAZY KANSAI MAGIC GROUP IS AFTER OUR CLASS 3-A!?
THAT'S RIGHT. THEY'RE CALLED THE KANSAI MAGIC ASSO-CIATION.
NO WONDER! WELL, THAT EXPLAINS THE FROGS.
FIGURES IT WAS MORE MAGIC STUFF.
ふぅ HUMPH
I'M SORRY, ASUNA-SAN.

NEGI-SENSEI, THE TEACHERS ARE GONNA FINISH THE DAY EARLY WITH A BATH, OK?

EEYAH!

I MEAN, AH, YEAH... OK, SHIZUNA-SENSEI.

GROUP 5 IS GONNA TAKE A BATH SOON.

THE EVENING'S FREE AFTER THAT, RIGHT?

Y-YEAH.

OK, ANE-SAN.

男湯
MEN'S BATH

THIS IS GREAT! JAPANESE OUTDOOR BATHS...

AHHH...

CLANK CLANK
カラカラカラ...
SSSHHH ザァッ...

HUH?

SOMEONE'S HERE. I WONDER IF IT'S ONE OF THE MALE TEACHERS?

YEAH. SWORDS-MEN ARE THE SWORN ENEMIES OF WIZARDS.

ON TOP OF THAT, SHE'S SOMEONE WHO USES ONMYOU GODS...

SHE'S ALWAYS CARRYING THAT SWORD CASE. A GOOD KATANA COULD BISECT YOU BEFORE YOU GET A SINGLE SPELL OUT.

IF WE CAN AVOID FIGHTING HER, LET'S.

IF ONLY WE DIDN'T HAVE THIS SETSUNA SAKU-RAZAKI HANGING OVER US.

THE BREEZE FEELS GOOD.

HYP...
WSSSH

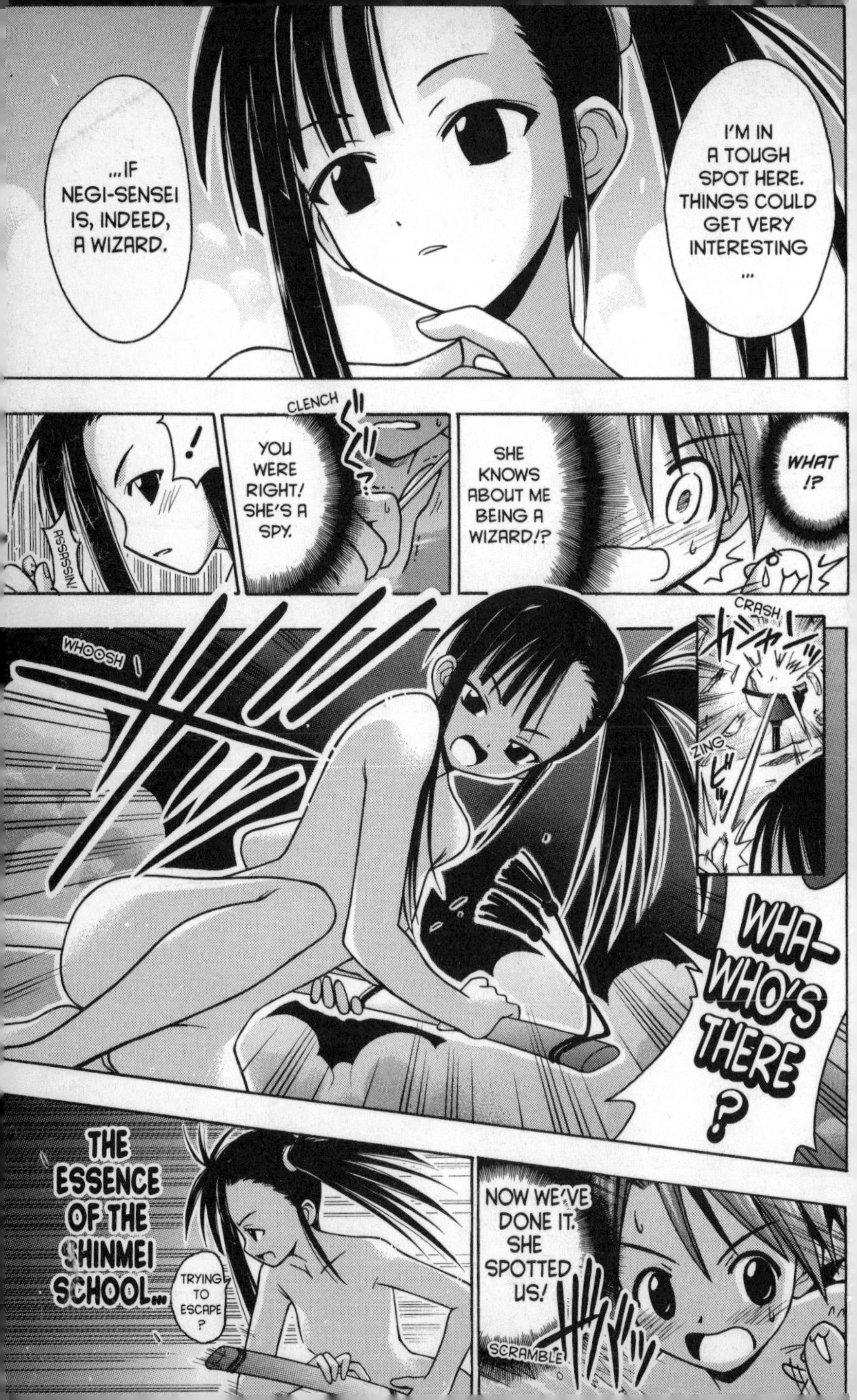
I'M IN A TOUGH SPOT HERE. THINGS COULD GET VERY INTERESTING ...
...IF NEGI-SENSEI IS, INDEED, A WIZARD.
WHAT!?
SHE KNOWS ABOUT ME BEING A WIZARD!?
CLENCH
YOU WERE RIGHT! SHE'S A SPY.
ASSASSIN!
!
CRASH
ZING
WHA-WHO'S THERE?
WHOOSH
NOW WE'VE DONE IT. SHE SPOTTED US!
SCRAMBLE
TRYING TO ESCAPE?
THE ESSENCE OF THE SHINMEI SCHOOL...

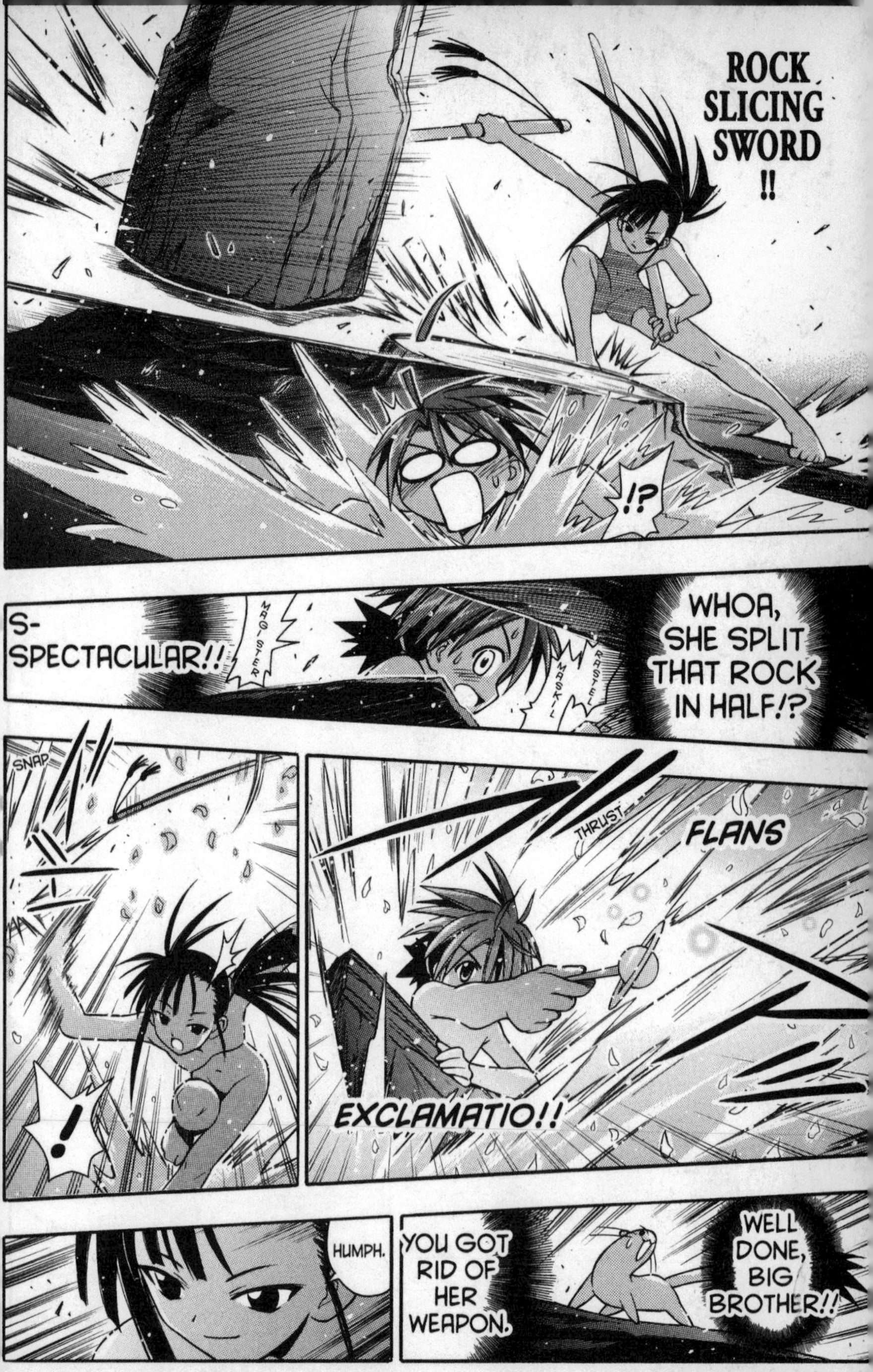
ROCK SLICING SWORD !!
!?
WHOA, SHE SPLIT THAT ROCK IN HALF!?
RASTEL MASKIL
MAGISTER
S- SPECTACULAR!!
THRUST
FLANS
EXCLAMATIO!!
SNAP
!
WELL DONE, BIG BROTHER!!
YOU GOT RID OF HER WEAPON.
HUMPH.

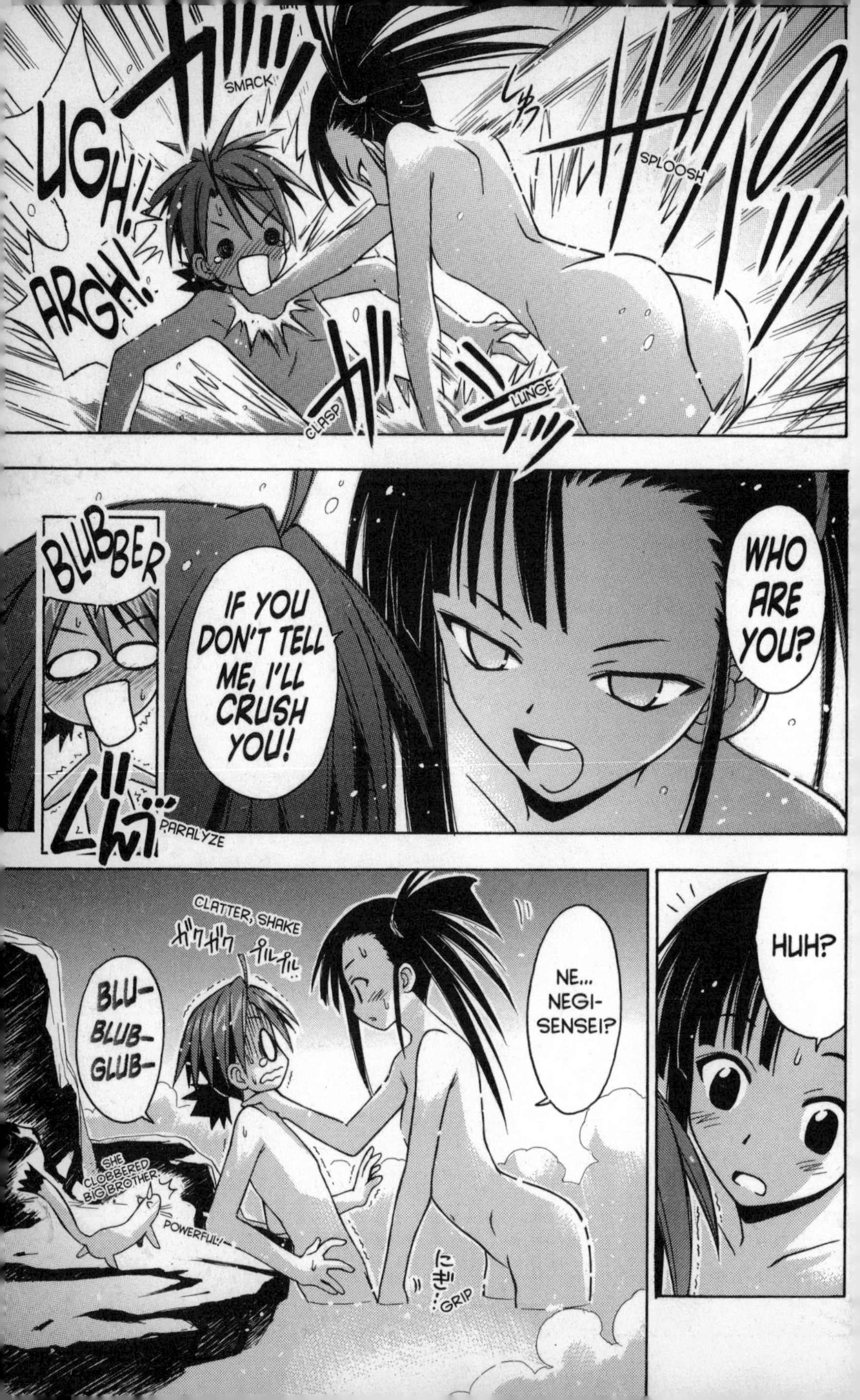
SPLOOSH
SMACK
UGH!
ARGH!
LUNGE
CLASP
WHO ARE YOU?
IF YOU DON'T TELL ME, I'LL CRUSH YOU!
BLUBBER
PARALYZE
HUH?
NE... NEGI-SENSEI?
CLATTER, SHAKE
ガクガク プルプル
BLU- BLUB- GLUB-
SHE CLOBBERED BIG BROTHER
POWERFUL!
にぎっ
GRIP

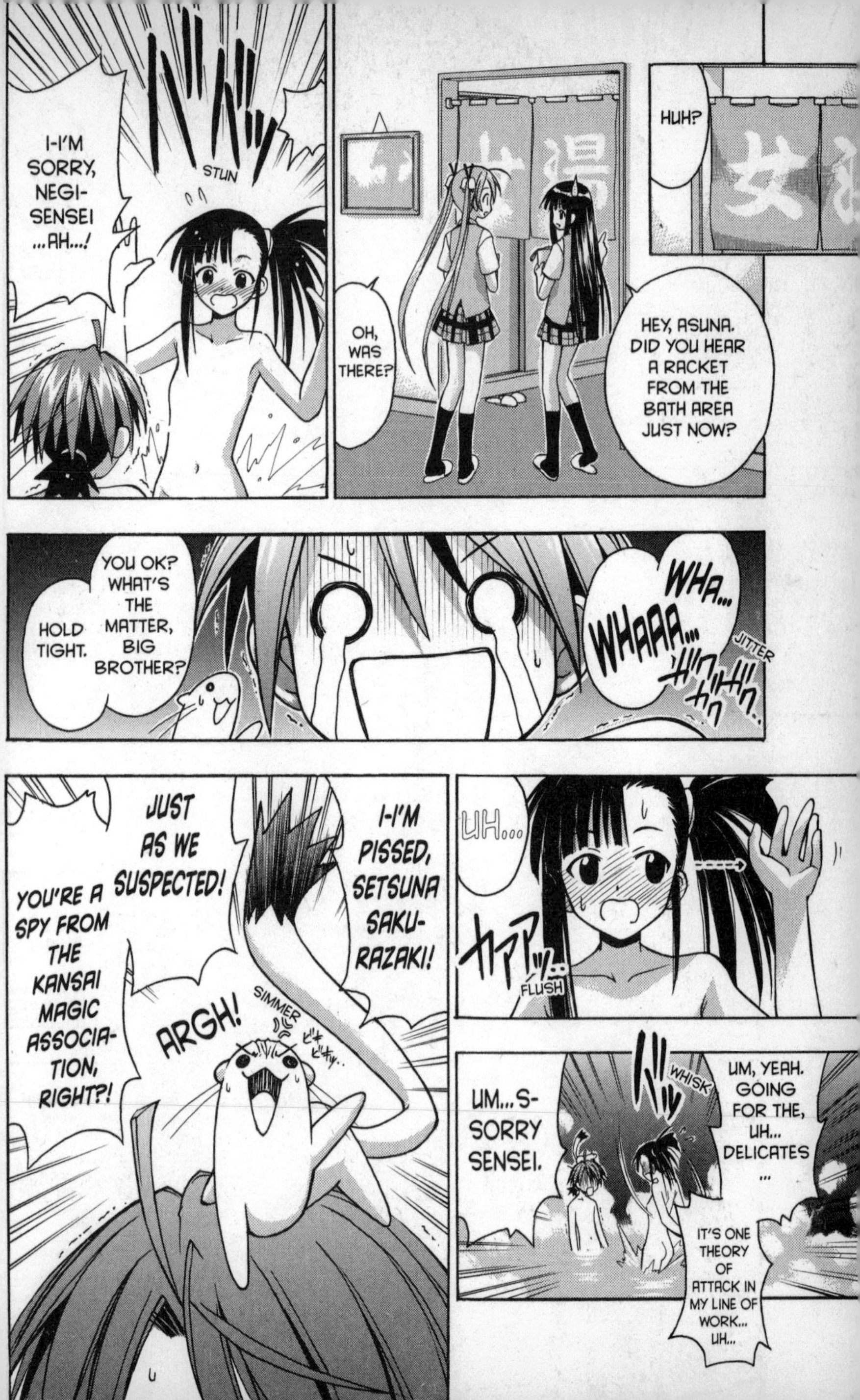
HUH?
HEY, ASUNA. DID YOU HEAR A RACKET FROM THE BATH AREA JUST NOW?
OH, WAS THERE?
STUN
I-I'M SORRY, NEGI-SENSEI ...AH...!
WHA... WHAAA...
JITTER
YOU OK? WHAT'S THE MATTER, BIG BROTHER?
HOLD TIGHT.
UH...
FLUSH
UM, YEAH. GOING FOR THE, UH... DELICATES ...
WHISK
UM... S-SORRY SENSEI.
IT'S ONE THEORY OF ATTACK IN MY LINE OF WORK... UH...
I-I'M PISSED, SETSUNA SAKURAZAKI!
JUST AS WE SUSPECTED!
YOU'RE A SPY FROM THE KANSAI MAGIC ASSOCIATION, RIGHT?!
ARGH!
SIMMER

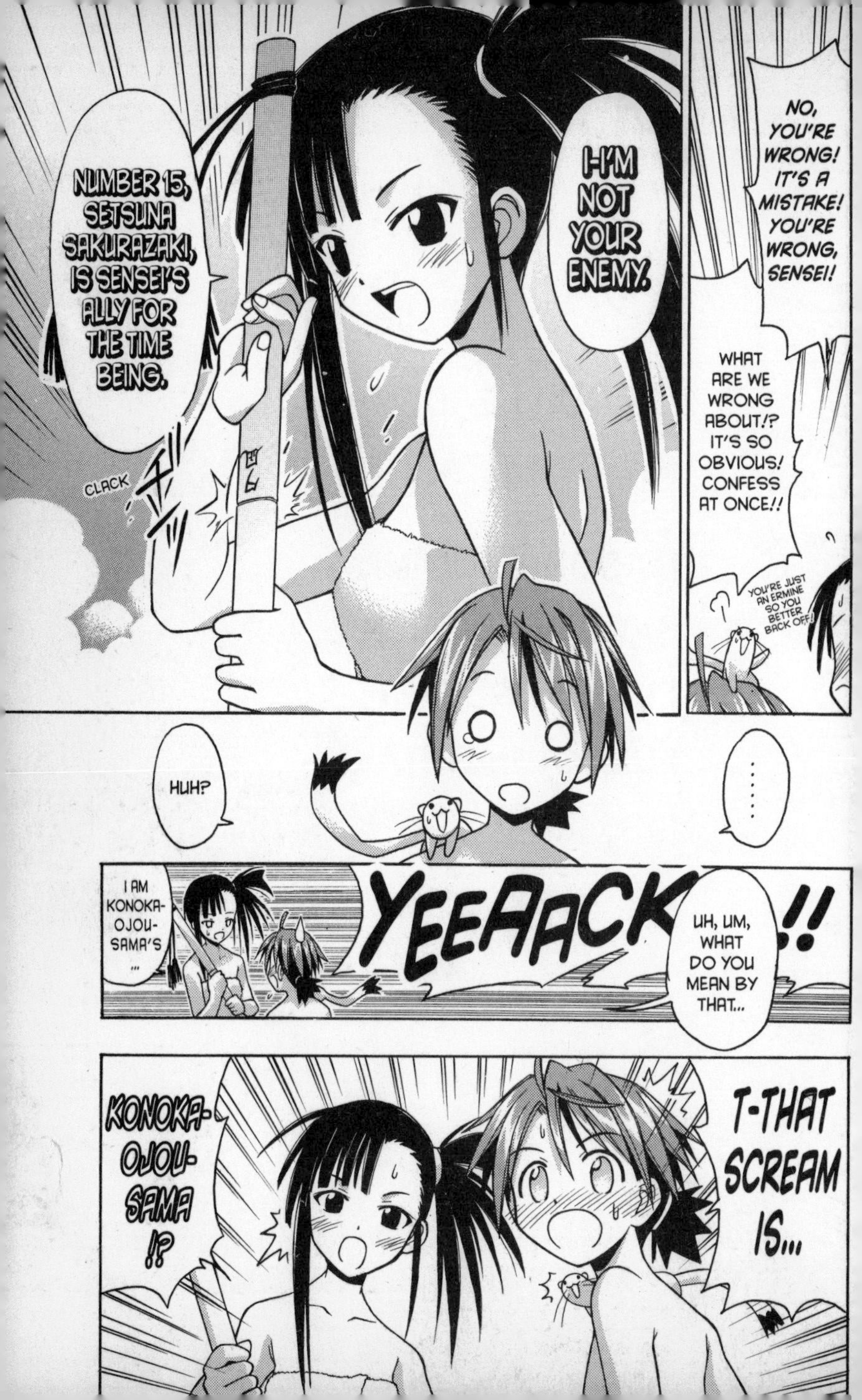
NO, YOU'RE WRONG! IT'S A MISTAKE! YOU'RE WRONG, SENSEI!
WHAT ARE WE WRONG ABOUT!? IT'S SO OBVIOUS! CONFESS AT ONCE!!
YOU'RE JUST AN ERMINE SO YOU BETTER BACK OFF!
I-I'M NOT YOUR ENEMY.
NUMBER 15, SETSUNA SAKURAZAKI, IS SENSEI'S ALLY FOR THE TIME BEING.
CLACK
......
HUH?
UH, UM, WHAT DO YOU MEAN BY THAT...
YEEAACK!!
I AM KONOKA-OJOU-SAMA'S ...
T-THAT SCREAM IS...
KONOKA-OJOU-SAMA!?

3-A FIELD TRIP GROUP NUMBER 1

(GROUP LEADER)
MISA KAKIZAKI

MADOKA KUGIMIYA
SAKURAKO SHIINA
FUKA NARUTAKI
FUMIKA NARUTAKI

NEGIMA!

MAGISTER NEGI MAGI

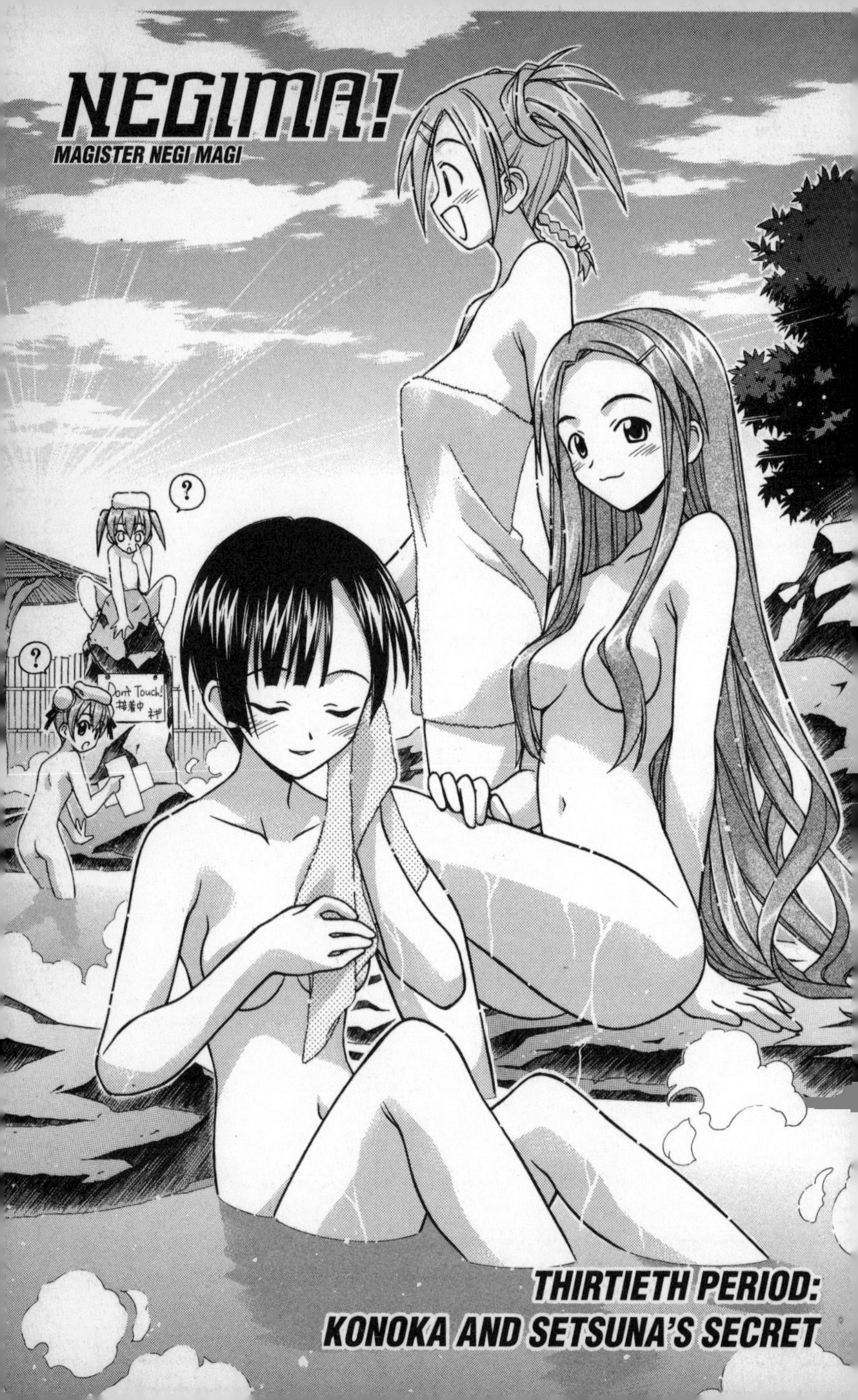
?
?
Don't Touch!
接着中

THIRTIETH PERIOD:
KONOKA AND SETSUNA'S SECRET

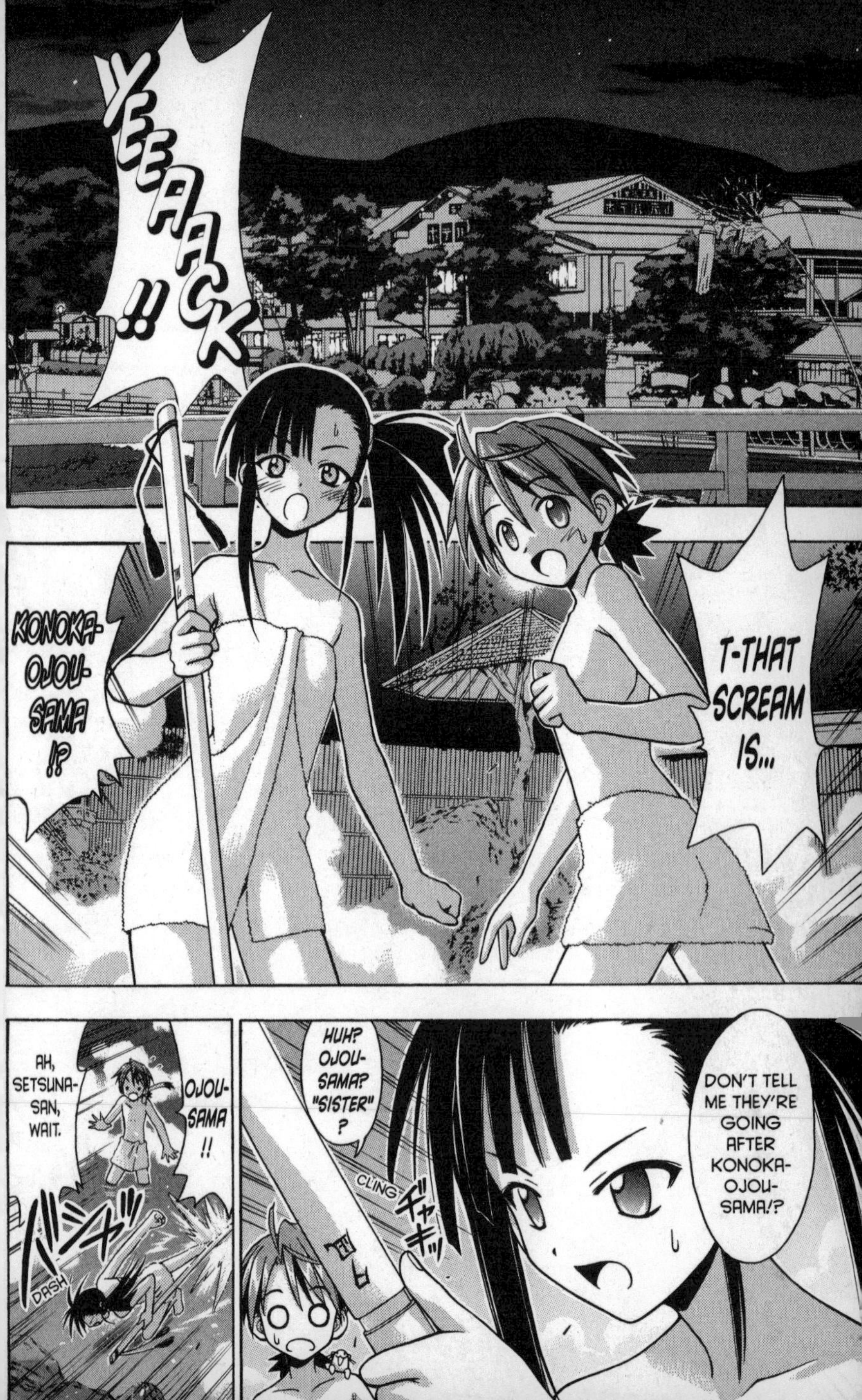

YEEAAACK!!
T-THAT SCREAM IS...
KONOKA-OJOU-SAMA!?
DON'T TELL ME THEY'RE GOING AFTER KONOKA-OJOU-SAMA!?
HUH? OJOU-SAMA? "SISTER"?
CLING
ギャキッ
OJOU-SAMA!!
AH, SETSUNA-SAN, WAIT.
DASH

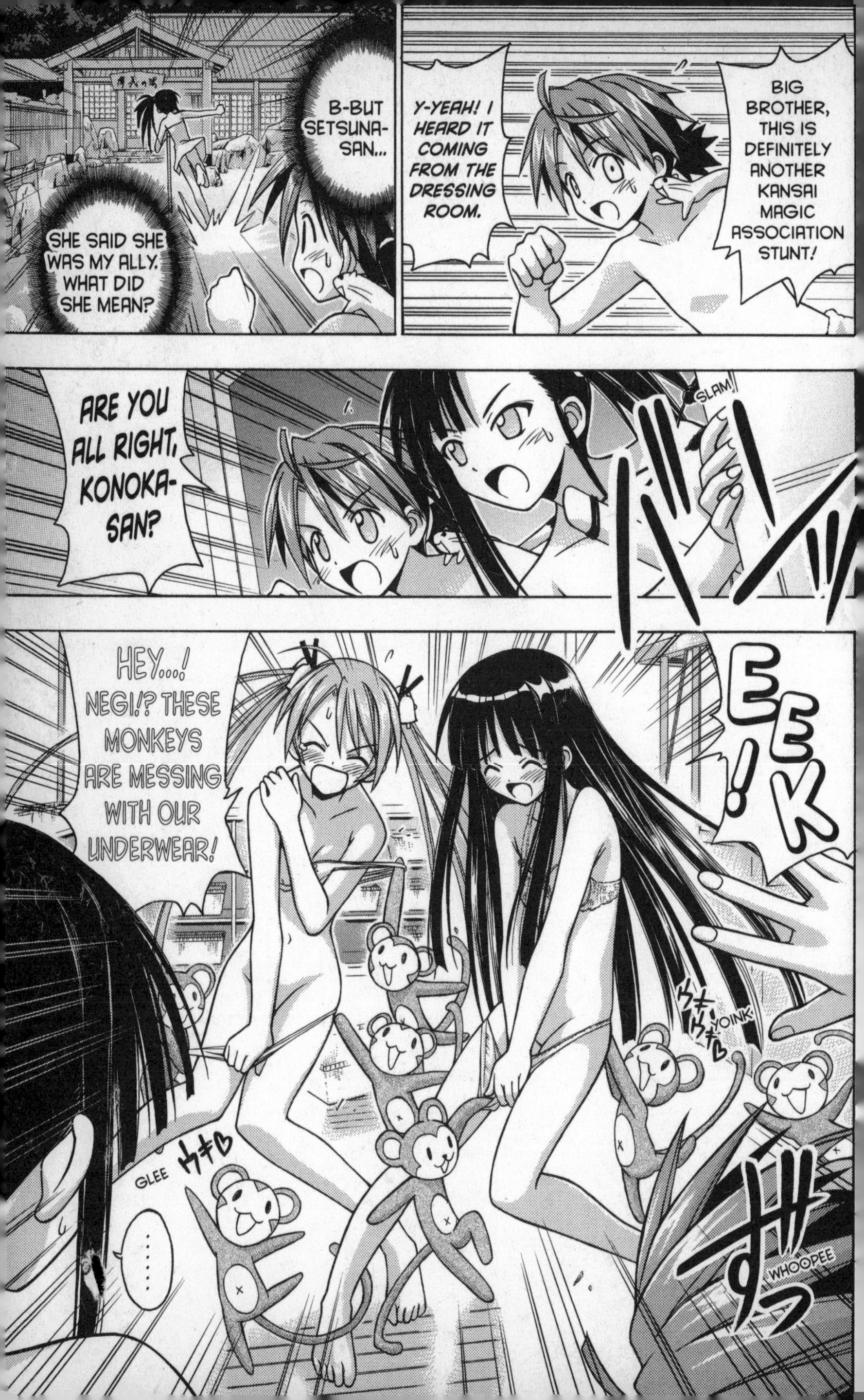
BIG BROTHER, THIS IS DEFINITELY ANOTHER KANSAI MAGIC ASSOCIATION STUNT!
Y-YEAH! I HEARD IT COMING FROM THE DRESSING ROOM.
B-BUT SETSUNA-SAN...
SHE SAID SHE WAS MY ALLY. WHAT DID SHE MEAN?
SLAM!
ARE YOU ALL RIGHT, KONOKA-SAN?
EEEK!
HEY...! NEGI!? THESE MONKEYS ARE MESSING WITH OUR UNDERWEAR!
YOINK
WHOOPEE
GLEE
......

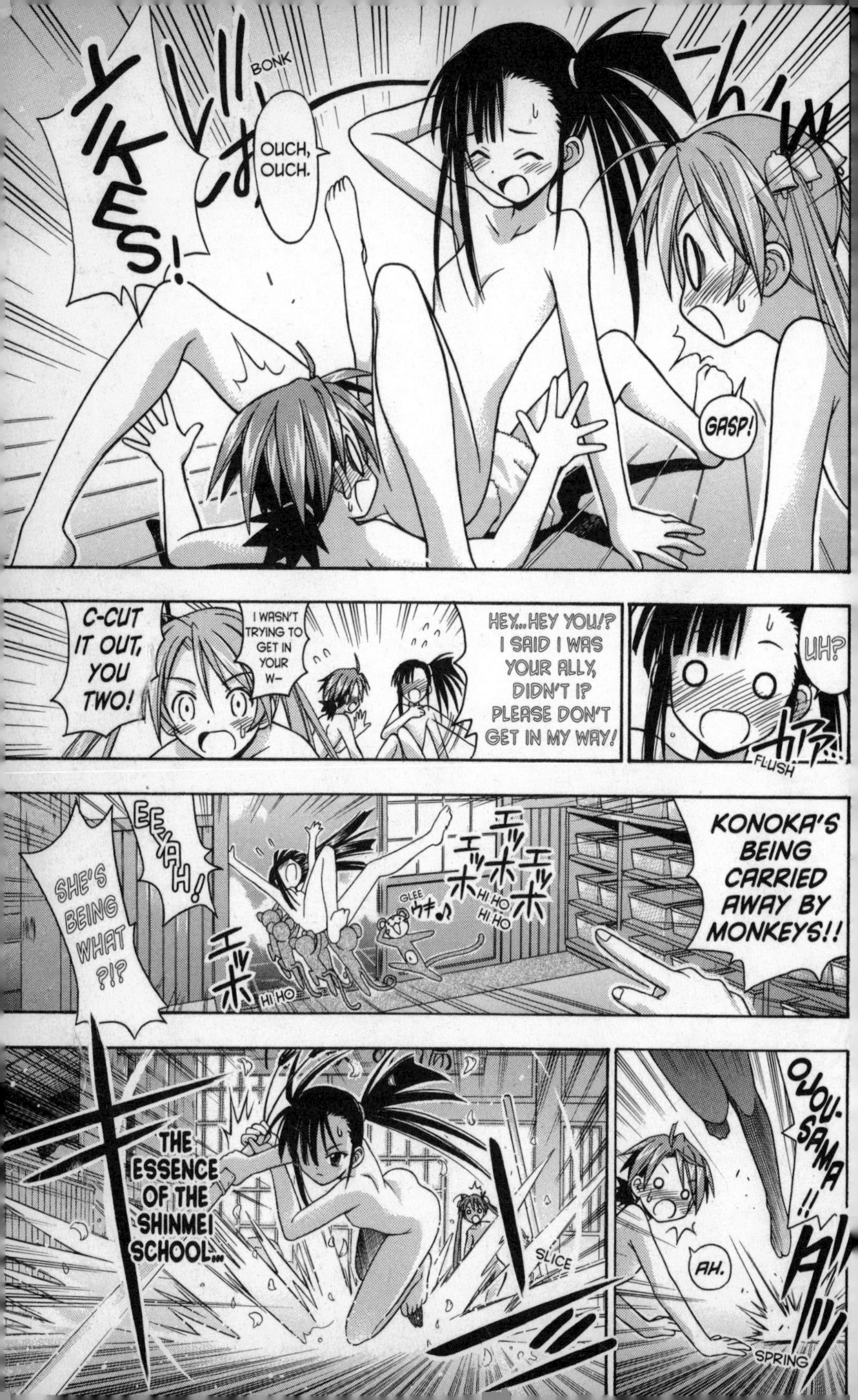
OUCH, OUCH.
BONK
YIKES!
GASP!
UH?
FLUSH
HEY...HEY YOU!? I SAID I WAS YOUR ALLY, DIDN'T I? PLEASE DON'T GET IN MY WAY!
I WASN'T TRYING TO GET IN YOUR W–
C-CUT IT OUT, YOU TWO!
KONOKA'S BEING CARRIED AWAY BY MONKEYS!!
エッホエッホ
HI HO HI HO
GLEE
ウキ♪
EEYAH!
エッホ
HI HO
SHE'S BEING WHAT?!?
OJOU-SAMA!!
AH.
SPRING
THE ESSENCE OF THE SHINMEI SCHOOL...
SLICE

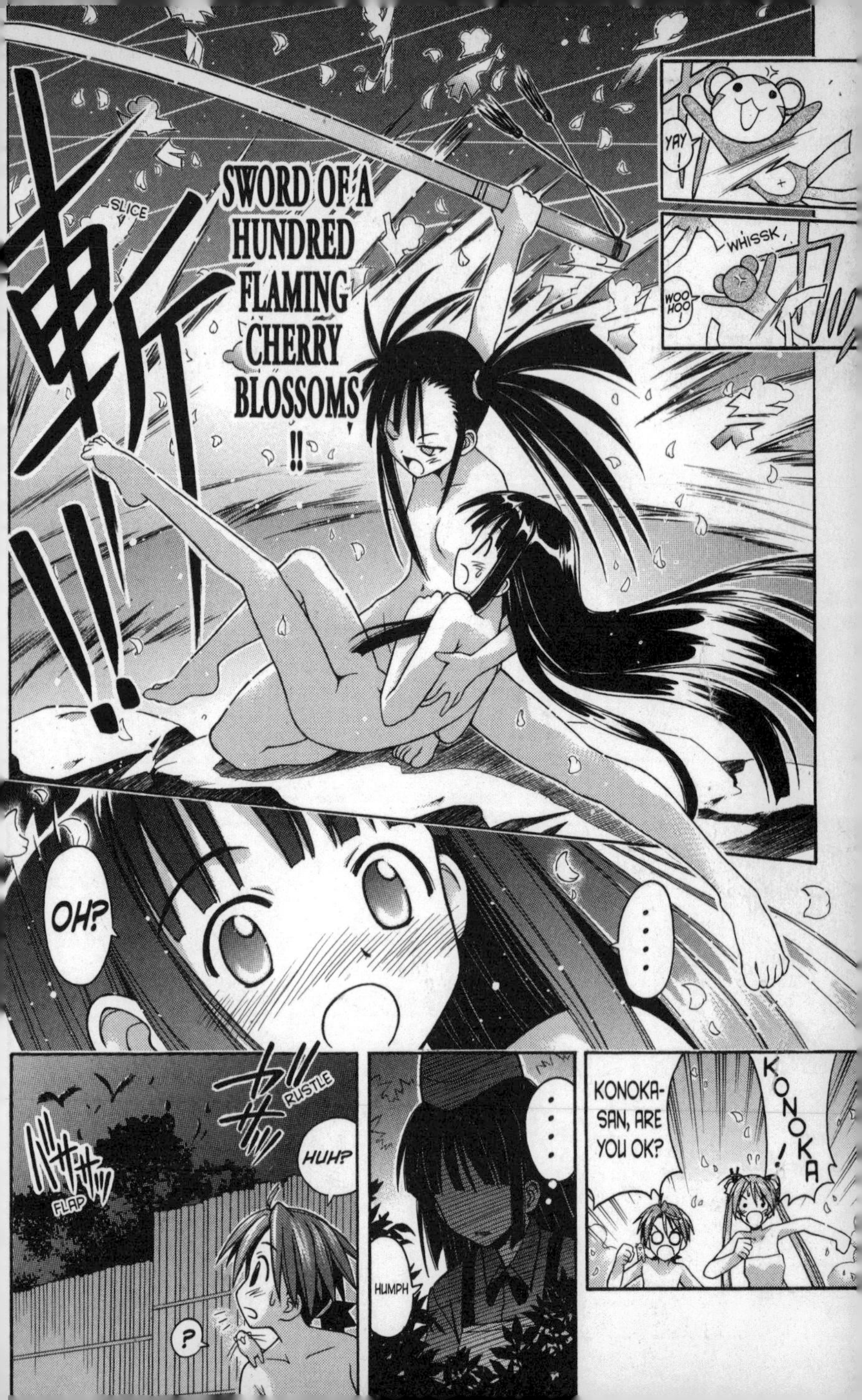
YAY!
WHISSK
WOO HOO!
SWORD OF A HUNDRED FLAMING CHERRY BLOSSOMS!!
SLICE
....
OH?
KONOKA!
KONOKA-SAN, ARE YOU OK?
....
HUMPH
RUSTLE
HUH?
FLAP
?

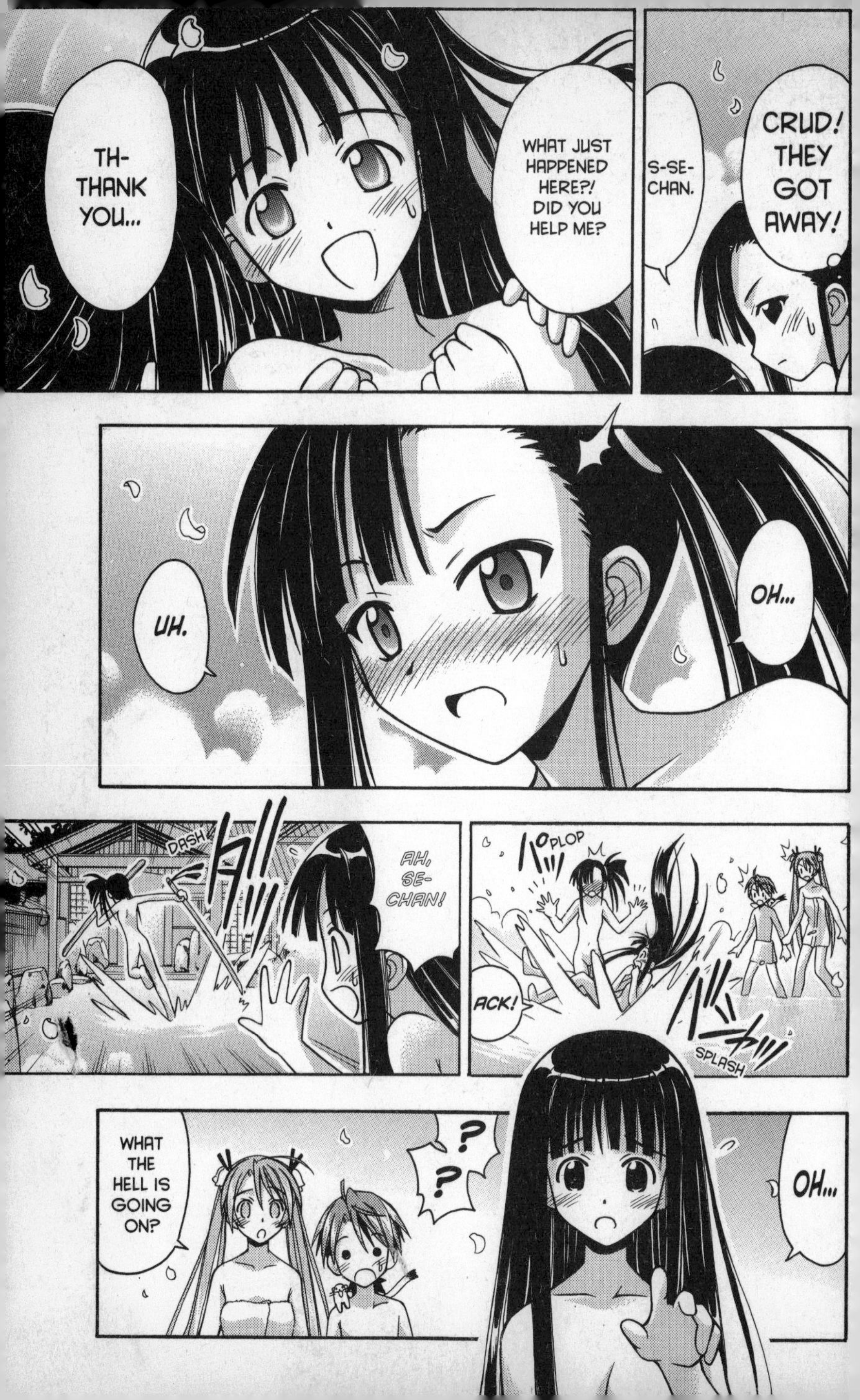
CRUD! THEY GOT AWAY!
S-SE-CHAN.
WHAT JUST HAPPENED HERE?! DID YOU HELP ME?
TH-THANK YOU...
OH...
UH.
PLOP
ACK!
SPLASH
AH, SE-CHAN!
DASH
OH...
? ?
WHAT THE HELL IS GOING ON?

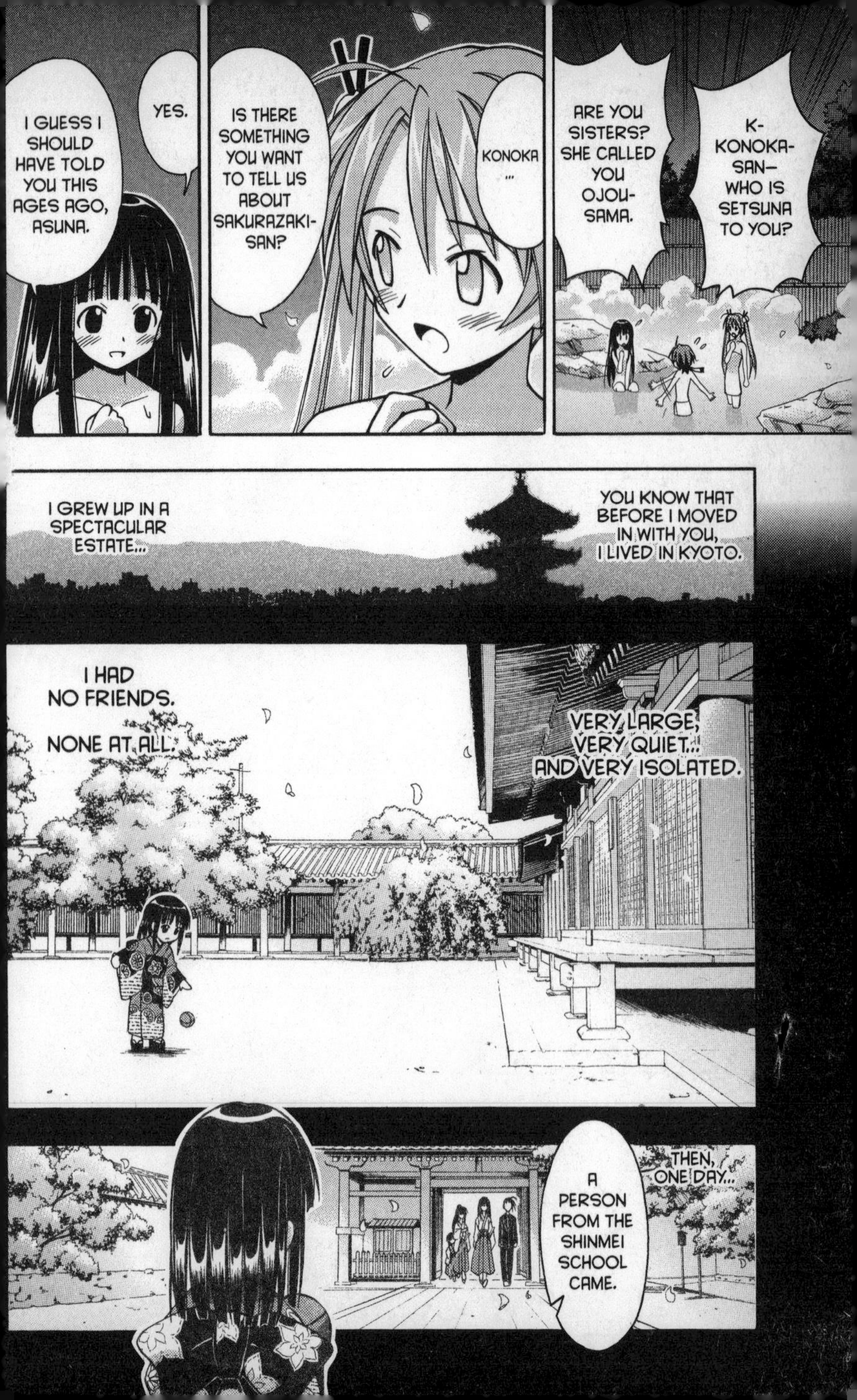
K-KONOKA-SAN— WHO IS SETSUNA TO YOU?
ARE YOU SISTERS? SHE CALLED YOU OJOU-SAMA.
KONOKA ...
IS THERE SOMETHING YOU WANT TO TELL US ABOUT SAKURAZAKI-SAN?
YES.
I GUESS I SHOULD HAVE TOLD YOU THIS AGES AGO, ASUNA.
YOU KNOW THAT BEFORE I MOVED IN WITH YOU, I LIVED IN KYOTO.
I GREW UP IN A SPECTACULAR ESTATE...
VERY LARGE, VERY QUIET... AND VERY ISOLATED.
I HAD NO FRIENDS.
NONE AT ALL.
THEN, ONE DAY...
A PERSON FROM THE SHINMEI SCHOOL CAME.

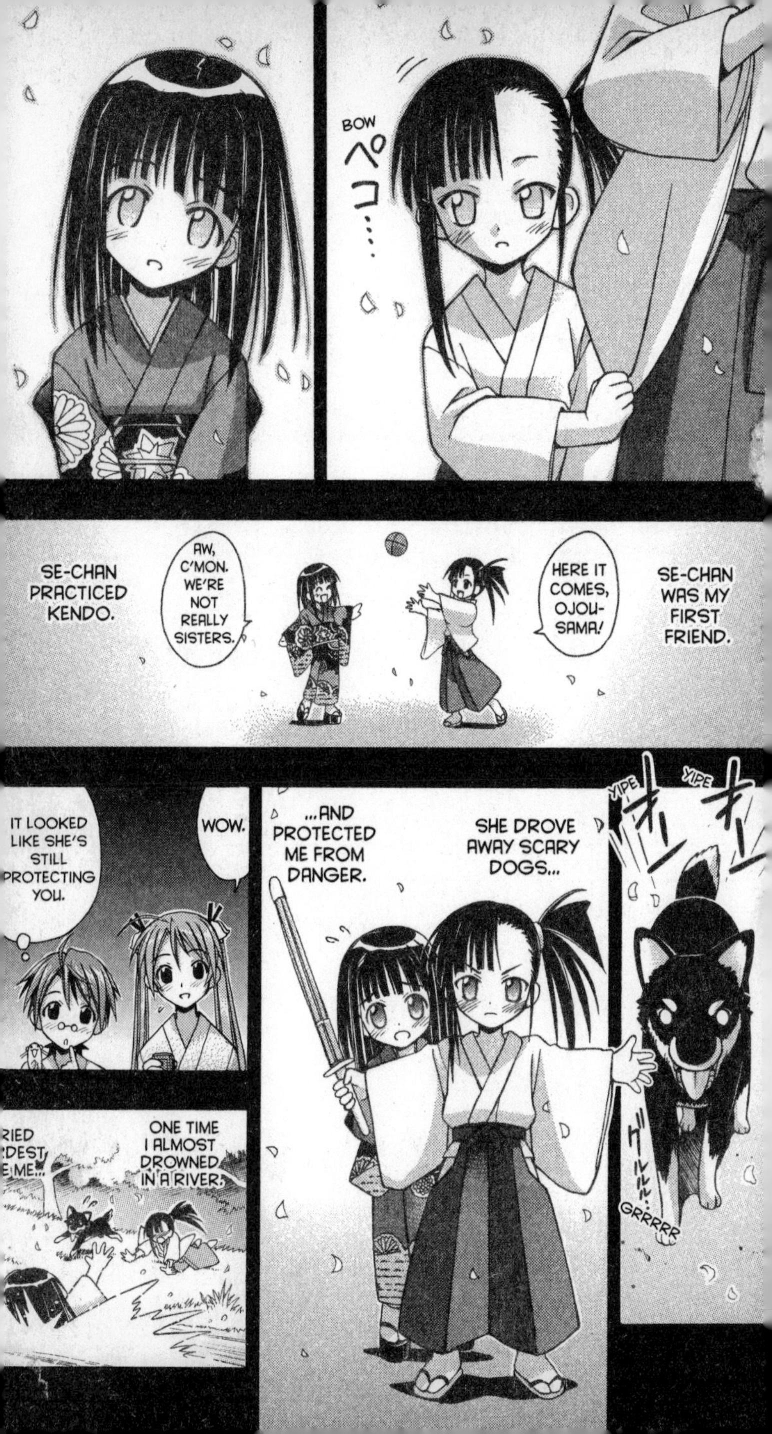

BOW
ペコ…
SE-CHAN WAS MY FIRST FRIEND.
HERE IT COMES, OJOU-SAMA!
AW, C'MON. WE'RE NOT REALLY SISTERS.
SE-CHAN PRACTICED KENDO.
YIPE
YIPE
GRRRRR
SHE DROVE AWAY SCARY DOGS...
...AND PROTECTED ME FROM DANGER.
WOW.
IT LOOKED LIKE SHE'S STILL PROTECTING YOU.
ONE TIME I ALMOST DROWNED IN A RIVER.

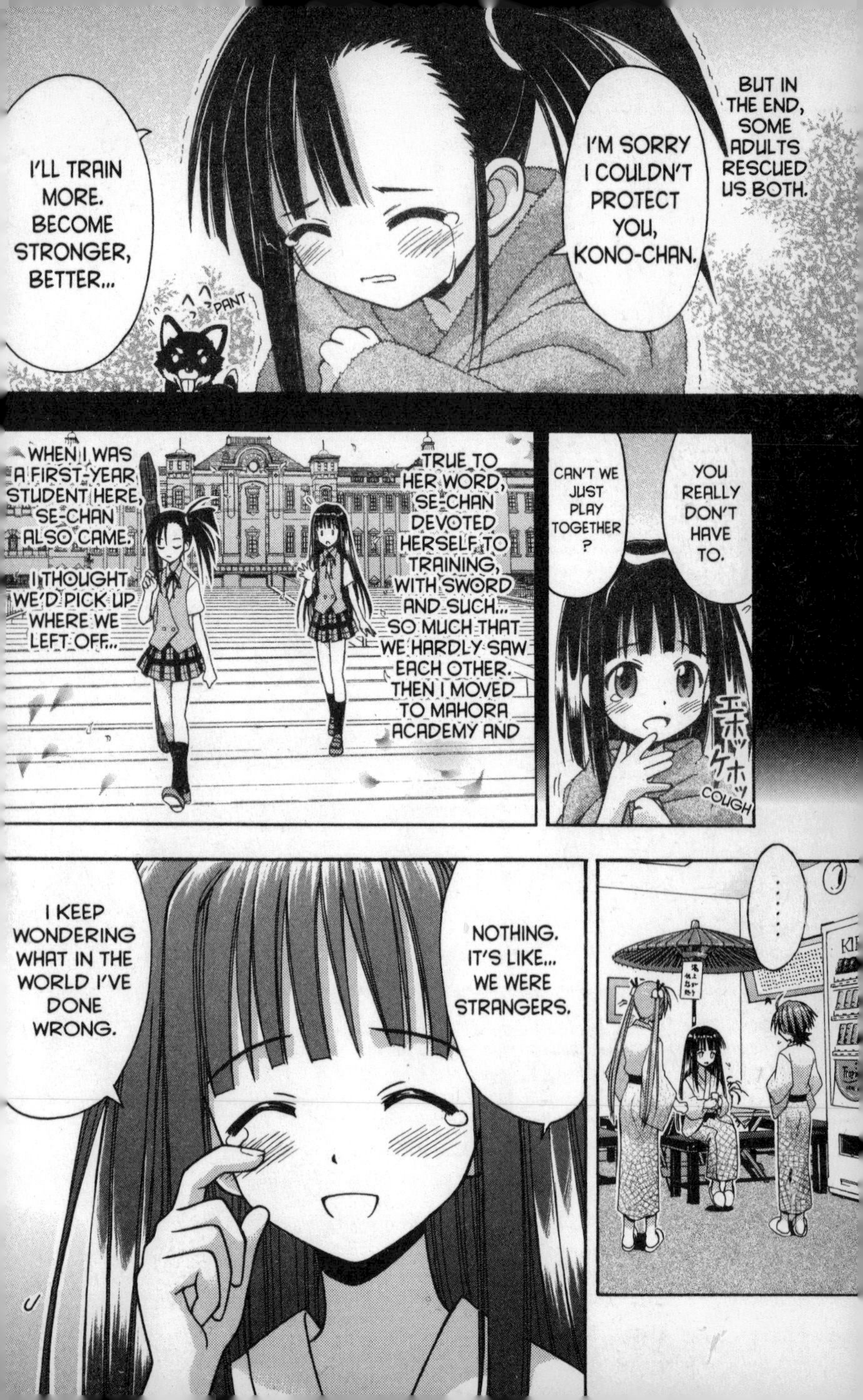
BUT IN THE END, SOME ADULTS RESCUED US BOTH.
I'M SORRY I COULDN'T PROTECT YOU, KONO-CHAN.
PANT
I'LL TRAIN MORE. BECOME STRONGER, BETTER...
YOU REALLY DON'T HAVE TO.
CAN'T WE JUST PLAY TOGETHER?
エホッケホッ
COUGH
TRUE TO HER WORD, SE-CHAN DEVOTED HERSELF TO TRAINING, WITH SWORD AND SUCH... SO MUCH THAT WE HARDLY SAW EACH OTHER. THEN I MOVED TO MAHORA ACADEMY AND
WHEN I WAS A FIRST-YEAR STUDENT HERE, SE-CHAN ALSO CAME.
I THOUGHT WE'D PICK UP WHERE WE LEFT OFF...
......
NOTHING. IT'S LIKE... WE WERE STRANGERS.
I KEEP WONDERING WHAT IN THE WORLD I'VE DONE WRONG.

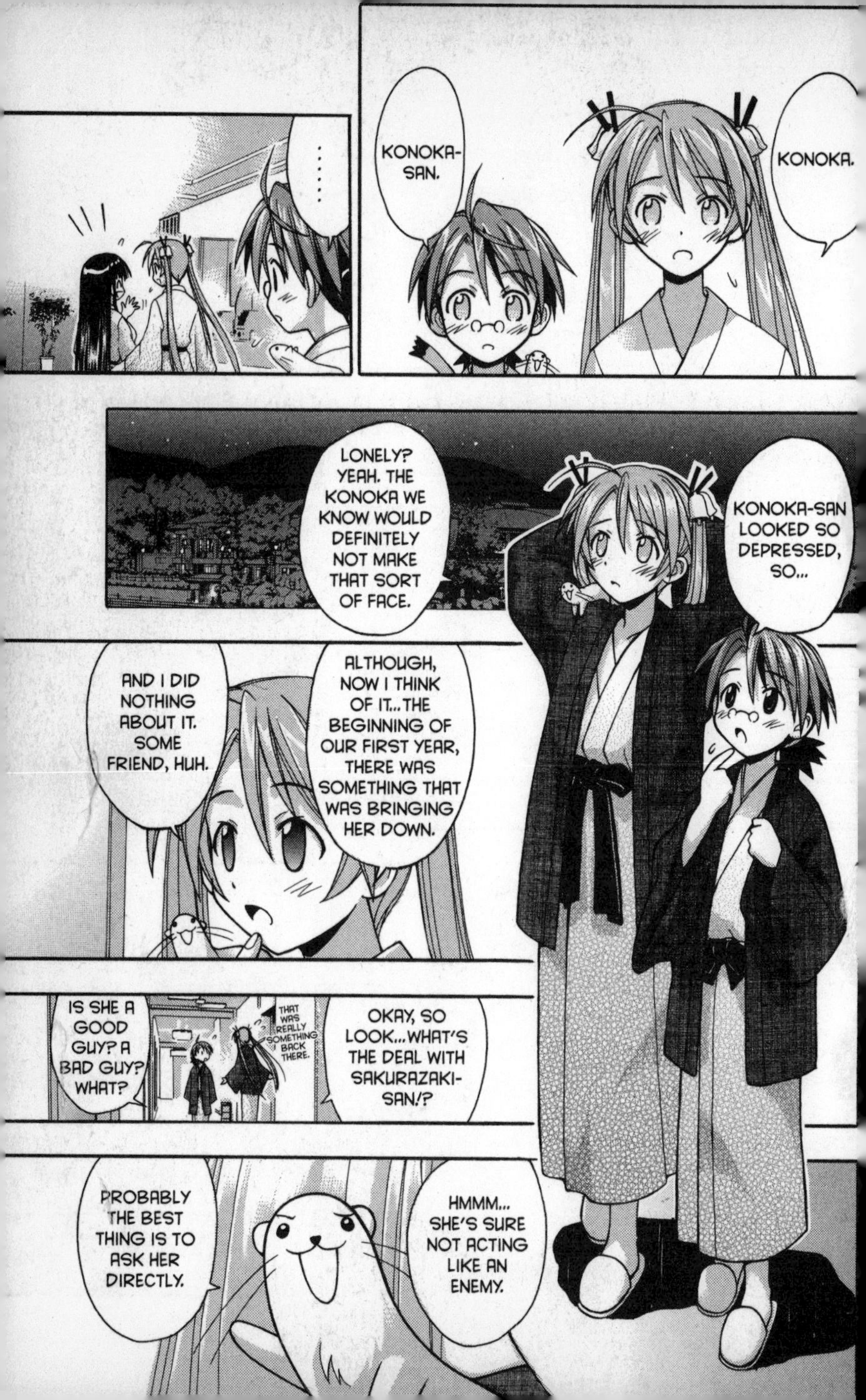
KONOKA.
KONOKA-SAN.
......
KONOKA-SAN LOOKED SO DEPRESSED, SO...
LONELY? YEAH. THE KONOKA WE KNOW WOULD DEFINITELY NOT MAKE THAT SORT OF FACE.
ALTHOUGH, NOW I THINK OF IT... THE BEGINNING OF OUR FIRST YEAR, THERE WAS SOMETHING THAT WAS BRINGING HER DOWN.
AND I DID NOTHING ABOUT IT. SOME FRIEND, HUH.
OKAY, SO LOOK... WHAT'S THE DEAL WITH SAKURAZAKI-SAN!?
THAT WAS REALLY SOMETHING BACK THERE.
IS SHE A GOOD GUY? A BAD GUY? WHAT?
HMMM... SHE'S SURE NOT ACTING LIKE AN ENEMY.
PROBABLY THE BEST THING IS TO ASK HER DIRECTLY.

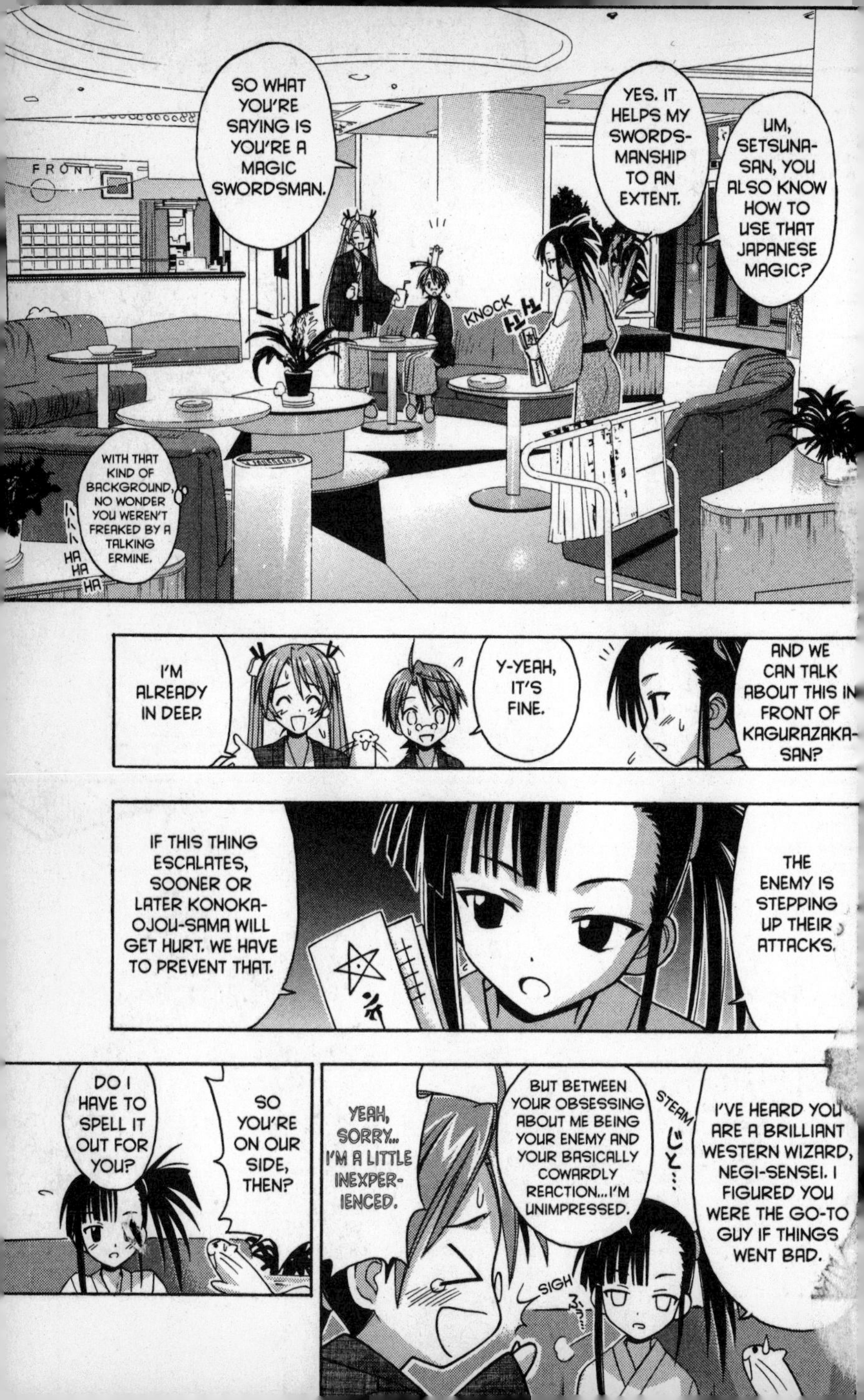
UM, SETSUNA-SAN, YOU ALSO KNOW HOW TO USE THAT JAPANESE MAGIC?
YES. IT HELPS MY SWORDSMANSHIP TO AN EXTENT.
KNOCK
SO WHAT YOU'RE SAYING IS YOU'RE A MAGIC SWORDSMAN.
FRONT
WITH THAT KIND OF BACKGROUND, NO WONDER YOU WEREN'T FREAKED BY A TALKING ERMINE.
HA HA HA
AND WE CAN TALK ABOUT THIS IN FRONT OF KAGURAZAKA-SAN?
Y-YEAH, IT'S FINE.
I'M ALREADY IN DEEP.
THE ENEMY IS STEPPING UP THEIR ATTACKS.
IF THIS THING ESCALATES, SOONER OR LATER KONOKA-OJOU-SAMA WILL GET HURT. WE HAVE TO PREVENT THAT.
I'VE HEARD YOU ARE A BRILLIANT WESTERN WIZARD, NEGI-SENSEI. I FIGURED YOU WERE THE GO-TO GUY IF THINGS WENT BAD.
STEAM
BUT BETWEEN YOUR OBSESSING ABOUT ME BEING YOUR ENEMY AND YOUR BASICALLY COWARDLY REACTION...I'M UNIMPRESSED.
SIGH
YEAH, SORRY... I'M A LITTLE INEXPERIENCED.
SO YOU'RE ON OUR SIDE, THEN?
DO I HAVE TO SPELL IT OUT FOR YOU?

OUR ENEMY IS LIKELY A FACTION OF THE KANSAI MAGIC ASSOCIATION. SINCE IT INVOLVES ONMYOU GODS, IT'S PROBABLY A TALISMAN USER.

......

SORRY, SETSUNA-SAN. BUT WE'RE ALLIES NOW. SO TELL ME: WHO'S BEHIND THESE ATTACKS?

SORRY, ANE-SAN. BIG BROTHER WAS SUSPICIOUS BECAUSE I KEPT SUSPECTING YOU.

MY BAD!!

... JUST LIKE YOU WESTERN WIZARDS, NEGI-SENSEI, THEIR WEAKNESS IS THAT THEY ARE DEFENSELESS WHILE RECITING SPELLS.

TALISMAN USERS CAME FROM KYOTO LONG AGO AND USED THE ORIGINAL JAPANESE MAGIC ONMYOUDOU AS THEIR BASIS BUT...

IT'S COMMON FOR AN ADVANCED PRACTITIONER TO PLACE A POWERFUL ONMYOU GOD— A "SUPERIOR" DEMON OR "GOKI," AND A "PROTECTIVE" DEMON—ON A CARD.

THAT APPLIES TO THEM ONLY, SO IT'S PROBABLY BEST TO THINK THAT IT DOESN'T APPLY TO OUR SPELLS, SWORDS, ETC.

ONMYOU WIZARDS

WESTERN WIZARDS

THEREFORE, FOLLOWING THE WIZARD/ PARTNER RELATIONSHIP,

LAST LINE OF DEFENSE, TALISMAN USER

LAST LINE OF DEFENSE, SHRIMPY VAMPIRE

FIRST LINE OF DEFENSE, ROBOT

FIRST LINE OF DEFENSE, SUPERIOR DEMON, PROTECTIVE DEMON

LAST LINE OF DEFENSE, CHILD SENSEI

FIRST LINE OF DEFENSE, JUMP-KICKING FEMALE JUNIOR HIGH STUDENT

THE SWORDSMAN LEADER, SHINMEI RYU, WAS MADE GUARD OF THE TALISMAN USERS, MAKING THEM VERY DANGEROUS IN A MAGIC WAR.

THE SHINMEI SCHOOL WAS ORIGINALLY A COMBAT TROOP WITH UNPARALLELED POWER, FORMED TO PROTECT KYOTO AND AVENGE MISUSED MAGIC.

THIS PANEL IS A DRAMATIZATION

GOKIBURI!? ISN'T THAT A COCKROACH?

ALSO, THERE'S A DEEP RELATIONSHIP BETWEEN OUR KYOTO'S SHINMEI RYU AND THE KANSAI MAGIC ASSOCIATION.

A SUPERIOR DEMON AND A PROTECTIVE DEMON. THAT SOUNDS PRETTY STRONG.

THEN... THEN WASN'T THE SHINMEI SCHOOL AN ENEMY?

WELL, SUCH WARS ARE RARE THESE DAYS.

I DON'T REALLY GET IT... —BUT WHATEVER

WHOA! THIS IS GETTING WORSE AND WORSE...

I... I'LL BE SATISFIED WHEN I'M ABLE TO PROTECT OJOU-SAMA.

BUT SINCE I WANTED TO PROTECT KONOKA-OJOU-SAMA, I HAD NO CHOICE.

THAT'S RIGHT... FROM THEIR POINT OF VIEW, LEAVING THE WEST AND GOING EAST MAKES ME A TRAITOR, SO TO SPEAK.

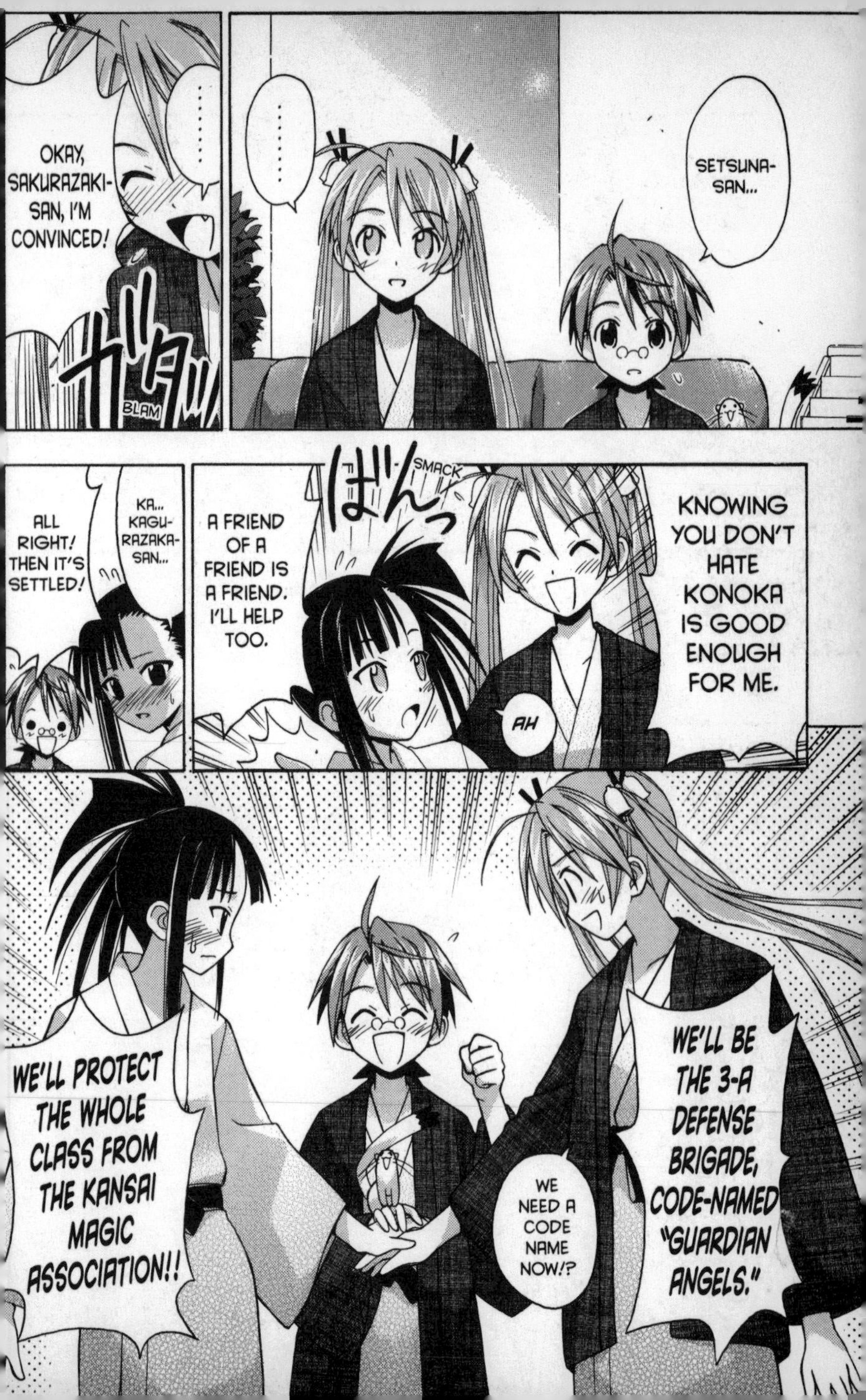
SETSUNA-SAN...
......
......
OKAY, SAKURAZAKI-SAN, I'M CONVINCED!
BLAM
KNOWING YOU DON'T HATE KONOKA IS GOOD ENOUGH FOR ME.
SMACK
AH
A FRIEND OF A FRIEND IS A FRIEND. I'LL HELP TOO.
KA... KAGURAZAKA-SAN...
ALL RIGHT! THEN IT'S SETTLED!
WE'LL BE THE 3-A DEFENSE BRIGADE, CODE-NAMED "GUARDIAN ANGELS."
WE NEED A CODE NAME NOW!?
WE'LL PROTECT THE WHOLE CLASS FROM THE KANSAI MAGIC ASSOCIATION!!

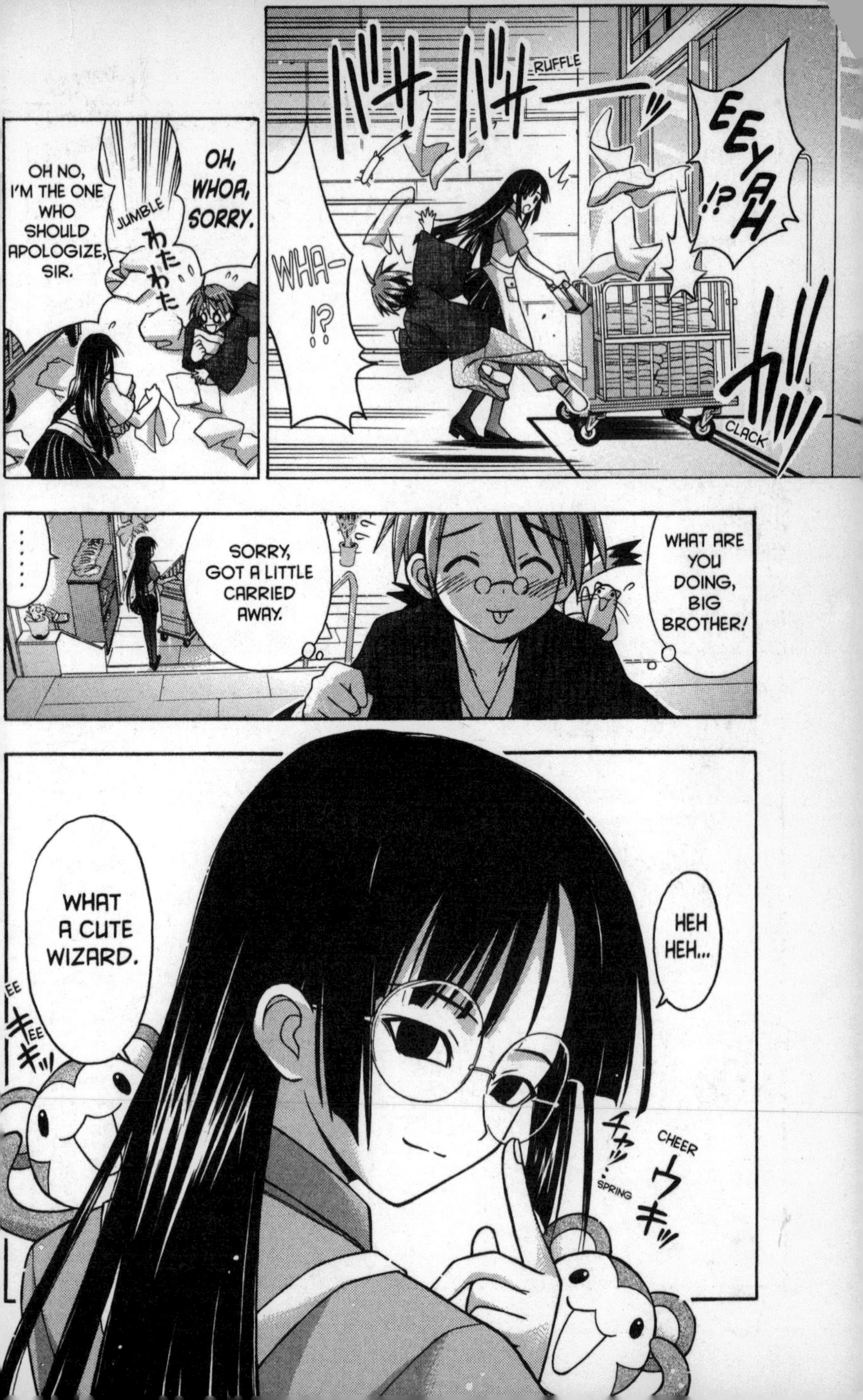
EEYAAH!?
RUFFLE
CLACK
WHA-!?
OH, WHOA, SORRY.
JUMBLE
わたわた
OH NO, I'M THE ONE WHO SHOULD APOLOGIZE, SIR.
WHAT ARE YOU DOING, BIG BROTHER!
SORRY, GOT A LITTLE CARRIED AWAY.
......
HEH HEH...
WHAT A CUTE WIZARD.
CHEER
SPRING
EE
EE

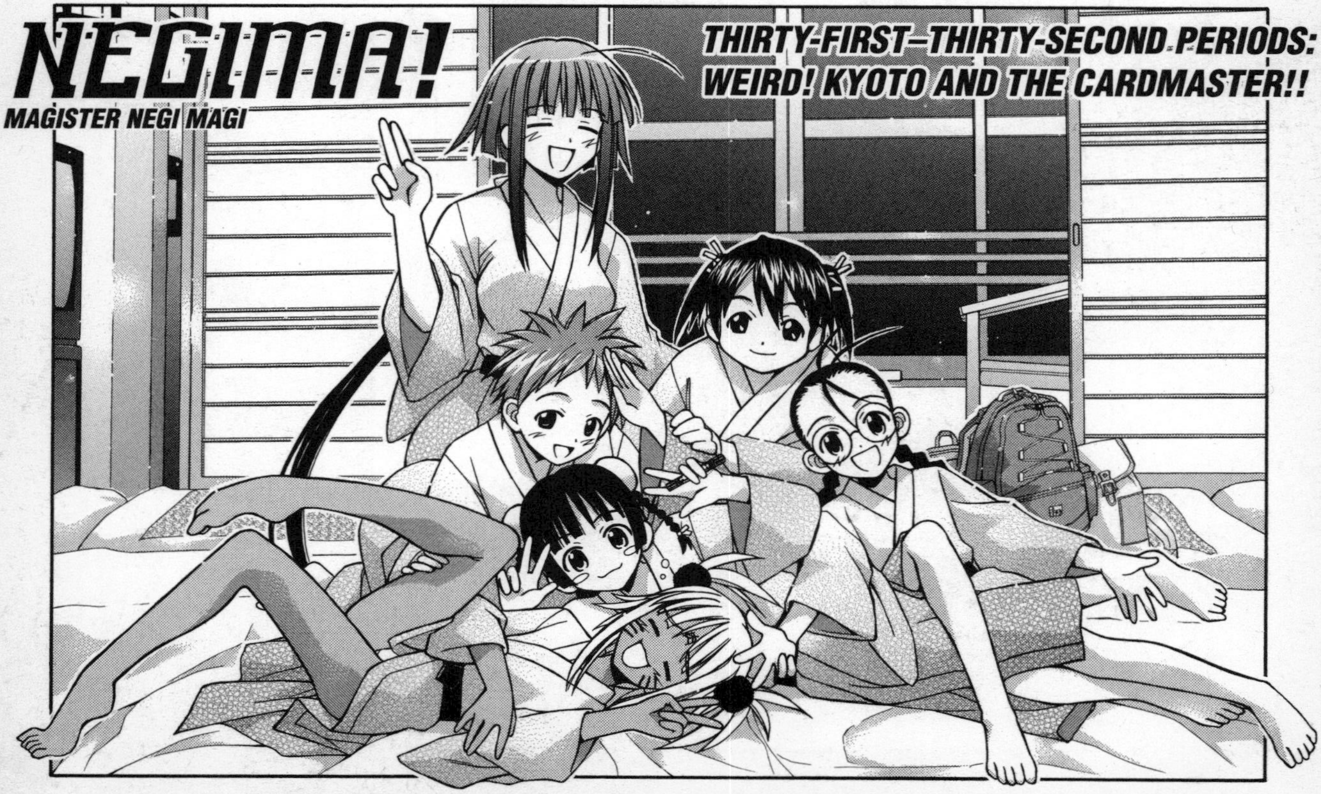
NEGIMA!
MAGISTER NEGI MAGI
THIRTY-FIRST–THIRTY-SECOND PERIODS:
WEIRD! KYOTO AND THE CARDMASTER!!

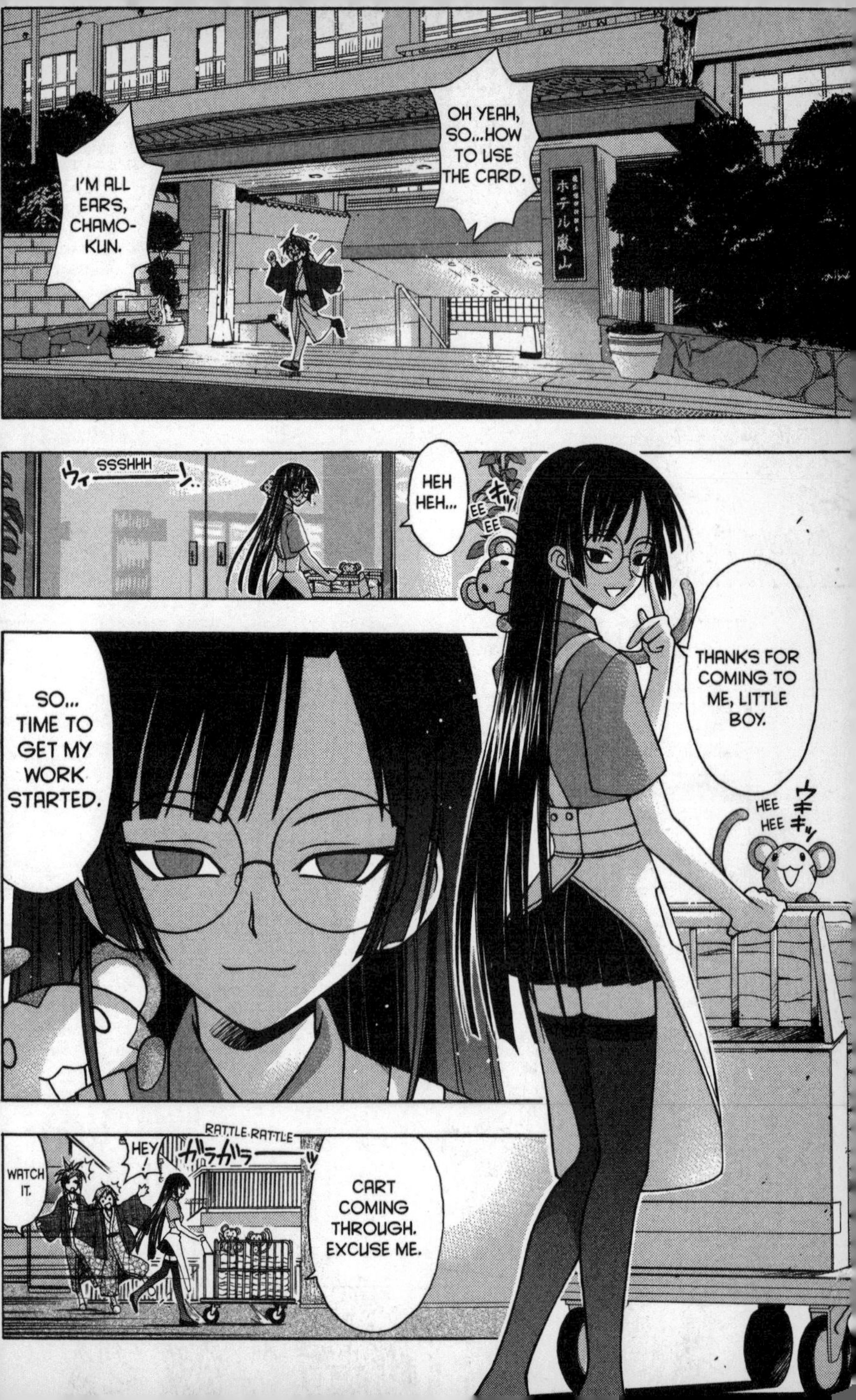
OH YEAH, SO...HOW TO USE THE CARD.
ホテル嵐山
I'M ALL EARS, CHAMO-KUN.
HEH HEH...
キッ EE EE
THANKS FOR COMING TO ME, LITTLE BOY.
ウキキッ HEE HEE
ウィーン SSSHHH
SO... TIME TO GET MY WORK STARTED.
CART COMING THROUGH. EXCUSE ME.
ガラガラーッ RATTLE RATTLE
HEY!
WATCH IT.

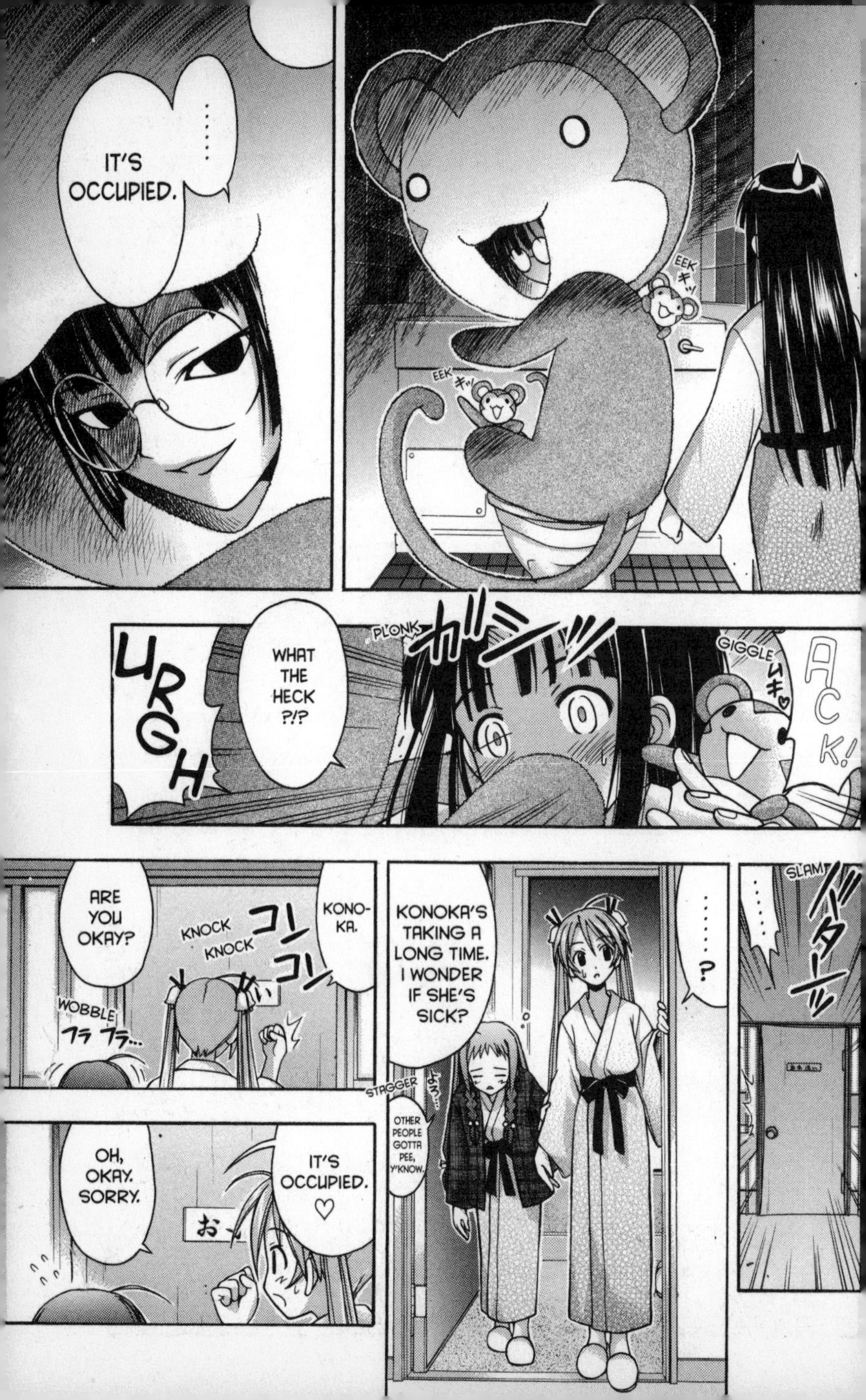

EEK キッ
EEK キッ
......
IT'S OCCUPIED.
ACK!
GIGGLE ムキ♥
PLONK カシーッ
WHAT THE HECK ?!?
URGH
SLAM バターッ
......
......?
KONOKA'S TAKING A LONG TIME. I WONDER IF SHE'S SICK?
STAGGER よろ...
OTHER PEOPLE GOTTA PEE, Y'KNOW.
KONO-KA.
KNOCK KNOCK コンコン
ARE YOU OKAY?
WOBBLE フラフラ...
IT'S OCCUPIED. ♡
OH, OKAY. SORRY.

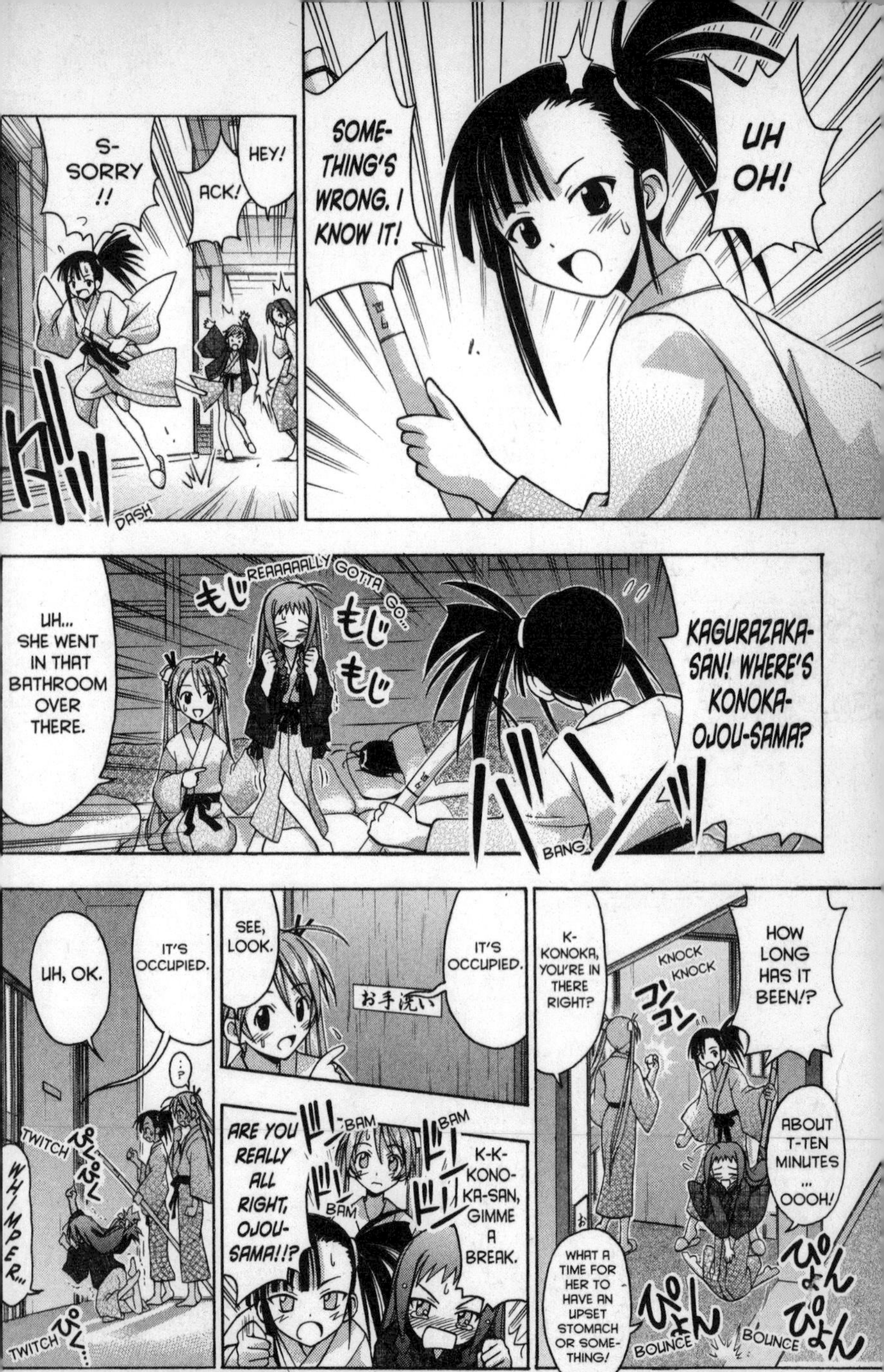
UH OH!
SOME-THING'S WRONG. I KNOW IT!
HEY!
ACK!
S-SORRY!!
DASH
KAGURAZAKA-SAN! WHERE'S KONOKA-OJOU-SAMA?
BANG
REAAAAALLY GOTTA GO...
もじ
もじもじ
UH... SHE WENT IN THAT BATHROOM OVER THERE.
HOW LONG HAS IT BEEN!?
K-KONOKA, YOU'RE IN THERE RIGHT?
KNOCK KNOCK
コンコン
ABOUT T-TEN MINUTES... OOOH!
ぴょんぴょん
WHAT A TIME FOR HER TO HAVE AN UPSET STOMACH OR SOME-THING!
BOUNCE
ぴょん
BOUNCE
IT'S OCCUPIED.
SEE, LOOK.
お手洗い
BAM
K-K-KONOKA-SAN, GIMME A BREAK.
BAM
ARE YOU REALLY ALL RIGHT, OJOU-SAMA!!?
BAM
IT'S OCCUPIED.
UH, OK.
...?
TWITCH
ぴくぴく
WHIMPER...
TWITCH
ぴく...

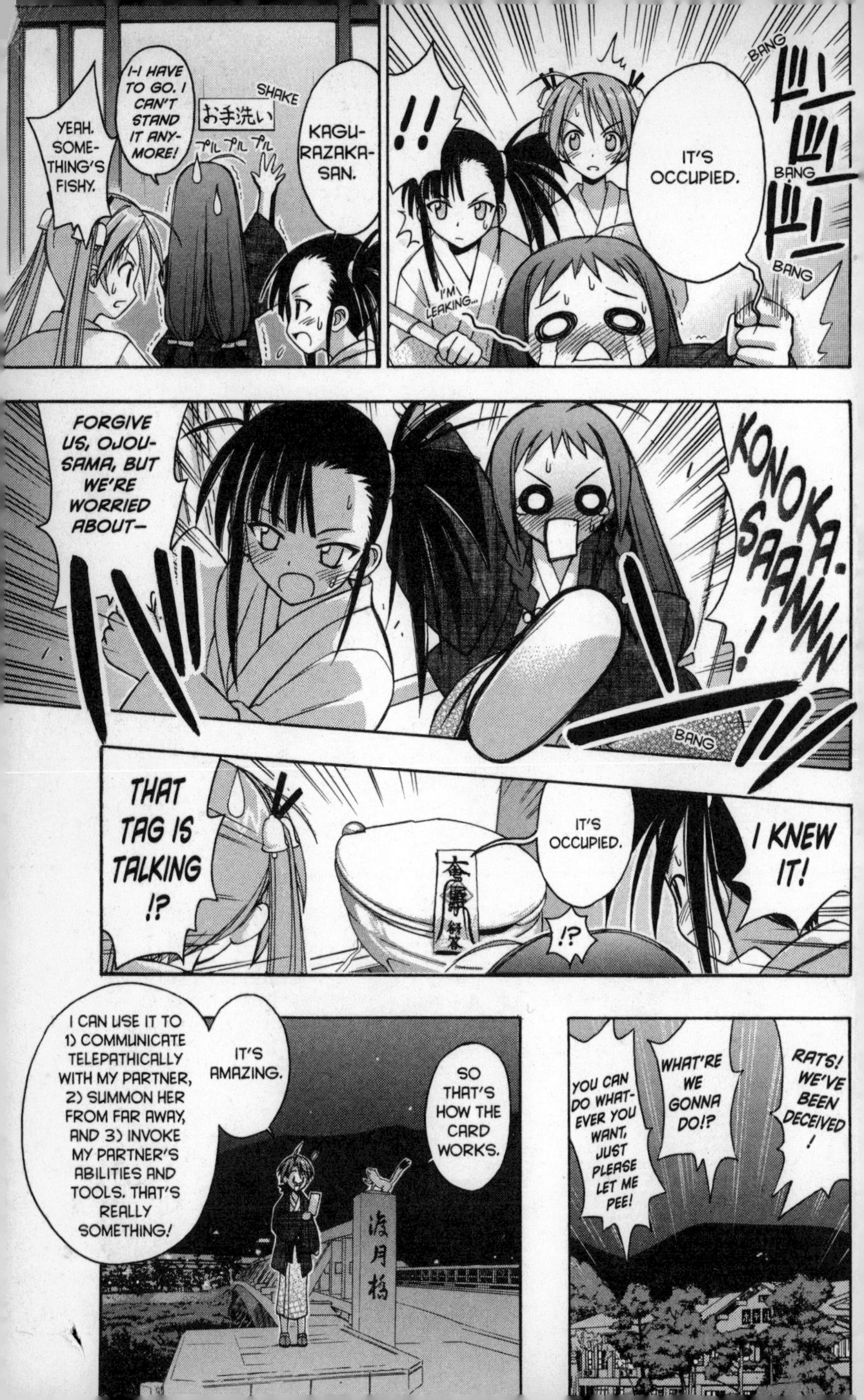
BANG
IT'S OCCUPIED.
BANG
BANG
!!
I'M LEAKING...
KAGURAZAKA-SAN.
SHAKE
I-I HAVE TO GO. I CAN'T STAND IT ANYMORE!
お手洗い
プルプルプル
YEAH. SOMETHING'S FISHY.
KONOKA-SAANNN!
FORGIVE US, OJOU-SAMA, BUT WE'RE WORRIED ABOUT—
BANG
I KNEW IT!
IT'S OCCUPIED.
!?
THAT TAG IS TALKING!?
RATS! WE'VE BEEN DECEIVED!
WHAT'RE WE GONNA DO!?
YOU CAN DO WHATEVER YOU WANT, JUST PLEASE LET ME PEE!
SO THAT'S HOW THE CARD WORKS.
IT'S AMAZING.
I CAN USE IT TO 1) COMMUNICATE TELEPATHICALLY WITH MY PARTNER, 2) SUMMON HER FROM FAR AWAY, AND 3) INVOKE MY PARTNER'S ABILITIES AND TOOLS. THAT'S REALLY SOMETHING!
渡月橋

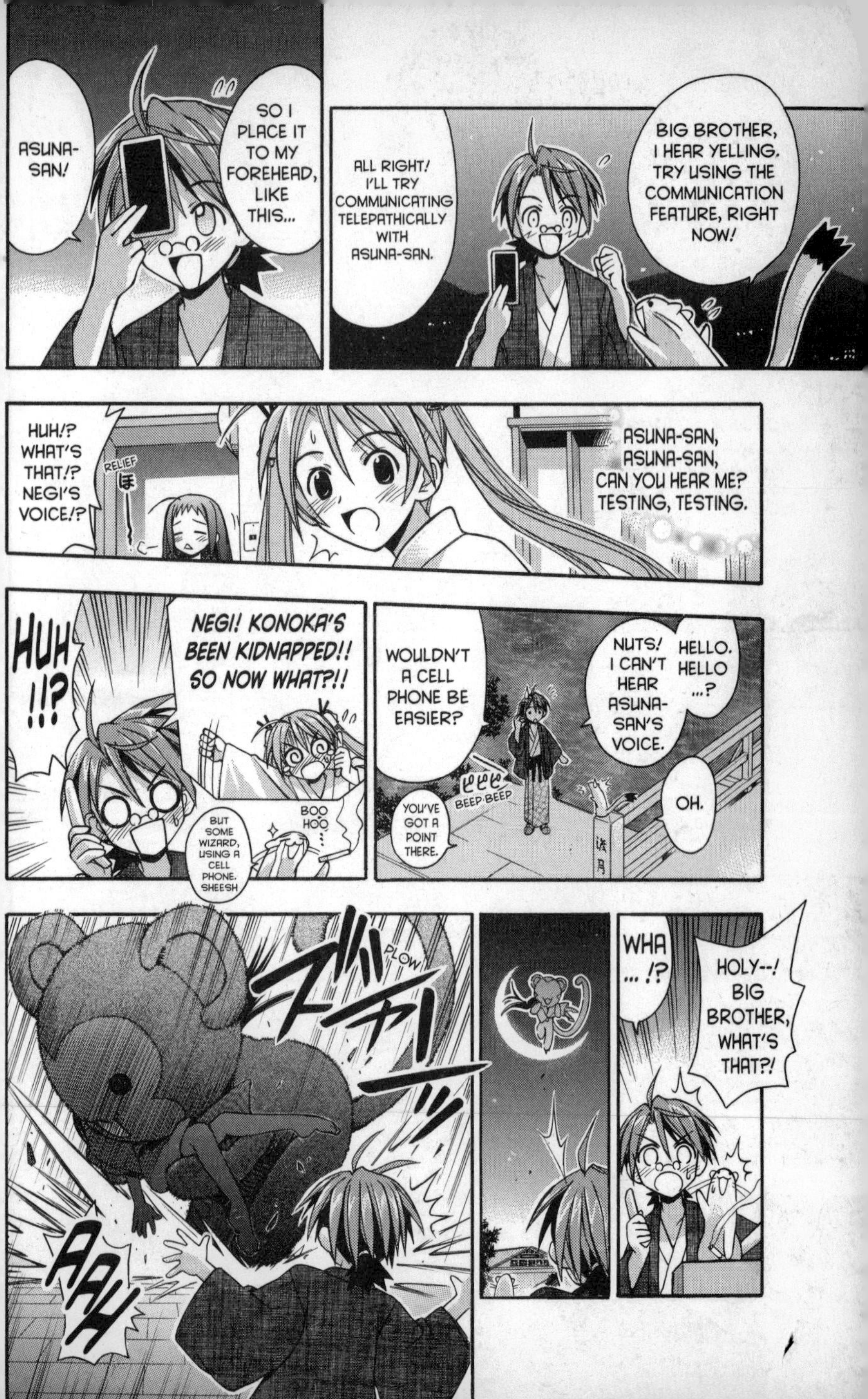
BIG BROTHER, I HEAR YELLING. TRY USING THE COMMUNICATION FEATURE, RIGHT NOW!
ALL RIGHT! I'LL TRY COMMUNICATING TELEPATHICALLY WITH ASUNA-SAN.
SO I PLACE IT TO MY FOREHEAD, LIKE THIS...
ASUNA-SAN!
ASUNA-SAN, ASUNA-SAN, CAN YOU HEAR ME? TESTING, TESTING.
HUH!? WHAT'S THAT!? NEGI'S VOICE!?
RELIEF
HELLO. HELLO ...?
NUTS! I CAN'T HEAR ASUNA-SAN'S VOICE.
OH.
WOULDN'T A CELL PHONE BE EASIER?
BEEP BEEP
YOU'VE GOT A POINT THERE.
NEGI! KONOKA'S BEEN KIDNAPPED!! SO NOW WHAT?!!
HUH !!?
BOO HOO...
BUT SOME WIZARD, USING A CELL PHONE. SHEESH
HOLY--! BIG BROTHER, WHAT'S THAT?!
WHA ...!?
PLOW
AAH

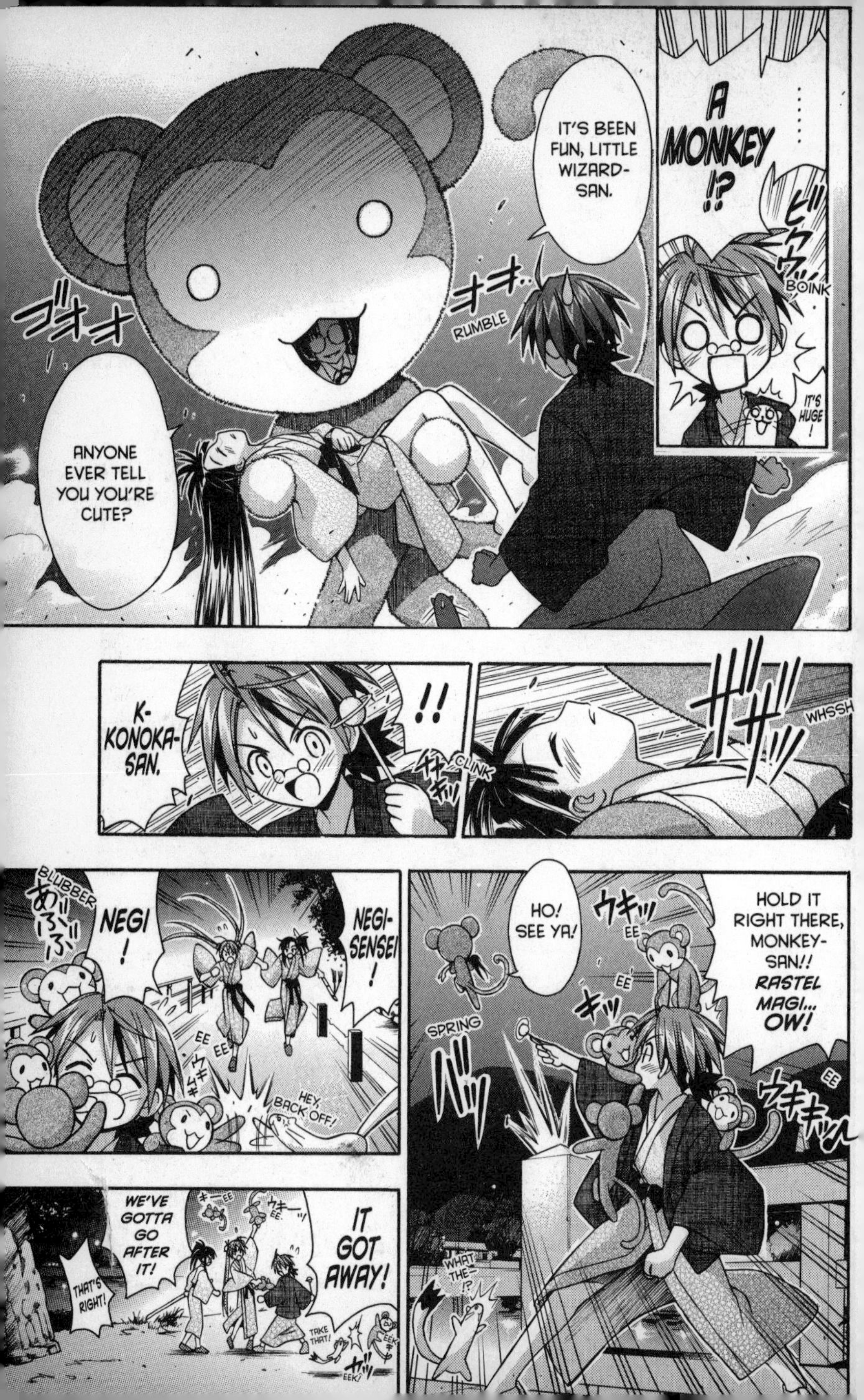
A MONKEY !?
BOINK
IT'S HUGE!
IT'S BEEN FUN, LITTLE WIZARD-SAN.
RUMBLE
ANYONE EVER TELL YOU YOU'RE CUTE?
WHSSH
!!
CLINK
K-KONOKA-SAN.
HOLD IT RIGHT THERE, MONKEY-SAN!! RASTEL MAGI... OW!
EE
HO! SEE YA!
EE
SPRING
EE
WHAT THE—!?
NEGI-SENSEI!
NEGI!
BLUBBER
EE EE
HEY, BACK OFF!
IT GOT AWAY!
EE
WE'VE GOTTA GO AFTER IT!
THAT'S RIGHT!
EEK
TAKE THAT!
EEK!

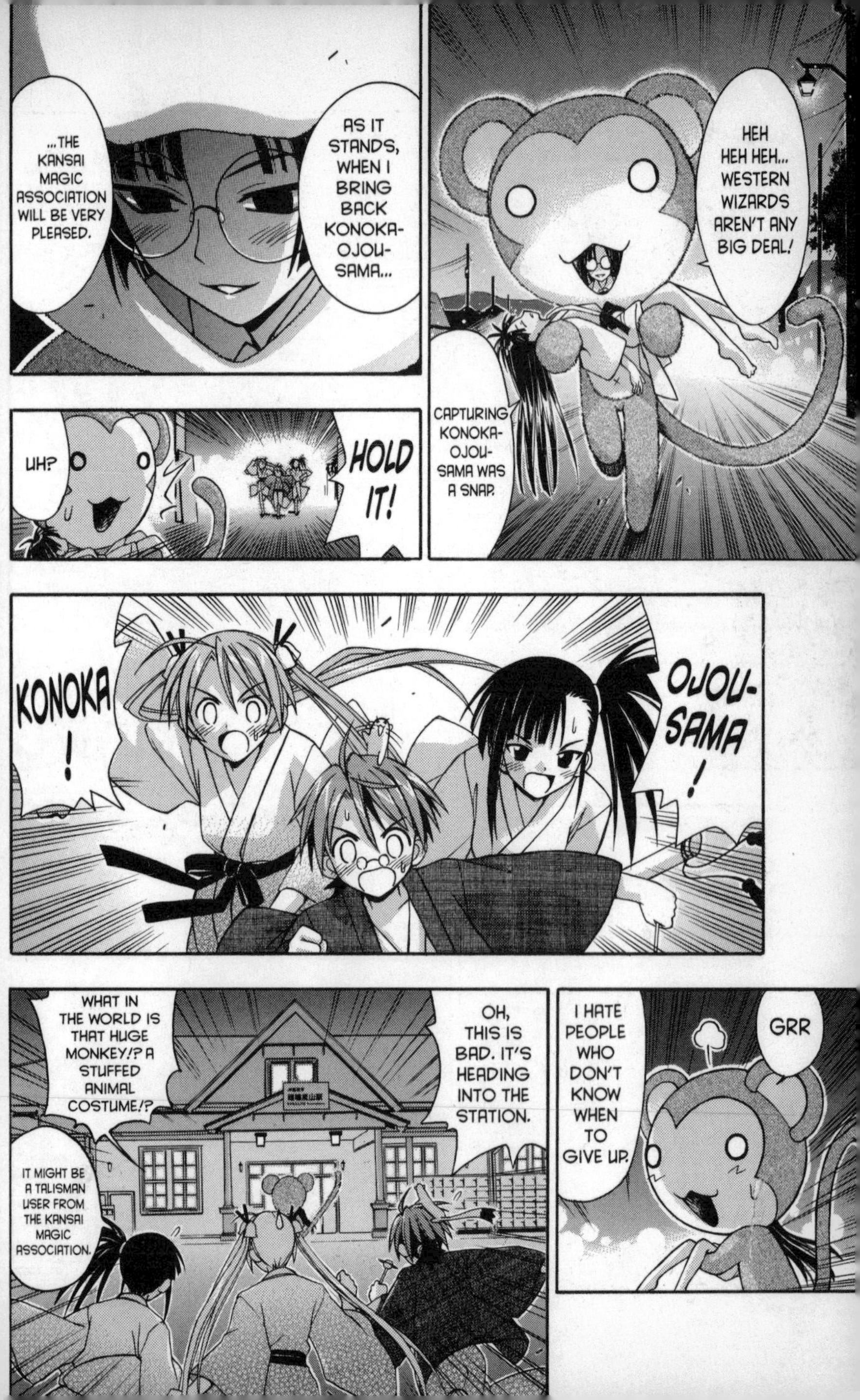
HEH HEH HEH... WESTERN WIZARDS AREN'T ANY BIG DEAL!
CAPTURING KONOKA-OJOU-SAMA WAS A SNAP.
AS IT STANDS, WHEN I BRING BACK KONOKA-OJOU-SAMA...
...THE KANSAI MAGIC ASSOCIATION WILL BE VERY PLEASED.
HOLD IT!
UH?
OJOU-SAMA!
KONOKA!
GRR
I HATE PEOPLE WHO DON'T KNOW WHEN TO GIVE UP.
OH, THIS IS BAD. IT'S HEADING INTO THE STATION.
WHAT IN THE WORLD IS THAT HUGE MONKEY!? A STUFFED ANIMAL COSTUME!?
IT MIGHT BE A TALISMAN USER FROM THE KANSAI MAGIC ASSOCIATION.

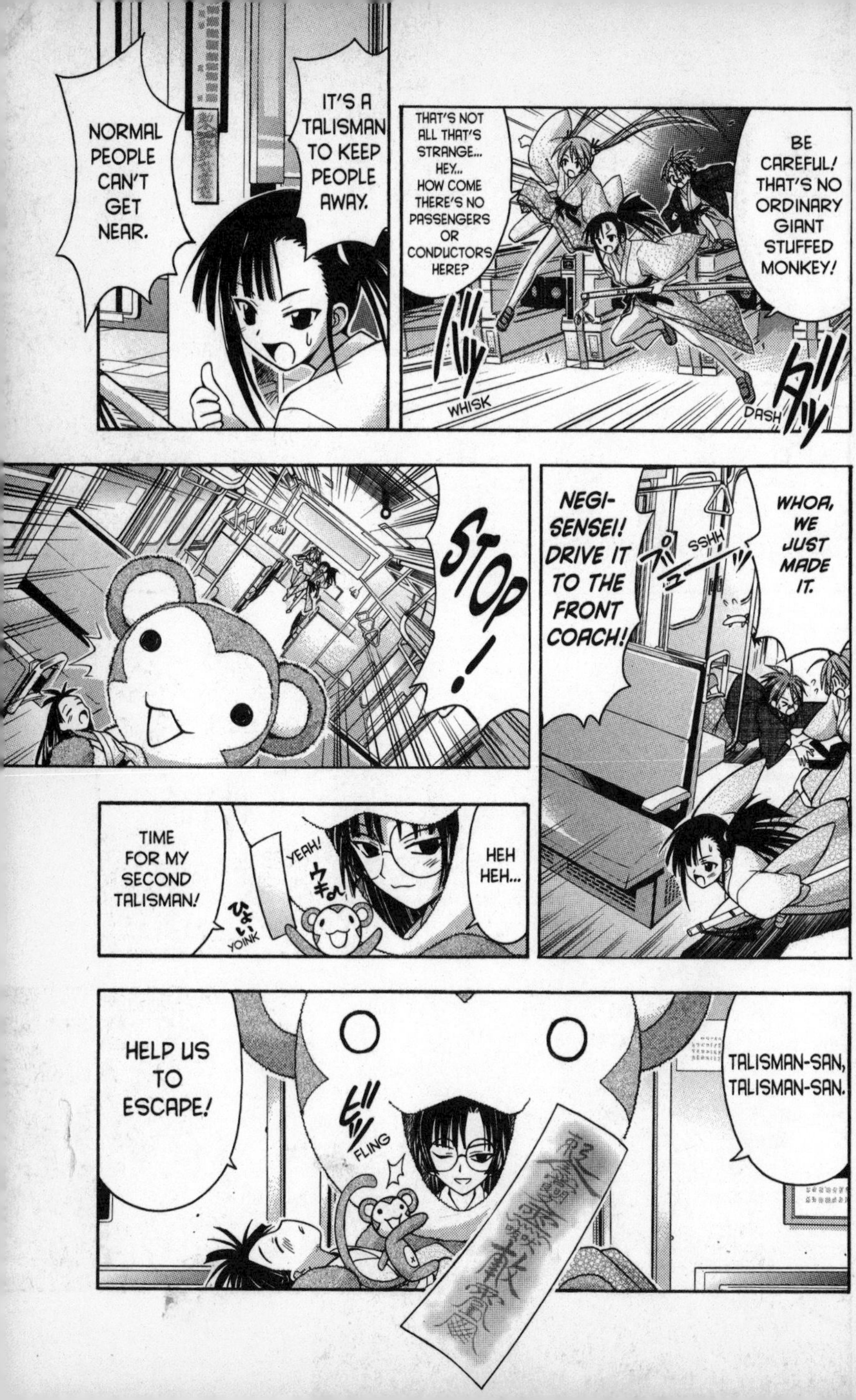
BE CAREFUL! THAT'S NO ORDINARY GIANT STUFFED MONKEY!
THAT'S NOT ALL THAT'S STRANGE... HEY... HOW COME THERE'S NO PASSENGERS OR CONDUCTORS HERE?
DASH
WHISK
IT'S A TALISMAN TO KEEP PEOPLE AWAY.
NORMAL PEOPLE CAN'T GET NEAR.
WHOA, WE JUST MADE IT.
SSHH
NEGI-SENSEI! DRIVE IT TO THE FRONT COACH!
STOP!
HEH HEH...
YEAH!
TIME FOR MY SECOND TALISMAN!
YOINK
TALISMAN-SAN, TALISMAN-SAN.
FLING
HELP US TO ESCAPE!

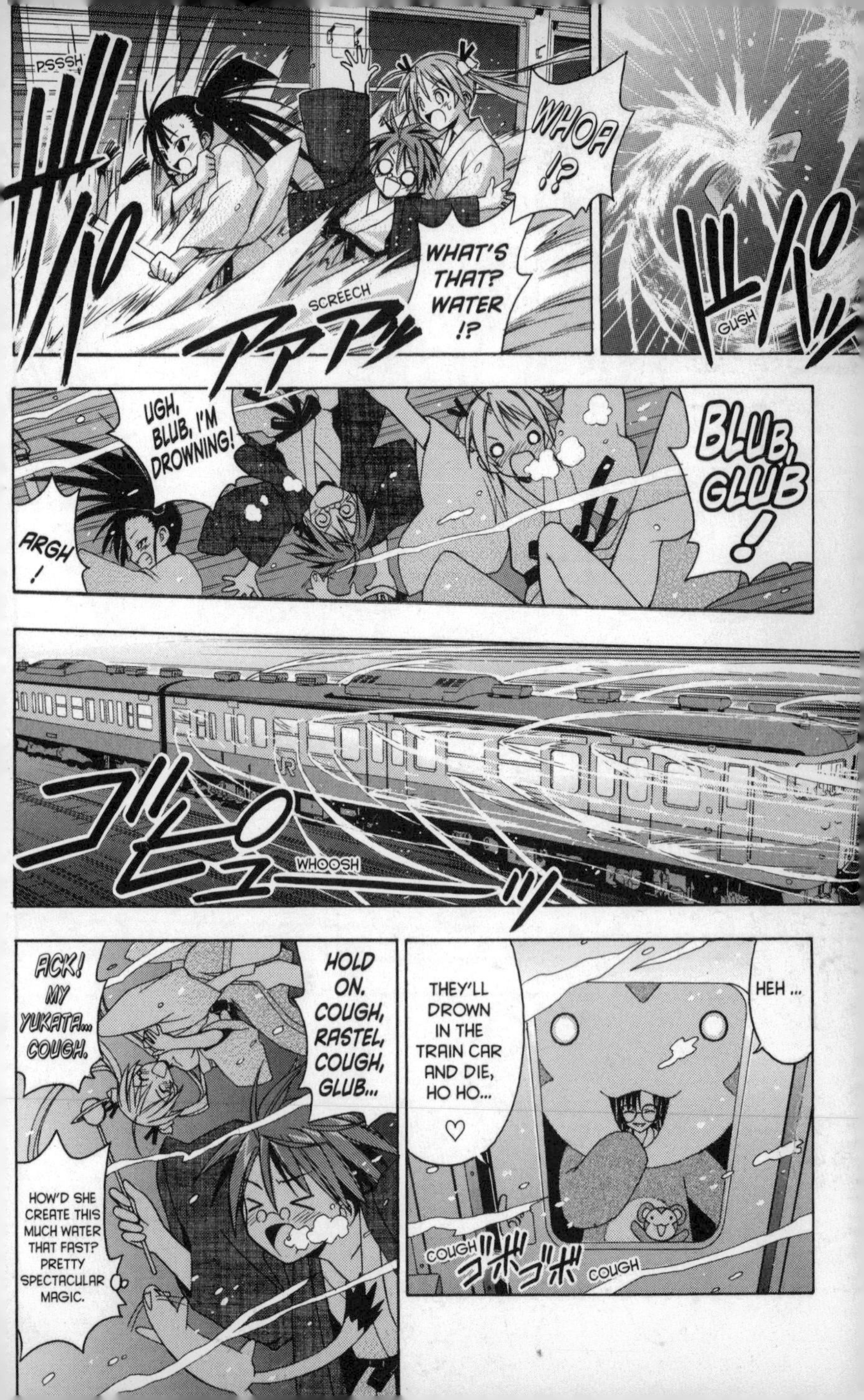
GUSH
WHOA !?
WHAT'S THAT? WATER !?
PSSSH
SCREECH
BLUB, GLUB !
UGH, BLUB, I'M DROWNING!
ARGH !
WHOOSH
HEH ...
THEY'LL DROWN IN THE TRAIN CAR AND DIE, HO HO... ♡
COUGH
COUGH
HOLD ON. COUGH, RASTEL, COUGH, GLUB...
ACK! MY YUKATA... COUGH.
HOW'D SHE CREATE THIS MUCH WATER THAT FAST? PRETTY SPECTACULAR MAGIC.

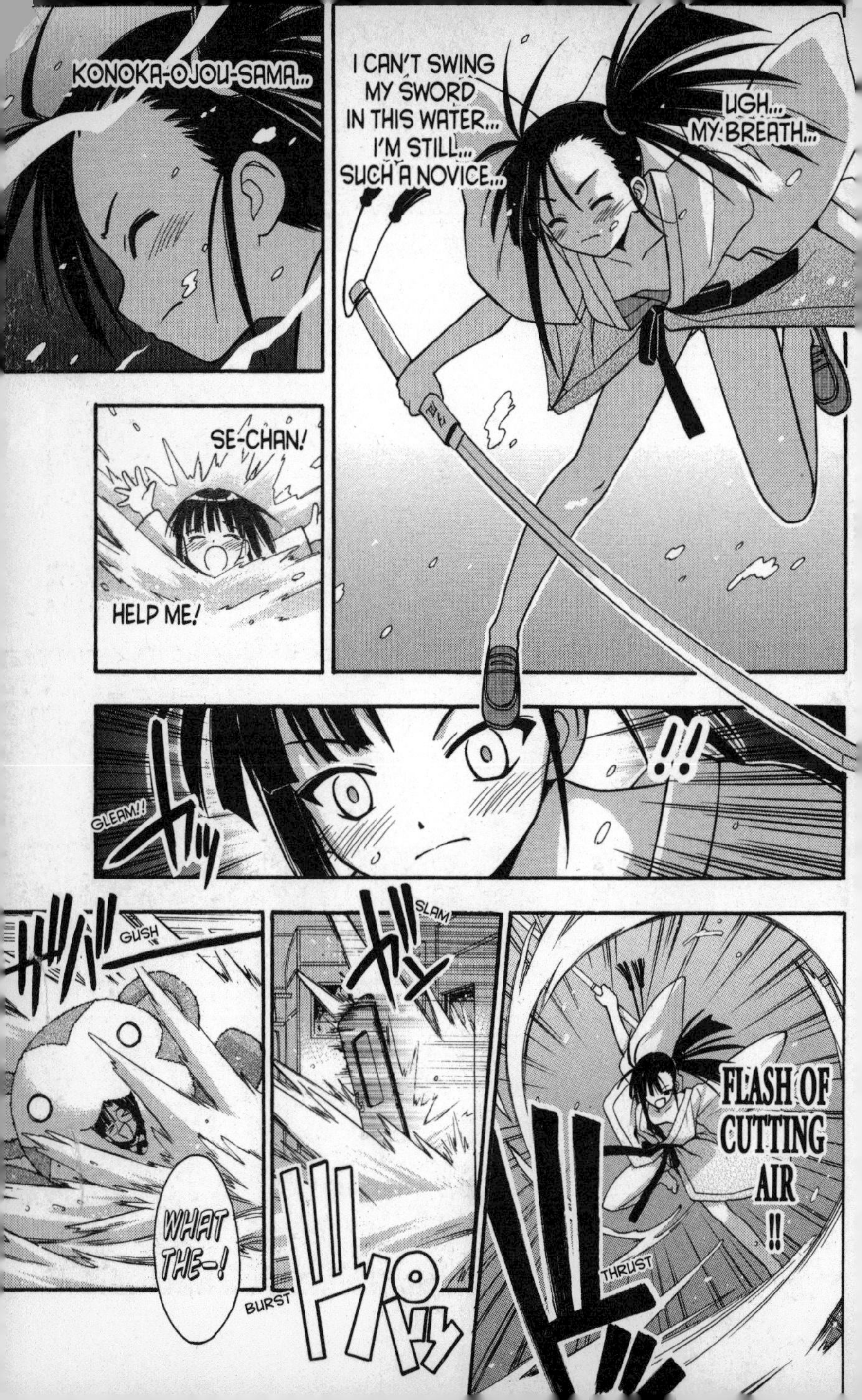

UGH... MY BREATH...
I CAN'T SWING MY SWORD IN THIS WATER... I'M STILL... SUCH A NOVICE...
KONOKA-OJOU-SAMA...
SE-CHAN!
HELP ME!
!!
GLEAM!!
FLASH OF CUTTING AIR !!
THRUST
SLAM
BURST
GUSH
WHAT THE-!

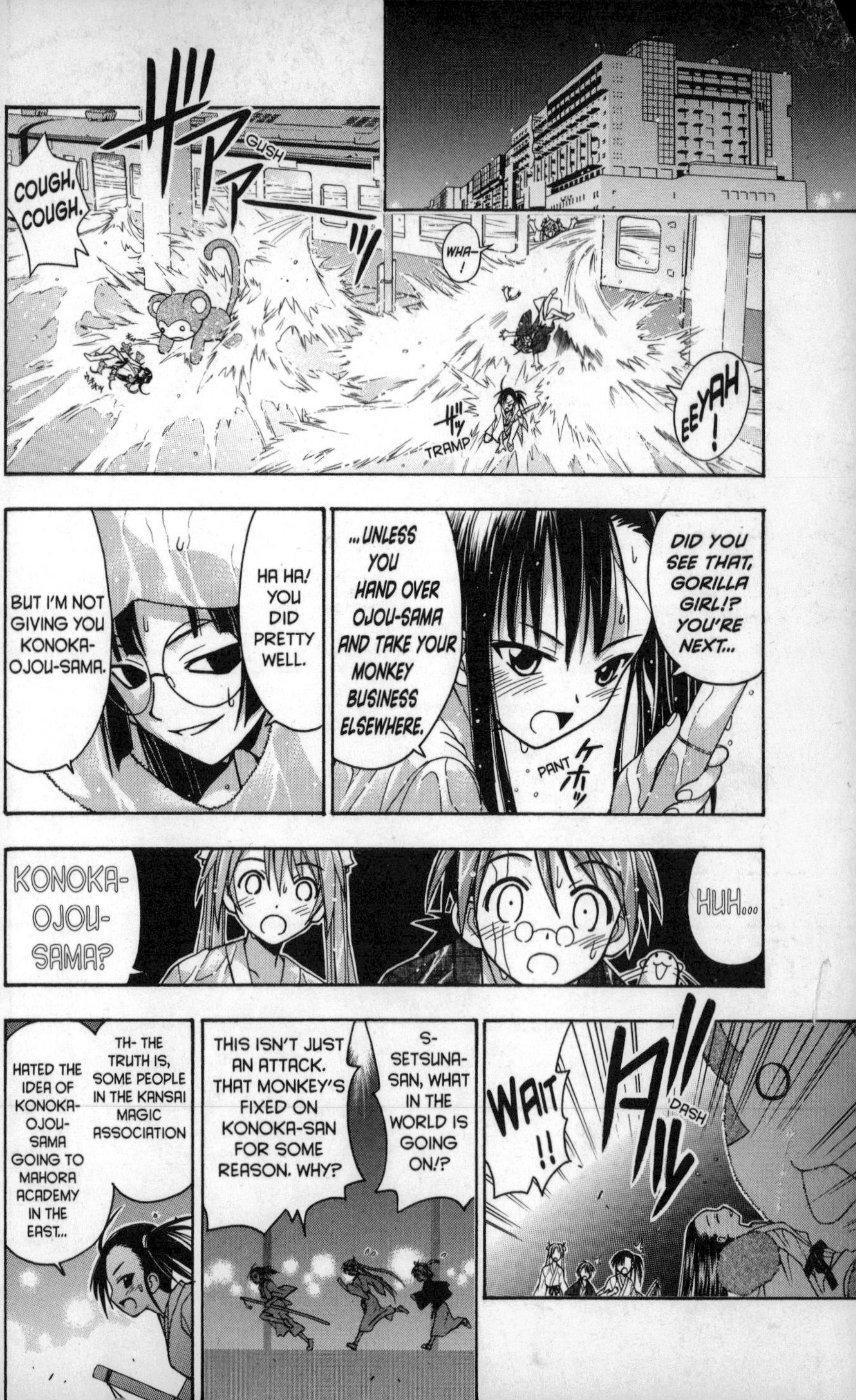
EEYAH!
TRAMP
WHA-!
GUSH
COUGH, COUGH.
DID YOU SEE THAT, GORILLA GIRL!? YOU'RE NEXT...
...UNLESS YOU HAND OVER OJOU-SAMA AND TAKE YOUR MONKEY BUSINESS ELSEWHERE.
PANT
HA HA! YOU DID PRETTY WELL.
BUT I'M NOT GIVING YOU KONOKA-OJOU-SAMA.
HUH...
KONOKA-OJOU-SAMA?
WAIT!!
DASH
S-SETSUNA-SAN, WHAT IN THE WORLD IS GOING ON!?
THIS ISN'T JUST AN ATTACK. THAT MONKEY'S FIXED ON KONOKA-SAN FOR SOME REASON. WHY?
TH- THE TRUTH IS, SOME PEOPLE IN THE KANSAI MAGIC ASSOCIATION
HATED THE IDEA OF KONOKA-OJOU-SAMA GOING TO MAHORA ACADEMY IN THE EAST...

PERHAPS
...

PERHAPS THOSE PEOPLE ARE TRYING TO USE KONOKA-OJOU-SAMA'S POWER TO TAKE CONTROL OF THE KANSAI MAGIC ASSOCIATION.

WHAT IN THE WORLD !?

WHAT THE... !?

SOMEONE'S BEEN PLANNING THIS CRIME FROM EVERY ANGLE.

LOOK! ANOTHER TALISMAN TO TRY AND KEEP US OUT.

AH!

SETSUNA-SAN, WAIT!

DASH

NOT WHILE I'M AROUND !

TO PEOPLE WHO DON'T CARE WHO GETS IN THEIR WAY OR WHO GETS HURT.

BUT FROM THE BEGINNING, THE KANSAI MAGIC ASSOCIATION HAS CONTRACTED OUT THEIR MORE "SORDID" JOBS...

ARGH...

WE NEVER THOUGHT THERE'D BE DIRECT ATTACKS, LIKE A KIDNAPPING, WHILE ON THE FIELD TRIP.

BOTH THE HEAD-MASTER AND I DIDN'T BELIEVE IT WOULD GET THIS FAR.

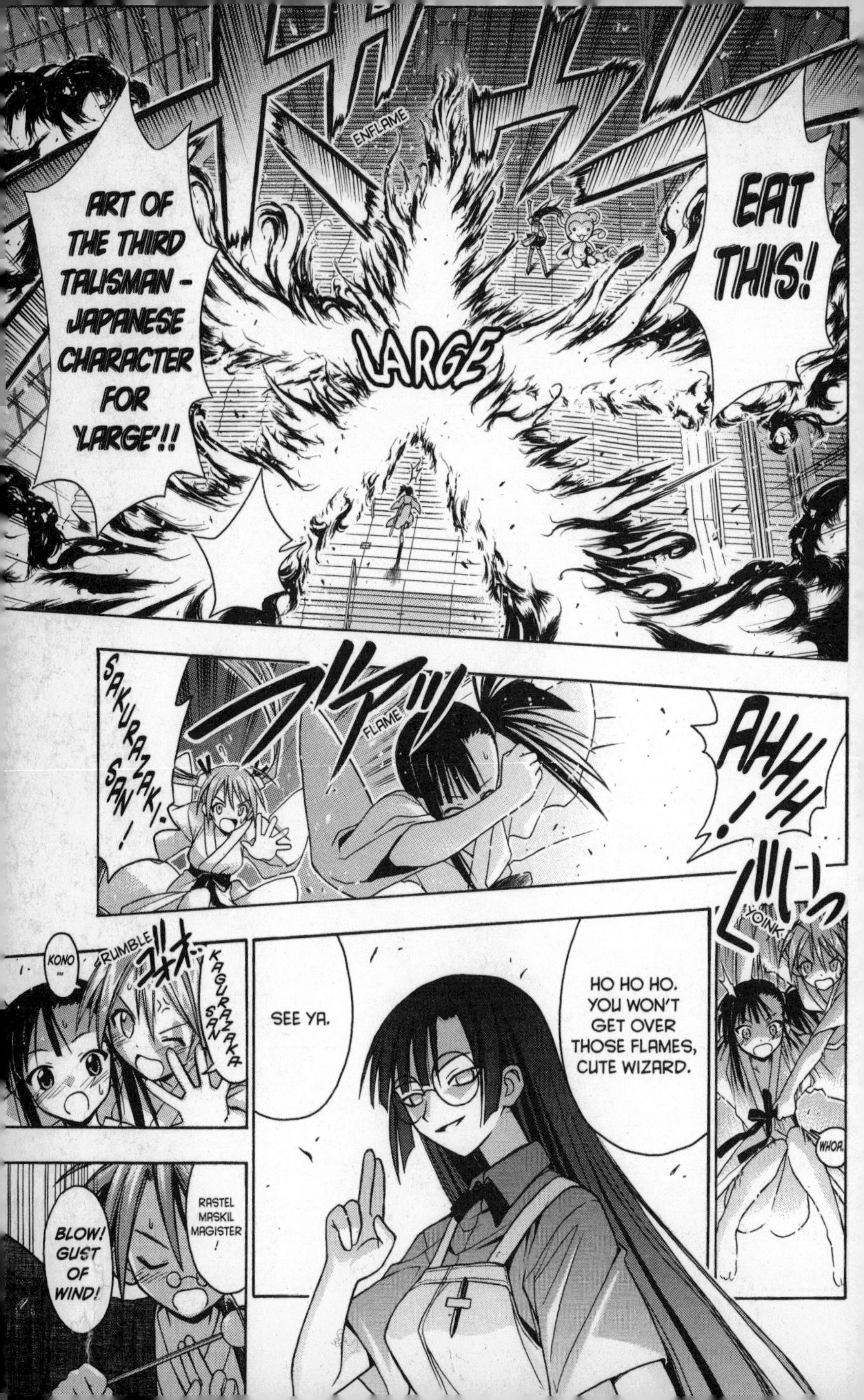
EAT THIS!
ENFLAME
LARGE
ART OF THE THIRD TALISMAN - JAPANESE CHARACTER FOR 'LARGE'!!
AHHH!!
FLAME
SAKURAZAKI-SAN!
YOINK
WHOA.
HO HO HO. YOU WON'T GET OVER THOSE FLAMES, CUTE WIZARD.
SEE YA.
KAGURAZAKA-SAN
RUMBLE
KONO...
RASTEL MASKIL MAGISTER!
BLOW! GUST OF WIND!

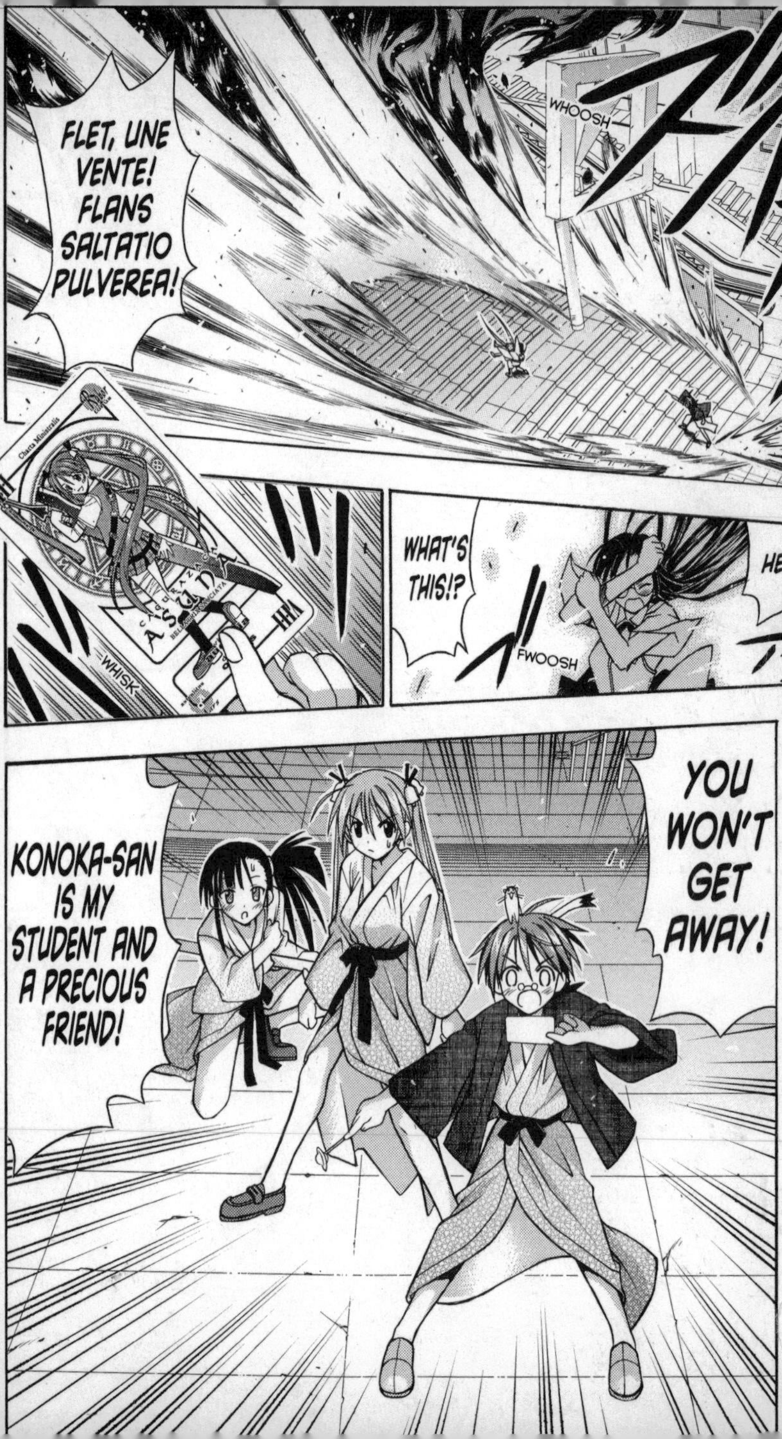
FLET, UNE VENTE! FLANS SALTATIO PULVEREA!
WHOOSH
WHISK
HEY...
WHAT'S THIS!?
FWOOSH
YOU WON'T GET AWAY!
KONOKA-SAN IS MY STUDENT AND A PRECIOUS FRIEND!

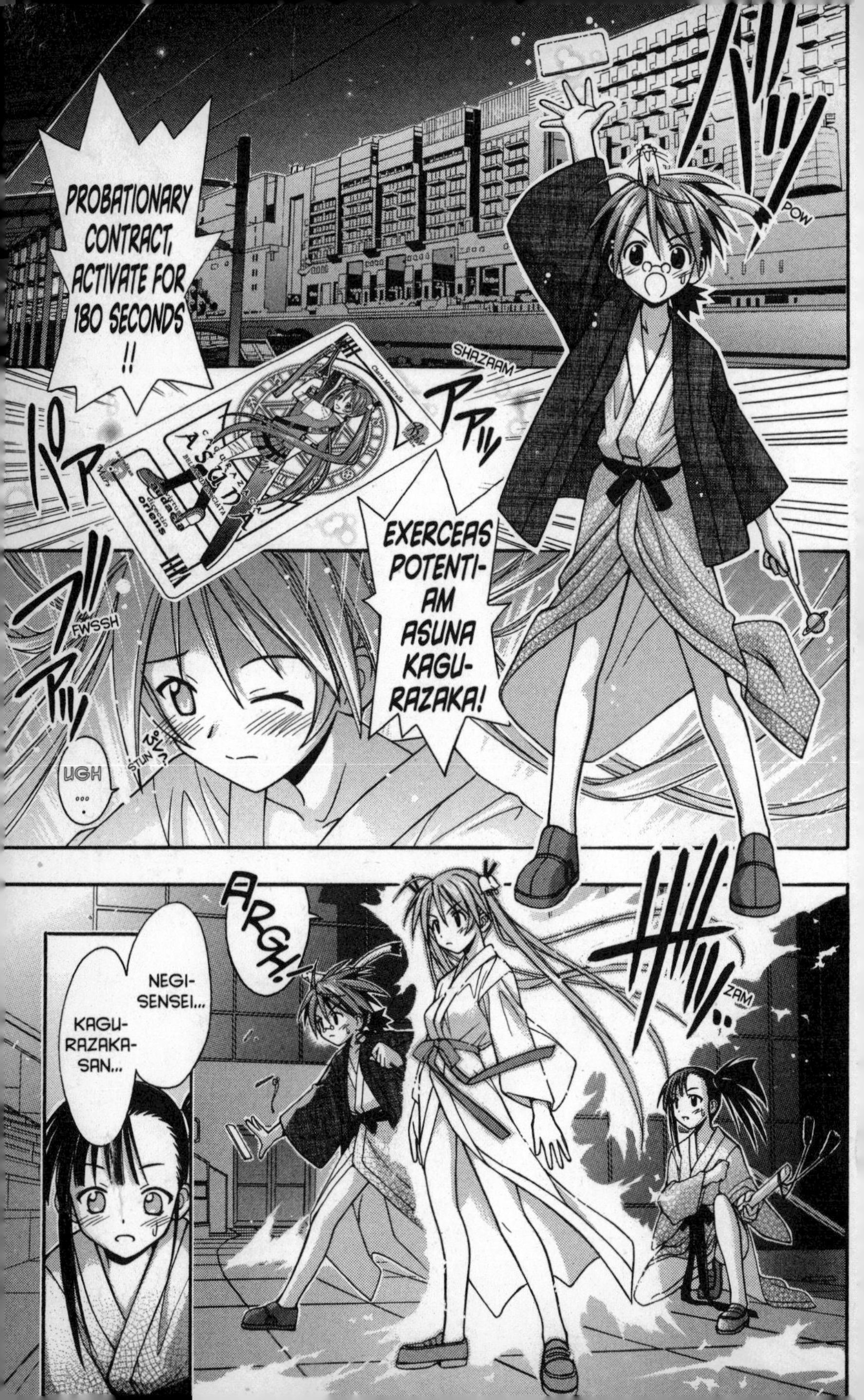
POW
PROBATIONARY CONTRACT, ACTIVATE FOR 180 SECONDS !!
SHAZAAM
EXERCEAS POTENTI-AM ASUNA KAGU-RAZAKA!
FWSSH
STUN
UGH ....
ZAM
ARGH!
NEGI-SENSEI...
KAGU-RAZAKA-SAN...

NO HEAT! WHAT A JOKE!

THAT FIRE WAS ALL SHOW,

TRAMP-

UH... OKAY!

SAKURAZAKI-SAN, LET'S GO!

YO! MONKEY GIRL! HAND OVER KONOKA, RIGHT NOW!

TROMP

OKAY!

BIG BROTHER, USE THE CARD!

THAT WESTERN WIZARD AND HIS PARTNER DID THAT!?

THEY SNUFFED MY FIRE...? AND WHAT WAS THAT LIGHT?

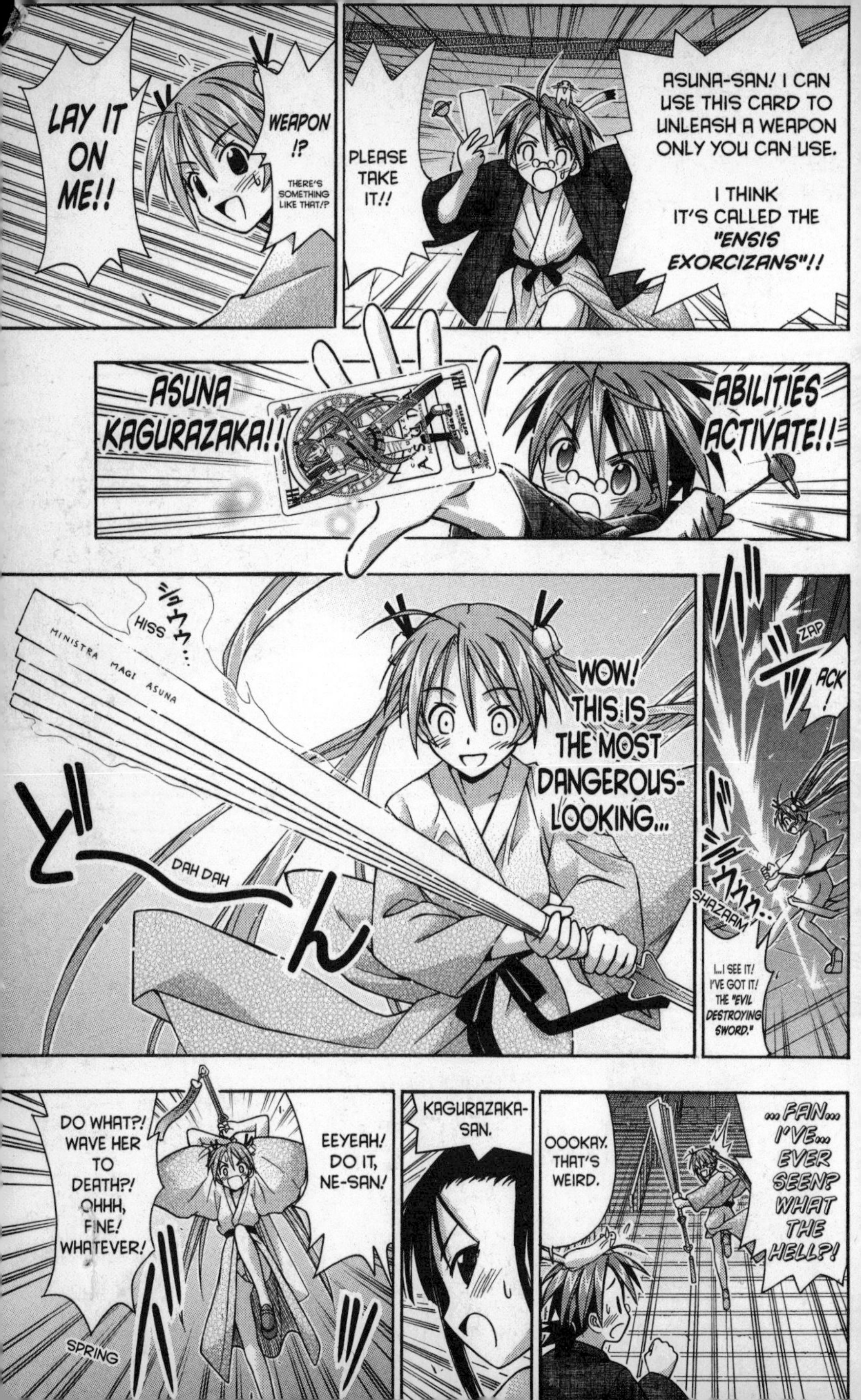
ASUNA-SAN! I CAN USE THIS CARD TO UNLEASH A WEAPON ONLY YOU CAN USE.
I THINK IT'S CALLED THE "ENSIS EXORCIZANS"!!
PLEASE TAKE IT!!
WEAPON !?
THERE'S SOMETHING LIKE THAT!?
LAY IT ON ME!!
ABILITIES ACTIVATE!!
ASUNA KAGURAZAKA!!
ZAP
ACK !
SHAZAAM
I...I SEE IT! I'VE GOT IT! THE "EVIL DESTROYING SWORD."
WOW! THIS IS THE MOST DANGEROUS-LOOKING...
HISS
MINISTRA MAGI ASUNA
DAH DAH
...FAN... I'VE... EVER SEEN? WHAT THE HELL?!
OOOKAY. THAT'S WEIRD.
KAGURAZAKA-SAN.
EEYEAH! DO IT, NE-SAN!
DO WHAT?! WAVE HER TO DEATH?! OHHH, FINE! WHATEVER!
SPRING

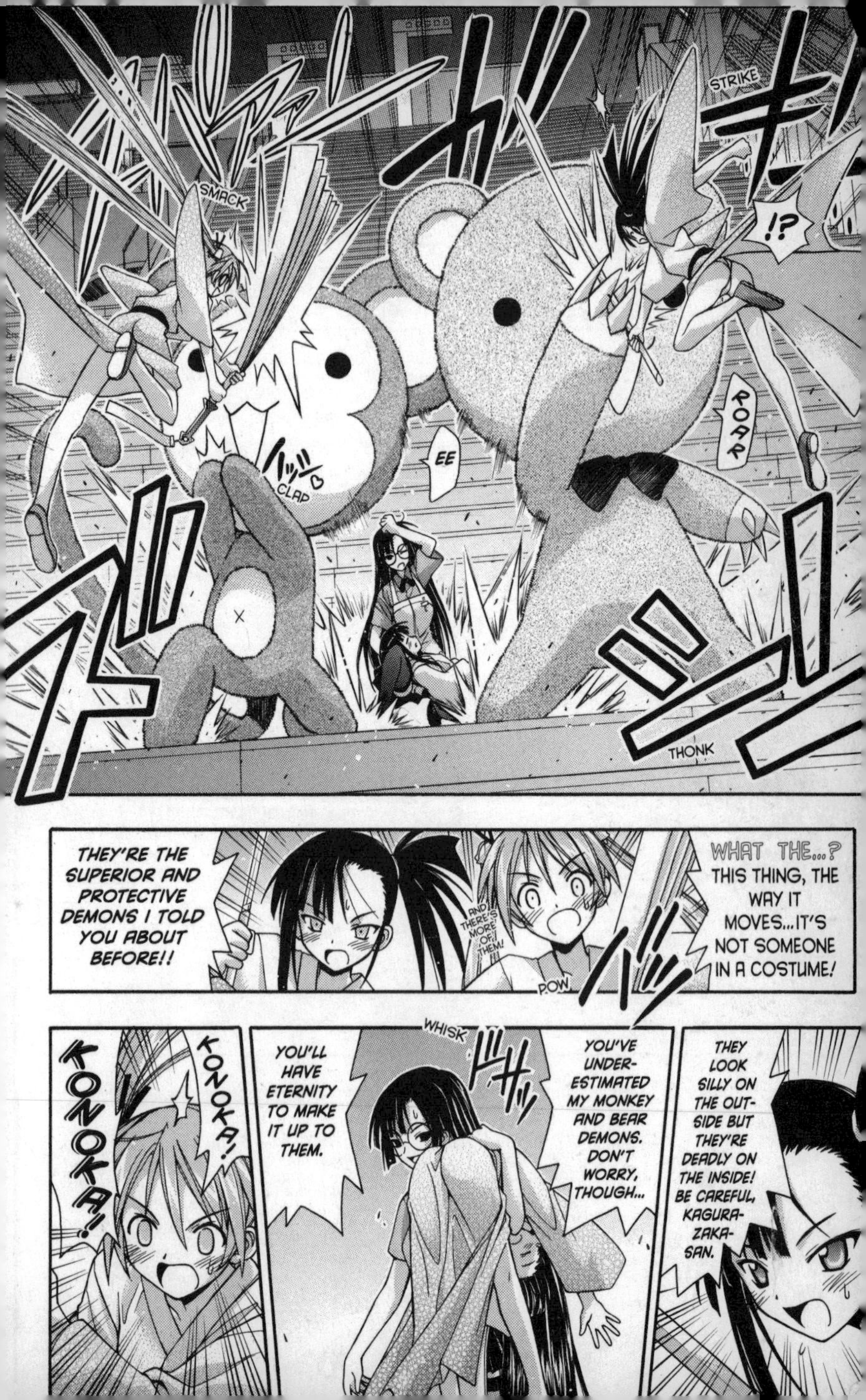
STRIKE
!?
ROAR
EE
SMACK
CLAP
THONK
WHAT THE...? THIS THING, THE WAY IT MOVES...IT'S NOT SOMEONE IN A COSTUME!
AND THERE'S MORE OF THEM!
POW
THEY'RE THE SUPERIOR AND PROTECTIVE DEMONS I TOLD YOU ABOUT BEFORE!!
THEY LOOK SILLY ON THE OUT-SIDE BUT THEY'RE DEADLY ON THE INSIDE! BE CAREFUL, KAGURA-ZAKA-SAN.
YOU'VE UNDER-ESTIMATED MY MONKEY AND BEAR DEMONS. DON'T WORRY, THOUGH...
WHISK
YOU'LL HAVE ETERNITY TO MAKE IT UP TO THEM.
KONOKA!
KONOKA!

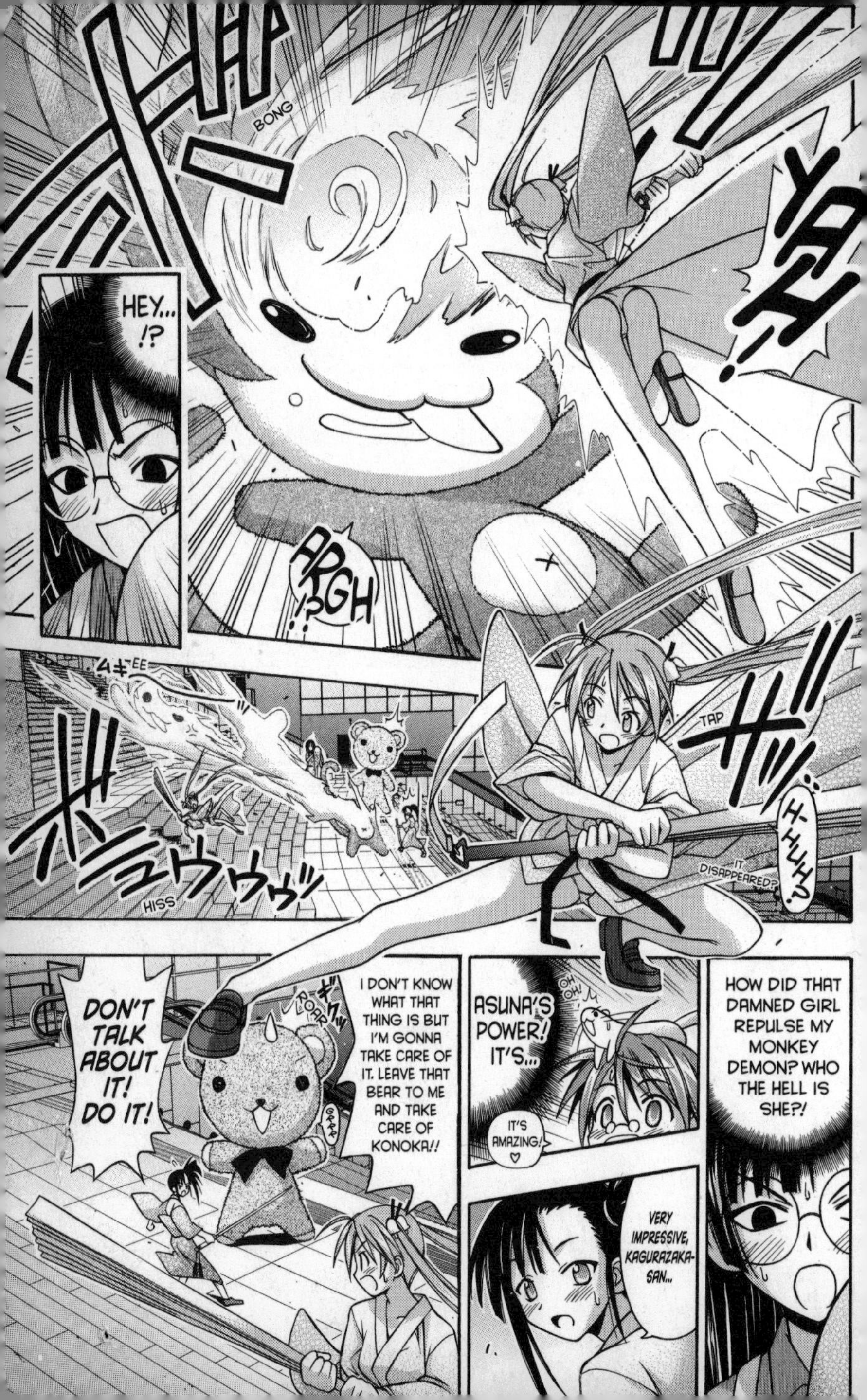
BONG
ARGH !?
HEY... !?
TAP
H-HUH?
IT DISAPPEARED?
HISS
HOW DID THAT DAMNED GIRL REPULSE MY MONKEY DEMON? WHO THE HELL IS SHE?!
ASUNA'S POWER! IT'S...
OH OH!
IT'S AMAZING! ♡
VERY IMPRESSIVE, KAGURAZAKA-SAN...
I DON'T KNOW WHAT THAT THING IS BUT I'M GONNA TAKE CARE OF IT. LEAVE THAT BEAR TO ME AND TAKE CARE OF KONOKA!!
ROAR
DON'T TALK ABOUT IT! DO IT!
GRRR

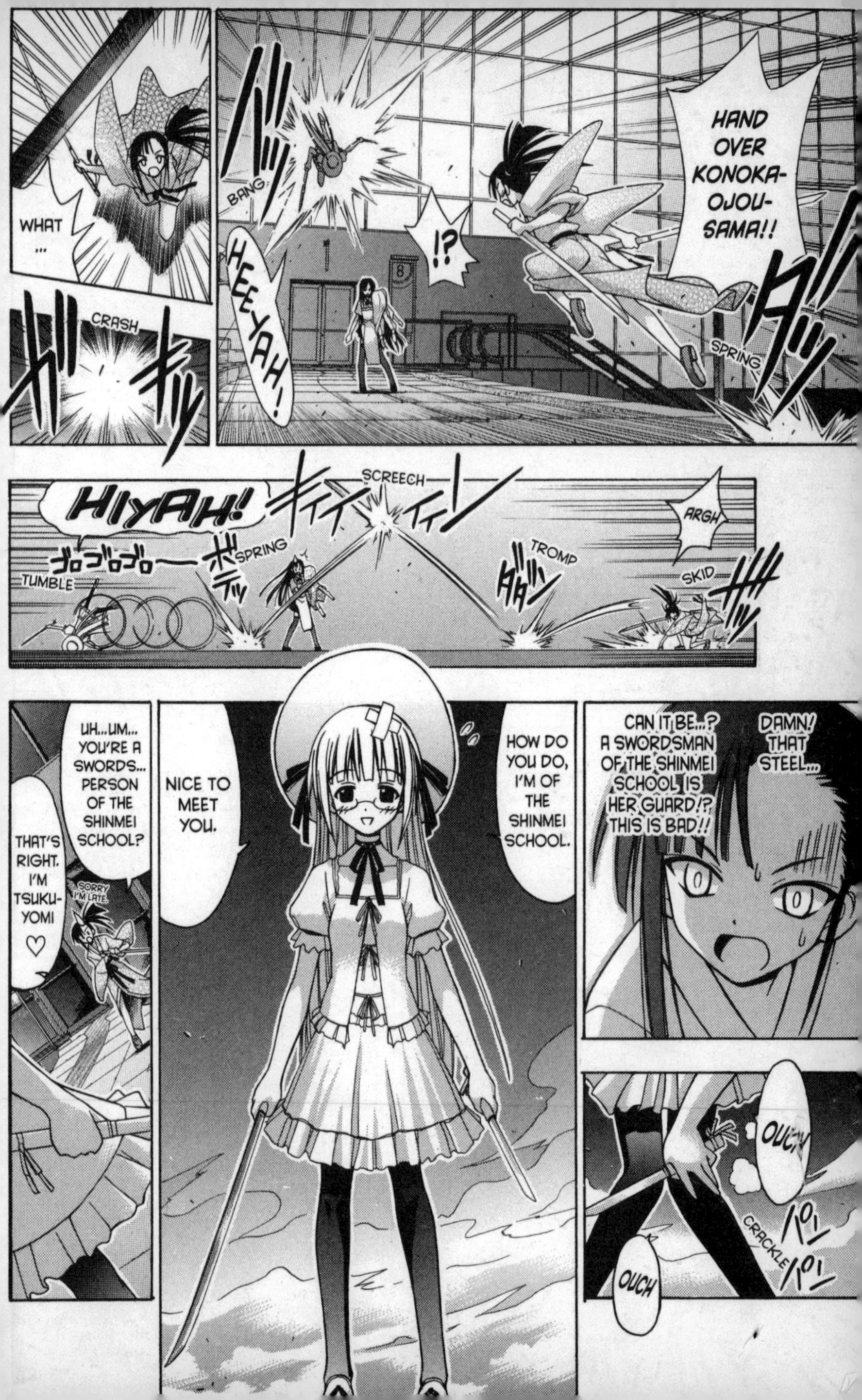
HAND OVER KONOKA-OJOU-SAMA!!
SPRING
!?
BANG
HEEEYAH!
WHAT ...
CRASH
ARGH
SKID
TROMP
SCREECH
SPRING
HIYAH!
TUMBLE
DAMN! THAT STEEL...
CAN IT BE...? A SWORDSMAN OF THE SHINMEI SCHOOL IS HER GUARD!? THIS IS BAD!!
OUCH
CRACKLE
OUCH
HOW DO YOU DO, I'M OF THE SHINMEI SCHOOL.
NICE TO MEET YOU.
UH...UM... YOU'RE A SWORDS... PERSON OF THE SHINMEI SCHOOL?
THAT'S RIGHT. I'M TSUKU-YOMI ♡
SORRY I'M LATE.

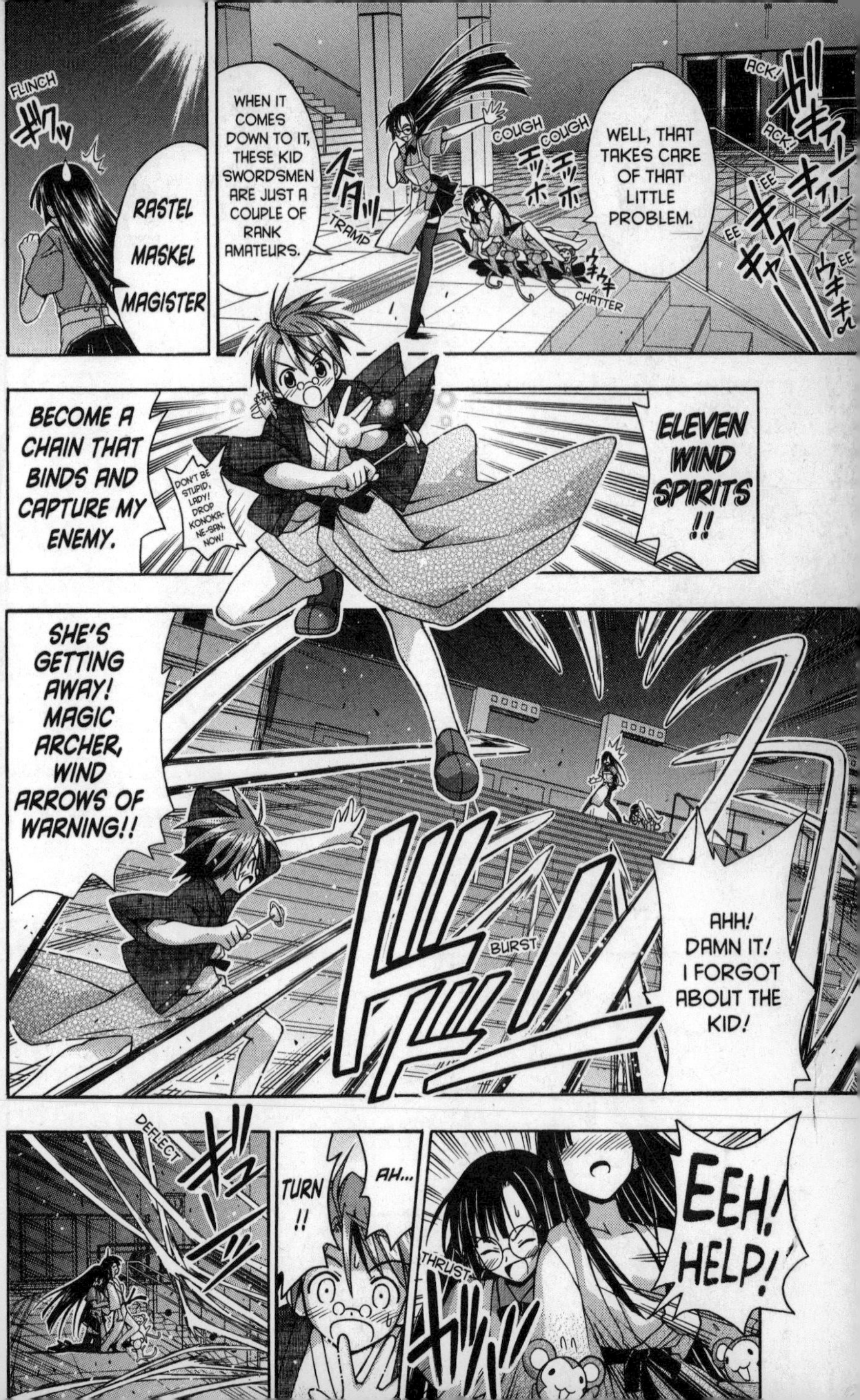
ACK!
ACK!
EE
EE
WELL, THAT TAKES CARE OF THAT LITTLE PROBLEM.
COUGH
COUGH
CHATTER
WHEN IT COMES DOWN TO IT, THESE KID SWORDSMEN ARE JUST A COUPLE OF RANK AMATEURS.
TRAMP
FLINCH
RASTEL MASKEL MAGISTER
ELEVEN WIND SPIRITS!!
DON'T BE STUPID, LADY! DROP KONOKA-NE-SAN, NOW!
BECOME A CHAIN THAT BINDS AND CAPTURE MY ENEMY.
AHH! DAMN IT! I FORGOT ABOUT THE KID!
BURST
SHE'S GETTING AWAY! MAGIC ARCHER, WIND ARROWS OF WARNING!!
EEH! HELP!
THRUST
AH...
TURN!!
DEFLECT

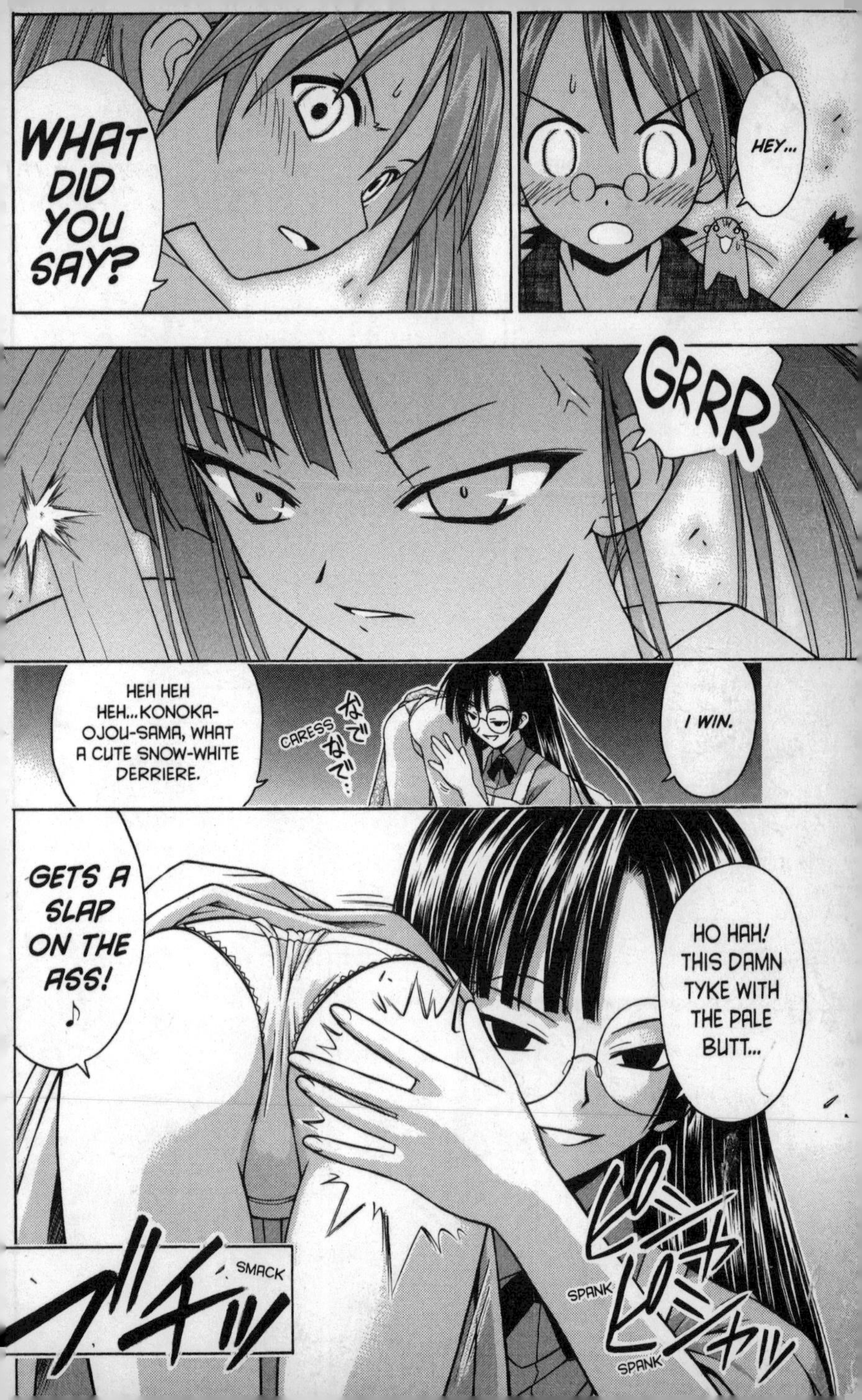
HEY...
WHAT DID YOU SAY?
GRRR
I WIN.
なで なで…
CARESS
HEH HEH HEH...KONOKA-OJOU-SAMA, WHAT A CUTE SNOW-WHITE DERRIERE.
HO HAH! THIS DAMN TYKE WITH THE PALE BUTT...
GETS A SLAP ON THE ASS! ♪
SPANK
SPANK
SMACK

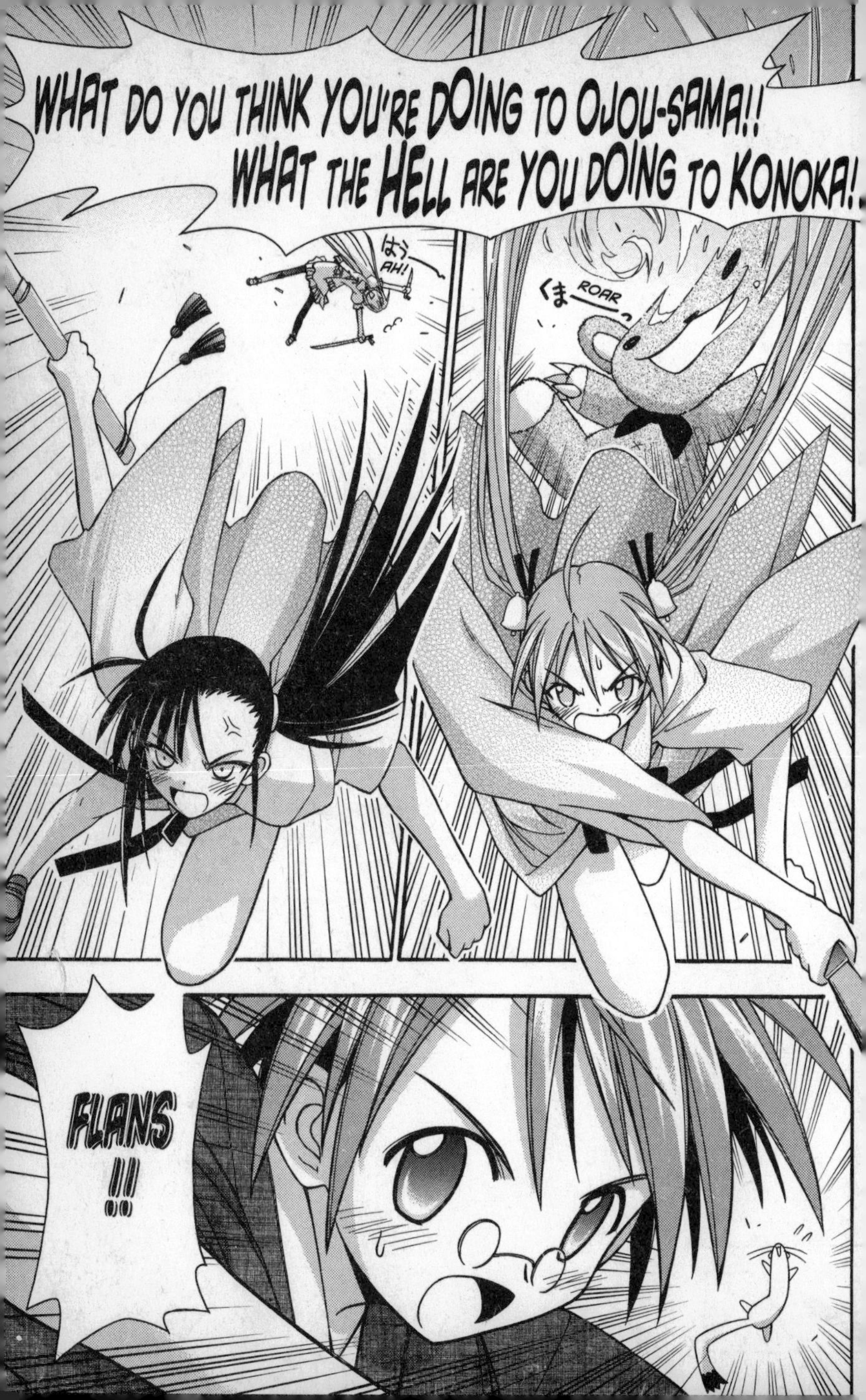
WHAT DO YOU THINK YOU'RE DOING TO OJOU-SAMA!!
WHAT THE HELL ARE YOU DOING TO KONOKA!!
くま ROAR
はう AH!
FLANS !!

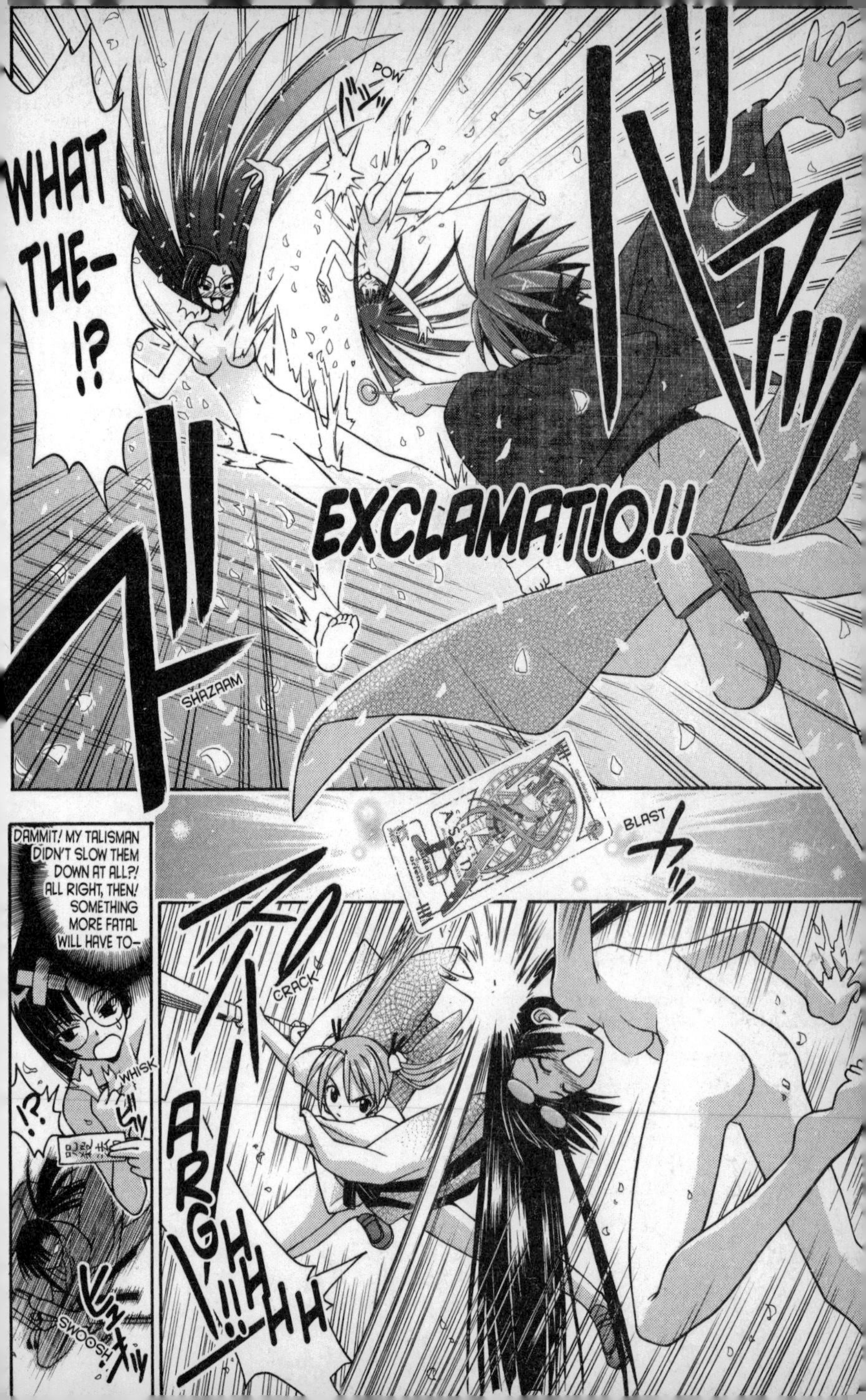
POW
WHAT THE-!?
EXCLAMATIO!!
SHAZAAM
BLAST
CRACK
ARGHHHH!!!
DAMMIT! MY TALISMAN DIDN'T SLOW THEM DOWN AT ALL?! ALL RIGHT, THEN! SOMETHING MORE FATAL WILL HAVE TO–
WHISK
!?
SWOOSH

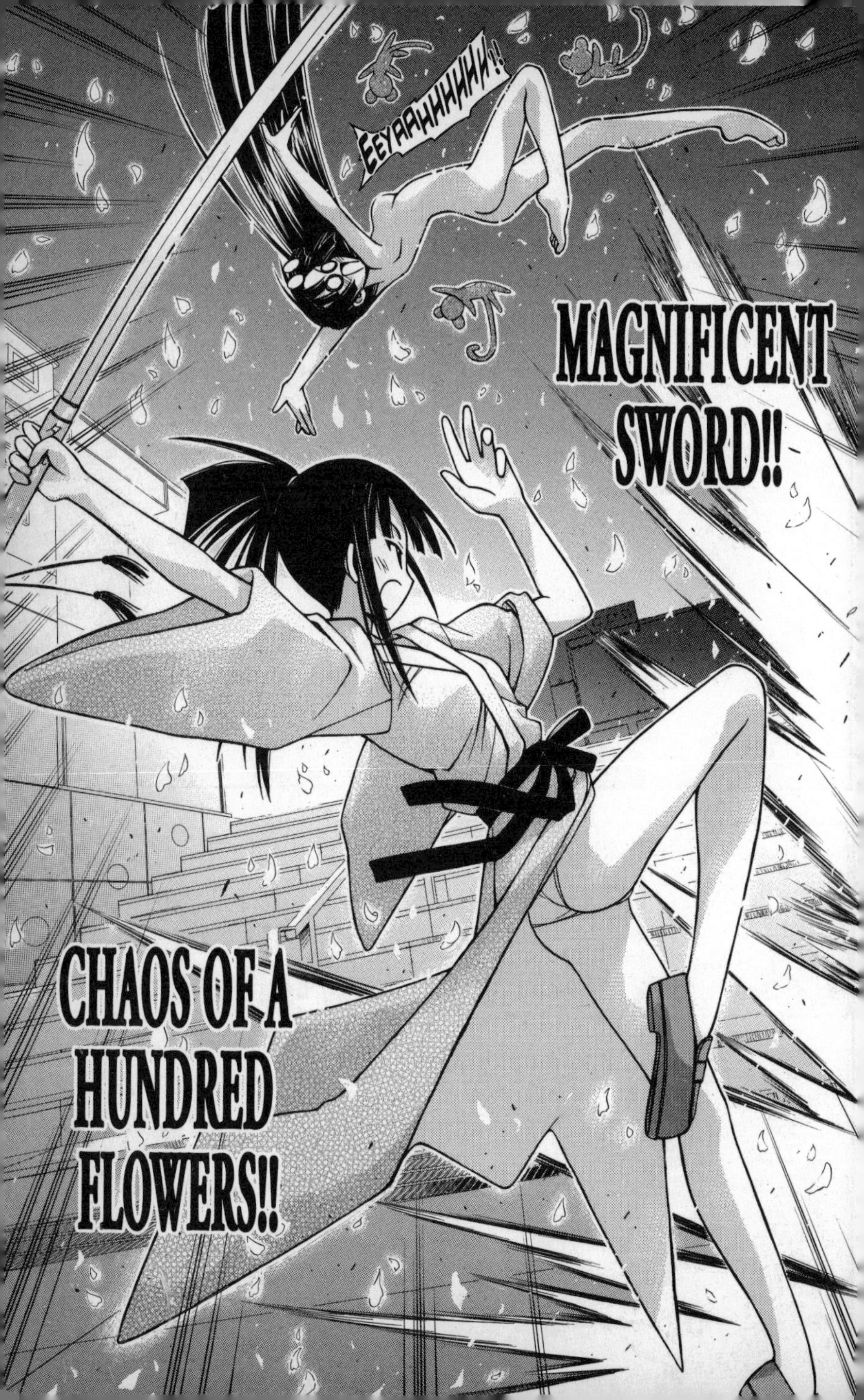
EEYAAHHHHHH!!
MAGNIFICENT SWORD!!
CHAOS OF A HUNDRED FLOWERS!!

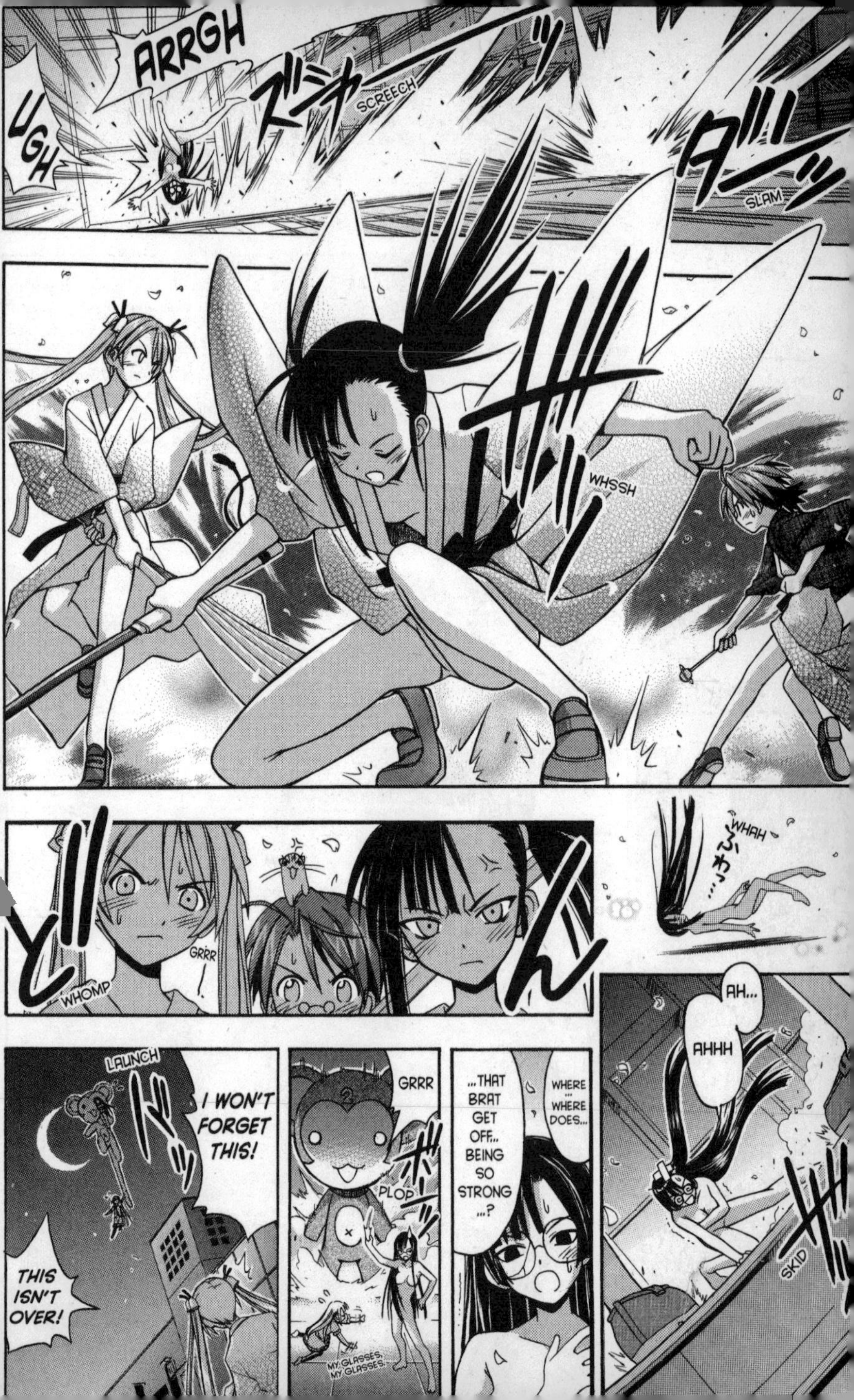
SLAM
SCREECH
ARRGH
UGH
WHSSH
WHAH
GRRR
WHOMP
AH...
AHHH
SKID
WHERE... WHERE DOES...
...THAT BRAT GET OFF... BEING SO STRONG ...?
GRRR
PLOP
MY GLASSES, MY GLASSES.
LAUNCH
I WON'T FORGET THIS!
THIS ISN'T OVER!

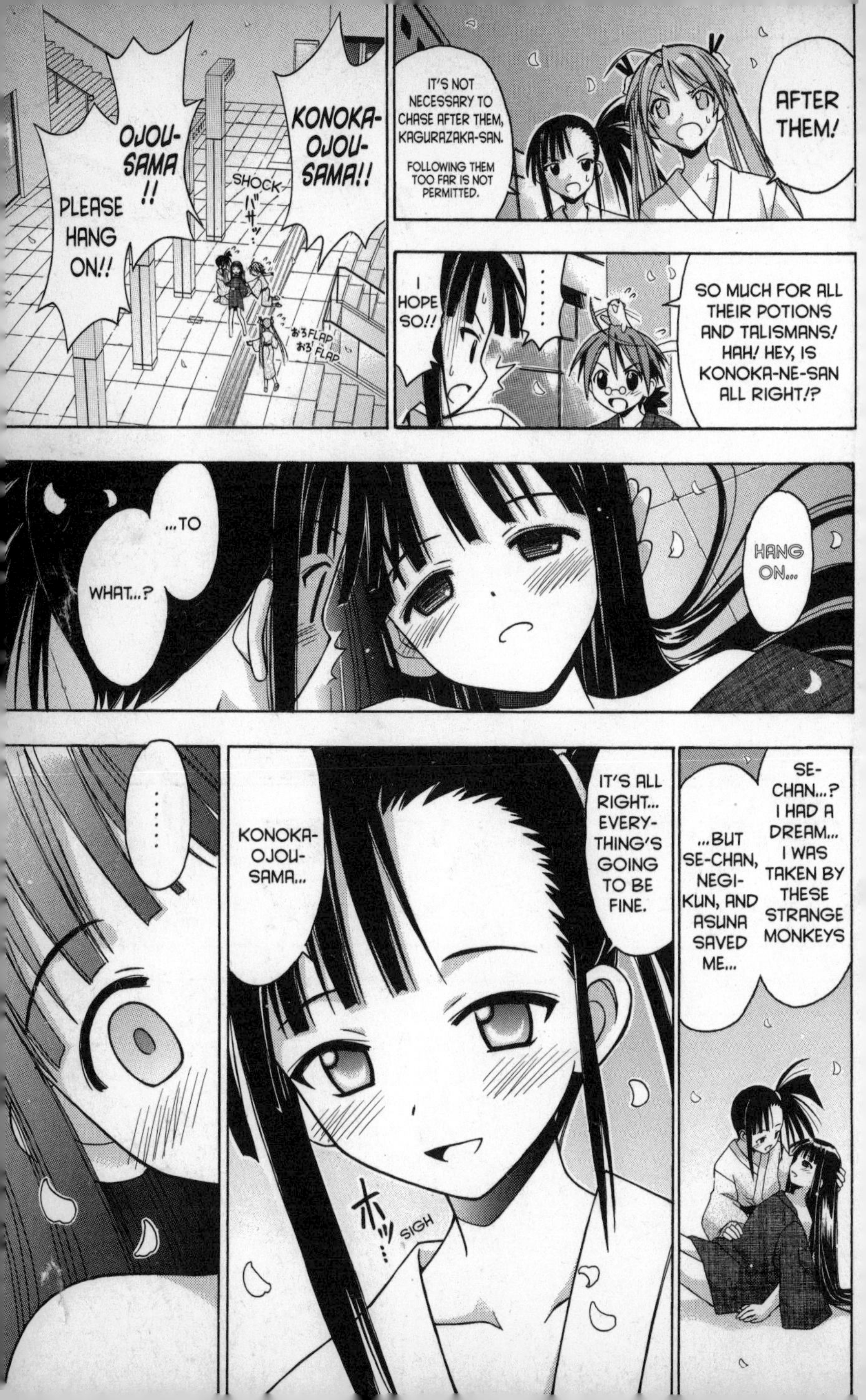
AFTER THEM!
IT'S NOT NECESSARY TO CHASE AFTER THEM, KAGURAZAKA-SAN.
FOLLOWING THEM TOO FAR IS NOT PERMITTED.
SO MUCH FOR ALL THEIR POTIONS AND TALISMANS! HAH! HEY, IS KONOKA-NE-SAN ALL RIGHT!?
......
I HOPE SO!!
KONOKA-OJOU-SAMA!!
SHOCK
OJOU-SAMA!!
PLEASE HANG ON!!
FLAP
FLAP
HANG ON...
...TO WHAT...?
SE-CHAN...? I HAD A DREAM... I WAS TAKEN BY THESE STRANGE MONKEYS
...BUT SE-CHAN, NEGI-KUN, AND ASUNA SAVED ME...
IT'S ALL RIGHT... EVERYTHING'S GOING TO BE FINE.
KONOKA-OJOU-SAMA...
SIGH
......

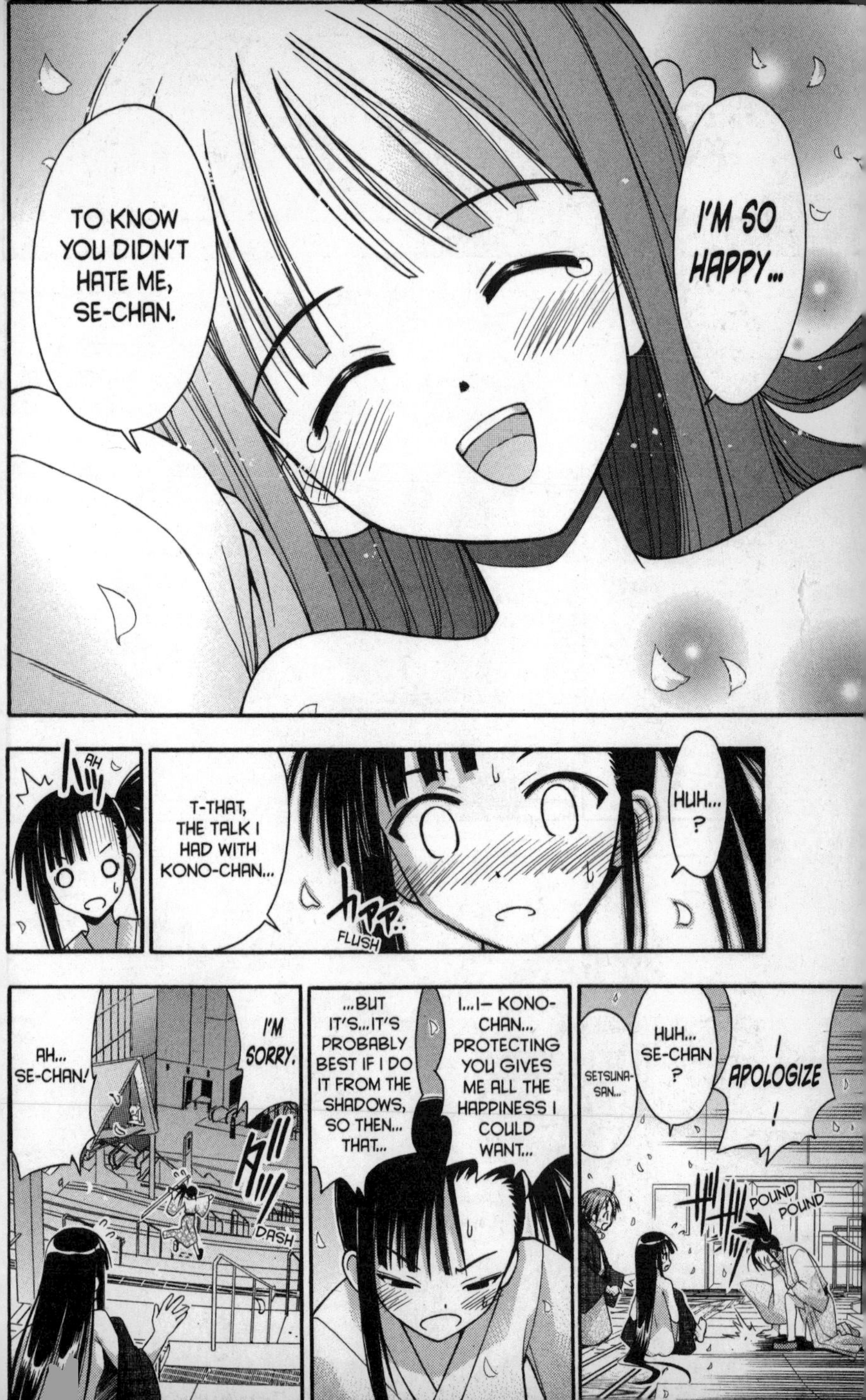
I'M SO HAPPY...
TO KNOW YOU DIDN'T HATE ME, SE-CHAN.
HUH...?
T-THAT, THE TALK I HAD WITH KONO-CHAN...
FLUSH
AH
I APOLOGIZE!
HUH... SE-CHAN?
SETSUNA-SAN...
POUND POUND
I...I— KONO-CHAN... PROTECTING YOU GIVES ME ALL THE HAPPINESS I COULD WANT...
...BUT IT'S...IT'S PROBABLY BEST IF I DO IT FROM THE SHADOWS, SO THEN... THAT...
I'M SORRY.
AH... SE-CHAN!
DASH

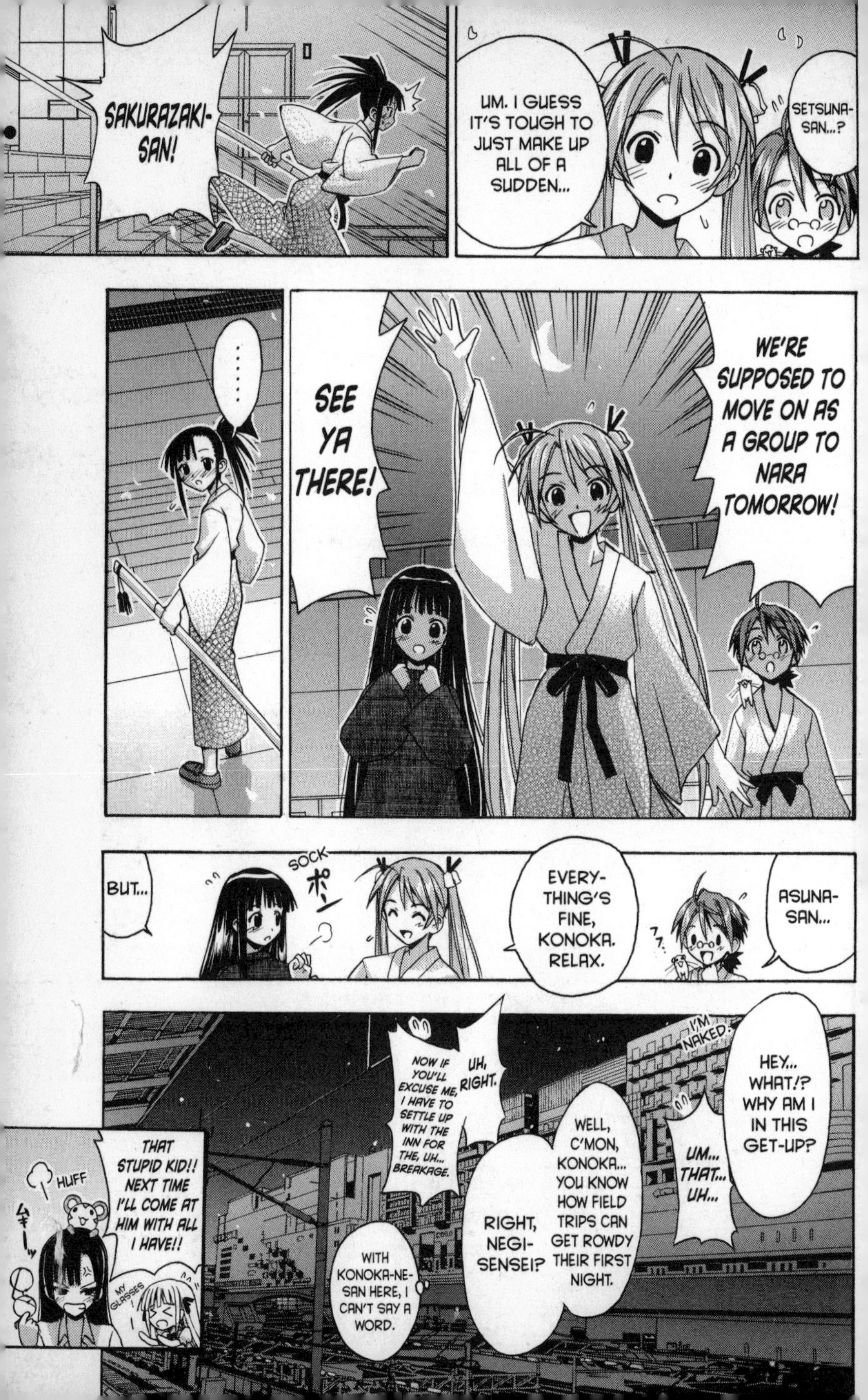
SETSUNA-SAN...?
UM. I GUESS IT'S TOUGH TO JUST MAKE UP ALL OF A SUDDEN...
SAKURAZAKI-SAN!
WE'RE SUPPOSED TO MOVE ON AS A GROUP TO NARA TOMORROW!
SEE YA THERE!
......
ASUNA-SAN...
EVERY-THING'S FINE, KONOKA. RELAX.
SOCK
BUT...
I'M NAKED.
HEY... WHAT!? WHY AM I IN THIS GET-UP?
UM... THAT... UH...
UH, RIGHT.
NOW IF YOU'LL EXCUSE ME, I HAVE TO SETTLE UP WITH THE INN FOR THE, UH... BREAKAGE.
WELL, C'MON, KONOKA... YOU KNOW HOW FIELD TRIPS CAN GET ROWDY THEIR FIRST NIGHT.
RIGHT, NEGI-SENSEI?
WITH KONOKA-NE-SAN HERE, I CAN'T SAY A WORD.
THAT STUPID KID!! NEXT TIME I'LL COME AT HIM WITH ALL I HAVE!!
HUFF
MY GLASSES!

3-A FIELD TRIP GROUPS 2 AND 3

GROUP 2

(GROUP LEADER)

FEI KU

MISORA KASUGA

SHEN RIN

KAEDE NAGASE

SATOMI HAKASE

SATSUKI YOTSUBA

GROUP 3

(GROUP LEADER)

AYAKA YUKIHIRO

KAZUMI ASAKURA

CHITSURU NABA

CHISAME HASEGAWA

NATSUMI MURAKAMI

ZAZIE RAINYDAY

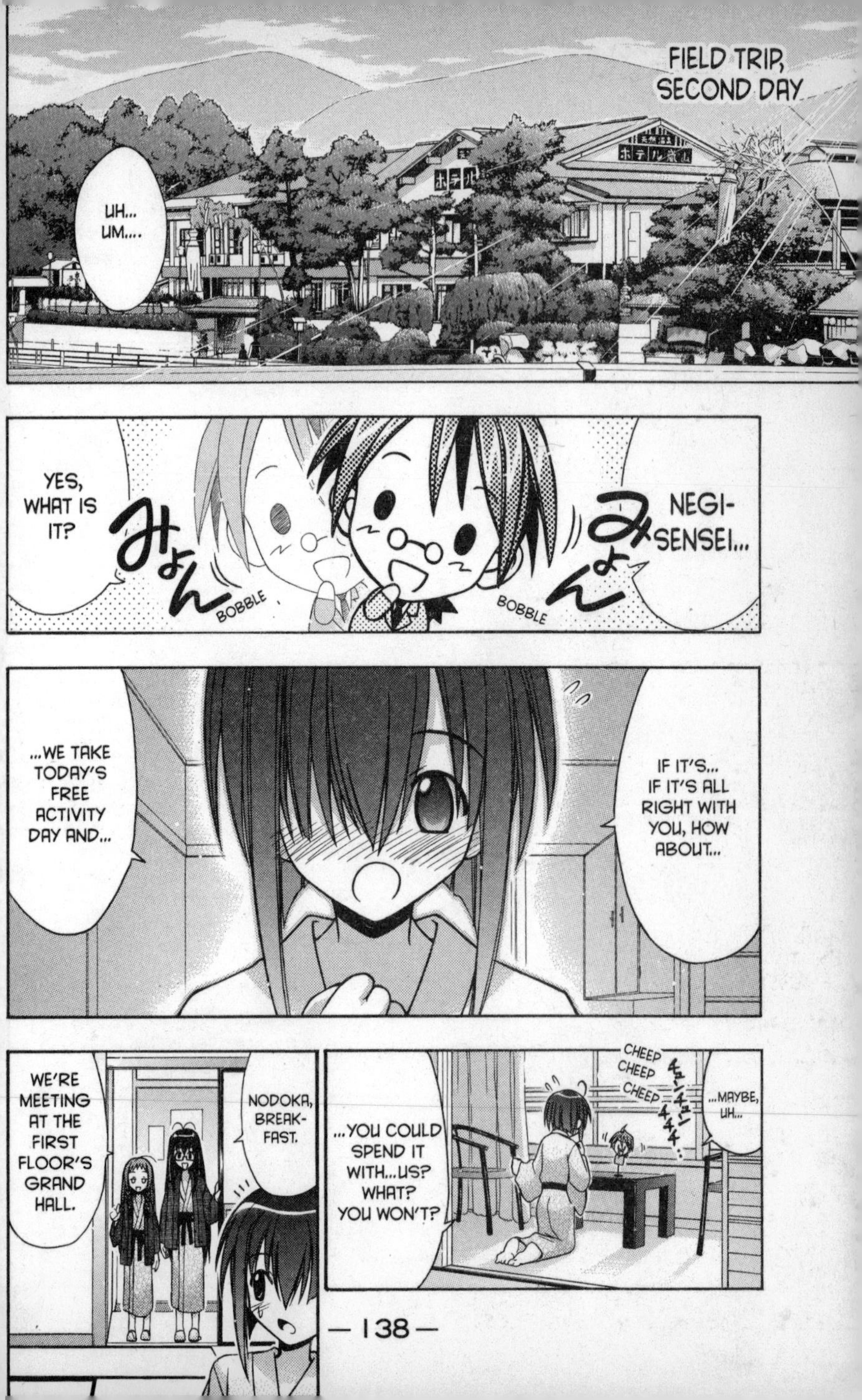
FIELD TRIP, SECOND DAY
UH... UM....
NEGI-SENSEI...
みょん
BOBBLE
YES, WHAT IS IT?
みょん
BOBBLE
IF IT'S... IF IT'S ALL RIGHT WITH YOU, HOW ABOUT...
...WE TAKE TODAY'S FREE ACTIVITY DAY AND...
...MAYBE, UH...
CHEEP CHEEP CHEEP
チュンチュンチチチ…
...YOU COULD SPEND IT WITH...US? WHAT? YOU WON'T?
NODOKA, BREAK-FAST.
WE'RE MEETING AT THE FIRST FLOOR'S GRAND HALL.

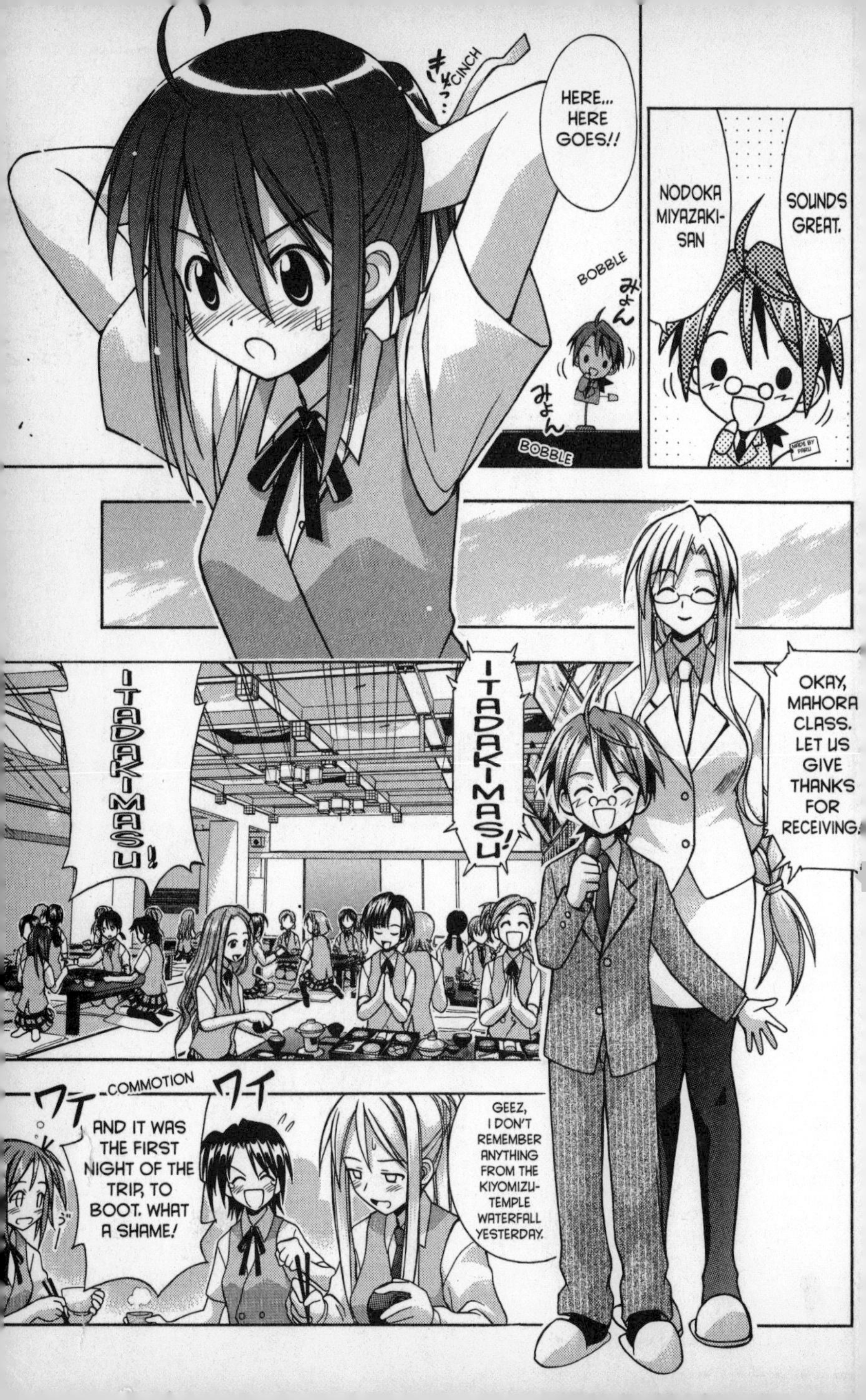
SOUNDS GREAT.
NODOKA MIYAZAKI-SAN
MADE BY PARU
HERE... HERE GOES!!
きゅっ
CINCH
みょん
BOBBLE
みょん
BOBBLE
OKAY, MAHORA CLASS. LET US GIVE THANKS FOR RECEIVING.
ITADAKIMASU!
ITADAKIMASU!!
GEEZ, I DON'T REMEMBER ANYTHING FROM THE KIYOMIZU-TEMPLE WATERFALL YESTERDAY.
ワイ
COMMOTION
ワイ
AND IT WAS THE FIRST NIGHT OF THE TRIP, TO BOOT. WHAT A SHAME!

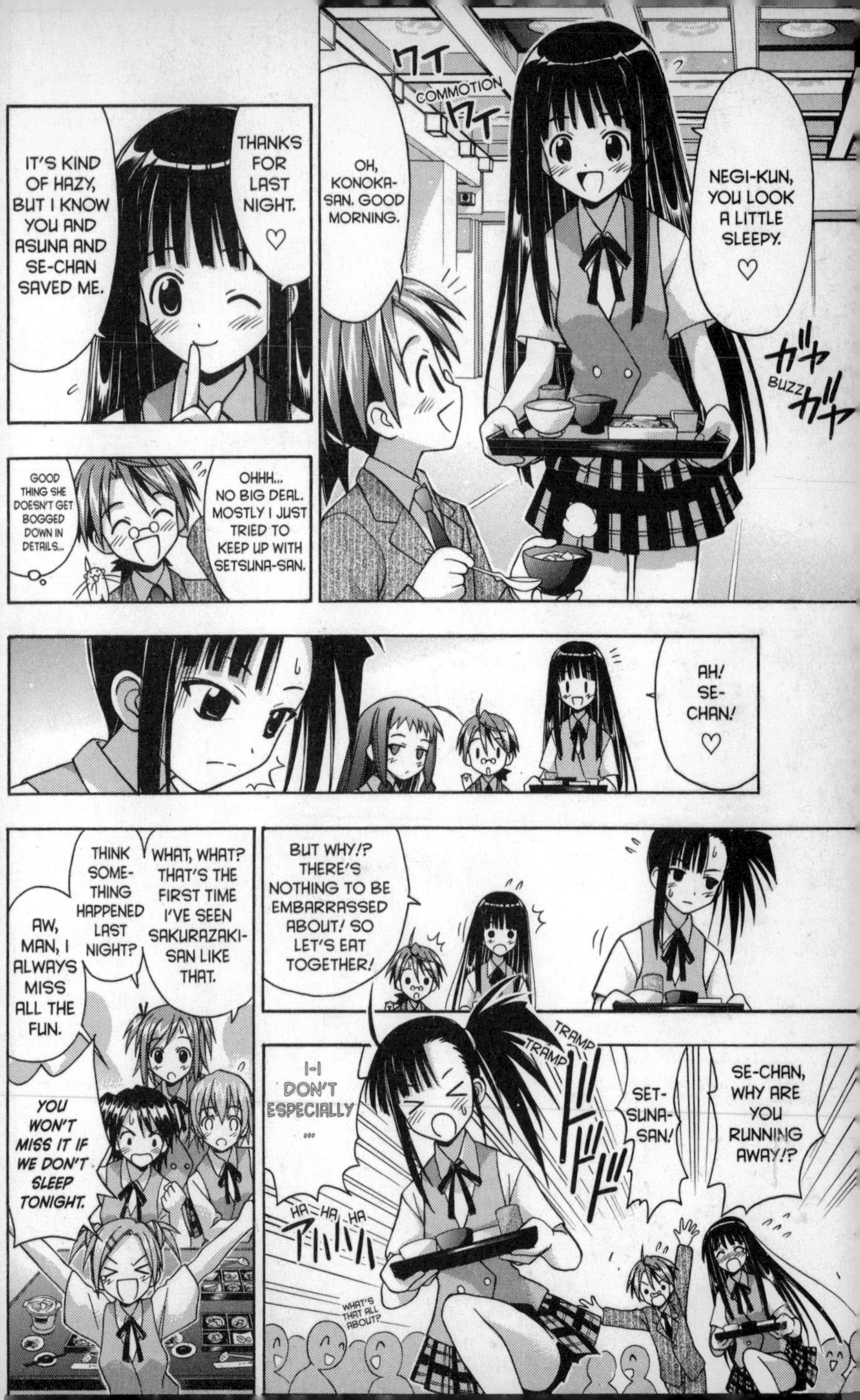

NEGI-KUN, YOU LOOK A LITTLE SLEEPY. ♡
BUZZ
COMMOTION
OH, KONOKA-SAN. GOOD MORNING.
THANKS FOR LAST NIGHT. ♡
IT'S KIND OF HAZY, BUT I KNOW YOU AND ASUNA AND SE-CHAN SAVED ME.
OHHH... NO BIG DEAL. MOSTLY I JUST TRIED TO KEEP UP WITH SETSUNA-SAN.
GOOD THING SHE DOESN'T GET BOGGED DOWN IN DETAILS...
AH! SE-CHAN! ♡
BUT WHY!? THERE'S NOTHING TO BE EMBARRASSED ABOUT! SO LET'S EAT TOGETHER!
SE-CHAN, WHY ARE YOU RUNNING AWAY!?
SET-SUNA-SAN!
TRAMP TRAMP
I-I DON'T ESPECIALLY ...
HA HA HA
WHAT'S THAT ALL ABOUT?
WHAT, WHAT? THAT'S THE FIRST TIME I'VE SEEN SAKURAZAKI-SAN LIKE THAT.
THINK SOMETHING HAPPENED LAST NIGHT?
AW, MAN, I ALWAYS MISS ALL THE FUN.
YOU WON'T MISS IT IF WE DON'T SLEEP TONIGHT.

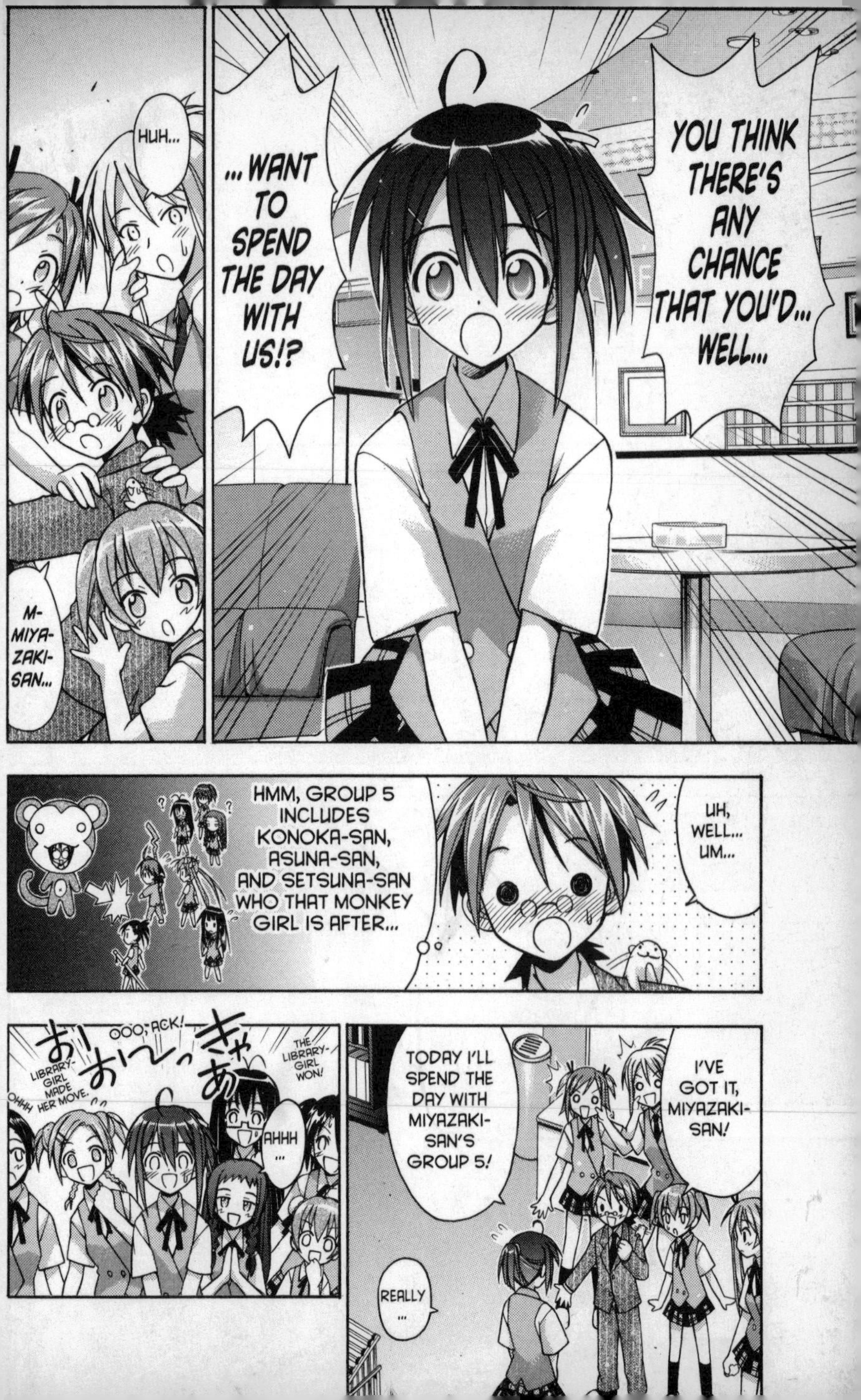
YOU THINK THERE'S ANY CHANCE THAT YOU'D... WELL...
...WANT TO SPEND THE DAY WITH US!?
HUH...
M-MIYAZAKI-SAN...
UH, WELL... UM...
HMM, GROUP 5 INCLUDES KONOKA-SAN, ASUNA-SAN, AND SETSUNA-SAN WHO THAT MONKEY GIRL IS AFTER...
I'VE GOT IT, MIYAZAKI-SAN!
TODAY I'LL SPEND THE DAY WITH MIYAZAKI-SAN'S GROUP 5!
REALLY ...
THE LIBRARY-GIRL WON!
OOO, ACK!
LIBRARY-GIRL MADE HER MOVE.
OHHH
AHHH ...

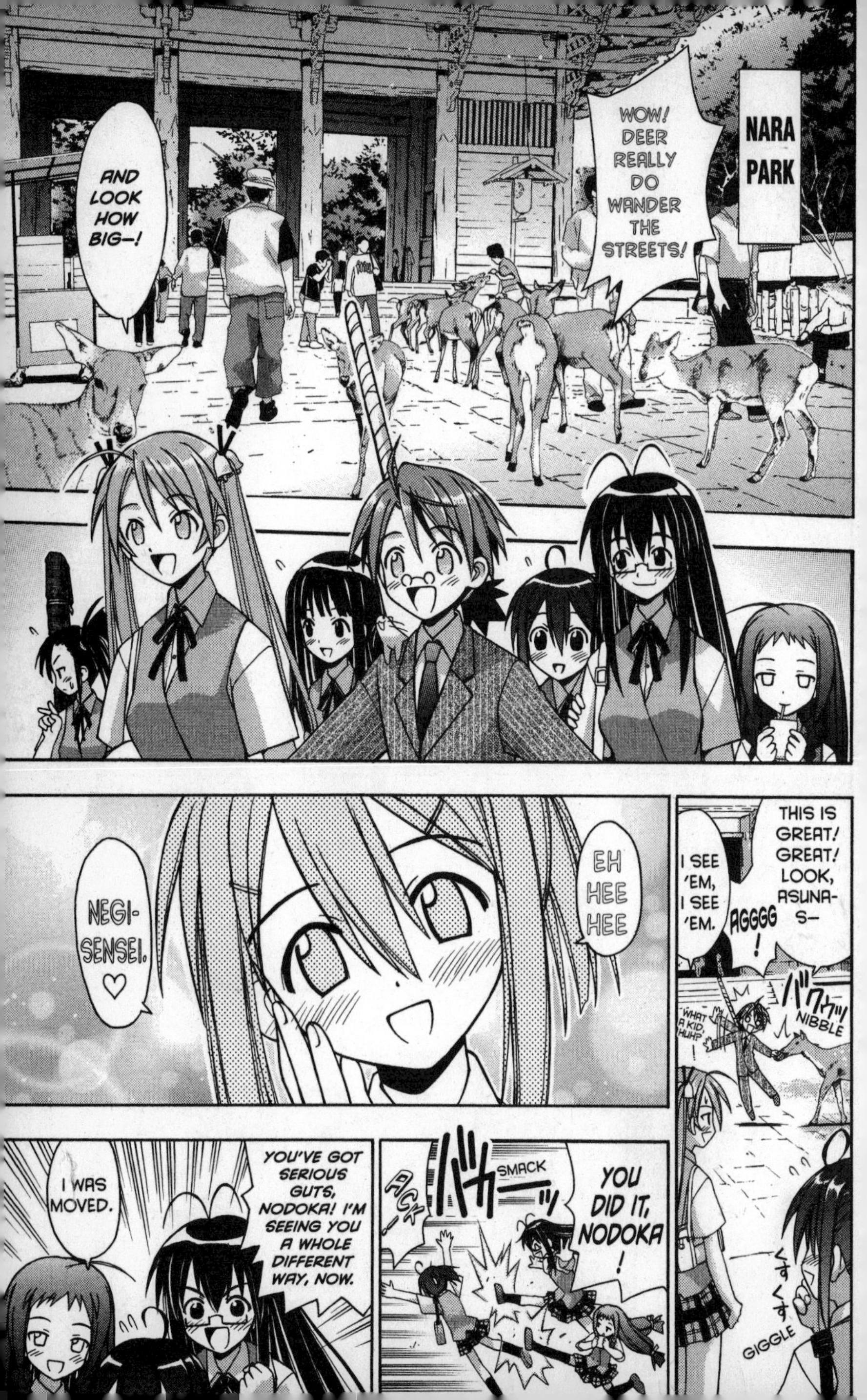
NARA PARK
WOW! DEER REALLY DO WANDER THE STREETS!
AND LOOK HOW BIG—!
THIS IS GREAT! GREAT! LOOK, ASUNA-S—
I SEE 'EM, I SEE 'EM.
AGGGG!
バクッ NIBBLE
WHAT A KID, HUH?!
くすくす GIGGLE
EH HEE HEE
NEGI-SENSEI. ♡
YOU DID IT, NODOKA!
バカーッ SMACK
ACK!
YOU'VE GOT SERIOUS GUTS, NODOKA! I'M SEEING YOU A WHOLE DIFFERENT WAY, NOW.
I WAS MOVED.

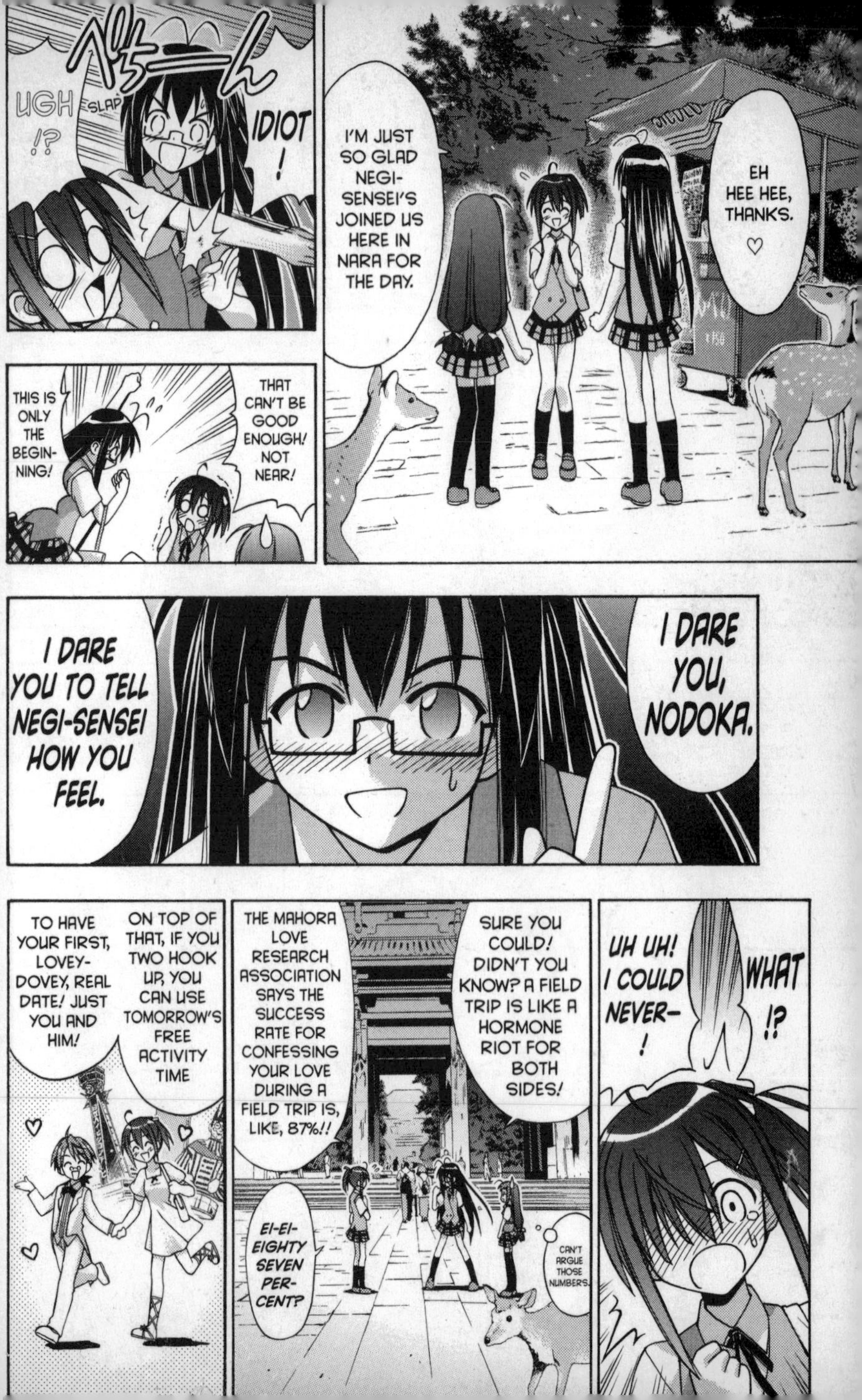
I'M JUST SO GLAD NEGI-SENSEI'S JOINED US HERE IN NARA FOR THE DAY.
EH HEE HEE, THANKS. ♡
ぺちーん
IDIOT!
SLAP
UGH !?
THAT CAN'T BE GOOD ENOUGH! NOT NEAR!
THIS IS ONLY THE BEGINNING!
I DARE YOU, NODOKA.
I DARE YOU TO TELL NEGI-SENSEI HOW YOU FEEL.
WHAT !?
UH UH! I COULD NEVER-!
SURE YOU COULD! DIDN'T YOU KNOW? A FIELD TRIP IS LIKE A HORMONE RIOT FOR BOTH SIDES!
THE MAHORA LOVE RESEARCH ASSOCIATION SAYS THE SUCCESS RATE FOR CONFESSING YOUR LOVE DURING A FIELD TRIP IS, LIKE, 87%!!
EI-EI-EIGHTY SEVEN PER-CENT?
CAN'T ARGUE THOSE NUMBERS.
ON TOP OF THAT, IF YOU TWO HOOK UP, YOU CAN USE TOMORROW'S FREE ACTIVITY TIME
TO HAVE YOUR FIRST, LOVEY-DOVEY, REAL DATE! JUST YOU AND HIM!

I'M SORRY, OJOU-SAMA, BUT I'M TOO BUSY TO—

UH, WHY DO YOU CALL ME OJOUSAMA?

WHAT'S UP WITH YOU GUYS !?

UP? UP!? NOTHING! WHY?

WAIT! まって—!

?

?

SE-CHAN, I BROUGHT SOME DANGOS... YOU KNOW, RICE BALLS. WANNA GO EAT 'EM TOGETHER?

びくっ STUN!?

HEY —!?

キュ RECOIL

アーグ! ARGH!

THWACK

ASUNA! ASUNA! LET'S GO CHECK OUT THE BIG BUDDHA!

SSSSSS ぽっん

AH.

ハッ ハッ TAP TAP

HUH?

PANT PANT

AH, MIYAZAKI-SAN.

AH, UM,

NEGI-SENSEI...

THUMP THUMP

YEAH, I'LL TRY HARD!

TREMBLE ふるふる

YES!

HUH... AH, YEAH! I'D BE HAPPY TO.

WELL...WELL EVERYONE TOOK OFF. YOU WANT TO CHECK THIS PLACE OUT?

PANT PANT ハァ

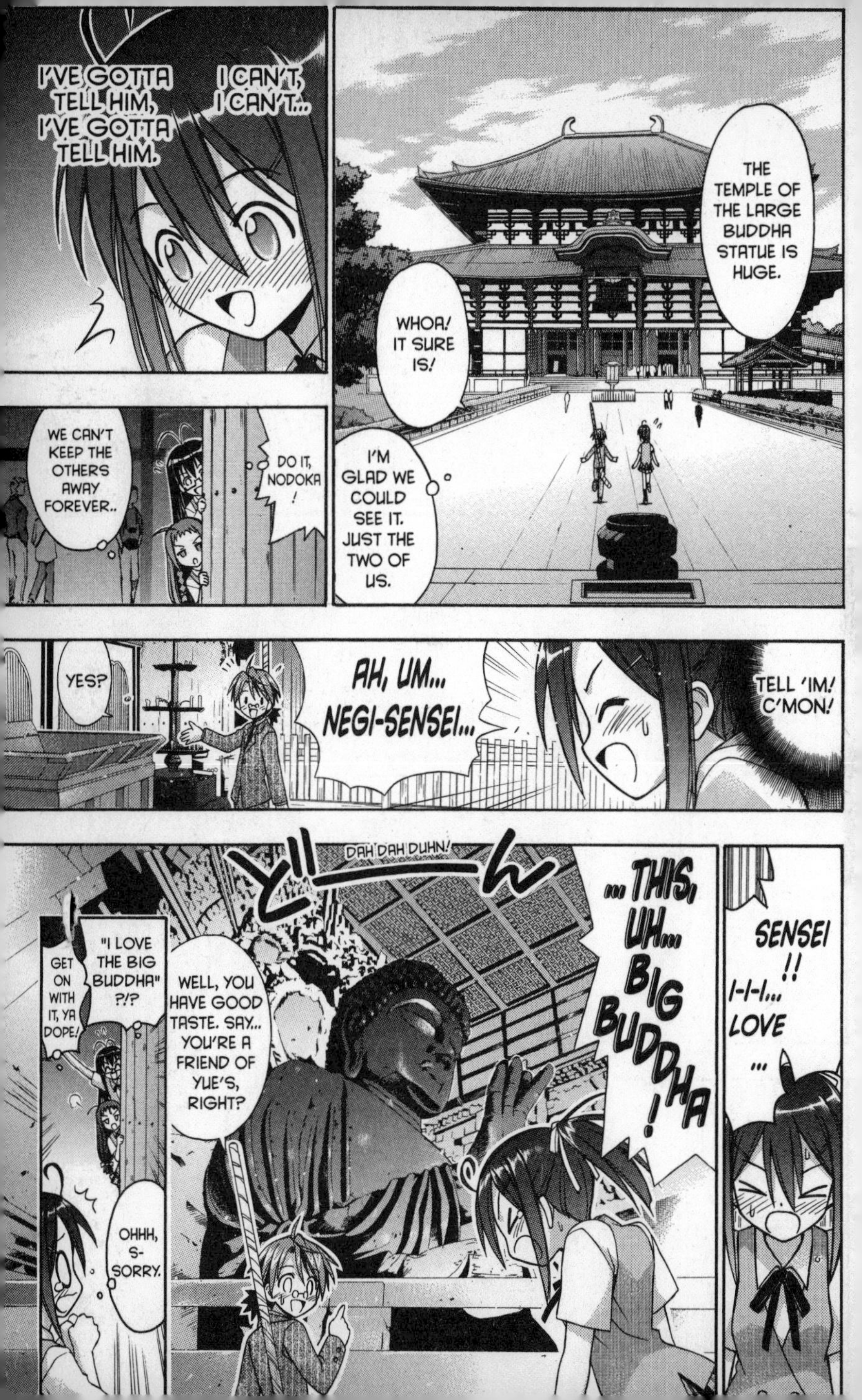
THE TEMPLE OF THE LARGE BUDDHA STATUE IS HUGE.
WHOA! IT SURE IS!
I'M GLAD WE COULD SEE IT. JUST THE TWO OF US.
I CAN'T, I CAN'T...
I'VE GOTTA TELL HIM, I'VE GOTTA TELL HIM.
DO IT, NODOKA!
WE CAN'T KEEP THE OTHERS AWAY FOREVER..
TELL 'IM! C'MON!
AH, UM... NEGI-SENSEI...
YES?
SENSEI!! I-I-I... LOVE...
...THIS, UH... BIG BUDDHA!
DAH DAH DUHN!
WELL, YOU HAVE GOOD TASTE. SAY... YOU'RE A FRIEND OF YUE'S, RIGHT?
OHHH, S-SORRY.
"I LOVE THE BIG BUDDHA" ?!?
GET ON WITH IT, YA DOPE!

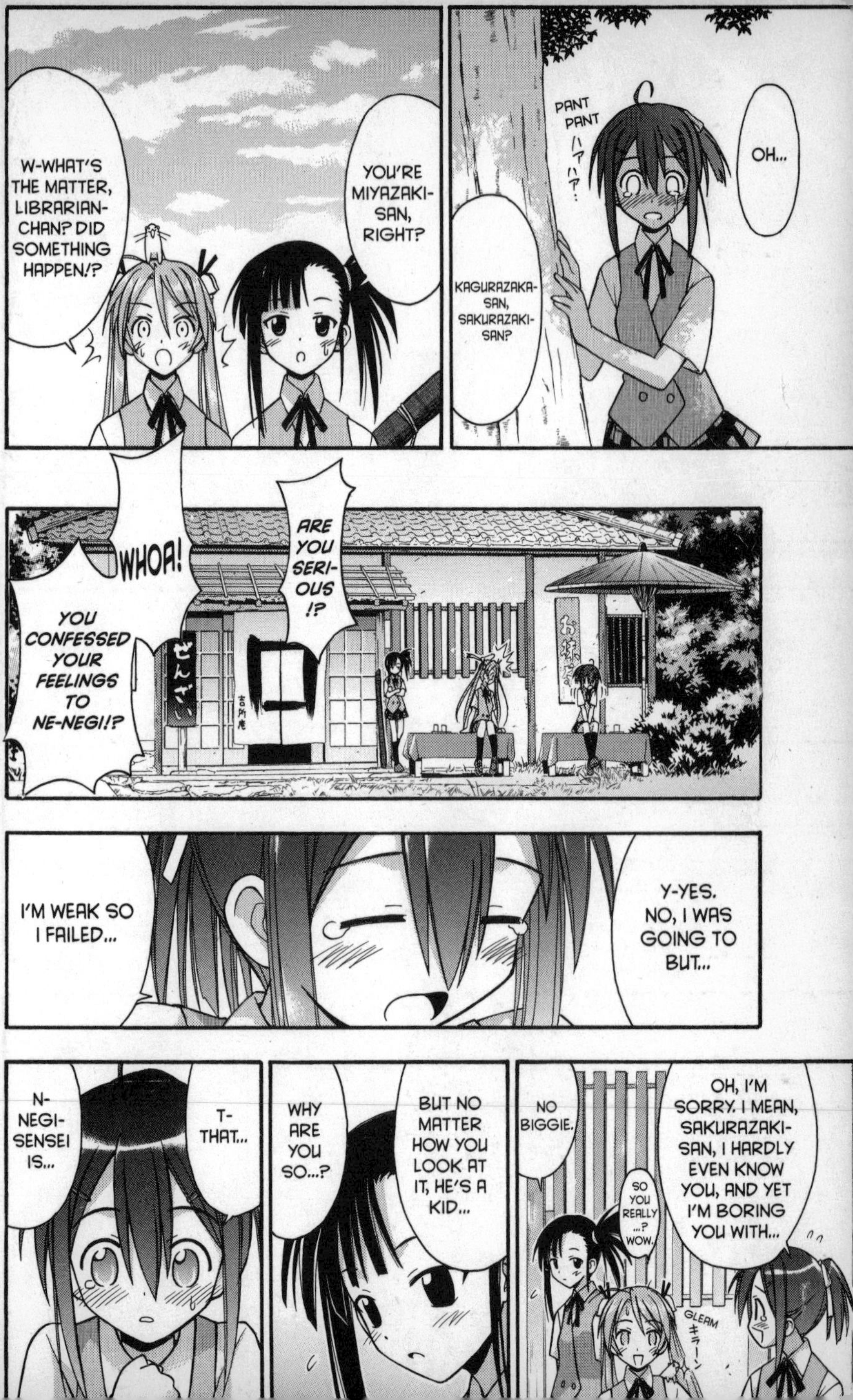
PANT PANT
ハァハァ…
OH...
KAGURAZAKA-SAN, SAKURAZAKI-SAN?
YOU'RE MIYAZAKI-SAN, RIGHT?
W-WHAT'S THE MATTER, LIBRARIAN-CHAN? DID SOMETHING HAPPEN!?
ARE YOU SERIOUS !?
WHOA!
YOU CONFESSED YOUR FEELINGS TO NE-NEGI!?
ぜんざい
Y-YES. NO, I WAS GOING TO BUT...
I'M WEAK SO I FAILED...
OH, I'M SORRY. I MEAN, SAKURAZAKI-SAN, I HARDLY EVEN KNOW YOU, AND YET I'M BORING YOU WITH...
NO BIGGIE.
SO YOU REALLY ...? WOW.
GLEAM
キラーン
BUT NO MATTER HOW YOU LOOK AT IT, HE'S A KID...
WHY ARE YOU SO...?
T-THAT...
N-NEGI-SENSEI IS...

I... I LOVE YOU, NEGI-SENSEI!!

NEGI-SENSEI, I'VE LIKED YOU SINCE THE DAY WE MET.

HUH?

......

I WANTED YOU TO KNOW HOW I FELT.

HITTING YOU WITH THAT OUT OF THE BLUE, IT'S BEGGING FOR TROUBLE. YOU'RE MY TEACHER, AND IT'S...I JUST...

I KNOW...

UH... AH...

......

SHE SAID IT!?

STUDENT NUMBER 3
KAZUMI ASAKURA

BORN: JANUARY 10, 1989
BLOOD TYPE: O
ASTROLOGICAL SIGN: CAPRICORN
LIKES: THE BIG SCOOP, HUMAN-INTEREST
    STORIES, CAMERAS
DISLIKES: GREAT EVIL
AFFILIATIONS: JOURNALISM CLUB, REPORTER
    FOR THE MAHORA NEWSPAPER
NOTES: KNOWN AS THE HUMAN DATABASE
    OF 3-A, SHE HAS A TALENT FOR
    GATHERING INFORMATION. SHE HAS
    EXCELLENT GRADES AND THE FOURTH
    LARGEST BREASTS IN CLASS.

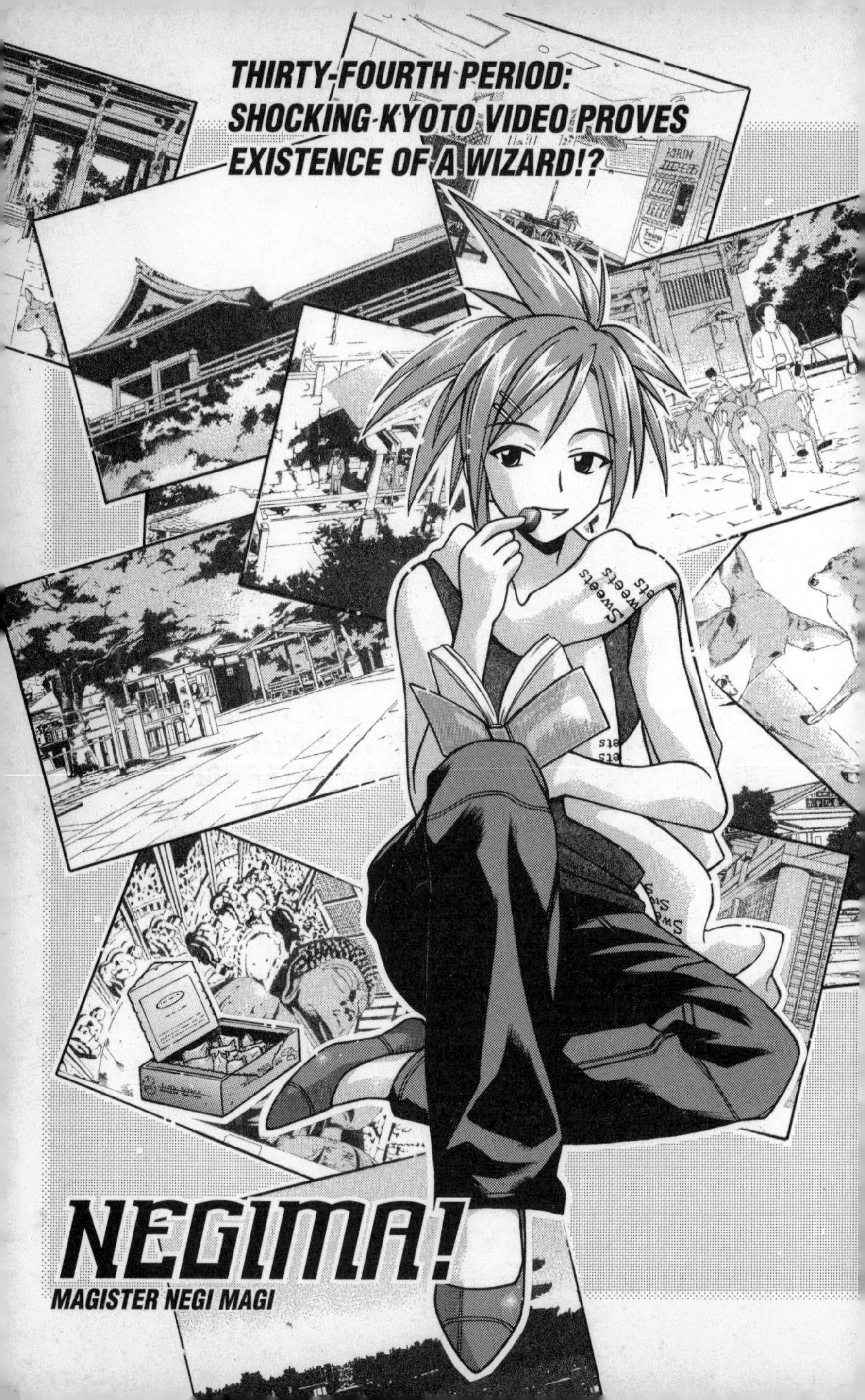
THIRTY-FOURTH PERIOD:
SHOCKING KYOTO VIDEO PROVES
EXISTENCE OF A WIZARD!?
KIRIN
NEGIMA!
MAGISTER NEGI MAGI

CAW
CAW

I... I LOVE YOU, NEGI-SENSEI!!

NEGI-SENSEI, I'VE LIKED YOU SINCE THE DAY WE MET.

CRUNCH
CRUNCH

MIYAZAKI-SAN...

...TOLD ME SHE LOVED ME.

YOU KNOW A TEACHER CAN'T TAKE ADVANTAGE OF A STUDENT LIKE THAT.

COME ON, NEGI...

NEGI'S OLDER SISTER.

I'LL BE BANNED FROM TEACHING!

WHAHH! I CAN'T DO IT!

AS AN ENGLISH GENTLEMAN, I...I HAVE TO DEAL WITH THIS AS AN ADULT...

DONG
DONG

JAPANESE GIRLS... THEY'RE SUPPOSED TO BE SO... I DUNNO... SHY! AND SHE COMES RIGHT OUT AND TELLS ME THIS... THIS HEARTFELT...

B-BUT I'M STILL TEN YEARS OLD...

ザワ HULLABALOO ザワ

ON TOP OF THE LETTER THING, NOW I GOTTA DEAL WITH THIS?!

TUMBLE ゴロゴロ

AW MAN!

MAYBE HE ATE SOMETHING BAD?

SOMETHING'S UP. THIS DOESN'T SEEM LIKE AN ORDINARY MATTER.

WHAT'S WRONG WITH NEGI-KUN?

HE'S BEEN ACTING STRANGE SINCE WE GOT BACK.

NOBODY TOLD ME THEY LOVED ME OR ANYTHING...

N-NO, NOTHING AT ALL...

DID SOMETHING HAPPEN THIS AFTERNOON AT NARA PARK, NEGI-KUN?

NEGI-SENSEI, WHAT'S THE MATTER?

WHAT!? 何!?

WHOA! NO KIDDING, NEGI-KUN! WHO WAS IT?

WHAT!? LOVED YOU?!

N-NOW I'M IN THE SOUP!!

EEYAH!

AND A MAJOR SCOOP...

...IF IT'S TRUE.

YEP, YEP.

T-THAT'S RIGHT. IT'S AN INDECENT SITUATION, ASAKURA.

LEAVE IT TO ME: 3-A'S OFFICIAL CAMERAMAN, KAZUMI ASAKURA OF THE MAHORA JOURNALISM CLUB'S STORM SQUAD.

IF THERE'S A SCOOP, WE CHECK IT OUT WITHOUT DELAY!

WHAT!? HOW THE HELL IS THAT INDECENT!?

SOMEONE TOLD NEGI-SENSEI THEY LOVED HIM.

W-WHAT ARE YOU SAYING!? THAT'S INDECENT ENOUGH!!

SEE, DURING THE WHOLE GROUP ACTIVITY AT NARA PARK...

UH HUH...

WELL, ABOUT THAT...

OKAY, SO... WHO'S DOING WHO? NITSUTA? SERUHIKO?

WE KNEW WE COULD TRUST YOU TO GET THE JOB DONE.

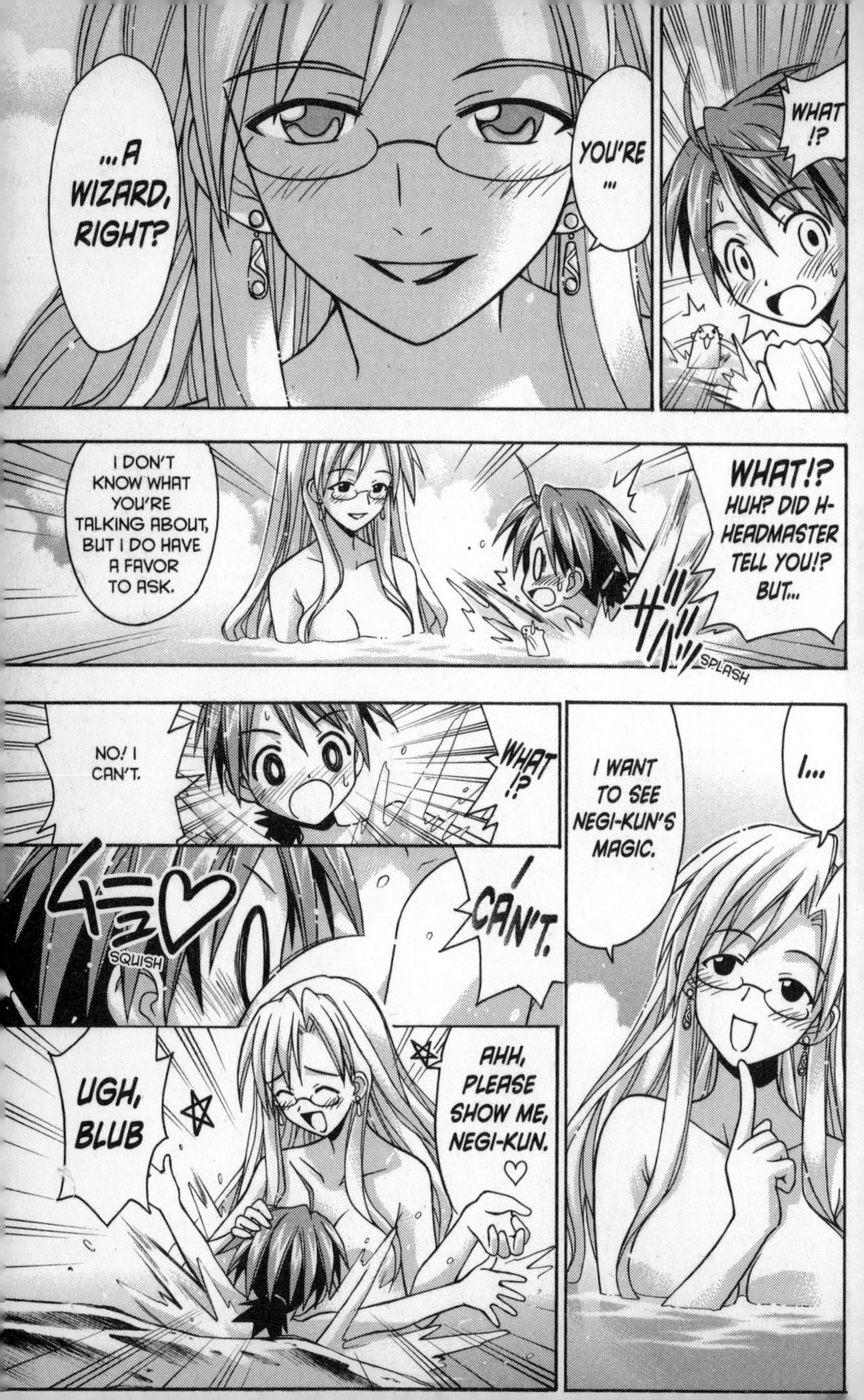
WHAT !?
YOU'RE ...
...A WIZARD, RIGHT?
WHAT!? HUH? DID H-HEADMASTER TELL YOU!? BUT...
SPLASH
I DON'T KNOW WHAT YOU'RE TALKING ABOUT, BUT I DO HAVE A FAVOR TO ASK.
I...
I WANT TO SEE NEGI-KUN'S MAGIC.
WHAT !?
NO! I CAN'T.
I CAN'T.
ムニュ♡
SQUISH
AHH, PLEASE SHOW ME, NEGI-KUN. ♡
UGH, BLUB

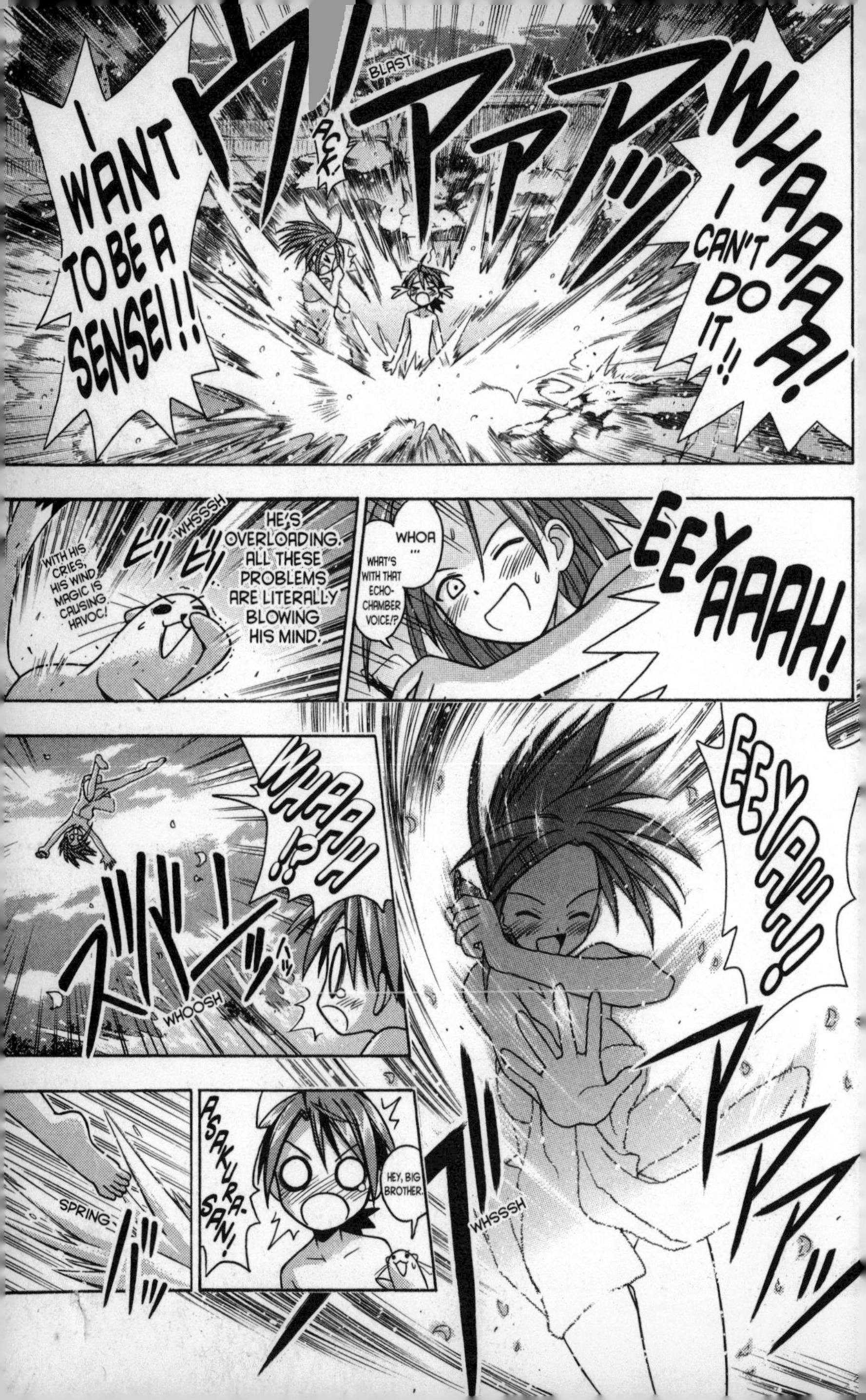

WHAAAAA!
I CAN'T DO IT!!
BLAST
ACK!
I WANT TO BE A SENSEI!!
EEYAAAH!
WHOA...
WHAT'S WITH THAT ECHO-CHAMBER VOICE!?
HE'S OVERLOADING. ALL THESE PROBLEMS ARE LITERALLY BLOWING HIS MIND.
WHSSSH
WITH HIS CRIES, HIS WIND MAGIC IS CAUSING HAVOC!
EEYAAAA!
WHSSSH
WHAAA!!?
WHOOSH
HEY, BIG BROTHER.
ASAKURA-SAN!
SPRING

BANG BANG BANG

HEY, WAIT A SEC. WHAT? THOSE SOBS JUST NOW...!?

AH...

NUTS! MY CELL PHONE IS BROKEN.

UH... ...HUH?

······

SPLASH

OH, NO. THIS IS...

ASAKURA-SAN!?

NEGI-KUN!?

BONG!!

UH!?

WHAT THE?

OH, ASUNA-SAN.

NEGI! WHAT'S GOING ON HERE?

ACK! HELP ME!

GETTING NAKED WITH THE SUBJECT?

SHRIEK SHRIEK SHRIEK

IS THIS YOUR IDEA OF JOURNALISTIC INVESTIGATION?

FLUTTER

YOU'VE GOT SPUNK. I LIKE SPUNK.

NOT NECESSARILY, NE-SAN!!

WIZARDS ARE A MAJOR PAIN.

SMART

BOP!!

OWWWW. WELL, I BLEW THAT SCOOP.

(CONTINUED IN VOLUME 5)

– STAFF –

Ken Akamatsu
Takashi Takemoto
Kenichi Nakamura
Masaki Ohyama
Keiichi Yamashita
Chigusa Amagasaki
Takaaki Miyahara

Thanks To

Ran Ayanaga

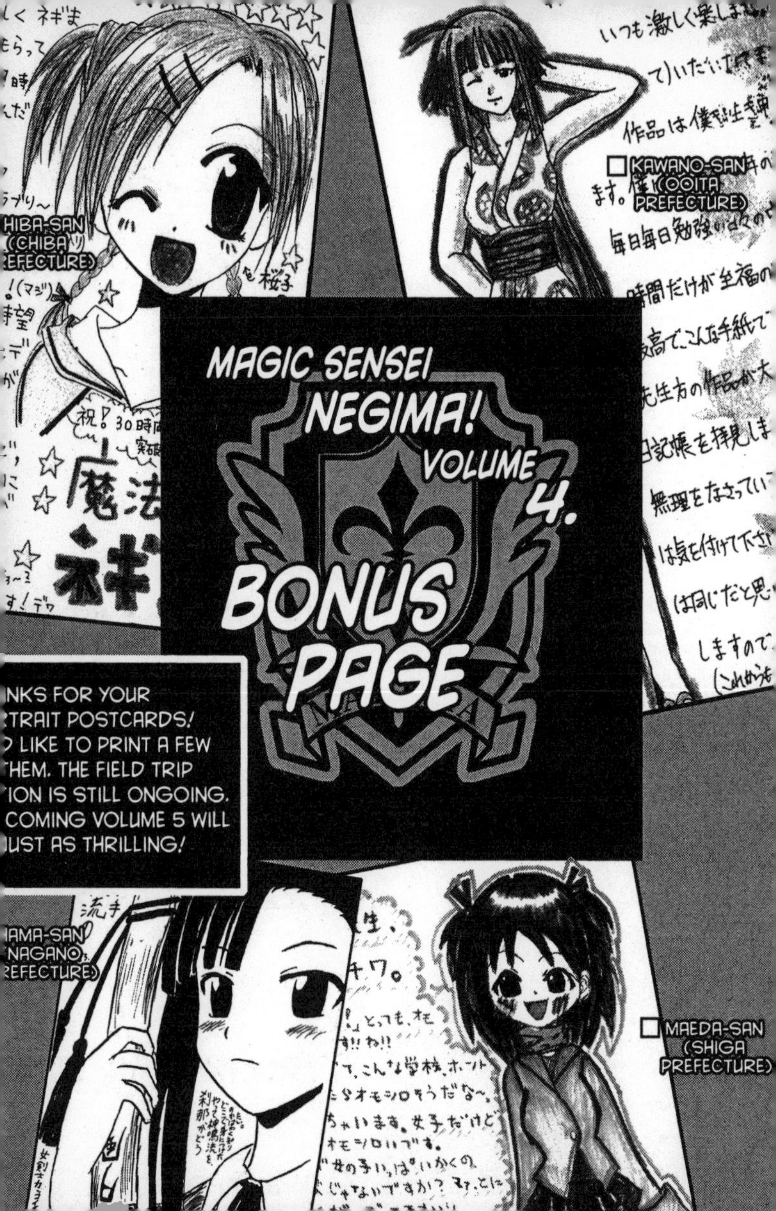
MAGIC SENSEI NEGIMA! VOLUME 4.
BONUS PAGE
NKS FOR YOUR
RTRAIT POSTCARDS!
D LIKE TO PRINT A FEW
THEM. THE FIELD TRIP
TION IS STILL ONGOING.
COMING VOLUME 5 WILL
UST AS THRILLING!
KAWANO-SAN (OOITA PREFECTURE)
HIBA-SAN (CHIBA REFECTURE)
HAMA-SAN (NAGANO REFECTURE)
MAEDA-SAN (SHIGA PREFECTURE)

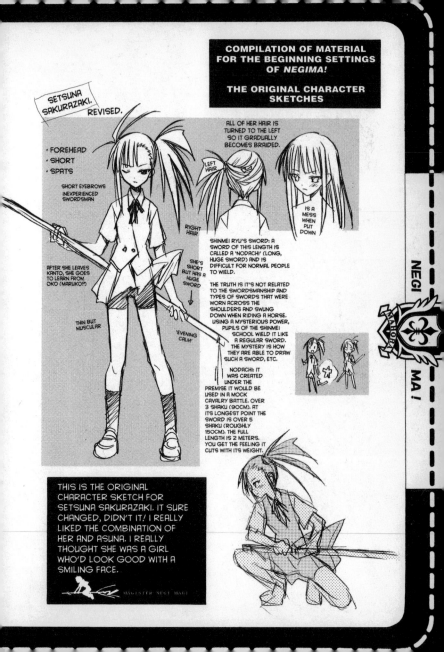

SETSUNA SAKURAZAKI. REVISED.

- FOREHEAD
- SHORT
- SPATS

SHORT EYEBROWS
INEXPERIENCED SWORDSMAN

AFTER SHE LEAVES KANTO, SHE GOES TO LEARN FROM OKO (MARUKO?)

THIN BUT MUSCULAR

ALL OF HER HAIR IS TURNED TO THE LEFT SO IT GRADUALLY BECOMES BRAIDED.

LEFT HAIR

RIGHT HAIR

IS A MESS WHEN PUT DOWN

SHE'S SHORT BUT HAS A HUGE SWORD

'EVENING CALM'

SHINMEI RYU'S SWORD: A SWORD OF THIS LENGTH IS CALLED A 'NODACHI' (LONG, HUGE SWORD) AND IS DIFFICULT FOR NORMAL PEOPLE TO WIELD.

THE TRUTH IS IT'S NOT RELATED TO THE SWORDSMANSHIP AND TYPES OF SWORDS THAT WERE WORN ACROSS THE SHOULDERS AND SWUNG DOWN WHEN RIDING A HORSE. USING A MYSTERIOUS POWER, PUPILS OF THE SHINMEI SCHOOL WIELD IT LIKE A REGULAR SWORD. THE MYSTERY IS HOW THEY ARE ABLE TO DRAW SUCH A SWORD, ETC.

NODACHI: IT WAS CREATED UNDER THE PREMISE IT WOULD BE USED IN A MOCK CAVALRY BATTLE. OVER 3 SHAKU (90CM). AT ITS LONGEST POINT THE SWORD IS OVER 5 SHAKU (ROUGHLY 150CM). THE FULL LENGTH IS 2 METERS. YOU GET THE FEELING IT CUTS WITH ITS WEIGHT.

THIS IS THE ORIGINAL CHARACTER SKETCH FOR SETSUNA SAKURAZAKI. IT SURE CHANGED, DIDN'T IT! I REALLY LIKED THE COMBINATION OF HER AND ASUNA. I REALLY THOUGHT SHE WAS A GIRL WHO'D LOOK GOOD WITH A SMILING FACE.

MAGISTER NEGI MAGI

NEGI

MA!

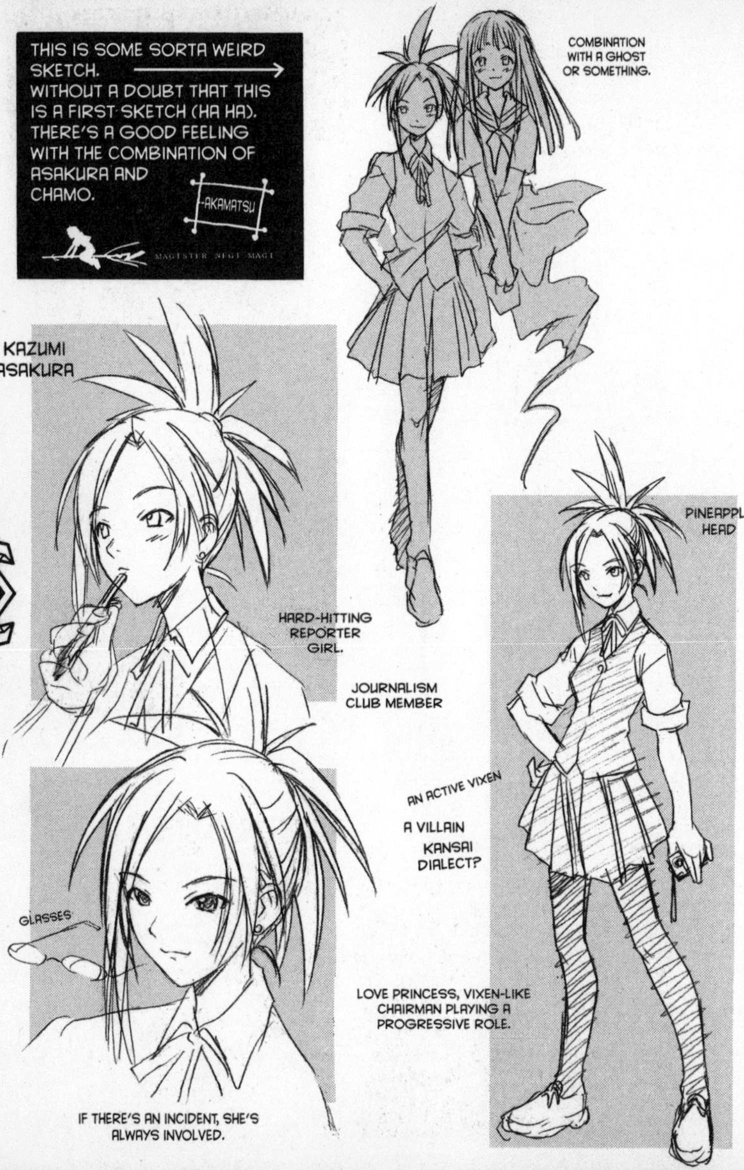
THIS IS SOME SORTA WEIRD SKETCH. →
WITHOUT A DOUBT THAT THIS IS A FIRST SKETCH (HA HA).
THERE'S A GOOD FEELING WITH THE COMBINATION OF ASAKURA AND CHAMO.
-AKAMATSU
MAGISTER NEGI MAGI
COMBINATION WITH A GHOST OR SOMETHING.
KAZUMI ASAKURA
HARD-HITTING REPORTER GIRL.
JOURNALISM CLUB MEMBER
PINEAPPLE HEAD
AN ACTIVE VIXEN
A VILLAIN
KANSAI DIALECT?
GLASSES
LOVE PRINCESS, VIXEN-LIKE CHAIRMAN PLAYING A PROGRESSIVE ROLE.
IF THERE'S AN INCIDENT, SHE'S ALWAYS INVOLVED.

NEGIMA! FASHION CONCEPTS

EXAMPLES OF CLOTHING PROPOSALS.

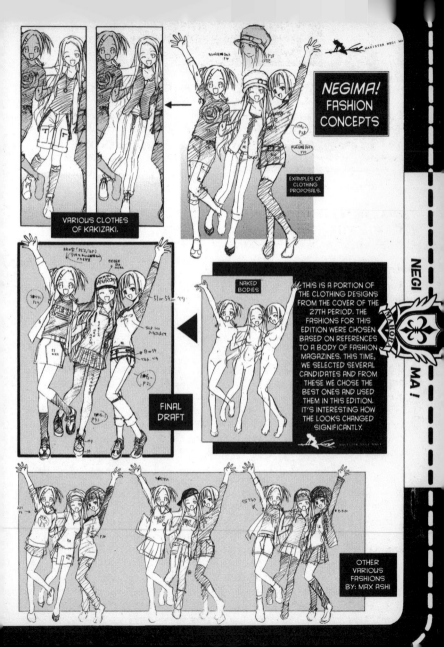

VARIOUS CLOTHES OF KAKIZAKI.

NAKED BODIES

THIS IS A PORTION OF THE CLOTHING DESIGNS FROM THE COVER OF THE 27TH PERIOD. THE FASHIONS FOR THIS EDITION WERE CHOSEN BASED ON REFERENCES TO A BODY OF FASHION MAGAZINES. THIS TIME, WE SELECTED SEVERAL CANDIDATES AND FROM THESE WE CHOSE THE BEST ONES AND USED THEM IN THIS EDITION. IT'S INTERESTING HOW THE LOOKS CHANGED SIGNIFICANTLY.

ANARCHY

FINAL DRAFT

OTHER VARIOUS FASHIONS BY: MAX ASHI

LEXICON
NEGIMARIUM DE CANTU
Negima! Glossary Of Spells

Thirty-first and Thirty-second Periods

Telepathia. (Telepathic Communication.) Telepathia comes from the Greek and means here "a remotely distant sensitivity." Wizards and their partners are able to use their card's power to communicate. However, Negi and Asuna couldn't communicate with each other both ways. It appears that two-way communication needs to have some sort of additional requirement filled.

Flet, une vente. Flans saltatio pulverea. (Blow! Gust of Wind! Wind Flower! Wind And Dirt, Dance Wildly!) Magic that causes a powerful wind. "Dance of wind blown dirt."

Exerceas potentiam Cagurazaca Asuna. (Abilities Activate, Asuna Kagurazaka.) With the establishment of a contract, the wizard's partner gains strength in both body and mind. Depending on each one's unique destiny, they receive different benefits and powers. *Potentia* indicates the powers (related to that, the overt powers are referred to as "*vis*"). The folding fan that Asuna was given is one of those powers.

Ensis exorcizans. (Evil Destroying Sword.) As per the contract, this is the exclusive tool given to Negi's partner, Asuna Kagurazaka. *Exorcizans* means "exorcise magic" and *ensis* is a long sword. In short, "Evil Destroying Sword" can also be called a "Magic Destroying Sword." However, for some reason, Asuna's tool is a folding fan. Additionally, Negi refers to this exclusive item as an artifact, which comes from the Latin, *artifactum,* something made by a skilled craftsman.

Thirty-fourth Period

Flans paries aerialis. (Wind Flower! Wall of Wind!) It's common for wizards to protect themselves from physical harm by surrounding the area around themselves with a magic barrier (refer to the Evangeline story in the Twenty-fourth and Twenty-fifth Periods in *Negima!* Volume 3). In the First Period, Negi also did this when he made the blackboard eraser that was going to fall on his head float in the air. However, it is necessary for Negi (who learned an important lesson when Asuna found out about his magic this way) to recite the spell over again in order to disperse it and not surround himself with the barrier in everyday life.

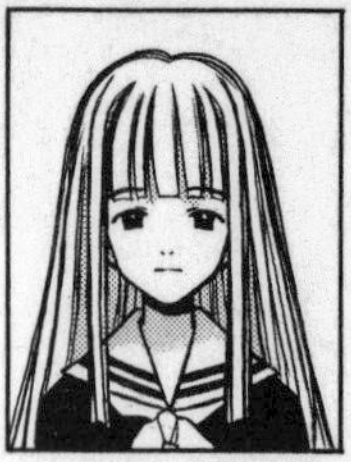

1. SAYO AIZAKA

1940~
DON'T CHANGE HER SEATING

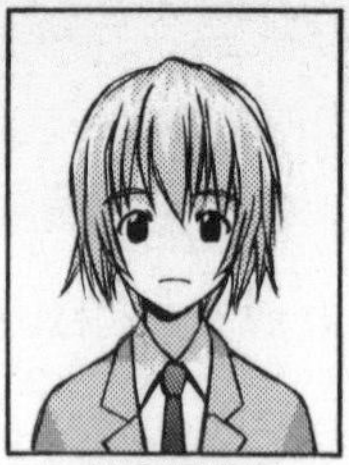

5. AKO IZUMI

NURSE'S OFFICE
SOCCER TEAM
(NON-SCHOOL ACTIVITY)

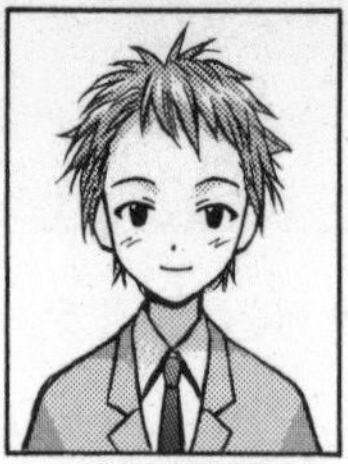

9. KASUGA MISORA

GRANDAUGHTER OF
SCHOOL DEAN

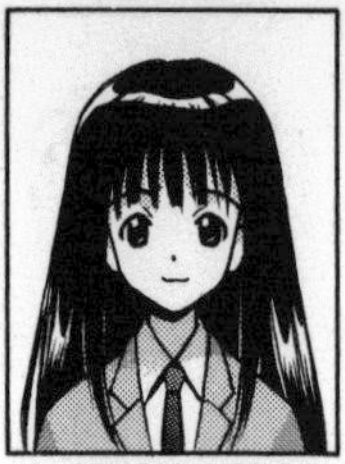

13. KONOKA KONOE

SECRETARY
FORTUNE-TELLING CLUB
LIBRARY CLUB

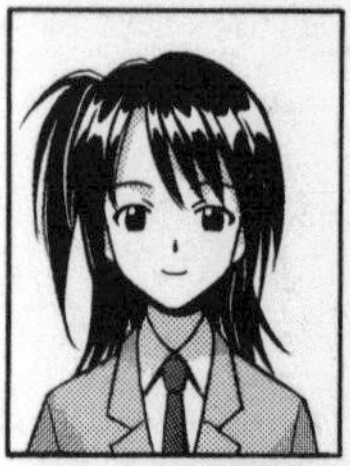

2. YUNA AKASHI

BASKETBALL TEAM

PROFESSOR AKASHI'S DAUGHTER

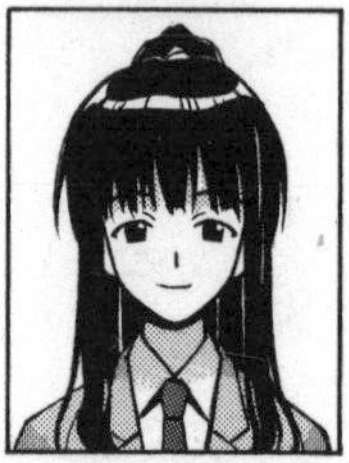

6. AKIRA OKOCHI

SWIM TEAM

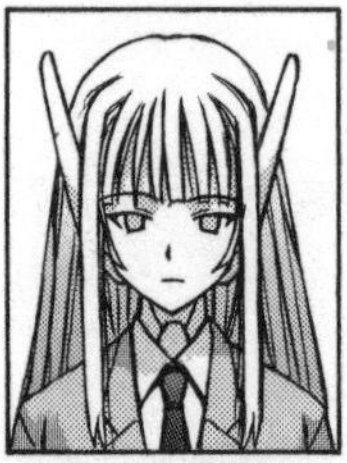

10. CHACHAMARU RAKUSO

TEA CEREMONY CLUB
GO CLUB

CALL ENGINEERING (ext. A08-7796)
IN CASE OF EMERGENCY

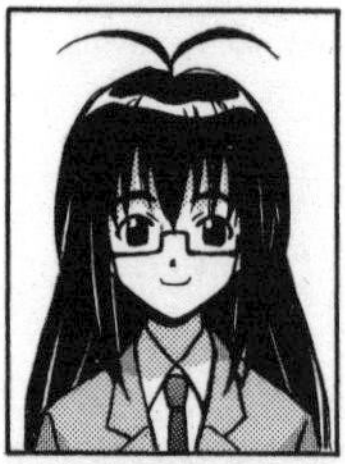

14. HARUNA SAOTOME

MANGA CLUB
LIBRARY CLUB

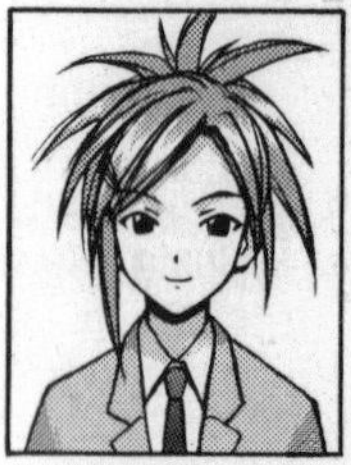

3. KAZUMI ASAKURA

SCHOOL NEWSPAPER

MAHORA NEWS (ext. B09-3780)

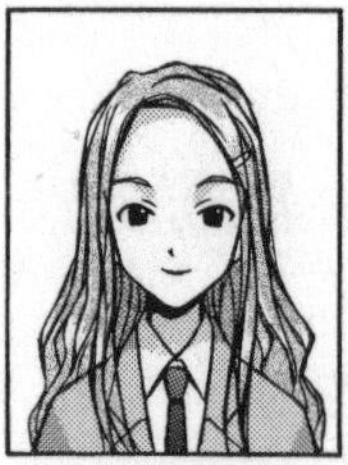

7. KAKIZAKI MISA

CHEERLEADER
CHORUS

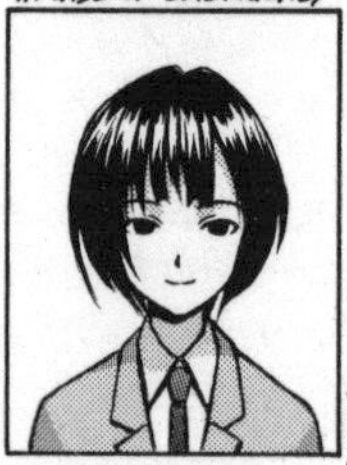

MADOKA

11. MADOKA KUGIMIYA

CHEERLEADER

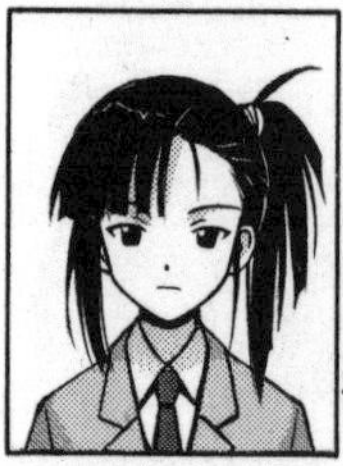

SETSUNA SAKURAZAKI

15 SETSUNA SAKURAZAKI

JAPANESE FENCING

KYOTO SHINMEI STYLE

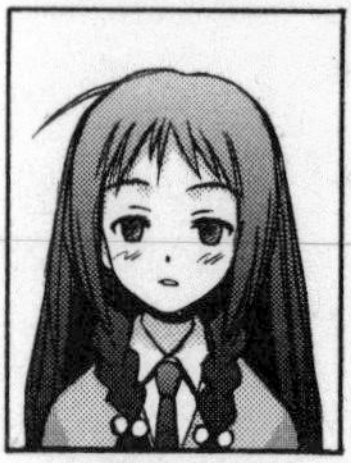

4. YUE AYASE

KID'S LIT CLUB
PHILOSOPHY CLUB
LIBRARY CLUB

A GOOD PERSON JUST
AS I THOUGHT.

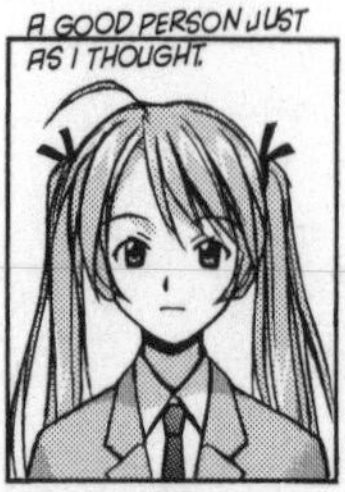

8. ASUNA KAGURAZAKA

ART CLUB

HAS A TERRIBLE KICK

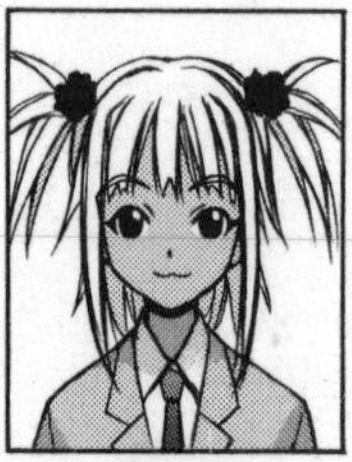

FEI KU

12. FEI KU

CHINESE MARTIAL ARTS
GROUP

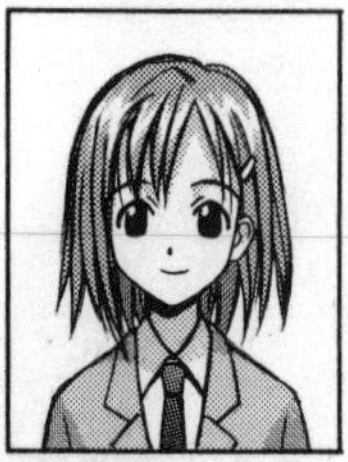

16. MAKIE SASAKI

GYMNASTICS

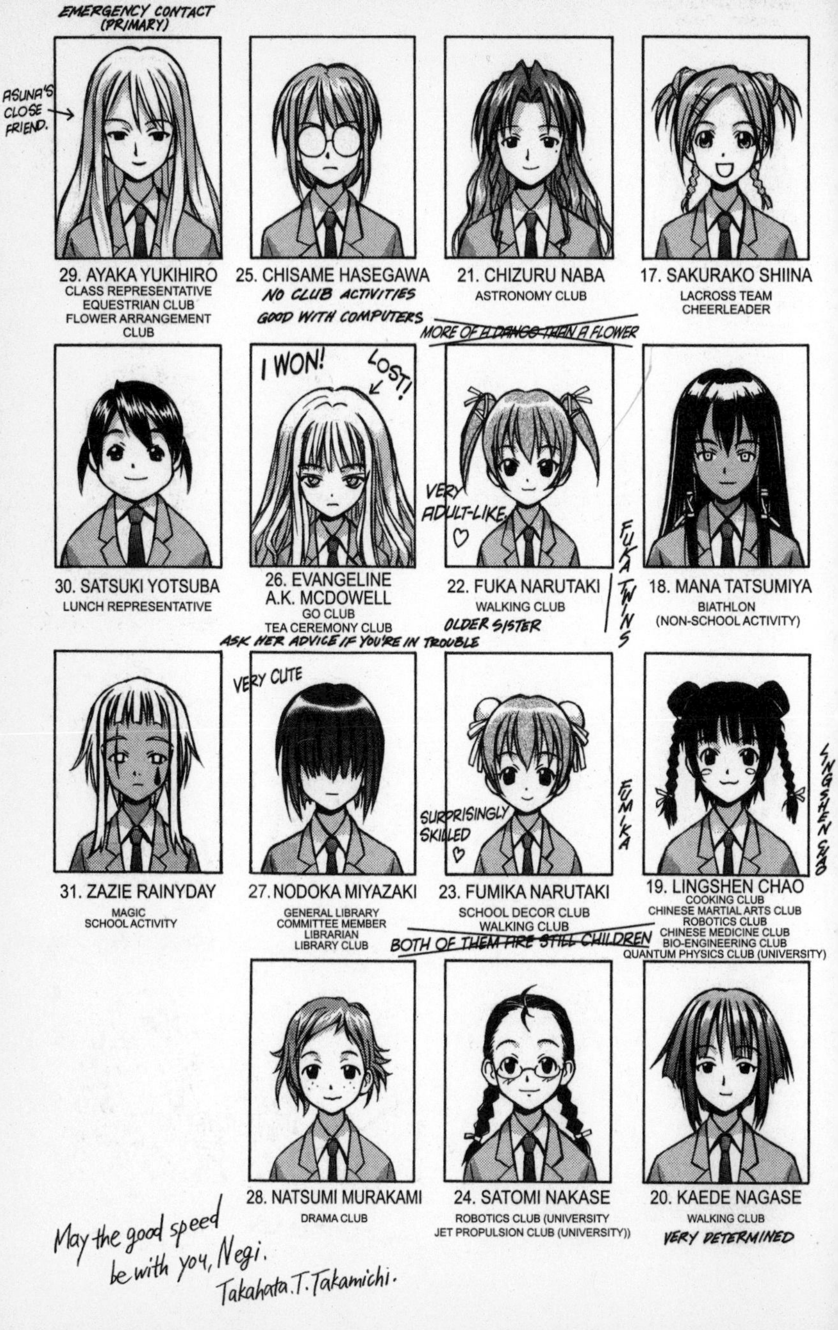
17. SAKURAKO SHIINA
LACROSS TEAM
CHEERLEADER
21. CHIZURU NABA
ASTRONOMY CLUB
MORE OF A DANGO THAN A FLOWER
25. CHISAME HASEGAWA
NO CLUB ACTIVITIES
GOOD WITH COMPUTERS
EMERGENCY CONTACT (PRIMARY)
ASUNA'S CLOSE FRIEND.
29. AYAKA YUKIHIRO
CLASS REPRESENTATIVE
EQUESTRIAN CLUB
FLOWER ARRANGEMENT CLUB
18. MANA TATSUMIYA
BIATHLON
(NON-SCHOOL ACTIVITY)
FUKA TWINS
VERY ADULT-LIKE ♡
22. FUKA NARUTAKI
WALKING CLUB
OLDER SISTER
I WON!
LOST!
26. EVANGELINE A.K. MCDOWELL
GO CLUB
TEA CEREMONY CLUB
ASK HER ADVICE IF YOU'RE IN TROUBLE
30. SATSUKI YOTSUBA
LUNCH REPRESENTATIVE
LINGSHEN CHAO
19. LINGSHEN CHAO
COOKING CLUB
CHINESE MARTIAL ARTS CLUB
ROBOTICS CLUB
CHINESE MEDICINE CLUB
BIO-ENGINEERING CLUB
QUANTUM PHYSICS CLUB (UNIVERSITY)
FUMIKA
SURPRISINGLY SKILLED ♡
23. FUMIKA NARUTAKI
SCHOOL DECOR CLUB
WALKING CLUB
BOTH OF THEM ARE STILL CHILDREN
VERY CUTE
27. NODOKA MIYAZAKI
GENERAL LIBRARY
COMMITTEE MEMBER
LIBRARIAN
LIBRARY CLUB
31. ZAZIE RAINYDAY
MAGIC
SCHOOL ACTIVITY
20. KAEDE NAGASE
WALKING CLUB
VERY DETERMINED
24. SATOMI NAKASE
ROBOTICS CLUB (UNIVERSITY
JET PROPULSION CLUB (UNIVERSITY))
28. NATSUMI MURAKAMI
DRAMA CLUB
May the good speed
be with you, Negi.
Takahata.T.Takamichi.

About the Creator

Negima! is only Ken Akamatsu's third manga, although he started working in the field in 1994 with *AI Ga Tomaranai*. Like all of Akamatsu's work to date, it was published in Kodansha's *Shonen Magazine*. *AI Ga Tomaranai* ran for five years before concluding in 1999. In 1998, however, Akamatsu began the work that would make him one of the most popular manga artists in Japan: *Love Hina*. *Love Hina* ran for four years, and before its conclusion in 2002, it would cause Akamatsu to be granted the prestigious Manga of the Year award from Kodansha, as well as going on to become one of the best-selling manga in the United States.

Translation Notes

Japanese is a tricky language for most Westerners, and translation is often more art than science. For your edification and reading pleasure, here are notes on some of the places where we could have gone in a different direction in our translation of the work, or where a Japanese cultural reference is used.

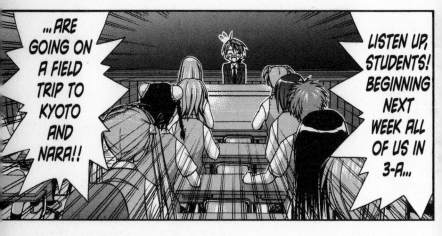

Kyoto and Nara, page 9

Kyoto was Japan's capital and the emperor's home from 794 until 1868. It is rich in historical sites and buildings — so much so that the city was specifically avoided by American air raids during World War II. Like Kyoto, Nara has historical significance to the Japanese. It was the location of the country's first permanent capital in the year 710. It features some of Japan's oldest Buddhist temples and is about an hour from Kyoto.

Kansai, page 11

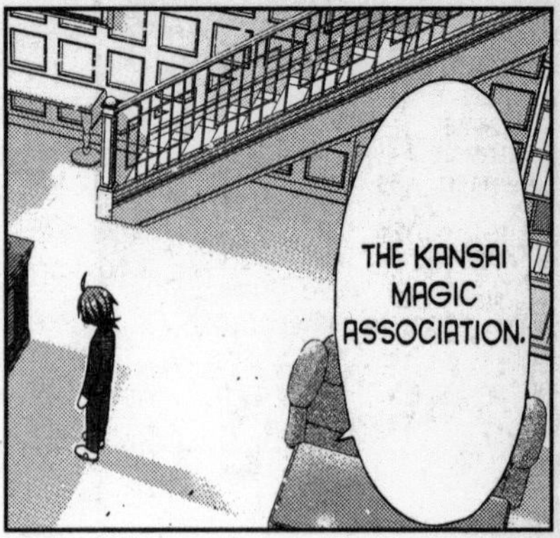
THE KANSAI MAGIC ASSOCIATION.

Kansai is the area of Japan that encompasses Osaka, Kobe, and the surrounding area. Japan is officially divided into the following eight regions: Hokkaido, Tohoku, Kanto, Chubu, Kansai (also known as Kinki), Chugoku, Shikoku, and Kyushu.

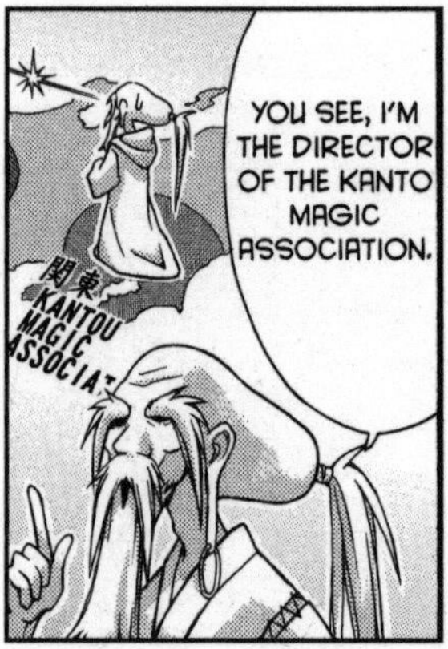
YOU SEE, I'M THE DIRECTOR OF THE KANTO MAGIC ASSOCIATION.
関東
KANTOU MAGIC ASSOCIAT

Kanto, page 11

The Kanto region encompasses Tokyo and the surrounding area.

Matsuya, page 22

Matsuya is a fast-food beef bowl restaurant, very similar to Yoshinoya, which has franchises across Japan and California.

STUDENT NUMBER 11
MADOKA KUGIMIYA (RIG

BORN: MARCH 3, 1989
BLOOD TYPE: AB
ASTROLOGICAL SIGN: PISCES
LIKES: MATSUYA BEEF BOWL, SILV
ACCESSORIES, WESTERN M
(LATELY, IT'S AVRIL LAVIGN
DISLIKES: SHOWY GUYS THAT COM
HIT ON HER. HAS A COMPL

Gouya, page 25

Crepe stands are popular and very common across Japan. When you order a crepe, it is folded and placed in a cardboard cone, making it look a lot like an ice cream cone. Often, the crepe is filled with ice cream, fruit, or some other sweet concoction. In the Japanese text, Sakurako is asking for a *gouya* crepe. *Gouya* is a type of bitter-tasting gourd.

Harajuku, page 27

Harajuku is a part of Tokyo where the trendiest shops are and many young people come to hang out.

O-miai, page 31

An *O-miai* is a date set up usually by one's parents, where information about each person is exchanged. Somewhat like a blind date, it leads ideally to marriage. *O-miai* are becoming less popular in Japan as people seek to find their own partners. However, they are still used for people who for one reason or another have trouble finding a mate.

Ryokan, page 46

The Japanese text says that the students are going to visit a *ryokan*, but we decided to just call it an inn. A *ryokan* is a traditional family inn. Guests stay in traditional Japanese-style rooms with tatami floor and a *kutatsu* (low table), and sleep on futons.

Onmyou, page 58

Onmyou or *Onyou* is the way of yin and yang, an occult divination system based on the Taoist theory of the five elements. Shinmei Ryu appears to be a mythical character that was an expert in the way of *Onyou*. *Onmyouji* were sorcerers who served as mediators between humans and gods in ancient Japan. For a superficial look, check out the 2001 movie *Onmyouji*.

Gokiburi, page 97

While a *goki* is a protective demon, a *gokiburi* is a cockroach. It's a play on words that loses its effect when it's not in Japanese. If we were to try the same thing in English, we'd have to call the demon a . . . um . . . forget we said anything.

Preview of Volume 5

Here is an excerpt from Volume 5, on sale in English now.

THE GAME STARTS AT 11!

WOO-HOO!

ALL RIGHT THEN! EACH GROUP LET ME KNOW WHO YOUR TWO PLAYERS ARE BEFORE 10:30!

I WOULDN'T EXPECT ANY LESS FROM YOU, BIG SISTER. OUR PLAN IS BEING EXECUTED TO THE LETTER.

HMM... WHAT DO YOU THINK? I THOUGHT THAT WENT WELL.

ぴょこ
BOING

AND ANOTHER THING... YOU'RE PRETTY CHEEKY FOR HIDING ME HERE.

WANNA MAKE A BET!?

OH WELL, I'M THROWING MY HAT IN.

DUH!!

AS YOU MIGHT EXPECT, I THINK I'LL CHEER THEM ON.

CHATTER
ァァ
ァァ

I'M GONNA DO IT! I'M GONNA BE ONE OF THE TWO!

#ァ #ァ
CLATTER

WOW! THINGS ARE REALLY HEATING UP.

OPERATION: GET A TON OF THEM!!

13

8

VIII
Chartis Ministralis
CAGURAZAKA
ASUNA
BEL
ministra
dada
directio
oriens

ばーーん

THE PROBATIONARY CONTRACT CARDS!

OO HOO HOO. OPERATION KISS NEGI-KUN IS ONLY THE FIRST STAGE...

THE HEART OF THE MATTER IS REALLY...

THAT'S THE IDEA. BIG BROTHER NEGI HAS THE ORIGINALS, BUT THESE ARE COPIES I MADE WITH MY OWN POWER TO BE USED BY PARTNERS.

UP TO NOW, BIG BROTHER'S GOT TWO BOTCHED CARDS, WHICH MAKES THREE ALL TOGETHER.

THE MORE OF THEM YOU COLLECT, THE BETTER, RIGHT?

OH HO, SO THIS IS THE LUXURIOUS PRIZE, HUH? THESE CARDS...

OH HO HO, I'LL BE A MILLIONAIRE, BIG SIS!

IF WE GET EVERYBODY, THAT'S 30 PEOPLE TIMES 50,000...

THE CARDS PAY 50,000 ERMINE DOLLARS EACH, WHICH MEANS...

HEE HEE!

AS A RESULT, A PROBATIONARY CONTRACT WILL BE FORMED IF ANYONE KISSES BIG BROTHER ON THE GROUNDS!!

I'VE ALREADY TAKEN THE LIBERTY OF DRAWING UP A MAGIC CIRCLE AROUND THE PERIMETER OF THE INN.

HA HA! CUT IT OUT ALREADY! I'M GONNA POP A STITCH!

?

THEY'RE STILL IN THERE...

TOILET

OOEH HEH HEH

GEEYA! HA HA

AND WE'VE GOT A POOL GOING ON THE GROUP AND INDIVIDUAL WINNERS!!

CLACK

SNEAK

WE DIDN'T FIND ANYTHING ESPECIALLY WEIRD, AND THE GROUNDS ARE SECURE.

CHAMO-KUN'S DRAWN UP SOME KIND OF STRANGE MAGIC CIRCLE. WHAT'S UP WITH THAT?

NEGI, WE CHECKED AROUND.

I'VE GOT THE FEELING SOMETHING STRANGE IS GOING ON.

IT WOULD BE BETTER FOR US NOT TO STICK AROUND HERE TOO LONG.

THAT DOES IT. I'M GOING OUT ON THE NEXT PATROL.

TEACHERS' PRIVATE ROOM

NEGI-SENSEI

AHH, IT'S GONNA BE 11 SOON. ANOTHER TOUGH DAY AT THE OFFICE.

PAPER DOUBLES?

HMM...IN THAT CASE, I'LL LEND YOU THESE PAPER DOUBLES.

#RUSTLE

BUT WON'T THE OTHER TEACHERS NOTICE IF NEGI TAKES OFF IN THE MIDDLE OF THE NIGHT?

RUMBLE

BUT I DON'T THINK IT WANTS TO DO US ANY HARM.

NOW THAT YOU MENTION IT, I DEFINITELY FEEL SOMETHING ODD AS WELL.

LEAVE THE STUDENT PATROL UP TO US.

YOU'RE JUST TEN, SO WHY DON'T I COME BACK LATER AND KEEP YOU COMPANY.

HO HO HO

OH, HI SHIZUNA-SENSEI. I WAS JUST ABOUT TO HIT THE HAY.

UH OH...

WHISK

ARE YOU ASLEEP ALREADY?

OH, NEGI-SENSEI!!

NOW DON'T LEAVE YOUR ROOM, OKAY? BYE NOW. ♡ OH, SO MUCH TO DO!

DASH

ALL RIGHT...

BURST

KA-CHICK

TICK TICK TICK TICK...

I'VE GOT THE VIDEO CAMERAS SET UP, AND EVERYTHING'S UNDER CONTROL.

OKAY OKAY. KEEP YOUR SHIRT ON, CHAMO.

SNAP

WHISK

HURRY, BIG SIS!! THE GAME'S ABOUT TO START!

ROLL

GROUP 1

GROUP 2

GROUP 3

SCHOOL FIELD TRIP EXTRA-CURRICULAR ACTIVITY!!

GROUP 4

GROUP 5

SCHOOL FIELD TRIP'S EXTRACURRICULAR ACTIVITY. LIP SCRAMBLE!! OPERATION: KISS NEGI-KUN PASSIONATELY ON THIS SCHOOL FIELD TRIP! ♥

"OPERATION: KISS NEGI-KUN PASSIONATELY ON THIS SCHOOL FIELD TRIP!!!"

SOMY

TAH DAH

THEY'RE TAKING THIS SERIOUSLY.

EEK! IT'S STARTED!

CLASS REP IN GROUP 3 IS A LOCK!

WHO'S YOUR MONEY ON?

WELL THEN, LET'S INTRODUCE OUR CONTESTANTS. FIRST UP IS GROUP 1...

AND I'VE GOT A LITTLE SIDE BET ON GROUPS 2 AND 4!

CHATTER

JEEE

Subscribe to

DEL REY'S MANGA
e-newsletter—

and receive all these exciting exclusives directly in your e-mail inbox:

• Schedules and announcements about the newest books on sale

• Exclusive interviews and exciting behind-the-scenes news

• Previews of upcoming material

• A manga reader's forum, featuring a cool question-and-answer section

For more information and to sign up
for Del Rey's manga e-newsletter,
visit www.delreymanga.com

VOLUME 3
BY CLAMP

Kimihiro Watanuki is haunted by spirits—and the only way to escape his curse is to become the indentured servant of the mysterious witch, Yûko Ichihara. But when his beloved, beautiful Himawari-chan, asks him for a favor, he and his eternal rival, the exorcist Dômeki, must go on a spirit-busting adventure without Yûko there to save them!

Meanwhile Yûko gives a young woman a precious cylindrical box from her treasure room. There's just one caveat: She must never open it. Inside is a magical device with a terrifying reputation! Can Kimihiro save an ambitious young lady from her own overconfidence?

Volumes 1-6 are now available in bookstores.

 For more information and to sign up for Del Rey's manga e-newsletter, visit www.delreymanga.com

xxxHOLiC © 2003 CLAMP. All rights reserved.

TSUBASA

VOLUME 4

BY CLAMP

Young Syaoran embarks on a worlds-spanning adventure to restore the memory of the most important person in his life, the princess Sakura—even though he knows that she'll never remember her love for him. The trail leads to a small town reminiscent of Europe at the turn of the nineteenth century, a place where the ghostly image of a golden-haired woman comes in the night to steal the town's children. Syaoran and his band of outrageous friends—affable Fai D. Flowright, loose cannon Kurogane, the odd creature Mokona, and Sakura herself—mount their horses and venture into forbidding, barren woods to solve a mystery, rescue the children, and retrieve one more piece of Sakura's missing memories.

4
RESERVoir CHRoNiCLE
TSUBASA
CLAMP
NEW FROM THE CREATORS OF CHOBITS!

Volumes 1-7 are now available in bookstores.

DEL REY

For more information and to sign up for Del Rey's manga e-newsletter, visit www.delreymanga.com

GUNDAM SEED
VOLUME 4

ART BY MASATSUGU IWASE
ORIGINAL STORY BY HAJIME YATATE
AND YOSHIYUKI TOMINO

Devastated by the cruel realities of war, Flay, Athrun, and Miriallia grieve, believing that Kira and Tolle are dead. Even as they mourn and question themselves, the fighting intensifies. Coordinator leader (and Athrun's father) Patrick Zala gains political control over the Plant, and the battle between Zaft and the Earth Army shifts to a military base. When the crew of *Archangel* realize that Earth has used them as bait and betrayed them, they decide to embark on a journey to the neutral state of Aube to start new lives. But on the horizon are new, more powerful mobile suits that may just turn the tide in this war!

Volumes 1-5 are now available in bookstores.

For more information and to sign up for Del Rey's manga e-newsletter, visit www.delreymanga.com

Gundam SEED © 2004 Hajime Yatate, Yoshiyuki Tomino and Masatsugu Iwase. All rights reserved.
Copyright © 2004 by Sotsu Agency, Sunrise, MBS. First published in Japan in 2004 by Kodansha Ltd., Tokyo.

VOLUME 3

BY SATOMI IKEZAWA

Timid Yaya is the victim of every bully in school, but she has a secret kept even from herself: She has another personality named Nana, who is all too willing to kick butt. While nice-guy guitarist Moriyama begins a tentative romance with Yaya, the constant appearances of brash Nana reveal the truth about his would-be girlfriend. And soon Moriyama's charismatic professional-musician friend Shôhei takes too much of an interest in Nana's killer singing voice…and body! Can Nana resist the very man Yaya has idealized all her life?!

Volumes 1-5 are now available in bookstores.

For more information and to sign up for Del Rey's manga e-newsletter, visit www.delreymanga.com

Othello © 2004 Satomi Ikezawa. All rights reserved.

VOLUME 2

BY TOMOKO HAYAKAWA

Four fabulous guys must completely transform a high school girl if they want to keep living rent-free in her aunt's luxurious mansion. But Sunako Nakahara, the most fashion-hopeless girl in Japan, would rather live like a hermit and watch her favorite horror movies than undergo a makeover.

When the guys stumble upon the mansion's secret sub-basement, they discover the ghost of a prim and proper lady who (thankfully) begins to possess Sunako's soul. It seems their problem is solved. Too bad that Sunako's now-suitable personality includes a desire to lock the boys up in the mansion's dungeon!

Volumes 1-5 are now available in bookstores.

For more information and to sign up for Del Rey's manga e-newsletter, visit www.delreymanga.com

The Wallflower © 2004 Tomoko Hayakawa. All rights reserved.

TOMARE!

[STOP!]

You're going the wrong way!

Manga is a completely different type of reading experience.

To start at the *beginning*, go to the *end*!

That's right! Authentic manga is read the traditional Japanese way—from right to left. Exactly the *opposite* of how American books are read. It's easy to follow: Just go to the other end of the book, and read each page—and each panel—from right side to left side, starting at the top right. Now you're experiencing manga as it was meant to be.